Shattered Barriers Copy

Aaron D Yoder

AARON YODER

This book contains graphic content, including strong language, alcohol use, graphic violence, and scenes of mutilation. Reader discretion is advised.

Also by

Shattered Divinity– Book one in the Shattered Divinity Series

AARON D YODER

SHATTERED DIVINITY

BOOK ONE

To the readers.
You are the reason these worlds live beyond my imagination.
Every page you turn, every late night you spend in Kalazaar,
every moment you share these stories with others keeps the fire
alive. This book is for you, the ones who believe in adventure, in
struggle, in hope, and in the power of stories to carry us beyond
ourselves.

Contents

Shattered Barriers

B ^y
Aaron Yoder

Chapter One

L eper stepped into the sparring square, his muscles taut with purpose. Across from him stood a man he loathed more than any other. Blank Face. His brother. Rin's murderer.

Not a day passed without thoughts of her, her golden hair, her soft, sweet voice, the scent of lilacs she'd loved so much. She had been his everything, his best friend, and, at one point, the love of his life.

Leper had been practicing relentlessly in the two weeks since the War of Tudela, and the night she died. He wouldn't lose another loved one. Not ever. Day after day, he sparred with the guards and defeated them with ease. Then came the larger challenge: Leighth's bulwark. It took a little time, but he learned to best the hulking warrior every single time, even in hand-to-hand combat. Yet here, facing Blank Face, he was reminded of his limits. He hadn't beaten him. Not once. But today, Theora willing, he'd drive Blank Face's head straight into the dirt.

Hundreds of tanned elves had gathered to watch the spar, their voices a low murmur of excitement and speculation. Leper and Blank Face had become something of a spectacle in Kundry, and bets were already flying on whether this would be the day Leper finally beat him. The two of them were the undisputed strongest warriors around, and the elves loved these matches—loved watching two titans clash.

Leper prowled around Blank Face, taking in everything around them. He refused to let the assassin have any sort of edge. The sparring square sat within the barracks of Kundry, surrounded by towering forests. A gentle floral aroma drifted on the cool breeze, mingling with the faint scent of wood and leather. Wooden gates marked the city's edge, while massive tree trunks stretched skyward, some seamlessly integrated into the city's structures. Kundry's homes were built into the trees, the elves refusing to harm nature unnecessarily. The castle itself was a marvel—several colossal, fifty-foot-wide trees, interconnected and fortified to form a single, unified stronghold.

When they'd first arrived in Kundry, the city had been a mess. Leighth's uncle, Crux, had the place in a chokehold. Criminals roamed unchecked, and instead of planting crops to feed the people, Crux used the fields to plant illicit drugs. Sure, it might've made him richer, but the city suffered under his greed. *Typical bastard.*

Leper, Petrovana, Blank Face, and Leighth had put an end to it. Together, they overwhelmed Crux's forces. Leighth took charge immediately, and she had her uncle executed for his failures. Now, Kundry was thriving in the short time under her leadership. The people were in good spirits, and she'd made it clear: Leper, or any Chernzerk, was to be treated with dignity and respect.

Leper appreciated her for that. The elves had adapted well to her orders, though a few still gave him cold, lingering stares. But they kept their distance. No one dared challenge him directly. Blank Face remained hidden beneath his hood, as always. Leper wasn't even sure if the crowd knew he was Chernzerk or not. *Typical coward.*

Petrovana and Leighth sat on a dais just outside the sparring square's white barrier. Petrovana, stunning as ever, wore a yellow sundress that showed plenty of leg and more than a hint of cleavage. She smiled and winked at Leper, earning a brief nod in return. Beside her, Leighth cut a regal figure in her formal gown of yellow and silver, its full skirt puffed around her in stately elegance. On her head rested the crown of Kundry, a delicate circle of twigs and sticks plated in gold and silver, with two small wheat stalks rising from the sides just above her ears.

Unfortunately, the crown didn't hide the fact that they'd never found a healer to regrow the ear The Latter had sliced off a few weeks ago. The wild mohawk man who transformed into smoke every time they tried to subdue him.

Leighth clapped her hands together, her voice cutting through the crowd. "FIGHT!"

"Come on, lover boy," Blank Face sneered, his voice dripping with mockery. "Stop gawking at your girlfriend and focus. It's why you always lose." His daggers flashed into his hands so quickly it seemed they'd appeared from thin air.

"Why don't you just fuck right off, murderer?" Leper shot back, holding out his hands. Maka Kura floated into his palms, the weapon humming faintly with power.

If magic were allowed, this would be over in seconds. But it wasn't. These fights were about raw skill—close-quarters combat. Besting him was the last thing Leper needed to finally move past Blank Face murdering Rinawen. At least, he hoped it was. Right now, nothing seemed more satisfying than beating Blank Face to a pulp—again and again.

After all, he had taken the only person Leper had ever truly known and trusted. The only person he'd ever felt comfortable turning to in times of trouble.

Leper lunged first, leading with his left for a change instead of his usual right-to-left pattern. Blank Face deflected the swing and ducked under the follow-up, his movements impossibly quick.

That was always the problem. If Leper could get his hands on the scrawny bastard, it'd be over. But Blank Face was just too damn slippery, darting out of reach before Leper could land a blow or lock him in a grapple.

Leper had decided beforehand he wasn't going to press the offensive this time. Let Blank Face come to him. That way, he could draw him in close and finally end this. He took a few halfhearted swings, trying to bait his opponent into attacking. They circled each other, testing the waters like predators waiting for the other to make a mistake. But patience wasn't Leper's strong suit, and after several rounds of evasive footwork, he grew restless.

"If yer not goin' to fight, then hurry up and kiss already!" Petrovana hollered from her seat.

The crowd erupted into laughter and cheers, their energy crackling around the sparring square.

Blank Face darted in at last, his daggers flashing. Leper side-stepped the attack with practiced ease, shoving Blank Face on the shoulder to throw him off balance. He followed up with a swing aimed squarely at his opponent's back, sure this time he had him.

But Blank Face was already dropping to the ground, rolling away in one smooth motion. Before Leper could capitalize, he flipped upright in a burst of agility that made Leper's blood boil.

Gods, I hate this guy.

Leper charged, fury fueling his strikes, but Blank Face met him head-on. Steel clashed in a furious rhythm, the sound sharp and deafening. Leper's arms burned as he blocked and parried, sweat rolling down his face. Around them, the crowd gasped, then cheered, then gasped again, their reactions rising and falling with each exchange.

Every time Leper thought he had an opening, Blank Face twisted, ducked, or performed some ridiculous maneuver that seemed to defy the laws of nature. It was infuriating. The man was *impossible* to hit.

Then Leper spotted it—a high swing coming straight at him. He deflected the strike upward, stepped in, and drove his elbow into Blank Face's face. The impact sent a shock of satisfaction through him. Without hesitation, he swung for all he was worth, his blade arcing toward Blank Face with deadly intent.

He wasn't supposed to aim for fatal blows in these matches. He didn't care. This man had murdered Rinawen. Brother or not, Blank Face deserved to die.

Leper's lips curled into a feral grin. Finally. After all this time, his first taste of victory against Blank Face was within reach.

Somehow, that snake ducked the blow. Leper barely had time to register it before Blank Face slammed into his chest, driving him off balance. A sharp kick to the back of his shin sent him crashing to the ground with a heavy thud.

The impact blasted the air from his lungs, leaving him gasping as he struggled to breathe. Blank Face was on him in an instant, kneeling beside him, his dagger cool against the exposed skin of Leper's neck.

Another loss.

His blood boiled. Sweat dripped from Leper's face, sliding down his bare torso. The three jagged scars across his left pectoral—souvenirs from a bear attack—burned with a dull ache, only fueling the storm of rage building inside him. That familiar fog crept in, the same suffocating haze of anger he'd felt the day Rinawen died.

"Almost," Blank Face said, his tone smug. "Maybe next time."

"Fuck you," Leper snarled, his voice raw with fury. He lashed out, his fist connecting with Blank Face's jaw.

Crack.

His lips twisted upward at the satisfying sound.

Before Blank Face could recover, Leper grabbed the front of his brown robe and yanked him close. Wrapping an arm around his neck, he locked him into a chokehold.

"You worthless murderer," Leper growled through clenched teeth, his voice a venomous rasp. "Fuck the rules of sparring. I'll kill you."

Leper tightened his grip around Blank Face's neck, but his opponent blinked away, vanishing into thin air. Leper knew the trick well enough by now. He'd reappear behind and above him, like always. Unfortunately, this had happened more times than Leper cared to admit. After the match ended, he'd lose his temper, try to kill Blank Face, and—like always—Blank Face would use his stupid blinking ability to stay alive.

If a participant went feral, ignored the rules, or intentionally tried to kill someone, that was when an overseer stepped in. Or, if you had magic, you could use it to defend yourself. These weren't life-or-death battles—just a place to hone your skills and improve your skill with a weapon.

Rolling onto his stomach, Leper surged to his feet, already anticipating the next move. His muscles coiled, his mind clouded with rage.

"Leper! Not again!" Petrovana squealed from the sidelines, racing toward him with Leighth close behind.

Just as expected, Blank Face materialized behind him. But this time, Leper was ready. Already in motion, his fist connected with Blank Face's cheek the moment he reappeared, the impact cracking like a thunderclap. Blank Face growled in pain, but Leper didn't stop.

He drove his knee into Blank Face's midsection, then followed up with a crushing blow to his back. Blank Face hit the dirt hard before blinking out of sight again, only to reappear standing in front of him, blood dripping from the corner of his mouth.

Blank Face wiped his face with the back of his hand, his expression a mix of exhaustion and resignation. "You want to beat the shit out of me to make yourself feel better? Fine." He spread his arms wide. "I owe you that."

Leper's chest heaved with each ragged breath. "I don't just want to beat the crap out of you, killer." His voice was a low, dangerous growl. "I want you to *feel* what Rinawen felt when you stabbed her to death!"

He lunged again, his fist poised to strike, but before he could make contact, Petrovana and Leighth stepped between them.

"Leper, yer out of control... again." Petrovana jabbed an accusatory finger in his direction, her voice sharp. "It's been two weeks. When are ya goin' to realize he's not yer enemy?"

"He *is* my enemy," Leper snarled through clenched teeth, his hands trembling with fury.

Leighth stepped in, placing firm hands on his chest. Her tone was calm but commanding. "Come on, mister. Get your shit. We're going for a walk."

"No." Leper shoved her hand off him. "I'm not going for a damned walk with you. I've got business to finish."

Petrovana grabbed his wrist. "Hey. Listen to yer queen. This ain't like you. What would Rinawen think if she saw you right now?"

"She'd probably think I need better friends," Leper grumbled.

Petrovana's soothing touch and soft voice always helped calm him down. If it weren't for her, he'd probably walk around in a constant state of rage.

"She'd probably think you're out of control," Leighth snapped, slapping his shoulder. "She wouldn't let Zanera and Kelindra around someone acting like this, would she?" Her eyes narrowed.

She has a point. There's no way I'd act like this around Zanera, Kelindra, or Rinawen herself.

Leper paused but relented, yanking his crumpled brown shirt over his head. It clung uncomfortably to his sweat- and dirt-streaked body. He scratched at his beard, scowling, disgusted with everything, Blank Face, himself, and this whole damned day.

"Why do I have to leave? Take Ass Face for a walk, shove him off a cliff, and be done with it," Leper whined, crossing his arms.

"Hey!" Leighth spun on her heel, fixing him with a piercing glare. "Who is your queen?"

"You are," Leper gritted out, his jaw tight.

"Your queen is requesting your company on a walk. Are you going to deny her that?" She placed her hands on her hips, exuding authority.

Leighth fit the queenly role masterfully, as though she'd been born to it. Even at eighteen, her wisdom and presence commanded respect. The people already loved her, seeing her as a natural leader. She had not only avenged her parents, Jaynoh and Kendra—rulers of Kundry before her—by stabbing Borlden, but she had also led people back to overthrow Crux and his band of mercenaries. She had cleaned up the city, and despite losing her entire family, she held her head high, never spiraling into chaos the way Leper often feared he was. He never understood how she handled it so well.

Leper's glare remained, but he finally spat, "No." He offered a curt, reluctant bow.

"Then walk with me." Her smile softened her tone, her perfect teeth flashing briefly. The jagged edges of her hair—still not fully grown back after Blank Face had cut it a few months ago—framed her face like a crown of resilience.

She led him out of the city, dismissing the guards and bulwark who trailed behind. They stared momentarily, their protective instincts warring with her authority. The way they eyed Leper made it clear they didn't trust him, but Leighth's assurance silenced their protests.

As they stepped into the orchard, the air filled with the crisp scent of apples and peaches. Leighth stopped occasionally to inspect the trees, running her fingers over the leaves and bark. For a solid thirty minutes, she walked in silence, leaving Leper alone with his swirling thoughts of disgust and vengeance.

Finally, she reached for a low-hanging apple, her voice breaking the quiet. "We don't spend a lot of time together, you and I."

"There's a reason for that," Leper muttered, his eyes shifting to the golden wheat field ahead. "And I've been openly expressing why."

"Yes, you've made your feelings abundantly clear." Leighth plucked the apple and took a bite, the crunch loud in the stillness. "You don't want to be around... him."

Leper stopped, his fists clenching at his sides. "I can't just get over it, Leighth. Even if you demand it as my queen, I can't unsee her dying face." His voice cracked with barely contained anger, his growl like a wounded animal.

"I know, Leper. More than anyone, I know." Leighth took another bite of the apple, her voice cracked slightly, before continuing toward the field.

"How can you just forgive him like that? Like nothing happened? Surely you were fond of Rinawen, too?" Leper pressed, his tone biting.

Leighth slowed, her gaze drifting to the distant wheat swaying in the breeze. "I didn't know her nearly as well as you did," she admitted quietly. "I knew Zanera and Kelindra better, but yes, she carried a special place in my life." She motioned for him to follow, her steps steady.

Leper grumbled under his breath as he trudged after her. "He killed her. For no other reason than an honest mistake."

Leighth let out a long, dejected sigh, her shoulders sagging. "I know you don't believe this, but I can relate. I lost my entire family, Leper. I still see their faces, hear their voices... but I'll never truly see or hear them again."

"Yeah, but you killed Borlden, remember?" Leper shot back, shrugging as though it were obvious. "You got your justice. I was there when you stabbed him. Repeatedly."

"I did." Leighth's voice hardened, her steps halting as she turned to face him. "Do you know how much that helped?" She raised her hands, her expression sharp.

Leper frowned, shaking his head.

"None." Her voice pitched high. "It didn't help at all, Leper. Because they're still fucking dead. Sure, the world's a better place without him. Sure, it felt good in the moment to take all that anger, pain, and resentment out on him. But guess what?" Her voice broke entirely as a tear slid down her cheek. "After all that, I still miss my family more than I ever cared about vengeance. I hate him for what he did, but getting justice didn't fill the enormous amount of emptiness I feel. It never will."

"What's your point?" Leper snapped, flicking his hand dismissively. "That I should just move on? Get over it?"

The fog of anger clouded his mind, burning hotter with every breath. Her words only seemed to stoke the fire, fueling the memories of Rinawen. Her dying face. Her blood. Blank Face walking free after what he'd done.

The injustice of it all churned in his gut. Borlden had died, sure, but that bastard hadn't suffered nearly enough for what he'd done to Leighth. The thought of him escaping true punishment twisted Leper's rage tighter.

"My point is, I'm trying," Leighth said, her eyes darting nervously. She paused at the edge of the tree line, and he could see her hands trembling. "Trying to figure out how to handle all of this. Trying to find people in my life that I can trust like I trusted them."

She swallowed hard, her gaze distant. "Nobody will ever replace them, but holding on to all that hatred, anguish, and pain—it isn't good for anyone. And the way you act when you get angry... it isn't right. It isn't like anyone else. You don't just want to kill, harm, or hurt." She sighed deeply. "That's not natural, and it scares the shit out of everyone.

"You can't bring Rinawen back, Leper, but you have friends here who'd help you. Blank Face... he honestly wants to be your brother, your friend. Once you lose your family—" Her voice cracked, and she sniffled. "You don't get them back."

Leper clenched his jaw, his chest tight. Leighth would never understand how he felt about Blank Face. Sure, Blank Face was his brother, and in another life, one where he hadn't taken

Rinawen, the one thing Leper held most dear, he could have embraced that bond. But Rinawen's death was senseless. Blank Face, as skilled and calculating as he was, didn't need to kill her. It wasn't justifiable. It was unforgivable, and that fueled Leper's hatred more than anything else.

He stepped forward and embraced Leighth. "I'm sorry about your family. I'm sorry for everything you've been through. But I can't let it go. Maybe I'm too stubborn, maybe I'm vengeful, but I just... can't."

She wrapped her arms around him, letting out a long sigh. "At least you're honest about it," she said quietly. She pulled back, placing her hands on his shoulders, her expression thoughtful.

Leper raised a brow, his frustration simmering just beneath the surface. The fog of anger clung to him, unrelenting, even after an hour of walking. He wished he could shake it off—or at least control these fits of rage and reckless actions.

What truly scared him was the thought that he'd always be this way, trapped between two versions of himself.

"When I was younger," Leighth began, her voice softening with the memory, "Rinawen used to visit my parents to talk about crop growth and all that boring stuff. I'd get so excited because I knew Zanera and Kelindra would be there too. Being the only girl in a family of three with two older, insufferably annoying brothers, it was such a relief to have their company." She smiled faintly, her hand resting on his shoulder as she gestured toward the castle. "Come on. Let's head back."

Leper followed her lead, a faint grin tugging at his lips. "Zanera and Kelindra told me a lot about you. They looked up to you—you know that? They still do. You don't know how many times I wanted to meet you, just from the way they talked about you."

Leighth smiled, a spark of amusement lighting up her face. "They used to tell me all these wild tales about this guy named Leper. How he experimented with making vials, played all sorts of crazy games... and even how he was mad enough to fight a bear for them." She giggled as Leper instinctively touched the scars on his chest, a sheepish grin spreading across his face.

"They carried on about you so much, I was dying to meet you," she continued. "But when I asked if I could see you the next time my family visited Kordry, they both stiffened up and got all tight-lipped."

"Ugh." Leper groaned, running a hand through his hair. "I caused them so much misery."

Leighth burst out laughing. "Oh, misery? Those two covered for you better than anyone I've ever met. One time when I was visiting, they actually took me to see your house."

Leper's brows shot up, his stomach dropping. "What? They took you to my hidden cabin?"

"Oh no." Her eyes twinkled. "They led me through town to an abandoned house, banged on the door, and screamed your name. Of course, you weren't there. Next time, they claimed you'd been arrested and dragged me to your "cell." Big shock—no Leper there either. I was starting to think you were just some imaginary friend they made up."

Leper couldn't stop the laughter that burst out of him. The tension in his chest finally loosened. "Wow. I had no idea."

Leighth chuckled, shaking her head. "That's the guy you need to be, Leper. The one Zanera and Kelindra loved so much that they couldn't stop bragging about him. The guy who, Zanera said, would wait outside the city walls, hidden in the trees, every single day—just to catch a glimpse of her."

His smile faltered, and he stared at her. "I *am* that guy."

"Not when you're around Blank Face or in that... fog of yours." Her tone grew serious, her brow creasing. "When you're like that, you're someone else entirely. And it's scary. Don't lose that guy, Leper. Don't lose *you*."

Her words struck him deep, carving through the layers of anger and guilt that had consumed him. As they walked the rest of the way to the castle, the fog in his mind finally cleared, replaced by a sliver of calm. He was grateful to Leighth for pulling him back, but the fear lingered—fear of what might happen if he truly lost control one day. Fear that he might become more like Blank Face—an unloved murderer, an assassin.

Fear that he'd drive away everyone he loved because of these actions he couldn't control, including Petrovana, Zanera, and Kelindra.

He swallowed hard. That was something he could *never* live with

Reconstruction was progressing, but not fast enough.

Madislak strode down the dirt paths of Lantess, his gaze sweeping over the rising walls and skeletal frames of buildings clawing their way back from ruin. Hammers rang through the air, mingling with the shouts of laborers hauling stone and timber. The city was rebuilding itself, yet all he could think about was how quickly it could all be torn down again.

Harmony walked beside him, her arm looped through his. "Lantess will see its former glory restored."

He wanted to believe that. Needed to. "Not if Nalecht or Tamara have their way."

Two weeks had passed since Tudela was attacked. Madislak spent those two weeks of frantic effort gathering survivors and salvaging what they could. The people of Lantess had returned, throwing themselves into the work, but Madislak knew better than to think that momentum alone would save them. Nalecht had already reduced this city to ashes once. With the shards he had now—and Tamara's involvement—it could happen again and at any time.

His fingers brushed the shield strapped to his back, a gift from Leper. His new armor, forged from the rare plethocyte, gleamed under the sun. Colored in black and red, the armor bore an intricate engraving of the kingdom's emblem—a lion's head—at the center of the chest. Surrounding it, delicate patterns shaped like various weapons stretched across the rest of the armor, running down the sleeves.

Harmony squeezed his hand. "You're sure about... us?"

Madislak turned to her, catching the way her violet robe swayed in the breeze, the silver constellations on her sleeves shimmering in the light. She had always been striking, but now, cloaked in the deep colors of her new station, she looked every bit the queen she would be.

"Maybe this will answer your question," he murmured, cupping her face and kissing her deeply. Her lips tasted of blueberries, her hands threading into his hair, pulling him closer. When they finally parted, her breath was warm against his ear.

"I'll take that as a yes, then," she whispered.

He smiled, but it was fleeting. "I know the people might not agree with how fast this is happening, but they'll come around."

"I just don't want them to resent me," she admitted, voice quieter. "Or your children to hate me."

"They don't hate you." He tightened his grip around her shoulders. "They adored Gwen. They'll warm up to you in time. Trust me."

If his family could find happiness in this union, he would embrace it. But as much as he wanted this—wanted her—his mind remained fixed on the city's defenses.

"Lantess was the first civilization ever built, the first true stronghold," he said as they passed a group of workers laying fresh stone. "It's been in my family's hands since its foundation. I won't be the one to lose it."

Harmony's brow furrowed. "You think you could?"

"Not if I prepare properly." He kicked a loose stone from his path. "Nalecht has nearly every shard. If he gains the last two, nothing will stop him. We have to be ready."

"Then I'll help you," she said firmly, pressing a kiss to his cheek. "Especially after we're married."

Madislak exhaled slowly. "We should wait. Until Nalecht is dealt with."

Harmony stopped walking. "Wait?"

"It's not the right time. The city is still exposed. If word of our wedding spreads, Tamara and Nalecht will use it as an opportunity to strike."

Her jaw tightened. "You think I don't understand the threat? We don't even know when we'll be able to go after him. A wedding could raise morale. Give the people something to celebrate after everything they've lost."

"And what's the point of that if it's followed by utter doom?" He shrugged. "I want to marry you, Harmony, but we have to be realistic."

Her expression darkened. "We already announced our engagement. People are expecting it. I thought we could do it during the primordial equinox. The sky observers say it will happen in a few months—colors filling the sky, magic surging. It would be the perfect moment."

The equinox. His father had spoken of it, the alignment of the moons, a rare and powerful event. A wedding under those skies would be unforgettable. But by then, where would they stand in this war? Would Lantess even be standing?

"Harmony," he said carefully. "There's something you need to understand. What we want and what we get are two different things. Our duty comes first. The city. The children. Then us."

She stared at him. "Your children, I understand." Her voice was measured, but something in it was fraying. "Never mind."

Madislak sighed, running a hand down his face. "Let's just see how Lillian's doing. I don't want another argument right now."

Chapter Two

A grin spread across Madislak's face as he watched Lillian in the midst of one-on-one training sessions. She was simply embarrassing every man and woman who dared to step into the sparring square. Her scimitars were extensions of her arms, manipulated with absolute precision. Lillian maintained complete control over her body and the weapons. They approached the barracks, the first section of Lantess they had rebuilt to harbor any soldiers and people they could. The destruction Goreldea and Nalecht inflicted nearly decimated the entire city; the barracks and castle sustained the least amount of damage. If nothing else, Madislak could rest easy, knowing Lillian would show their troops how to fight. They would need it, going up against Nalecht, Tamara, and Goreldea, the queen of Kirilick, who had attacked Lantess when all this shard collecting began. At least that's what he figured.

"Have you heard anything from King Brebian or King Theodamar since the War of Tudela?" Madislak asked, trying to ease the tension. "I'm not sure we'll have either of their support, given how badly Brebian hated Leper and how quickly Theodamar's forces got crushed in the war."

"No," Harmony stated flatly. "Brebian hated any Chernzerk in general. Theodamar is so damned passive, I doubt he'll bother to help unless he is directly affected. So don't count on them."

Madislak glanced at Harmony, her scowl ever present. *Great. She's pissed.* He turned his attention back to the sparring square.

Most men entered the square with smirks or made smug remarks about teaching "this girl" a lesson, only to exit humbled and cowed, tails between their legs. Harmony continued to avoid his gaze and held her head high as Lillian dispatched yet another overconfident challenger with ease.

"No one at all?" Lillian hollered, her face covered in sweat and dirt. Her short-sleeve brown tunic was ruffled in places. She wore black pants and brown boots as she whipped her scimitars around in the air.

Madislak rolled his shoulders and stepped forward. "Enough showing off, Lillian. We have more important things to do than watching you humble every soldier here."

She sheathed her scimitars with a flourish, but her smirk remained. "If you say so."

Before Madislak could retort, a loud crash sounded behind him, followed by a startled cry. He turned to see a group of recruits stumbling back, their training dummies knocked aside. One of the men had evidently lost control of his weapon and sent it flying in their direction. The soldiers scrambled to right themselves, but their fumbling irritated Madislak.

He marched over, grabbed the discarded weapon, and shoved it back into the soldier's hands. "You think you can survive out there fighting like this? If you can't hold a damned sword properly, you'll be the first to die."

The soldier gulped, nodding stiffly, but Madislak wasn't finished. "Lillian's wasting her time with you lot. Maybe you should just start swinging blindly and hope you get lucky." His frustration boiled over, and in an attempt to emphasize his point, he raised his shield and slammed it into the ground.

A yellow pulse erupted from the shield's surface, and a concussive blast rippled outward. The force sent a nearby group of soldiers sprawling, but more horrifyingly, it struck Lillian square in the stomach when it shot back up off the ground. She was lifted off her feet and thrown backward, her scimitars flying out of the sheaths as her body flipped once before she landed hard on her side, coughing violently.

Madislak froze as a stunned silence overtook the training yard.

"Lillian!" Harmony rushed to her side, but Lillian shoved her away, struggling to push herself up. Her breath came in ragged gasps, and when she wiped her mouth, blood smeared across the back of her hand.

Madislak took a step forward. "Lillian, I—"

"Don't." Her voice was hoarse, raw with barely contained fury. She clutched her stomach, blinking rapidly, either from the pain or the sheer disbelief. "That what you call trainin' now? Knockin' people flat when they ain't expectin' it?"

"It was an accident," he said quickly. "I didn't know the shield could—"

"Bullshit." Lillian spat blood onto the dirt. "Doesn't matter what you knew. What matters is what you did."

Madislak clenched his fists, feeling his own frustration rising. "I didn't know it had that kind of power! I didn't—"

Lillian's glare cut through him sharper than her blades ever could. She grabbed her scimitars, wincing as she stood. "I ain't trainin' people just for you to knock 'em on their asses for no damn reason. If that's how you want to lead, you can find someone else to teach yer damned disappointments."

Madislak's stomach dropped. "Lillian, don't do this. We need you."

She exhaled sharply through her nose, shaking her head. "You holler at them fer fuckin' losin' control of their weapons when you can't control yer own damn shield." She coughed again, and blood splattered her hand. She looked up at Madislak with utter disgust on her face. "Fuck you, fuck yer city, and fuck yer damned soldiers."

Without another word, Lillian turned on her heel and strode away, shoulders stiff with fury. Blood still dripped from her lip, but she didn't wipe it away. Harmony halted for a moment, then shot Madislak a look, not anger, not disappointment, just quiet concern. Then she, too, walked away, her eyes hollow as if something in her had given up.

Madislak exhaled sharply, dragging a hand down his face. He knew Lillian had a temper, Petrovana had warned him, but he hadn't expected this. Not over a mistake. Not without even giving him a chance to explain. Now she was gone, and with her, the best warrior he had.

The training yard was silent. Soldiers shifted uncomfortably, uncertain whether to pick up their weapons or leave. Madislak stood there, watching the gates long after Lillian had vanished, a dull weight settling in his chest. This was going to make things a hell of a lot harder.

Leper's eyes fluttered open to the morning sunlight streaming through the bedroom window. A full month had passed since the War of Tudela. A full month since Rinawen's murder—yet her killer still walked free. The thought made his jaw tighten, but he shoved his brother, Blank Face, from his mind and focused instead on the beauty asleep on his chest.

Soon, he would leave for Kordry to find Rinawen's tree and pay his respects. He hadn't been able to attend her funeral, and this was something he needed to do alone. She had been the most important part of his life, and he wasn't sure how he would handle decorating her tree. He didn't want anyone else there. He needed time—to grieve, to think, to try to make sense of the emptiness she had left behind. His entire life, he handled adversity best on his own, and now would be no different.

The only people he could imagine sharing that moment with were her daughters, Zanera and Kelindra.

His greatest fear lay sprawled beside him, breathing deeply, and he wasn't sure how to tell her he'd be gone for a week—without her.

Since the war—no, since the moment he met Petrovana—she had accepted him completely. She defended him against Madislak and Brebian, always looking out for his well-being, especially in public spaces where his presence was still under scrutiny. That was something he absolutely loved about her, something she had in common with Rinawen when she was alive.

He inhaled deeply, savoring the scent of cinnamon and apples in her flowing black hair. Sleek and shimmering, it cascaded over her shoulder as he cupped the back of her head, running his nails lightly down her bare back. So. So soft.

"Mmm," she moaned into his ear, stirring as she nestled closer, draping a leg over his beneath the dark green blankets.

And gods, she was gorgeous. Morning or night, sweat-soaked and covered in dirt—it didn't matter. Somehow, she always looked beautiful, like a bouquet of flowers freshly picked and perfectly arranged.

Leper ran his fingers along the smooth crystal of the Theora hanging from his neck. The moment he touched it, Rinawen's face surfaced in his mind—her radiant smile, her long blond hair. Not a day passed that he didn't miss her.

Though Nalecht had retreated to Ambrosia to reorganize, they knew he'd make his next move soon—whether to resume his hunt for the shards or something else entirely. Leper glanced down at the shard, still thrumming faintly against his skin. It was the last piece not in the hands of Nalecht or Tamara, aside from the shard of Kasherri. The peace wouldn't last long, which was why they planned to meet with Madislak in a week to decide their next move.

No matter what, they couldn't let Nalecht claim either of the last two shards.

Leper gently kissed the top of Petrovana's head and slid out from under her. Walking over to his dresser, he threw on a green shirt and black pants. He considered starting to pack a bag for his trip but decided against it. No need to start the morning off that badly.

He grabbed a contraceptive vial from the top of his dresser, rolling it between his fingers as the dark brown liquid swirled inside. Lately, he couldn't imagine his life without Petrovana in it. She helped him control the fits of rage and mental fog that gripped him so often, and she helped him bear the loss of Rinawen. She truly was becoming a pillar in his life—one he couldn't remove.

"It's cold over here. Why'd you get out of bed?" Petrovana's groggy voice called out.

Leper sat back down beside her, extending the vial. "It's going to be a long day. But take this."

She batted her beautiful purple eyes. "Or what? Goin' to make me drink it?"

Leper grinned. "If I must."

She propped herself up on an arm. "Will you ever get over yer obsession with this? You'd make a great father."

Never. Not a chance. He would not risk endangering Petrovana's life for the chance to have a child. Not that he didn't want one, but if the cost was losing her...

"Until the day I am certain you won't die... No." Leper shook his head.

"What if I'm willin' to make that sacrifice... fer us? Fer you?" she smirked.

Leper placed his hand on her soft cheek, and she leaned into his touch. "Let's not go down this path right now. This week is going to be difficult for me, and I don't want to get into this right now."

He leaned in and kissed her soft lips, still tasting of cherries, but she pulled away.

"I don't mean right now, Leper." Her tone shifted, serious now. "But after this war is over, why not then? Why not try?"

Leper sighed. "Who knows how long this war will take or even if we'll both survive. Why not wait until after the threat of oblivion is dealt with before we have these conversations?"

"Bullshit! Yer only sayin' that because you want to find that Chernzerk girl that is still missin' and she can have yer damn babies and not die." She snarled.

"For the love of Theora. We have no idea where the last member of my race is at." Leper's toes curled against the floor. He hated these confrontations. "It could've been the girl that flew in on Fingin and saved Nalecht's life in Tudela, or she could be dead, or she could be anywhere else in the world."

"Just because we don't know where she is don't mean she ain't out there." Petrovana huffed. "Not to mention the fact that only a Chernzerk female can have a Chernzerk baby without the concern of dyin'. I ain't sayin' this for fun, but I adore everythin' about you. And I'm sorry if me wantin' some sort of future seems to get in the way, but I feel like I'm just some steppin' stone fer you."

Her words cut deep, the accusation stinging more than he could admit. She always pressed this issue, yammering on about having kids, living in some grand castle or palace. He wasn't even sure that was something he wanted. He liked the small hut in the woods where he grew up. Tucked away, private. They'd been together for a month now, and he wanted their relationship to deepen, but sometimes she made it hard, or it could've been his doing.

Leper rolled his eyes. "This again. You've shared my life since the war ended, and I love you for everything you've done for me. You helped me deal with losing Rinawen, and I will always love you for that, Petrovana."

"What about Lillian?" she hissed. "I know she has feelin's fer you."

Leper's mind drifted to Lillian, but he shook the thought away. "You are who I care about."

She yanked it from his hand and tossed it back quickly. "There... Happy!?"

"Almost." He exhaled, then finally dropped the news. "I'm leaving today for a week. And I'm going alone."

"What?" Her face contorted in confusion. "Where are ya goin'? Or am I not allowed to know that?"

"I'm going to Rinawen's tree to say goodbye to a friend." Saying it out loud hurt more than he anticipated. His throat tightened, and a tear slipped down his cheek before he wiped it away.

"Leper." She wrapped the blanket around herself and sat on her knees behind him. "I'm sorry, I didn't mean to pry or bring it up. I didn't realize that's what you were doin'. But with the bounty Larnadix put out and everyone else in the world searchin' for you or that shard, I think you should still let me go with you."

She slowly caressed his shoulders, her soft hands working his tense muscles. It felt good—comforting in a way few things were anymore.

"I know. I'll be careful, Petrovana." He leaned back into her touch, closing his eyes for a moment. "But I'm still going alone." He let out a sigh. "I just have to."

How could he make her understand? He appreciated that she wanted to go, that she cared—but he'd always dealt with hardship alone. It was the only way he knew how. No one else understood how to comfort him when he was upset. No one ever had—except Rinawen. And she was gone.

Petrovana was silent for a moment before resting her forehead against his shoulder. "I know how much she meant to you, and I ain't gonna push this anymore. I love you, and I want you to be happy. If this is what you want, I won't stop you. Just promise me you'll be safe." She wrapped her arms around him and squeezed.

He set his hand on her arm, leaning his head back against her. "I will be." He turned, pressing a kiss to her cheek. "Maybe you should keep this shard here—to make sure it's safe."

She pulled back slightly, studying him. "Don't you want to keep it in case somethin' happens? It'll protect you."

"No." He shook his head. "I've got Maka for that. If I run into Nalecht or Larnadix, I can't let them get their hands on this shard. It's safer with you."

"As long as yer sure." Petrovana rubbed his back, concern flickering in her purple eyes.

"I'm sure." He slipped the shard from around his neck, and the faint hum of its magic dissipated the moment it left his skin. "Keep it safe. When I get back, I'll come get it from you."

A small smirk tugged at her lips. "It's kinda intriguin', bein' with a wanted criminal."

He smiled back, though it faded quickly. "I gotta go. I don't know how I'm gonna face this, but delaying it will only make it worse."

His heart pounded as he packed, preparing to leave for Rinawen's tree. He wasn't sure what unsettled him more—that all of Kordry was hunting him, that Larnadix had lost his mind, or that he would be saying goodbye to Rinawen for the last time.

Ever.

A day after his brief argument with Petrovana, Leper approached his old hut, keeping low to avoid detection. He circled the woods several times, scanning every familiar clearing, every shadowed grove, searching for signs of civilians—or worse, Larnadix himself.

He knew all too well how much Larnadix hated him. That hatred had been made clear when they'd tried to attend Rinawen's funeral, only to find the banners offering five thousand gold for Leper's head. Excessive, considering he had nothing to do with Rinawen's death. But Larnadix didn't care. Grief had twisted him into something relentless.

None of it mattered now. Rinawen deserved his respect, and her tree deserved only the most glorious of decorations. Even a month after her death at the hands of his own brother, Leper's heart ached. The physical pain in his chest never went away, but he hoped that saying goodbye to the dearest friend he'd ever have might ease it, or at least quiet the anger that so often surged to the surface.

Sliding off Ghost's saddle, he stepped into the small, weathered house that had once been his. The wooden floor creaked beneath his boots, the air thick with memories. He pulled out the last chakram he had left from Rinawen—the one she'd given him when he was twelve. His fingers brushed over the worn leather hilt wrapped around the crescent-shaped blade, lingering. The other chakram had been lost on The Talon during the fight against Ace and his dragon, Voldahyl.

Leper exhaled, then set the weapon down. With Maka Kura, he no longer needed this blade.

For a moment, he stood still, letting the quiet of the home settle over him. It was strange—how a place could feel so empty and yet so familiar. Calm. Safe.

But he hadn't come here for nostalgia. He needed to find Rinawen's tree.

Tearing his gaze away, he grabbed a chunk of meat and bread from his pack, tossing it onto the ground for Ghost. The griffin purred, gobbling it up, then hopped around, squawking as she poked her beak into trees and investigated the house.

Leper chuckled softly, running a hand over her sleek feathers. "You helping me look?"

Ghost chirped in response, her sharp eyes scanning the forest.

Leper wasn't sure if she truly understood—but then again, she always seemed to.

And right now, that was enough.

"It won't be in this area, girl." He scratched under her beak. "It should be more north, by her parents."

Ghost popped her head north and sniffed. She then walked that way, checking every tree and squawking, before turning around and plowing into Leper, knocking him to the ground as her beak chittered along his neck. He laughed as she tickled him and playfully shoved her head off him as he got up and brushed himself off. He wrestled around with her for a few more minutes before getting himself back on track. He dismissed her to keep himself focused on finding her tree.

Over the next two days, Leper scoured the familiar forest for Rinawen's tree to no avail. He stopped only to eat and sleep. At first light on the third day, he gathered his supplies for another day of searching. Then, he would try to sneak into Kordry's castle to see Zanera and Kelindra on this near-impossible day. He set his vial pouch on top of the magically connected case, along with his daily travel pack, which held the book Rinawen had given him. He figured he wouldn't need it today. The shard of Theora was hopefully still safe in Petrovana's care.

"Sure, you don't want to take that with you?" Maka Kura popped into his head.

Leper stiffened as the voice startled him. "You know, a little warning when you're just going to ramble off some gibberish would be nice."

"Warning?" Maka Kura mocked. "Like this."

Leper felt his head tingle slightly, a little numbing sensation, then Maka screamed loudly. "HEY, LEPER!"

Leper jumped back at the booming echo in his mind, falling over and grabbing onto the bed. A fistful of brown covers came with him on his way down. The case and the vial pouch flew off the bed. Some of them crashed onto the floor and busted.

"Damn it, you idiot." Leper seethed. "No, that's not any better. Maybe you should just not talk altogether."

Maka laughed. "Sorry. Couldn't miss the opportunity. Maybe I'll do that when you're sleeping." Maka continued to chuckle. "Seriously, though. You're way too tense. Just trying to get you to loosen up a little bit. Sometimes it's good to not brood and be an uptight prude all the time."

"Uptight prude?" Leper scoffed. "I'm going to decorate the tree of a dead friend, you ignorant prick. Not exactly a great time to let loose and be happy."

"I get that, but just wanted to tell you that you've been unnecessarily rude and ignorant towards everyone lately. Petrovana especially. I wanted to let you know if you need to vent, I'm here. And it's not like I'll ever tell anyone."

"Thanks. I appreciate your concern, but I don't need your advice or counsel. I'm fine on my own." Leper retorted. As he picked up the mess, his hand slipped, and a small piece of glass pierced into the center of his palm.

"Son of a bitch!" He roared. "You see what you did now!?"

"If I would've known you were going to knock everything off the bed, I wouldn't have even bothered to try and joke with you," Maka said, sounding sort of like an apology.

"The worst part about you is I can't just leave you somewhere and not have to listen to your constant blabbing."

"Hmph." Maka snorted. "Judging by your actions and mood lately, I think you should take me up on that offer. You don't exactly talk to any of your friends about what's bothering you."

Leper shook his head as he put everything back like it was. "Just shut up. You already made this mess that you can't clean up because you're a weapon, you've done enough."

"I'm worried about you. That's it." Maka Kura's voice was deep and seemed oddly concerned.

"Well, I'm fine, just get out of my head and leave me alone for the next few days. If I wanted to be pestered, I would've asked Petrovana to come with me."

"If you say so." Maka poked, then went silent.

He scooped up his large pack, slung it across his back, and headed out the door. Stepping outside his old hut, the blue sky was refreshing, as was the familiar scent of home: pine, maple, apple trees, and lilacs—Rinawen's favorite. A sudden breeze pressed against the heavy pack on his back, making it sway. The shifting weight forced him to tighten his grip on the straps, adjusting his hold with more effort than he would have liked. Each step made the burden feel heavier, dragging against his shoulders.

Leper remembered nearly every nook and cranny of this forest as he marched to the north, grateful for his daily ex-

ercise regimen. Training every day, knowing Nalecht or his
forces could appear at any time, he continued to hone his abilities and practice with Maka Kura. He had trained so much
with Maka that no guards could oppose him, not even the lone
bulwark. Until Petrovana suggested he train with his brother,
Blank Face. Leper snarled at the thought. Thankful for the
sparring partner that truly challenged him—one he had yet to
best—Blank Face was also the main reason he was here today.

He shook the thought out of his mind. Today was not the
day to think about that wretched, vile soul, but the one laid to
rest a month ago. A physical pain seared across his chest as he
pictured her smile, her face, her hair... her voice.

His vision whirred to a blur, and his mind became a swirling
vortex of anger. He had another urge to kill Blank Face yet again
for what he had done, and if that bastard was here, he'd do it.
He slammed the pack on the ground in anger and screamed.

Maka Kura filled his mind with another booming echo. "Shut
your mouth! Are you trying to get caught out here!" He sighed,
and it sounded disappointed. "You're ruining all the golden
twine, knock it off!"

"You're nothing but a stupid weapon! You don't know what it
feels like to lose someone, asshole." Leper fired back.

Ghost plowed into Leper again and knocked him over playfully. Leper grabbed onto her neck and pulled on her head lightly.
She chittered her beak under his armpit, and he let out a bubble
chuckle. Perhaps Maka was right; he was too frequently letting
the anger get the best of him. Well, not entirely, Blank Face still
needed to die, and so did anyone else who was involved with her
death.

It was then he noticed it, a familiar and comforting scent that
cut through his rage. He looked up and saw the tree standing
before him, and without a doubt, he knew it was Rinawen's.

The tree wasn't as decorated as it should have been. Only a
few had shown their respect. Lilacs filled the air, and vibrant
flowers twisted around the trunk. Her embroidered shirt hung
from a branch, along with her wedding dress—both green, both
adorned with vines and flowers. Vines crept up the tree, and far
above, a crown rested—a simple thorny circlet, crowned in gold
and silver, with daisies, roses, and lilacs woven through it.

Leper fell to his knees and braced his hands on the tree, no longer able to hold back the sobs and dread that coursed through his body.

Talking came in spurts. "What..." He sobbed again. "What am I going to do without you? For the rest of my life..." He swallowed hard, his mouth dry and sapped of moisture as he tried to calm himself down and slow his breathing.

"I can't do this without you, Rin..." He looked up at the branches. "There's no one I can trust. Not like I trusted you. Even Petrovana... For all her kindness, I still don't know who would do for me what you have done."

Even when he learned she'd lied to him about Blank Face being his brother, it stung for a bit. But that paled in comparison to what she meant to him. He spent the rest of the time emptying the contents of his large bag. It was twine, colored gold, just like her hair, and Leper had made sure it was exactly her color. He had it redone several times because it didn't meet his standards. He would not—could not—bring lackluster gifts to her tree.

Utilizing Maka Kura, Leper floated the strands of twine through the tree, weaving them to mimic her long, flowing golden locks. He longed to hang the shard of Theora there, but knew Nalecht would somehow find it, and that was too risky. *Maybe once Nalecht was dealt with.*

A couple of hours passed, and he took in another breath of the lilac-scented air. A rustling noise caught his attention. He jolted up, listening, peering. He didn't see anyone, and he'd been out here for so long that anyone could have heard his pathetic scream earlier and reported his presence. The sun had nearly vanished, leaving only a sliver of light. *Probably a deer.* He folded his empty bag quickly, preparing to return to his hut one last time before attempting to sneak into the castle. His heart thundered in his chest, and his hands trembled as he picked the bag up and slung it over his shoulder.

A sudden rush of footsteps barreled toward him from behind. Before he could react, he was knocked to the ground.

Chapter Three

B y the time Leper turned around, two vicious girls had already knocked him over. Kelindra rammed into him full speed as Zanera helped push him the rest of the way to the ground. His lips curled upward at the sight of his two favorite people in the world. He was dying to know how they'd been, what they'd been up to this past month, or if they had forgotten about him entirely. From the looks of it, not likely. And all traces of his anger completely fluttered away as his lips curled upward.

Leper fell onto his back, and Kelindra sat on his chest. She grabbed his horns and pushed his head into the ground as she got inches from his face, barely able to control her growing grin but holding a serious face as best she could.

"You are in big trouble, mister!" She pointed her little finger at him.

Leper put his hands up in surrender. "You got me. I'm sorry."

"Unacceptable. First, you don't say bye. Now you are never home." She poked his cheek. "And no, notes back and forth in your stupid medicine vial holder thingy don't count!"

During his trip to The Talon, they had discovered a unique way to communicate—if they placed paper inside the magical metal container in his abandoned hut, it would appear in the pouch he usually carried at his side. They used this method as often as possible to stay in touch. But since they had to leave the castle to access the container, it wasn't exactly convenient. Worse, he never got to see them in person.

A shadow passed over them. A beat later, Ghost thudded to the earth behind Kelindra, massive wings folding in with a rustle of wind and feathers. She chirped happily and nudged Leper's shoulder, nearly rolling him over.

"Ghost!" Kelindra squealed and immediately jumped off Leper to pet the griffin's feathered neck. Zanera laughed and joined in, rubbing behind one of Ghost's ears while the beast playfully batted at Leper's foot with a taloned paw.

After returning from the War of Tudela, Leper had introduced Zanera and Kelindra to Ghost, and they immediately hit it off.

"Alright, alright—" Leper chuckled, pushing himself up. "Go on now, Ghost. Can't have you stomping around where someone might hear you."

Ghost huffed, gave Kelindra a final nuzzle, then flapped her wings once and took off into the sky with a low cry that echoed across the hills.

Laughter bubbled up from his chest, spilling out before he could stop it. Grinning, he wrapped his arms around Kelindra and playfully tickled her sides until she squirmed away. She wore a blue shirt and black pants, her brown hair now reaching just past her shoulders.

Zanera stepped toward him, tears welling in her eyes. He pulled her into a tight embrace and held her close.

"I've missed you both so much. You have no idea," he said.

Through her sniffles, she replied, "We've missed you, too. Everything has...changed."

A surge of rage rolled through his entire body. His disdain for Larnadix grew tenfold. If it wasn't for the bounty he placed on Leper's head and his general complete hatred for him, they would be able to visit whenever. However, since Rinawen's death, he no longer had her protection in Kordry, and Larnadix took complete advantage of being the sole ruler of the kingdom...for now.

"Meaning?" Leper kissed her forehead and then ruffled Kelindra's hair.

Her giggle told him everything he needed to know—that there were still people who cared about him as much as their mother did. Now nine years old, Kelindra was just a little taller than he remembered. Zanera handed him another blueberry tart, his favorite, and he wasted no time gobbling it down. The buttery crust and tang of blueberries always a delight on his tongue.

Zanera brushed some dirt off Leper's shoulder. "Meaning ever since Mom...well..." Another tear escaped her eye, and Leper's seething anger towards Blank Face deepened as Zanera finished, "It's just different around here."

Zanera rubbed her forearm and elbow, a sign that she was either nervous or had something she wanted to say.

"I'm sorry I can't be around more. I wish it was different, and maybe someday it will be, but until then we'll just have to see each other when we can." He knelt down and wrapped his arm around Kelindra.

Her blue shirt shifted, and he noticed a slight red mark on her shoulder. He pushed the shirt aside, revealing a mark that ran down her back. Like she'd been struck by something, or maybe had fallen? His eyes snapped to Zanera, and she glanced away. He stood up and looked her over. She had two marks on her that looked like the one Kelindra had.

"What the hell is that?" His voice was stern, and his mind swirled.

"It's nothing." Kelindra fixed her shirt. "Dad was mad we snuck out to go to your house in the evening one time."

"In the evening, like it is now?" He set his hand on Zanera's shoulder and turned her to face him.

She nodded yes, but still said nothing.

"He whipped you or hit you, or whatever the hell that is for being out in the evening?" He seethed.

"It's nothing, Uncle Leper, we are fine here, you don't need to worry about us," Kelindra argued as she walked towards him.

"Leper," Zanera said, squaring her shoulders.

He looked straight into her green eyes. "Yes?"

"Uhm..." She looked away to the ground.

Kelindra poked his gut. "Will you take the Oath of Blood and Spirit with us?"

"The oath!?" Leper jerked his head back. "That... would be extremely complicated and likely end with both of you being marked as traitors to the elves."

Leper glanced between the two girls, curiosity flickering across his face as he arched a brow. The Oath of Blood and Spirit was sacred, an unbreakable bond that tied non-family members together as kin. Once completed, it could never be undone; their blood became his, and his became theirs. It was most often used when adults adopted a child, sealing them as family forever. Betrayal was impossible. Once bound in the presence of a deity, the god or goddess overseeing the oath would sometimes intervene to punish any who dared break it.

As much as Leper wanted to take this oath with them, he knew it would only create more problems.

"I told you, Kelindra." Zanera shook her finger towards Kelindra. "It's not something we can just do."

"Why would you want to do that anyway? What about your father?" Leper rubbed the back of his neck. "What about your city. Your birthright?"

The biggest problem was their current father. What would Larnadix do if they were suddenly no longer bound to him? He was their father by blood, and that alone would make him even angrier than he already was.

Then there was the matter of their royalty. In three years, Zanera would have the right to rule Kordry if she chose. The city had never belonged to Larnadix—it had been Rinawen's. And under their laws, leadership didn't pass to him just because he had been married to her. It was Zanera's birthright.

But if she took the oath with Leper, everything could change. His being a Chernzerk would almost certainly lead Kordry to cast her out, stripping her of her claim to the throne. And then what? Would she live with him, Petrovana, and Kelindra in the woods? Did she even understand what she'd be giving up?

She and her sister would be sacrificing more than he could even fathom. And they wanted to do all this for him?

"He's not Dad. He's just not. He couldn't care less about us. We never leave the castle, he's always planning, or sleeping, or doing some stupid renovations in the basement." Zanera stomped her foot. "Something changed him when he disappeared. It's like he's not Larnadix anymore, but someone else entirely, and with Mom gone, it only gets worse. I couldn't care less about that stupid birthright Leper. I'd rather be poor and happy than rich and miserable."

He spoke softly. "Zanera, Kordry is next in line to provide the Anyth. Which will be you by that time, and you'll move to the capital."

"I don't really care. I don't want to move there, I don't want to be Anyth. I want to stay here with you." Zanera put her hands on her hips.

"Well, there's still like ten years left for Axeladdle to provide the Anyth, Zanera. If they can't provide a suitable one once Nalecht is either dead or removed, then it will fall to you." Leper brushed her hair back over her ears.

She stammered and shook her head. "So?"

"So, if you take that oath with me, I'm sure they won't let you be Anyth after bonding with a dirty Cherno." Leper gritted. "I don't like it, but it's the truth and you both know it."

"That's because everyone is stupid and mean," Kelindra shouted.

"Forget it. We can discuss it some other time. I missed you, and I don't want us to fight with what little time we have." Zanera smiled at Leper.

A gust of wind blew through as the sun disappeared, giving way to the moon's yellow light. Leper could smell lilacs on Zanera now, just like her mother. Her golden hair was braided over the top of her head and around her right ear, then hung down just beyond her shoulders. It was longer than the last time he saw her.

"Yeah, that stupid, mean man keeps showing up a lot, too," Kelindra blurted.

Leper's grin vanished. "What stupid, mean man?"

Zanera let out a sigh. "Nalecht."

"Does he threaten or hurt you?" Leper glowered at Zanera. "Why didn't you mention any of this in the notes?"

Rage surged through him, a blistering fog of fury ready to consume everything just to eliminate the threat. It was the same rage he'd felt when Blank Face stabbed Rinawen, when he'd fumbled for the revival vial too late. The same fury that had overtaken him when Ace had threatened Petrovana in that cell. He couldn't control it.

"No, he doesn't hurt us, but he comes around every week or so." Zanera fiddled with her hair, avoiding his gaze. "I didn't think it was that important, Leper. You were fighting off Crux's gang in Kundry and trying to keep the shard hidden. I didn't want you coming here, where there's a bounty on your head, and getting yourself killed trying to help us."

He heard her words, but they barely registered. His mind spun, suffocated under the weight of it all. Larnadix was manipulating them. Nalecht was coming around. There was a price on his head. And the two people he loved most were trapped in a danger he couldn't pull them from.

His eyes flicked from Zanera to Kelindra. He let out a slow breath. The rage ebbed, and his thoughts cleared. If there were a way to get them out of Kordry, he'd do it in a heartbeat.

But with a bounty on his head and half the world hunting for him, or for the shard he'd entrusted to Petrovana, it would put them in too much danger. He couldn't risk that. He couldn't risk them.

"Well, this is an unexpected surprise."

Leper tensed and turned. Nalecht stood casually against a tree, his long white hair flowing in the breeze.

"What are you doing here? Didn't you learn your lesson in Tudela?" Leper growled.

Nalecht pushed off the tree, his black and brown uniform clinging tightly to his slender frame. His elven ears jutted out just beyond his hair.

"My lesson?" Nalecht let out a low, cruel chuckle. "I may have lost that particular battle, but the war is far from over."

From behind him, Larnadix stepped into view. Short and chubby, their father, sure—but out here, parading around with Nalecht?

His shaggy brown hair flopped to the side as his gaze narrowed on Leper. "All this time, my wife and daughters told me about this strange man named Leper they go to see in the woods, and not once did they mention he was a dirty freaking Cherno!"

"What?" Zanera's voice bristled with exasperation. "You've known that forever—practically since you and Mom got married."

Larnadix stifled what Leper thought was either a scream or an insult, but something was off about him. Leper could see it in his face; something had changed. He hadn't even had the opportunity to confront him before all this. Petrovana had approached Larnadix about them attending the funeral, and that's when he put the bounty on Leper's head, blaming him for Rinawen's death and demanding he never return. But in truth, the last time Leper had stood face-to-face with Larnadix was eight years ago, the first time he'd seen Kelindra as a one-year-old baby. That had been the last time he'd laid eyes on him.

Maybe after being kidnapped five years ago, Larnadix had lost his memory?

Leper caught Zanera's gaze for a brief second. Something had definitely changed. Larnadix had known Leper before—never liked him, sure, but he'd never seemed this furious about it. Maybe he'd just masked his disgust for the Chernzerk because of Rinawen?

"It's not important," Nalecht cut in. "What is important is—who has the dead bitch's shard?"

Fury ignited in Leper's core. His face burned with rage so pure he thought his ears might catch fire. "Wouldn't you like to know, you senile old fuck," he said, voice low and sharp as a blade.

"You take that back!" Zanera spat, shoving past Leper's shoulder.

He caught her waist and pulled her behind him as she continued to scream, "My mom is not a bitch!"

Kelindra started sobbing.

Leper flicked a glance over his shoulder. "I'll handle them. You take care of Kelindra."

"I can help you." Zanera snapped.

"This is the Anyth," Leper said, shaking his head. "He's powerful—politically and physically. I won't have either of you risk your status or well-being for me. If your so-called fath—"

Leper didn't have time to finish as his head got wrenched backward by the horns. Nalecht's sneering face loomed in front of him, fingers trailing over Leper's chest.

"So, where's my shard?"

"Let him go!" Zanera shrieked, then drove her foot into Nalecht's groin.

Leper's heart pounded as Nalecht released his horns, doubling over in pain and dropping to one knee. Laughter threatened to bubble up, but fury smothered it—fury at how Nalecht spoke about Rinawen and her daughter, and how Larnadix just stood there like a clueless idiot and let him.

"Zanera! Don't attack the Anyth! What are you thinking?!" Larnadix barked, jabbing a sausage-like finger at her.

All traces of humor vanished, replaced by raw, seething hatred. As Nalecht reeled, Leper caught his wrist before he could strike Zanera—and drove his fist straight into Nalecht's nose.

The crack that followed sent waves of elation through Leper.

"You don't fucking touch them." He snarled, driving his fist into Nalecht's cheek with another satisfying snap. He loved every second of this.

"I have had it with you peasants disrespecting me!" Nalecht roared, staggering to his feet. Blood trickled from his nose. "I'm the Anyth! You don't attack me!"

"You do when he threatens your life and kills the people you love." Leper swung again. It didn't matter who he was—Anyth or not, he deserved this beating.

"I'm warning you," Nalecht growled. "You hit me again, and I'm going to—"

Crack.

Leper's fist slammed into his nose again. The sharp iron scent filled the air as blood streamed down Nalecht's face.

The shards of Ryollin and Hathor flared red and blue on his necklace as he whipped out his falchion. Leper had probably bitten off more than he could chew, but that didn't matter. Defending Rinawen's name mattered. Protecting those kids mattered. He wouldn't let them drag her through the mud. Wouldn't let them hurt Zanera and Kelindra.

He raised his palms, and Maka Kura glided into them like always. The dance of blades began.

Zanera and Kelindra shrieked as Larnadix ushered them away. Leper couldn't tell if he was ushering them away because of the fight, or to use them as leverage against him; he didn't have time to dwell on that right now. He could take care of Larnadix once he was done with Nalecht.

Leper had fought this battle before—he'd beaten Nalecht at Tudela barely a month ago. He could do it again. Maybe even reclaim the shards hanging from that bastard's neck and end this once and for all.

That thought shattered as cold steel bit into his abdomen.

Pain should have surged through him, but rage numbed it. He barely registered the wound.

He swung upward with the chakrams—both deflected. Adjusting instantly, he arced another toward Nalecht's neck.

Nalecht caught his wrist mid-air and squeezed.

"Not this time, asshole," he sneered.

Leper's fingers went numb under the crushing grip. Then the shard of Ryollin hummed, glowing an even brighter red.

With inhuman strength, Nalecht wrenched Leper up and slammed him into the ground.

Agony tore through his spine. His back arched as a dull, aching shock rippled through every nerve. He swore he could taste that blueberry tart Zanera had given him creeping back up his throat.

"Where's the shard of Theora, Leper?" Nalecht pressed his blade to Leper's throat.

Across the clearing, Zanera and Kelindra shrieked as Larnadix kept them pinned in place.

"I told you—I don't know." Leper gritted out, searching for an opening to shove the sword aside and launch upward.

"Maka, can you take his head off if I command you?"

"Not likely," Maka Kura replied. "With his augmented speed and strength from the shard, we could try, but you're only digging yourself a bigger grave, Leper. We're not strong enough to handle him... yet."

Leper debated ignoring Maka's warning. If he struck now, he might land a hit—but it could cost Zanera and Kelindra their lives. He simply wasn't strong enough. He needed shards. Shards that Nalecht had. His gaze flicked to the necklace still glowing faint red from Ryollin and blue from Hathor.

"I'm not messing around." Nalecht sneered. "Tell me where it is, or you die."

"I don't. Fucking. Know." Leper spat in his face.

Nalecht slammed his head against the ground. Leper's vision went white. Sounds blurred, the world muffled—he barely heard Zanera and Kelindra's cries as he struggled to stand. Even the forest scent was gone. Rinawen's lilacs? Faded.

Just as his senses started creeping back, a boot drove into his already gashed stomach.

The impact sent him flying backward, slamming into a tree beside Zanera and Kelindra.

"Stop it!" Kelindra screamed. "Don't hurt him—he's nice!"

Leper blinked, forced himself to a knee. His head pounded. Blood burned in his throat.

"Stay back. Both of you." He glanced at them—just for a second—and the fog of rage lifted enough for him to think clearly.

"Nalecht." Larnadix's voice cut through the tension. Deeper than Leper remembered.

He studied him again. Not just heavier than before, but different. Something had changed.

"What is it?" Nalecht snapped.

Larnadix folded his arms. "Perhaps there's another purpose for him." His tone was unreadable, offering nothing more.

Nalecht glanced down at Leper. "I must admit—I absolutely loathe you and your entire kind." He paced in front of him, slow, deliberate. "But you remind me of Xartazza."

Xartazza? I know I heard that name before. The name stirred something distant in Leper's mind. "Who's Xartazza?"

"Who he was doesn't really matter. What matters is how he fought." Nalecht ran his thumb along his jawline, studying him. "As much as I hate to admit it, you remind me of him. Slower—but your strength is your real asset."

Leper pushed himself to his feet, using the tree for balance. "What's your point?"

"My point is, he disappeared—five, maybe six years ago. Somewhere around there." Nalecht rolled the shards between his fingers, their glow flickering. "I wanted to find him. Needed him to get me the last shard, the one from the rain trials."

Leper scoffed. "Why don't you get the damn thing yourself? You've got all these other shards, and you're already a pain in the ass to fight."

Nalecht grinned, settling the shards back against his shirt. "I can't enter the trials with these shards. And I sure as hell don't trust anyone else to hold all of them." His gaze flicked to Larnadix. "And him... Well, you don't need to know why he can't go in."

Interesting.

He stepped forward, voice dropping to a deadly whisper. "All you need to know is how to get that shard."

Leper let out a sharp, humorless laugh. "Not happening. Ever."

Nalecht's sneer deepened. "Allow me to change your mind."

The green shard of Obidiah flared to life, sending a massive wave of fire blasting from Nalecht's hand. The flames engulfed Rinawen's newly decorated tree, the one he had spent so much time perfecting, and Leper's stomach plummeted. A boulder-sized lump formed in his throat. *No.* All the rage he'd fought down surged back, now twisted with gnawing dread and sadness that pricked at his very soul.

The tree burned with an intensity Leper had never witnessed. The scent of charred wood and melting twine filled the air as it went up in flames. The cold night vanished, replaced by searing heat that stung his skin.

Anger boiled into rock-solid dread as he felt two hands grasp each of his wrists. He turned to see Zanera on his left, holding him steady as she too fought the eruption of emotions inside. He pulled her close, his arm wrapping protectively around her. To his right, Kelindra was already sobbing. She was just nine—*Amarook's sake*, she shouldn't have to see this. This man was desecrating her mother's memory, burning the sacred grave she'd created.

Leper's heart pounded with the desire to tear Nalecht apart, to let out a guttural cry and become a feral beast. But he couldn't, not with Zanera and Kelindra there. So, he held them tighter, drawing comfort from their closeness as the ashes of Rinawen's tree floated away, her lilac scent vanishing into the smoke.

"You are the most despicable elf I've ever met," Leper's voice cracked.

"Despicable or not," Nalecht sneered, "you're going to get that shard for me from the rain trials. Until I can get my hands on Xartazza or Blank Face, you'll do."

He shoved the girls away from Leper. "Go to Costin. Take the oath to enter. If you survive, I'll give them to you in exchange for the shard."

"No!" Leper roared. "I don't trust you. I don't trust him! How do I know you won't hurt them? They should stay in Kundry with Queen Leighth."

"I'm a man of my word," Nalecht said, sticking his nose in the air. "I won't harm them. You have my word. Hell, I might even let you live if you bring me the shard of Kasherri. But they will remain here, with my... They will remain here with Larnadix until you succeed."

"And what if I don't? What if I die in these stupid trials?" Leper gritted.

"I guess it sucks to be you then, doesn't it?" Nalecht smiled. Leper would've loved to smack that grin right off his smug face.

"But then again, if you're dead, you won't know what happens to them, will you? And it won't matter anyway." He gracefully flicked his hair over his shoulder.

Leper turned to point at Larnadix. "He can't harm them either." He shook his head, frustration boiling over. "I need time to gather my things and prepare to leave. I..." He cut himself off, not needing to explain. "Never mind. Go fuck yourself, Nalecht. I'll get your damn shard, but I swear to Theora, if you hurt either of them, you'll have more than just me to worry about."

If anyone harmed these girls, he would let the fire inside him consume his every thought. He would utilize whatever darkness harbored inside of him to get his vengeance. And he would let it consume him until the entire world burned.

"Agreed." Nalecht sneered. "But one last thing. You've got two weeks to enter. I'll be waiting at the entrance. If you're not there in two weeks..." He backhanded both Zanera and Kelindra to the ground, his face twisted with malice. "They die."

Leper flicked his eyes to Zanera, then Kelindra, and nodded, a silent promise that he would return for them. Zanera nodded back, then jerked her head slightly to keep Nalecht and Larnadix from noticing, signaling toward his hut. They would continue sending notes through his magical pouch and vial box.

Chapter Four

F our weeks had passed since Lillian's departure, a full month since the War of Tudela. Madislak sat at a table in his throne room, his bride-to-be, Harmony, beside him, surrounded by stacks of both ancient and newly written books. Some of these volumes, more than three centuries old, chronicled the first war and the breaking of the talisman into seven pieces. They pored over the texts, searching for knowledge about the talisman and its shards—desperate to understand the threat Nalecht posed if he succeeded in reforging the ancient relic.

Madislak had been forced to appoint someone else to train his troops—an unfortunate necessity, but Lillian still hadn't returned, and he had no idea where she'd gone. He couldn't understand how she could be so upset over a mere mistake.

Madislak's throne, a grand wooden chair painted blue and yellow, featured a bright yellow lion's head at the top, mouth agape. It was cushioned and comfortable, set in a large gathering area with stone pillars and columns. Half the space housed chairs and tables, while the other half remained open for standing audiences.

Being in his kingdom felt right. His father and children were here, as was Harmony, his beautiful protégé and fiancée. Their relationship had blossomed since the War of Tudela. He still felt pangs of guilt over Gwen's fate, but he was determined to change the future. As king, he planned to abolish the rules of marriage for royalty, allowing future rulers of Lantess to marry for love, not for gold, resources, or power.

The city's rebuilding efforts were nearly complete, allowing him to focus on the shards. Despite the talisman's enigmatic power, they discovered one chilling fact: once reforged, it would be indestructible. At least that's what all the people who wrote these useless books seemed to think. Not a single one of them knew how to destroy it, or if it was even possible.

Madislak shuddered at the thought of Nalecht wielding such power. He glanced at Harmony, her focus intense on the book in her hands, and knew they had to find a way to prevent the unthinkable.

The heavy double doors to the connecting hallway swung open, and Nelaan, Madislak's father, barged in, a bottle of whiskey and two shot glasses in hand. His bald head and white beard spoke volumes of his age, but it was the hollowness in his brown eyes that hinted at something amiss.

Harmony closed her book, addressing Nelaan with a polite greeting, but Nelaan's focus was on Madislak. He poured each of them a drink, a silent invitation to a serious conversation.

"Hello, Mr. Idelth. How are you today?" Harmony inquired.

"Fine," Nelaan replied, taking a sip of whiskey. He glanced at Madislak, motioning for him to do the same. "I have something I need to discuss with my son... If you wouldn't mind."

Madislak interjected, refusing to exclude Harmony from the conversation. "She is to be my wife, and there will be no secrets between us. Whatever you have to say to me, you can say to her."

Nelaan exchanged a glance with Harmony before turning back to Madislak. "Even as your future wife, I don't know how she will react to what I'm about to say."

Madislak took a sip of whiskey, bracing himself for what was to come. "It doesn't matter. She's about to be part of this family, and you will treat her as such."

Nelaan leaned back, crossing his legs. "Very well, my king. You might want to finish that shot then and get her one too."

"Just spit it out already," Madislak urged, his leg bouncing under the table.

Nelaan didn't waste any time. "Coraidon and Finrod D'leon have been murdered by someone named The Latter. The King and Queen of Terynsipple are dead."

Madislak's leg stopped bouncing under the table. He remembered Leper mentioning The Latter after the War of Tudela, the mohawked freak who had cut off Queen Leighth's ear. Leper had said the man could transform into some kind of toxic smoke and was a formidable opponent. His mohawk had been... blue? Green? Madislak couldn't recall all the details. But last he knew, this man had been searching for Blank Face. And now he was killing royalty?

Nelaan explained. "According to my sources, he's working with Nalecht as long as it serves his own interests. They're attempting to force the shrews of Terynsipple to join them. What better way to do that than to exercise their power?"

"So I need to go over there and petition them for safe harbor in return for their assistance?" Madislak proposed, seeking a solution.

"Or send Petrovana?" Harmony suggested, offering an alternative. "Before her banishment, she was the heir to Terynsipple. She might be able to talk them into following her—or might even make herself queen."

"They won't lift her banishment if she goes on her own," Nelaan replied dryly.

"Then I'll go over and demand they lift her banishment. We don't have time for this crap." Madislak took another sip.

Nelaan shook his head, disagreeing. "No."

"No!?" Madislak protested. "Why not? I should do something."

"Showing up yourself or sending Petrovana will only get you so far," Nelaan countered. "They're shrews—strange and eccentric, but strict about their rules. They could still be swayed to fight for whoever they believe will win."

Frustration bubbled inside Madislak. "Then what would you have me do?"

"Marry Petrovana," Nelaan said bluntly. "It will guarantee their allegiance. She was once the heir to Terynsipple, with a strong noble lineage. They'll fight for her to be their queen and you, their king. The union would secure their place in the kingdoms, and I guarantee that if she's married to the King of Lantess... they'll lift that banishment and fight for you."

Madislak's refusal was swift and adamant. "No. Not in a thousand damned lifetimes. I can't... I won't."

"Look at me!" Nelaan's voice rose. "You can and you will! This world is being ripped apart piece by piece. Joining Lantess with the shrews will send a strong message and gain their support. Madislak, you don't have another option."

"What makes you so sure they will join us if I marry her? What do you know that I don't?" Madislak challenged as he narrowed his gaze on Nelaan.

Nelaan matched his intensity. "I've been alive for sixty years, son. I know how the world works and how to manipulate entire cities to get what I..." He stopped. "To get what we want."

Madislak's gaze bored a hole into his father. Yet again, wanting him to marry someone he didn't want to marry at all.

Madislak glanced at Harmony, her silence more powerful than words. Her eyes blazed with anger, her face a mask of steel. Their eyes met briefly before she buried her face in her hands, overwhelmed with emotion.

"I'm sorry. This is why I didn't want her here, but it makes the most logical sense," Nelaan persisted.

Madislak's fist slammed the table in frustration. "NO! I'm the damn king, and I say no. We'll find another way."

Nelaan let out a long, dejected sigh. "Fine. I can't force you to do this, like I did with Gwen. But you need to at least consider the implications, boy. You can't just power and hack your way through everything."

"Is that all?" Madislak gritted.

Nelaan shook his head as he took yet another shot of whiskey, then another.

"There's more." He poured them another round. "The real reason I got removed from the throne when Nalecht took power. I feel it's time for you to know the truth from me before you hear it somewhere else."

Madislak drilled his father with a look. Up until this point, Madislak believed his father was removed from the throne for incompetence. Now he's admitting that he'd lied to him all these years about why he had been removed? *Disgusting.* This man lied to him all that time. What kind of father would do that? What kind of nonsensical garbage would come out of his mouth now?

Nelaan's explanation flowed forth. "Many, many years ago, before your mother died, I knew Oubank and Samaja existed. Your horned friends' father."

Madislak knew exactly who Nelaan was talking about. Samaja was Leper and Blank Face's father, while Oubank was Ace's. They still hadn't found Ace's sister, but apparently she was out there somewhere.

Harmony interrupted, her tone serious. "His name is Leper."

"Right, anyway." Nelaan continued with a shrug. "Yusef, Nalecht's father, had battled against his grandfather Pasileveo and kept those two hidden from him when he was trying to exterminate them all. Before Samaja and Oubank's children were born, he told me he had to do something important on The Talon but didn't tell me what. Asked if I could hide the damn Cherno's in Lantess. So I did. After Yusef died, I may have helped the Chernzerk hide from Nalecht, because for some reason, he absolutely hates them."

Madislak's throat tightened. "You...you lied...you lied to me!" He seethed.

"The only reason Nalecht didn't say the real reason he re-moved me is because he's the one who orchestrated Goreldea's original attack on us when you were nineteen. I told him you could kill all three of her sons—her three sons who would've posed a threat to him claiming the title of Anyth."

Madislak's mouth hung open. "You used me!?"

Nelaan held his finger up. "I was dumb. It wasn't until Yusef told me he found two Chernzerk teenagers in Xaneth Harbor. He also told me the talisman isn't used for its power, but it's the key to something, but left out the details of what it was the key for." He rubbed the back of his neck. "So I went to Xaneth Harbor to find out what Tamara was up to. She was looking to manipulate the Chernzerk that could talk to the dragons for her own twisted reasons."

Nelaan's throat bobbed. "So, I set him free. Told him to seek out Kendra, she had something that might require his skill set. And keep him hidden."

All this time searching, and his father could've helped.

Madislak's grip on the table was iron, knuckles blanched to bone, the wood beneath his hand groaning. His heart fractured within his chest, pulsing with a fury previously unknown. The man he revered was nothing but a deceitful, self-serving relic. How dare he manipulate Madislak, the respected ruler, into his political machinations, reducing him to a mere puppet? Again and again, Madislak's fist hammered the table, the force enough to splinter wood and draw blood from his own flesh. Harmony reached out to place a calming hand on his shoulder, but he shrugged it off. His face was too hot, his anger too far over the edge to rein in.

"All this time... you knew..." His voice thundered, accusation laced with anguish. "You raised me to despise them, to fear them, yet you sheltered them! You vile, deceptive, manipulative wretch!" His words sliced through the air.

"I saved us all. My knowledge, my leverage, kept Nalecht at bay, spared Lantess from ruin long before your reign," Nelaan attempted to reason. "If I hadn't helped Nalecht become Anyth by having you kill Goreldea's sons eleven years ago, then he would've taken Lantess for himself. He would've taken it for the—"

Crack.

Madislak backhanded his father mid-sentence. He didn't need to hear any more of his treachery. The man had helped Nalecht become Anyth, setting this entire path in motion for him, the shards, the talisman, everything. He was literally aiding the enemy, nothing but a complete waste of space.

"Leave. I never want to see your face in my city again." Madislak's command was absolute, a decree forged in fury.

"Madislak, please—" Nelaan began, but was swiftly cut off.

"I said GET OUT!" Madislak bellowed, pointing towards the door. "And don't you dare return."

Nelaan rose, extending a hand in apology. "Son, I'm sorry—"

"Sorry?" Madislak scoffed, his voice dripping with contempt. "You're the reason Mom suffered, the reason she died! If not for your actions, she would never have endured that torment, knowing her fate for four long months. Was she just another pawn in your fucking political games?"

When his father didn't respond, Madislak knew there had to be more to his worthless existence than what he was saying. But he didn't have time to delve into that right now. The only thing Madislak knew was that he didn't want to see this man's face around here again. Hell, he probably helped Nalecht plan the first attack on Lantess when Madislak went to find the shard down in the Bay of Disdain. His core heated intensely.

Madislak grabbed the edge of the table, and Harmony dove out of the way as he upended the entire thing, scattering books and chairs as the table broke apart—glass shattering on the floor, the smell of whiskey filling his senses.

"Do not go near my children again. Do not come near me again."

"Please," Nelaan begged. "Please. Take time to process before making any rash decisions."

Madislak rushed towards Nelaan, ready to forcefully shove him out the front doors. "Get the fuck out and never come back. I'll not have you use your grandchildren as pawns in your life of lies."

Leper guided Ghost down onto Lantess' landing pad, already longing for the forests of Kundry, which always granted him a sense of serenity. His heart pounded. Zanera and Kelindra remained in Kordry, held by Larnadix. He didn't trust Nalecht or Larnadix to keep their word, but to ensure the girls' safety, he had to entrust the shard of Theora, which he just got back from Petrovana, to someone before setting off for the rain trials.

It had taken him two days to reach Lantess, one to pick up Petrovana, the other to fly here on Ghost, leaving him with only twelve days to reach Costin and enter the trials. He couldn't afford to linger. But first, he and Petrovana needed to meet with Madislak, Harmony, and Lillian to decide who would safeguard the shard in his absence.

He scanned the city of Lantess, amazed at the transformation. The last time he was here, the place had been in shambles, everything ablaze, and Madislak had just lost his betrothed wife. The sight before him now was a far cry from that grim memory. People lined the streets, bustling about, and the castle had been restored to its former glory, its four high peaks bearing the Lantess flag and insignia, flapping proudly in the wind. The scent of freshly cut wood and mixed concrete filled his nostrils as he took a deep breath.

He helped Petrovana off Ghost and stroked the great beast's feathered neck. She nuzzled her head into his chest, and he patted her furry brown head, his hand running the length of her beak. She squawked and ruffled her wings as she bounced around excitedly. She bumped Leper with her large body and nudged Petrovana, too. Leper chuckled and smoothed her feathered neck, then told her to be free for a while. With a lurch, she took flight, her great wings beating rapidly, and Leper watched in awe as she sped away.

Leper grabbed Petrovana's hand and kissed her cheek. "Let's go find our friends."

She grinned and brushed her cheek with the back of her hand. "Should we wait for Blank Face and Leighth?"

Leper shook his head. "Nah, they'll find us." He gestured toward the city. "Last time I was here, this place was burning and completely destroyed. I met Madislak out in Straggler's Forest for the first time. Hard to believe I was meeting my own brother and didn't even realize it."

Petrovana giggled. "Well, reckon it would've been hard to tell, y'all don't exactly look alike."

He gently squeezed her hand. "I was an insecure Chernzerk, just searching for some friends and a way to save Rin." His face hardened as he gazed at the ground. *Too bad no one was trying to help me save her, too.*

Petrovana kissed his cheek, then gazed out over the city with a longing expression.

"What are those beautiful eyes looking at?" Leper prodded. "Or what's that beautiful mind thinking?"

"Just... imaginin' if I were queen, I'd want somethin' like this." She smiled. "Could you imagine us havin' little kids runnin' around the castle, with large portraits of us on the walls—our family?"

The mention of kids pulled his thoughts back to Zanera and Kelindra, reminding him of the urgency to reach Costin. *Twelve days.*

"Reckon if there's kids, you wouldn't be alive," he teased, poking fun at her accent.

She slapped his shoulder with more force than he expected. "Hey! Don't make fun of my dreams, or how I talk—I can't help how I was raised."

"You're right, I'm sorry. I didn't mean any offense." Leper kissed her forehead. "Let's just find Madislak."

There it was again, always the arguments. He loved sharing their dreams and wanted kids of his own, but he wouldn't risk her life for that unless they found a way to ensure she'd survive. He knew if he kept resisting or spoke honestly, it'd just lead to more fighting, and he wasn't in the mood. He needed to see his brother, Harmony, and Lillian. Spending too much time with Blank Face took its toll, and even though he and Petrovana had lived alone in the woods for the last month, his refusal to stay in the same building as Blank Face remained.

He led Petrovana off the landing pad and down the steps toward the castle's foyer. The renovated castle looked immaculate as they descended the stone steps. Railings had been added for support, and the walls were lined with insignias and Lantess's colors of yellow and blue. In the foyer, several portrait banners hung, depicting Madislak, Rylin, Alissia, and Harmony.

"Is she the queen? Or just the proxy?" Leper mouthed to Petrovana, pointing at Harmony's painting.

Petrovana shrugged. "I don't know, love. She's probably there because she's the proxy now."

"Well, it looks like she's on the family side of the portraits. Right between Nelaan and Madislak." Leper gestured to the portraits.

"Maybe they got married? A lot can happen in a month." Petrovana linked her arm with his.

As they chatted, Madislak entered the room with Harmony at his side. He wore a sleek, leather-like ensemble that hugged his muscular physique—a source of mild jealousy for Leper. The black outfit, trimmed in red, resembled tiny dragon scales.

Harmony's purple robe was made from a similar material. Her blond curls bounced with each step.

Leper's grin widened. "Madislak, Harmony, it's so good to see you. It's been too long."

Madislak extended his hand. "It's been too long, brother."

Leper clasped his hand and pulled him in. "I've missed you."

He then moved over and wrapped Harmony in a hug. "And how have you been, blondie?"

Her grin mirrored his. "Amazing. How about yourself? And how are Kundry and Kordry? Find anything interesting over there?"

He noticed Madislak looking Petrovana up and down, like he's assessing her or something. Then hugged her. *Weird.* Not just the hug, but just the whole encounter seemed like he was scrutinizing her.

His body tensed. "Yes. Some very disturbing news that needs to be addressed." He grinned. "As far as Kundry though, they seem to have taken to Queen Leighth quite well."

"What exactly needs to be addressed? Is everything okay?" Harmony tilted her head.

"No, not really." His face heated thinking about having to leave Zanera and Kelindra in Kordry. "I have to go get the shard of Kasherri. Nalecht is keeping Zanera and Kelindra prisoner in Kordry until I get him that shard."

Madislak's jaw ticked. "Godsdamnit." He slammed the wall. "What about the shard of Theora? Does he have that?"

"No." Leper held it up. "I need you guys, or someone, to keep it safe while I go after that other shard. I only have two weeks to get there, and he said he'd be waiting by the entrance for me."

"Ya and didn't ya say they were huntin' fer some Xartazza fellow?" Petrovana added, leaning on him.

He put his arm around her. "Yeah, no idea who he is, but apparently can run the rain trials better than anyone?"

Harmony let out a disgusted sigh. "I never met him or saw him. But according to some recent rumors and hearsay from Xaneth Harbor, he was the best fighter ever. Never lost a battle in the arenas to beast or man. He's the main reason bulwarks stopped passing their training regimen years ago, and there's been a sharp decline in promoted bulwarks. They couldn't defeat him."

"What happened to him?" Leper locked his gaze with Harmony's.

She shrugged nonchalantly.

"There've been some... developments here, but we'll get into that once everyone's here," Madislak's gaze dropped to the ground, then back to Leper.

Leper arched a brow. "No Lillian?"

Madislak and Harmony exchanged uneasy glances, and Leper didn't miss Petrovana's sharp side-eye at his question.

"She, uh..." Madislak stroked his beard. "Won't be joining us."

Leper's shoulders sagged slightly. "Why not? You chase her off already?"

"Of course she's the first person you ask about," Petrovana snapped, then pulled her arm away.

Leper let out a dejected sigh. Perhaps he should've kept quiet. "Sorry. Didn't mean to have friends, Petrovana. Just because you both messed up your friendship doesn't mean everyone else should suffer."

Petrovana's eyes narrowed. "Dick." She shoved his shoulder.

Harmony quickly stepped between them. "On a good note, Madislak and I are getting married."

Leper's eyes widened. "Wow. Congratulations." He pulled Harmony into another hug. "When? Or did it already happen?"

"No date yet. Probably sometime after this shard business," Madislak added as Leper embraced him. "Speaking of which. Maybe while you're in the rain trials, we should try and find a way to destroy that shard?"

"Congratulations," Petrovana cooed. "At least someone can be happy and enjoy plannin' a future."

Leper ignored the jab. "I mean, it's kind of the last thing I have from Rinawen. I don't exactly want to destroy it."

Madislak's face slackened. "I see." He motioned towards the door. "But would you be willing to destroy it in the case that it's our only defense against him forging the talisman?"

He'd never really considered that before. Part of him always felt that he'd have this shard forever, his own memento he could keep and never let go of. But if it meant Nalecht not forging a relic weapon? It might hold weight to at least consider that possibility.

"I'll think about it." Leper followed them through the door. "Where's Lillian?"

Madislak grimaced. "Look, she's been gone for four weeks. I don't think she's coming back. I may have accidentally hit her with the magic in this shield, and she vomited blood." He shook his head. "I didn't mean to. I was upset, and I slammed it on the ground out of anger. It did something I did not expect."

"He truly didn't mean to," Harmony quickly added.

"You *what?*" Leper's pulse quickened, his thoughts spiraling. "You actually chased her off? One of the best fighters we've had on our side?" His frown deepened, rage creeping into every corner of his mind, a mental fog clouding his thoughts as he glared at Madislak.

"Psh," Petrovana murmured. "Probly was nothin' and her temper took over, and she ran off."

Leper felt a hot wave of anger rising, unsure why it hit him so hard. Madislak's carelessness and Petrovana's constant criticism of Lillian gnawed at him. He cared for Lillian as a friend, but Petrovana refused to see that. Did Madislak even try to find her, or did he just let her leave, feeling betrayed and used? Each thought stoked his boiling anger further. He wants to destroy the last remnant he has of Rinawen.

"Nice. Where're Blank Face and Leighth when you need them? Let's just get this over with so I can go," Leper snapped.

"Let's calm down. We haven't seen each other for a month. Let's not start fighting already," Harmony interjected.

Petrovana, as if sensing his anger, placed her hands on Leper's shoulders, her eyes reflecting the concern on her face. "I'm sorry, love. I shouldn't have said that. Let's forget it fer now. Calm down, handsome." She stroked his neck and cheek.

Her soft touch soothed him, and he pressed his lips to hers, the taste of cherries still lingering. He cupped her cheek as his anger melted away almost as quickly as it had flared up.

"You're right. I'm sorry. How are Rylin and Alissia?" Leper asked, keeping his arm around Petrovana.

"Come see them! They'll be happy to see their horned friend." Harmony cooed.

Leper followed them into Madislak's throne room. A large, polished oak throne stood at the head of the square room, surrounded by tables and supporting pillars.

A servant was scrubbing the floors when Madislak ordered her to fetch his children. She shot a timid glance at Leper before hurrying out of the room. They briefly discussed how Kundry was openly accepting Leper's presence as a Chernzerk, and he expressed how comfortable he felt among the public there. Madislak mentioned that he had issued a royal decree for Chernzerk to be treated with kindness and respect—unless they proved otherwise. While most people accepted the change, some embraced it enthusiastically, while others left the kingdom altogether, unwilling to accept the new order.

Leper grinned as Madislak told him about his royal decree. He'd come a long way since he'd abandoned him on The Talon. At first, Madislak had a strong dislike towards Chernzerk, but now he'd issued a royal decree to accept them. Leper couldn't help but feel a wave of appreciation for his brother's actions.

Rylin and Alissia soon entered, their eyes immediately locking onto Leper's head, widening with curiosity.

"Wow," Alissia said, staring at his horns. "They look cool, Mr. Leper."

Leper grinned. "Now you know why I didn't want you touching my hat?" He chuckled.

She giggled, her innocent brown eyes meeting his. "Yeah! But to me, you're still the hero who saved my dad and taught me a new game."

Leper glanced at Rylin. "You both have grown since then."

Rylin's eyes brimmed with determination. "Soon, I'll be fighting evil with you! I won't let anyone take away loved ones ever again!"

"If you'll have me, or if I'm not too old by then, I'd be glad to help you do that." Leper tapped one of his chakrams with a wink.

Rylin puffed out his chest. "Of course! I'd be honored to have the legendary Leper and my dad fighting by my side one day!"

Leper's smile softened, a genuine warmth in his expression. "Hopefully, by the time you're of age, the world will be peaceful. None of you will have to worry about war, evil, or losing loved ones."

As they caught up, Blank Face and Leighth entered the room. Leper immediately let out an audible sigh of disgust. Petrovana nudged him, narrowing her eyes as she whispered, "Try."

Petrovana was always urging him to be civil with Blank Face, but Leper just couldn't manage it. The mere sight of him drove him mad. Now Madislak wanted to destroy the shard of Theora, and he had no clue how he would get to the rain trials or get the shard of Kasherri or if he even trusted any of his friends to keep the shard of Theora safe the way he did.

"I just don't understand why he has to be here. Can't Leighth just fill him in?" Leper whispered back.

"Bashing me already?" Blank Face interjected, his tone sharp.

"U mixg fgixn ayed pimo," Leper jeered.

Blank Face stiffened. "Jo fryevn pymef yx gro luqqod grdoig gy fymuoga, unuyg."

He rocked back on his heels. *I didn't know Blank Face spoke Kordrarian. When would he have learned that?*

Leper glared at him but kept his mouth shut. He was trying, like Petrovana had asked, but the fog of rage crept up, and all he could think about was beating the daylights out of Blank Face. His nails dug into his palms as he tried to hold the rage back.

"Look, Leper, I know it's tough, but we need to work through this *together*," Madislak said, attempting to break the tension. "We've got some very, very bad news, and what you told us earlier only adds to it. So please, let's try to be civil."

Leper's eyes bore into Madislak. "Tell me, Madislak, what would you do if Nalecht were here right now? After everything he's done to your city and family?"

"Kill him!" Rylin growled through clenched teeth.

"Exactly," Leper replied. "Rylin gets it."

Madislak sighed and turned to the children. "You two are dismissed. Leave the room so the grown-ups can talk."

He wasn't prepared for the wave of anger that rolled over him, and he needed to leave the room before he lost complete control and started attacking Blank Face again.

Leper shrugged Petrovana's hand off his shoulder. "You all talk. I'll catch up later," he muttered, following Rylin and Alissia out of the room. The door slammed shut behind him.

Chapter Five

Madislak pressed a hand to his forehead, letting out a deep sigh. "So, he's still having those fits of rage?"

Petrovana shifted her weight uncomfortably. "Yeah. Reckon it's best to let him run off and cool down. Pushin' him just makes it worse."

Madislak studied her tense posture, noticing the stress brimming in her purple eyes. She seemed on the edge, like she might shatter with just one more push. They had barely reunited, and already, everything was unraveling. Maybe it was too much at once. His struggles to lead this group and to keep the tensions from spiraling felt laughable. Blank Face did whatever he pleased, Harmony constantly challenged him on trivial matters, and Leper kept everyone on edge. And Petrovana—she just absorbed it all, silently.

Maybe they were all better off keeping their distance, remaining friends from afar. But Leper and Blank Face were his brothers. Surely, they could find a way to share the same room without anger and resentment boiling over. Yet, seeing Leper's recent outburst, Madislak feared how he'd react to the news his father had dropped on him—and to the suggestion of marrying Petrovana. He swallowed hard.

"Maybe I should go spar with him," Blank Face offered with a half grin. "Usually, if I let him hit me a few times, it lightens his mood."

Leighth sighed heavily. "You shouldn't have to. We've all lost people. I have no family left, but I don't take that emptiness out on any of you."

Harmony's expression tightened. "You're right, Leighth, but how would you feel if you had to be around Borlden constantly, and we all expected you to just forgive him and act fine with his presence?"

Blank Face's jaw clenched. "That's different. He's evil."

Harmony tilted her head, her gaze piercing. "And you were so different?"

Blank Face glared at her but said nothing. The room fell into an uneasy silence.

"Enough." Madislak's voice rang out. "This gets us nowhere. The only constant is that we always have to overcome adversity."

He still couldn't quite grasp why Harmony was the only one who understood Leper's actions, but she did have a point. They were asking him to tolerate Rinawen's murderer—it wasn't entirely fair. But that didn't change the fact that he was an adult, and whether he liked it or not, Blank Face was his brother, someone who'd suffered through a horrible childhood. *He should at least try to accept that.*

"Petrovana, do you think you can convince him to sit down with us? We've got some serious matters to address," Madislak said. His shoulders rose in a shrug.

"I'll try." She exhaled heavily. "Maybe if we appeal to his softer side, like with yer kids. He's always been fond of children. There's a gentler side in there if we can find a way to reach it."

Blank Face scoffed. "Or just tell him to grow the fuck up."

"I don't think y'all understand how much Rinawen meant to him." Petrovana's shoulders sagged. "Yes, he's been gettin' much, much worse with random fits of just pure anger. It's concernin' me to the point he might run off and get himself killed."

"Don't forget that he could actually lose himself entirely. To that rage, it's what happened to our father, Samaja." Blank Face stated.

"You mean, like, permanently?" Madislak side-eyed Blank Face, seeking clarification.

"Yes." Harmony nodded, her curls bouncing forward. "It's what happened to Enoch and Ghendala as well. The ones that destroyed everything."

This is a disaster.

"Actually, I've got an idea." Madislak took a step toward the table.

Petrovana eyed him curiously. "What's that?"

"Who's thirsty?" He grinned.

"Really?" Leighth giggled. "At a time like this?"

Harmony nodded in agreement. "Yeah. Let's take the edge off, forget the world's problems for a bit. We can just catch up and relax."

Petrovana wiggled her hips playfully, bumping into Harmony's side. "Maybe do a little dancin'."

Blank Face rolled his eyes. "Fuck."

Madislak clapped him on the shoulder. "If I'm going, you're going, brother."

Harmony straightened up. "I'll go get Leper."

"Yeah. Maybe he won't yell at you," Petrovana nodded. "Somehow I always say the wrong thing."

"What if he attacks her?" Leighth asked, as she motioned towards Harmony.

Harmony winked. "I'm a pinnacle four shrew now, I'll just hold him in place or blast him with an ice shard."

Madislak winced, imagining his fiancée and his brother brawling in the streets of Lantess. "Meet us at Landry's Tavern. Or should I go with you?"

"I think I'll be fine. He's not a killer, guys, just angry." Harmony's tone was light.

Petrovana patted Harmony's shoulder. "Yer right, he's not a killer, but just be careful. I'm tellin' ya it's getting' bad."

"Very well then. I'm going to change, and I'll meet you all down there." Madislak motioned towards the town.

He watched Harmony march out through the doors, heading in the direction Leper went. He trusted her abilities, but the knot in his gut wouldn't go away. *What if Leper turns back into that guy—the one who attacked Blank Face after Rinawen died?* The thought sent a chill through him.

Leper barreled down the stairwells, storming through the double doors that led out of the castle. Most guards shifted aside as he passed, but none dared confront him. It was a step in the right direction. Yet, as the mental fog and anxiety engulfed him, his chest heaved with each purposeful stomp. He could feel the heat rising in his ears, blood boiling in his veins, as thoughts of Rinawen's last breaths replayed endlessly in his mind. How could he make them understand? Every time he laid eyes on Blank Face—especially now, after Nalecht just desecrated her tree—it felt like he was teetering on the brink of sanity.

When he was this angry, all he could see was Rinawen's face and his failure to protect her. The thought that her children would never see their mother again twisted like a dagger in his heart. Memories from their early days together surged, building tree hammocks out of large leaves, playing hide and seek in the woods, the sweet moment when he kissed her soft elven lips on the beach. Each recollection stoked the flames of his anger, reminding him of what he had lost.

He marched past the castle's outer stone walls and through the massive iron gates that swung open, entering the residential district. The houses, crafted from brick rather than wood, rose two stories high and gleamed with pristine condition. Alleyways lined with numbered signs sprawled for miles, their ends hidden from view. Guards clad in yellow and blue with lion's head patches patrolled the main road separating the alleys. Many civilians dressed in fine clothes paused to observe him, some offering cautious nods or halfhearted smiles.

A guard raised his hand, stopping him in his tracks. "Excuse me... Leper, right?"

Leper halted, turning his gaze toward the guard. "Yes."

The guard fidgeted, clearly unsettled. "You look angry. Is everything alright?"

"Fine," Leper grunted, annoyance creeping into his voice.

"We don't want any trouble," the guard said, resting a hand on his sword hilt.

"Pfft," Leper scoffed, irritation bubbled over. "I'm upset, asshole. If I were planning to attack my own brother's kingdom, don't you think I'd have done it by now?"

"I... I'm sorry, sir." The guard offered a half bow. "This... acceptance is new to us."

Interesting. They must really respect Madislak. Leper appreciated the guard's attempt to understand him better.

"Thank you for your concern," Leper said, his tone softened. "I just need to clear my mind right now."

"If you're looking to blow off some steam, they're doing weapon and hand-to-hand sparring at the barracks for training. I'm sure you'd be a welcome challenge, if what we've heard about you is true." He pointed toward the southwest corner of the city.

"Thanks. I might just do that." Leper nodded, and the guard reciprocated before heading back to his post.

Wow. This was easily the most positive encounter he'd had with strangers. He respected their concern for the city. Instead of pushing him away, they invited him to participate in an event where he could actually hit someone. *Yes, please.*

Leper reached the barracks about ten minutes later, greeted by a sea of people lined around the sparring squares—hundreds of them. The squares were marked with white lines on the dirt, two for weapon sparring and two for hand-to-hand combat. Dust kicked up around him, tickling his nose with its earthy scent. As the sun dipped low, shadows from the giant stone wall encircling the city began to stretch across the streets. Spring still lingered in the air, which was chilly, and most participants wore long sleeves or vests. Leper, however, felt no chill in his black pants and short-sleeved green shirt.

Normally, he'd don reinforced leather armor for sparring or combat, but his anger outweighed his caution, and his cockiness led him to believe it wouldn't matter against anyone here. After all, he dueled Blank Face frequently to hone his skills—strictly for skill-building. Plus, if anything went wrong, medics were nearby, equipped with bandages and healing vials.

One particular combatant caught Leper's eye immediately. He wielded two scimitars, just like Lillian, and was exceptional with them. Perhaps not as skilled as Lillian, but he dispatched his opponents quickly and easily, winning several matches in a row. After the fifth victory, the overseer raised his hand, declaring him the winner yet again.

"The winner, and still the undefeated champion of sparring!" the overseer shouted over the crowd.

"Anyone else want to challenge me?" the champion taunted, his voice dripping with arrogance.

Silence hung in the air as no one immediately stepped forward.

"Surely there's someone out there who can at least make me sweat!" he goaded.

Leper felt a spark ignite within him. He grinned as he stepped forward. "I'll fight you."

Despite the uncomfortable attention of the crowd, he reminded himself that nobody would dare try anything drastic with so many witnesses, right? He was already pushing his luck with this newfound acceptance just by walking through town, and now he was about to openly challenge someone in the sparring squares. They could attack him at any moment, but he was too pissed to care. If they did, he'd take as many of them down with him as he could.

The overseer and the champion exchanged wary glances, their brows furrowed. They whispered to each other for a moment as Leper continued walking toward them. The overseer finally held up his hand.

"You've never participated in these before. You can't challenge for a championship in your first match," he said.

"That's fine. I don't want the championship, just the fight," Leper replied, a grin spread across his face.

The overseer looked Leper up and down. "Chernzerk has never participated here before... You can't actually kill your opponent."

"I know. My brother, King Madislak, allows it." Leper quickly invoked Madislak's name. "I'm aware of how sparring works. I participate in Kundry frequently. My opponent is usually the same one over and over. I need a new challenge."

They whispered again.

"Fine," the overseer finally relented. "A non-champion battle. Please step into the center with Armand."

Leper stepped into the center alongside Armand and shook his hand. Armand's gaze flicked over him, scanning him cautiously. Leper sensed the man's distrust—the unspoken fear that he might try to kill him.

He drew in a deep breath. *As long as I keep proving I'm not evil or destructive, this will get better.*

Don't lose control. Don't lose control. He repeated to himself.

The overseer recited the rules, emphasizing the prohibition on magic, and Leper nodded in understanding. He'd been through this countless times before and knew the drill. As the overseer stepped back out of the twenty-foot-square arena, Armand slapped his scimitars together, sliding one blade down the other before raising them in a dramatic display, hollering like he was performing a war cry. The crowd erupted in cheers.

Leper held out his hands and began moving them in a circular motion. The holsters that secured Maka Kura on his back, a spring-loaded mechanism, released his weapon with his call.

Maka Kura zinged quickly in a circular motion, whirling around him several times before floating to his outstretched palms when Leper held his hands to the sides like a 'T.' He gripped the hilt and settled into a ready stance. However, the crowd seemed less impressed by his display.

As he circled Armand, Leper sized up his opponent. From previous battles, he knew Armand was quick, standing about an inch or two shorter than him but with a sturdy build. Sandy blond hair framed a clean-shaven face, and his brown eyes sparkled with determination—basically a thicker version of Blank Face, but much more handsome than that ugly assassin.

Leper snarled at the thought.

Suddenly, Armand lunged, swinging both blades in a wide arc. Leper batted them away with ease, causing Armand to momentarily retreat. Armand eyed him for a heartbeat before launching two thrusts. Leper deflected them downward, then spun and aimed for Armand's chest. In an impressive display of agility, Armand executed a backbend to avoid the blow and rolled away.

Leper furrowed his brow, surprised at Armand's nimbleness. But how would he handle a defensive maneuver? A grin spread across Leper's face as he pressed the attack, swinging hard with his right hand, then following up with a left. Their blades clashed, ringing with the sound of steel.

Armand smiled. "You thought this was going to be easy?"

"You're a lot better than I expected, I must admit," Leper replied, grinning back.

"Get ready to taste steel, Leper," Armand smirked.

Armand pressed forward, attacking with a flurry of strikes that Leper deftly batted away as he backpedaled. The sudden increase in speed caught him off guard, but he relied on the parrying and evasion techniques he'd honed, even if he wasn't as fast as Blank Face. He let Armand wear himself down, and the crowd responded with audible gasps and cheers at the display. Leper could hear Armand beginning to pant, frustration etched on his face as his strikes grew slightly slower and weaker. Still, he pressed on.

Leper noticed Armand suck in a breath and recognized an opening during his next attack. He ducked the blade, using his shoulder to buck Armand in the ribs before swiftly kicking the back of his legs. Armand landed on the ground with a thud. Leper brought Maka down, the pointed edge hovering at Armand's neck.

"Good match," Leper said, and the overseer promptly declared the match over.

"Good match," Armand echoed, still catching his breath.

Leper stood and, though the crowd remained quiet, he shrugged it off and offered his hand to Armand. "Who taught you to fight like that? You're very good."

"A girl named Lillian, before she left. I bet she'd kick your ass if she were still here," Armand huffed.

Leper chuckled. "She probably would."

"Do you know her?" Armand's head snapped up, eyes wide.

"You could say that. Haven't seen her in forever," Leper replied, as he dusted off his clothes.

"She kicked my ass so many times, but I didn't quit. One day, I'll be as badass as she is." Armand puffed out his chest.

"Well, keep it up. We'll need good people like you, Armand." Leper patted him on the shoulder.

"You too, Leper." Armand eyed him cautiously, then his shoulders sagged. "I won't lie, I was scared of you at first. But... you don't seem so bad. Maybe this integration thing isn't so bad after all."

"Thank you," Leper nodded. "I'm a normal person. I'm just like anyone else."

The overseer approached, proclaiming Leper the winner without raising his hand.

"Done showing off?" Maka Kura chided.

"Hey, I'm feeling better. Don't piss me off. I didn't hear you trying to cheer me up," Leper retorted.

"I am not your personal babysitter. I am a legendary weapon, you buffoon," Maka shot back.

"The only thing legendary about you is the wielder," Leper chuckled inwardly.

"Please. I could pick any one of these people to carry me around the world. You should feel lucky," Maka boomed in his mind.

"Help!" a girl's voice cried as she grabbed his wrist. "There's another one like you in the bar—attacking civilians!"

"What?" Leper tilted his head. "Who?"

The girl, no older than thirteen or fourteen, looked up at him with wide, frantic eyes. Her clothes were ragged, and her brown hair was a tangled mess, unwashed and unbrushed for who knew how long.

"The red-haired, horned man! I don't know his name!" she panted. "He's attacking my mom and dad! Please!"

Ace is here? Leper thought as she tugged on his wrist.

"Where are the guards?"

"They're all scared of him! Please!" She yanked again, desperation sharp in her voice. "Are you a good person or not?"

What the hell.

If there was ever a way to prove himself, this was it. But something about her felt... off.

He followed her through the winding streets, turning corner after corner until they slipped into a narrow alleyway.

Wham.

A fist—easily the largest he'd ever seen—slammed into him.

Chapter Six

T he massive fist slammed into Leper's chest. For a second,
    it felt like his ribcage might explode—then his fury took
over. He swung back, landing a solid blow to the brute's cheek,
but the man barely reacted, only grunting as if swatting away
an insect. Before Leper could strike again, the brute seized him,
pried his mouth open, and shoved a vial between his teeth. The
thick liquid oozed down his throat like honey, but it tasted far
worse—like swallowing ashes and burnt wood.

Then, the familiar hum of Maka Kura, always present in his
mind, faded.

Arms snaked around his torso, legs, and shoulders. Before he
could struggle, he was on his back, staring up at four faces. One
of them belonged to a cleaning wench—the same woman he'd
seen scrubbing floors in Madislak's castle.

"His magic should be cut now," said a man with short blond
hair and a high-pitched voice.

"Thanks, Farred." The cleaning girl patted his shoulder, then
gestured toward the alley's exit. "We'll take it from here."

Farred gave a curt nod and left.

The brute grinned, his wide, toothless smile stretching across his face. "What do we have here?" His deep voice rumbled like distant thunder.

Leper reached out for Maka Kura, desperately calling to the presence that had been with him since their excursion on The Talon, but nothing answered. He couldn't even sense the shard of Theora's power anymore. It was like someone had severed him from magic entirely.

"Good job, young one. Here's your five gold pieces—now run off, you worthless street urchin." The cleaning girl tossed a small pouch of coins to the ragged girl who had lured him here.

The girl halted, her blue eyes flicking to Leper, glistening with regret. Then she turned and ran.

"Should we cut off his horns first, Jandler?" one of the men asked.

Jandler shook his buzz-cut head. "No. We need to move him somewhere he won't be seen or heard. Some fools actually support these creatures."

Leper strained against the ropes biting into his wrists. "The King will have you all hanged," he snarled, his voice dripping with venom. His gaze locked on the cleaning girl. "And you—I'll make sure you get the worst of it." He meant every word.

"It appears he brought us the shard of Theora," said the gray-haired man.

Jandler's grin widened. "Imagine what we could do with that, Murdock." His beady eyes gleamed with greed. "Stephie, see if you can get one of the castle scholars to help us figure out how to wield this thing."

With a sharp tug, Jandler ripped the shard of Theora from Leper's neck.

Leper twisted against the ropes, rage boiling beneath his skin. No magic. No Maka Kura. He was cut off from everything that made him dangerous, left vulnerable to the sneering bastards surrounding him.

Jandler held up the shard of Theora, its surface gleaming even in the dim alleyway. "Imagine the power we'll have," he rumbled.

Leper snarled. "You don't know what you're holding, you idiot."

Jandler crouched, shoving a meaty hand into Leper's gut, pressing down hard enough to make him wheeze. "I know it's something you want back real bad. Which means I'm going to enjoy keeping it."

Murdock chuckled. "Maybe we should carve a few lessons into his skin before we go. He needs to learn what happens when monsters pretend to be men." His brown eyes gleamed at the sentiment.

"Start with his hands," Stephie suggested. "Can't use a weapon without fingers."

Leper thrashed, but they slammed him down again. A fist crashed into his jaw, snapping his head sideways. Another blow landed against his ribs, and then a boot drove into his stomach, knocking the air clean out of him. They were tearing him apart piece by piece, and he couldn't stop them.

A scream of fury built in his throat. His vision blurred with red. *Not like this.*

A sharp whistle cut through the alley. Then—

Thud.

Jandler staggered back, a dagger lodged in his shoulder. A second one buried itself in Murdock's arm.

The next moment, the air shimmered, and a blur of motion crashed into the group—Blank Face blinked in, reclaiming both his thrown daggers. He struck fast and vicious, blades flashing as he sliced a deep gash across Murdock's other arm. The man howled, staggering back.

"Get up," Blank Face snapped at Leper.

Leper struggled, but his body wasn't cooperating. Before he could move, hands touched his bindings, and a surge of familiar magic flared. The ropes crumbled.

Harmony.

She yanked him up, eyes darting over his bruised face. "You're an idiot. You should know better than to walk into a dark alley by yourself, dipshit."

"Yeah, well, I thought Ace was actually here." Leper wiped blood from his lip and turned, just as Jandler, still clutching his bleeding shoulder, made a break for it with the shard.

Leper didn't think. Didn't stutter. He charged.

"Why would you think Ace is here?" Harmony called, but Leper ignored her.

His body screamed in protest, but anger drove him forward. He tackled Jandler to the ground, fists hammering into his face, breaking flesh and bone.

Jandler roared, swinging wildly, but Leper barely felt it. His mind was fire, his fists unstoppable.

It wasn't enough.

He grabbed Jandler by the throat and slammed his head against the cobblestones. Once. Twice. The brute's struggles weakened. Blood pooled beneath him.

"Leper." Harmony's voice cut through the haze.

He panted, barely hearing her. His hands still pressed down, squeezing Jandler's throat.

"Leper."

His body tensed, and he felt Harmony's paralyzing grip coursing through his body.

"Let me go, Harmony. He needs to die." Leper gritted through his teeth.

Blank Face blinked in. "It's only fair." He held out his dagger to Jandler's throat.

"Not like this," Harmony argued as she stepped forward and motioned for guards to come over. "We'll make a public humiliation out of all of them."

He let go.

Jandler slumped, barely conscious, blood dripping from his nose and mouth.

Leper yanked the shard from his grip.

It pulsed in his hand, its energy crawling over his skin. The source of a war. The reason he'd nearly been broken tonight. The reason Rinawen died.

He clenched his fist around it.

"We need to destroy this."

Harmony blinked. "What?"

Leper turned to her, to Blank Face, his fury still burning, but his mind finally clear. "This thing's done nothing but ruin lives. We need to find a way to end it."

Blank Face stared at him for a long moment. Then he nodded. "About time."

Harmony exhaled. "Fine. Let's take care of these traitorous fools, and then we'll try."

Leper shoved the shard into his pocket. His body ached, his head throbbed, but for the first time, he knew exactly what needed to be done.

He would destroy the last piece he had left of Rinawen.

Leper pulled a healing vial from his bag and drank it. The ones he made himself were far better than anything he'd found around the world so far—smooth, with the taste of green tea and mint. Harmony handed him a rag, and he wiped his face clean. The potion dulled the aches, stopped the bleeding, and sealed the cuts—but it did nothing for the swelling or bruises. That would take time.

He took the shard from his pocket and looped it back around his neck. As he sat recovering for another thirty minutes, Harmony ordered the guards to throw the criminals in a cell until a public hearing could be arranged. By then, Leper could feel the thrum of the shard again, the familiar hum of magic from Maka Kura.

This day started to feel like it would never end. And they'd only just arrived six hours ago.

"Maka?" he called softly.

"I'm here. What the hell?" Maka barked. "That was too close, Leper. No more screwing around by yourself."

"Can't believe that beggar girl would do that." Leper shook his head, frustration tightening his jaw.

"What beggar girl?" Harmony's head snapped toward him.

He hadn't realized he'd said that part out loud.

"Nothing." He brushed off his clothes. "How do we destroy these stupid shards?"

"I don't know if it's possible." Harmony flicked her golden hair over her shoulder. "Only one way to find out."

She motioned for him and Blank Face to follow. Leper stuffed the bloodied rag into his pocket and fell in step behind her, keeping an eye out for the beggar girl—not to berate her, but to ask why. His instincts told him she'd either been threatened or was just desperate enough to need the five gold that badly.

Blank Face kept his hood up as usual. It would be nice if someone else helped in this damn quest to get people to accept the Chernzerk. But no, Blank Face hid like a coward. Another reason Leper couldn't stand him. Everything he did, he had to do alone.

They finally reached a room that looked more like a vault than anything else. The walls were solid stone, reinforced with rebar, and a massive iron door swung outward. The lion's head of Lantess was painted across the front.

"This used to be the coin vault, for gold, silver, and precious gemstones." Harmony gestured around the barren room.

"Where'd it all go? Madislak spend it all?" Blank Face let out a quiet chuckle.

"Of course, a professional assassin or thief would ask about its whereabouts immediately," Leper muttered, frowning.

"No!" Harmony jabbed a finger at him. "We're not doing that."

Leper rolled his eyes.

She held out her hand. "Let me see the shard, please. I don't know if it can be destroyed, but we'll see what happens."

"Should we get Madislak?" Leper asked.

"He'll find us when he's done getting primped and proper." She flashed her white teeth. "We're just going to try a couple of things real quick."

"Okay, let's get rid of this thing." Leper handed her the shard.

She took it and set it on the floor. Holding out her hand, she curled her fingers into a slow fist and dragged her arm downward. Frost sparkled across the shard's surface before it chittered against the ground, vibrating, and then the frost shattered off. Harmony jumped back, frowning, then tried again.

She opened her hand, fingers splayed, and aimed her palm at the shard. A thick layer of ice—about two inches—formed around it. Her brow furrowed as she clenched her fist, trying to crush it. Leper had seen Petrovana do this before, freezing something in a block of ice and then tightening her grip to squeeze whatever was inside. They used it to make orange juice. Harmony was trying to crush the shard.

The shard trembled again. Then, the ice exploded into a thousand tiny shards, and the entire castle seemed to shake. Blood trickled from Harmony's nose, and red rims formed around her piercing blue eyes.

Leper caught her by the shoulders. "Harmony?"

She stared through him, unfocused, like she wasn't all there.

Suddenly, she clutched the side of her head. "Ouch," she mouthed, then fell to her knees, grabbing her skull with both hands.

"Ow. OW. OWWWW."

Her screams grew louder and louder. His heart slammed against his ribcage as Harmony collapsed to her knees, wailing in long, high-pitched bursts—*AHHHHHHHH!*—then gasping for air before shrieking again. His ears trembled from the piercing sound, his mind spiraling into utter panic. The screams were so loud they had to shout just to be heard.

"What's happening!" Blank Face yelled. "Is it hurting her?"

"I don't know!" Leper spat.

He rifled through his pack of vials, grabbed a green rejuvenation potion, and handed it to her. Harmony's hands trembled as she downed the mixture, the sharp scent of ginger and turmeric filling the air.

She immediately clutched her stomach and keeled over. Thank the gods she stopped screaming.

"That didn't work!?" Leper tried to assess her state of mind, but she just shook her head, her face turning deathly pale as she writhed in agony.

"I don't know what to do!" He slammed a fist against the ground.

Blank Face pointed at the shard. "IS IT HURTING HER!?" he yelled again, glaring at Leper.

Leper ran back to the shard and grabbed it off the ground. Magic thrummed through him, but this time it felt... angry. Disappointed. Normally, it flowed through him like a current, like when he used Maka Kura. But now, it felt like it was... corrupting?

He dropped it and yanked Maka Kura off his back.

"I don't know if that's such a good idea, Leper," Maka warned.

"You got a better idea? I think it's killing her!"

Maka Kura didn't respond. Leper gritted his teeth and slammed the blade down on the shard.

Immediate regret.

A sharp, searing pain ripped through his head, like a nerve had been severed in his neck. He grabbed his skull, vision blurring white. His fingers fumbled through his pouch, but he couldn't even tell the difference between the vials—colors melted together in his fogged mind.

Then, someone wrapped their arms around him, holding him still.

Faint whispers curled in his ears, just beyond understanding.

After a few more seconds, his hearing started to return.

"Just sit still. It'll come back," Harmony murmured.

He blinked up at her—her face had regained some color, and she looked steadier.

"I'm going to take that as a no," Blank Face said flatly.

"Take what as a no?" Leper asked. "I couldn't hear anything until just now."

"That it didn't work."

Leper exhaled sharply. "What the hell was that?"

"I don't think they can be destroyed by magic or force," Harmony said.

"Yeah, I definitely agree." He pushed himself up to one knee, panting. "Maybe we try melting it in a forge or something?"

Harmony nodded. "Exactly what I was thinking."

The door burst open.

Madislak stormed in, flanked by his bulwark and a handful of guards. His gaze swept the room, his face twisted in disbelief.

"What the hell is going on down here?" he stammered. "Are you guys trying to bring down my damn castle!?"

Leper followed Harmony up the steps of the dais, the murmurs of thousands filling the city circle. They stood before the statue of Madislak, where water poured endlessly over its shoulders, splashing into the pool below. The floral scent of the surrounding blooms filled his nose, but all he felt was the heavy thud of his heartbeat. Sweat beaded on his brow under the weight of the crowd's gaze. He still wasn't used to large gatherings, and this trial wasn't just about justice—it was about him. It would cast a spotlight on both him and the Chernzerk race as a whole, right here in front of all these people. While the attempted murderers deserved punishment, the outcome of this trial would have a monumental impact on how he and his people were still being perceived.

Madislak had burst into their experimenting room just as they were attempting to destroy the shard. At first, he was a little angry—more about the castle's potential collapse than their plan itself. That, at least, he understood the logic behind. When he mentioned that the guards had escorted the culprits behind today's crime to the city center and were preparing for a public trial, he seemed a bit peeved.

Now, two hours later, they were headed to the center of the city. Blank Face had gone to fetch Petrovana and Leighth, planning to meet them at Landry's Tavern.

This entire trial could go very poorly. Everyone would be looking at him, judging him. If Madislak executed these three people, what would the people of Lantess think? Would they be mad at Leper for getting their fellow citizens killed, or would they be upset at these three citizens for attacking a peaceful member of their society?

A shrew in purple robes and a golden sash stepped forward, his gray hair and lined face betraying his age. At Madislak's signal, he lifted his tattooed palm—marked with a blue triangular shield encased in a green octagon. Vitalis magic, rare among the shrews. He arced his hand towards the sky like he was throwing a ball, and suddenly Madislak's throat-clearing echoed through the square, silencing the crowd.

Holy shit, that's loud. The entire crowd dropped to one knee.

Harmony stepped forward, her voice resonating over the kneeling crowd. "These three ignored a direct order from their king." She gestured sharply at the trio, then pointed to Leper. "They beat this man nearly to death. Had I not arrived, they would have killed him!"

"So? He's a Cherno." A woman's voice rang out.

Madislak straightened his shoulders, his gaze swept the crowd. "Who said that?"

Silence settled over the gathered faces, none willing to claim the words. Leper let out a disgusted sigh. No matter what he did, things would never change. He'd always be seen as some kind of evil, no matter how much good he did. His heartbeat ticked up a notch, his ears heating at the ignorance.

Harmony's lips pressed into a thin line as she stomped forward, planting herself in front of Leper. "This *Cherno*," she emphasized each word, "saved my life and the king's four months ago, along with the entire royal family. He defended Tudela with us and others. He's also the king's brother, and you'll treat him with the respect and kindness you'd show anyone else."

"Tell that to the other one on the dragon," Murdock muttered through clenched teeth.

Madislak's jaw tightened.

Leper finally spoke up, his voice low. "I'm just going to go. Nothing about this is going well. They'll just hate me even more."

Harmony spun around, her tone sharp. "No, they need to understand what'll happen. I'm putting my foot down with this bullshit."

She turned to Madislak and motioned with her eyes toward the captives. He glanced back at the crowd, mouthing, "Here? Now?" before heading over to the shrew. He leaned in and whispered something in the man's ear. The shrew nodded, waved a hand, and their voices returned to normal as they made their way back to Leper.

"Madislak, if you don't show them how serious you are about this decree, they'll keep pushing until Leper's dead," Harmony warned, her voice tight.

"Don't you think killing them without a full trial is a little harsh, Harmony?" Madislak replied, his tone strained. "People might start going elsewhere, leaving the kingdom. It could spark civil unrest—executing them for the sake of..." He glanced at Leper. "No offense." He turned back to Harmony. "Chernzerk. I can't run a kingdom and an army if I have deserters and people who resent me. You know those are vital to keeping things running."

Leper swallowed hard. "This is exactly what I didn't want—a big spectacle that's only going to widen the divide among the people. I'm just going to Costin, focus on getting the shard of Kasherri, and save Zanera and Kelindra. Clearly, whether I do any good or bad doesn't matter. I could save everyone here's life and no one would bat an eye, but if I destroy this place... well then, I'm a giant asshole."

"No, godsdamnit," Harmony spat, jabbing a finger into Madislak's chest. "What would you do if it was Rylin, Alissia, or me? You would execute them. So show these bastards what's at stake for him or any Chernzerk."

Madislak's jaw clenched as he looked between Leper and Harmony. "You know this is different. It's not that simple."

Harmony sputtered, words tripping over themselves. "If you won't, then I will." She turned sharply toward the criminals, taking determined strides.

Madislak snatched her arm, his grip firm. "Hey. I'm the damned king here, and you're not queen yet."

Leper's eyes widened at Madislak's words, and he couldn't help the wave of appreciation that surged for Harmony. But she was relentless, even when it grated on Madislak. He realized he had at least one person who'd stand by him, and he made a mental note to remember that. But there was something off about their exchange—he'd never seen this fiery, driven side of Harmony before. Usually, she stayed calm and collected, analyzing every situation. Now, she let her emotions flare in front of Madislak, even in the middle of this tense moment. It was his brother who was holding justice back.

"I'll just kill them myself." Leper grabbed Maka Kura and marched towards them, his face burning with rage.

Madislak grabbed his arm in a vice-like grip. "No, the fuck you won't." He looked him dead in the eye with a cold, calculating stare—one he never wanted to see from Madislak again. "That's how you get an entire city to attack you. Now go stand over there and shut your mouth. Both of you."

Leper was taken aback—surprised, really—then stepped back to where he was.

"Fine." Harmony huffed and stepped beside Leper. "Do what you want... *my king.*" The words dripped with emphasis. "Just remember—if you go easy on them and Leper ends up dead, you won't get another brother."

Leper understood Madislak's tough position, too. He wanted to be just and fair in this case, to make sure he wasn't executing his civilians based on a lie. Though Leper and Harmony knew these people deserved exactly what they would get with an execution.

This was a bold move, one that could put a target on Madislak's back. It might even drive a group of zealots to rally and try to overthrow him, simply for supporting a Chernzerk. Setting a rule for their free passage was one thing, but executing civilians for attacking them? That could split the kingdom right down the middle.

Madislak sucked in a breath through his nose, then gave the shrew a nod. The man cast the amplifying spell once more, his hands weaving through the air.

Stepping forward, Madislak addressed the gathered crowd. "Good people of Lantess. These are uncertain times. There are whispers of war, dragons, tyranny, and the Chernzerk have returned." He paced in front of the criminals, his boots thudding against the wood, and stopped. "But I can personally attest that two of the three Chernzerk I've met are good people."

Leper snorted quietly, but Madislak pressed on. "Two of them are, in fact, my brothers—born from the greatest queen, Svetlana Idelth. An unprovoked attack on them is an attack on the royal family, and it will be treated as such. It will not be tolerated."

Madislak drew Skyrunner. In a single, swift motion, he swung the blade, cleaving three offenders' heads from their shoulders. The bodies crumpled to the wooden floor with a sickening thud, and the crowd gasped—whether in awe, defiance, or shock was unclear. But one thing was certain: Madislak had drawn a clear line of tolerance for his people.

Chapter Seven

The crowd murmured in hushed tones as Leper watched Madislak wipe Skyrunner on the dead criminal's shirt, then march toward them, his glare fixed on Harmony. He stopped at the steps, extending a hand to her, his lips set in a thin line.

"C'mon. I'm ready for that damned drink," he muttered, his tone flat.

"Me too," Harmony huffed.

Harmony nodded, took his hand, and gestured for Leper to follow. He descended the steps gingerly, struggling to match Madislak's determined stride. Every step sent a dull ache through his body.

He wanted to figure out how to destroy the shard. If they could get rid of it, that would solve a lot of their problems. Without one of the seven shards, Nalecht wouldn't be able to reforge the talisman at all. But their first attempt had gone horribly wrong, and they needed a different approach.

Both Madislak and Harmony moved with stiff irritation, whether at him or at each other, he couldn't tell. Madislak had changed into more regal attire—a fine brown shirt paired with dark blue pants.

"Slow down," Harmony quipped. "You're leaving Leper behind."

"He can meet us there. Both of you have caused me enough trouble today," Madislak shot back, keeping his pace.

Leper, feeling the strain of the unfamiliar city, spoke up. "Actually, I have no idea where it's at. This is my first time in Lantess since the attack."

Harmony yanked her hand from Madislak's grasp, her voice sharp. "I can't believe you, Mad. He's your brother—get it together. If we don't show people the way forward, they'll never change their perceptions."

"Change takes time, woman!" Madislak hollered, jabbing a finger towards her. "You can't just expect people to forget everything they know or were taught overnight. It doesn't work like that."

Leper's pulse quickened; heat surged to his ears. "Shut up!" he snapped, stepping between them.

Something was off with both of them. He didn't even want to go to the tavern—he was going because they insisted, and he could use a drink after that beating. But the constant bickering between Madislak and Harmony grated on him, pushing his patience to the brink.

"No more talk about what just happened. I know I'm a huge pain in the ass everywhere I go, and you have to be seen with me, and it's a big problem. I get it. Now, where's the damned tavern?" Leper growled, his gaze flicking between them.

"You—" Madislak began.

"NO!" Leper shouted.

"He—" Harmony tried to interject.

"Tavern!" Leper bellowed, silencing them both. "Now."

Madislak and Harmony exchanged a look, their lips pressed into tight lines. Maybe with a few drinks and some nerves calmed between them, they could sensibly broach the subject of destroying the shard of Theora again.

Without another word, he followed them into Landry's Tavern. As Leper entered, he took in the scene: the glossy brown tables and two L-shaped bar counters, their surfaces pristine. The deep green walls and cupboards gave the place a natural, forest-like ambiance. Straight ahead, a door led to a separate dining area, ready for any overflow crowd.

Glasses, plates, and dishware sparkled like tiny stars scattered through a forest canopy.

"Over here!" Petrovana called from a table on their right.

Leper turned toward her, but before he could speak, she covered her mouth in shock, shot up from her seat, and rushed over to him. "What happened, sweetie?" She reached to touch his face, but he groaned, and she quickly withdrew her hand. "Sorry, sorry!"

"It's nothing," Leper said, casting a glance at Madislak. "I told Madislak I was smarter and stronger than him, and he beat me up."

"Some people tried to beat him to death," Harmony corrected with a scowl. "But they're punished now."

Petrovana pressed her forearm, marked with its distinctive swirl, against Leper's chest. A soothing, healing energy flowed through him. He wrapped an arm around her waist, pulling her into a kiss. Meanwhile, Madislak and Harmony made their way over to Leighth and Blank Face, who were still seated at the table.

"Stop," Leper whispered in her ear. "I'd love the healing, but if my face suddenly looks normal, they'll know you've got three types of magic, and we could be in another sticky situation."

She cupped the nape of his neck, leaning back to look at him, her purple eyes sparkling with concern as they swept over his injuries.

"I'm fine," he assured her, trying to ease her worry. He inhaled sharply, taking in her sweet floral scent, and closed his eyes.

"Yer my big tough guy, huh?" She smiled, then leaned in, her breath hot against his ear. "Maybe I can make you feel better later?" She kissed his cheek, then his lips.

A shiver ran down his spine, goosebumps rising on his arms. "Or," he teased with a grin, "we could just go to our room now?"

Petrovana burst out laughing. "C'mon, let's have fun before the... fun." She entwined her fingers with his and pulled him toward the table. He couldn't help but steal a glance at her irresistible frame. She wore tight leather pants—the same ones she'd worn when they flew in the chariot, catching his eye for the first time. Her deep purple top, with its shoulder cutouts and a back opening, hugged her curves. The front plunged in a V-shape, buttoned just above a slit that revealed a glimpse of her smooth navel. He was certain she'd caught the attention of every man in the tavern.

As they approached the table, he noticed how the room seemed to tense—patrons and staff alike stiffened at the presence of their king, queen, and the Chernzerk. He took a seat to Madislak's left, who sat at the head of the table with Harmony beside him. Leighth sat next to Harmony, and Blank Face beside her. Petrovana settled in next to Leper, resting a hand on his leg.

For a moment, Leper's mind flashed to Lillian, and he wished she were there too. A smile tugged at his lips as he imagined her tearing into the men who had tried to kill him.

"What's so funny?" Petrovana squeezed his leg gently.

"Nothing," he said, shaking his head. "Just glad to see how far Lantess has come since I was last here." It was only half a lie.

Harmony offered him a warm smile. "Thanks to you."

He grinned back at her, but his mind stayed locked on the shard of Theora—whether they could destroy it, how they'd even manage it, or if it was possible at all. But regardless of the shards, he still had to enter the rain trials to keep Zanera and Kelindra safe.

He ground his teeth. Twelve days didn't seem like enough time to destroy the shard and still make it to Costin. The flight on Ghost alone would take at least a full day. That left him eleven. If he left right now, he might have a couple of days to find the entrance, which would put him in the trials with eight or nine days left. And he had to make sure Nalecht knew he was there—he wasn't going in without guaranteeing the girls were still safe.

Which meant he'd have to look at that bastard's stupid face again.

A waitress, dressed in a purple apron, white undershirt, and brown pants, appeared beside them, pulling Leper from his thoughts. "C..." She caught sight of Madislak and quickly bowed.

"None of that in here," he commanded, his voice firm but kind. "I'm just a normal person."

"Ye... yes, my king." She straightened up. "What can I get you?"

Madislak stroked his beard, glancing around the table before speaking. "Two night kickers, four roasted hens with the honey

glaze, and two orders of baked potatoes with roasted asparagus."

"Right away, sir. Anything else?" she asked, her voice quick
and nervous.

"Yes, actually, a bottle of wine and two pitchers of beer. I'm
thirsty." He winked at her and added, "Oh, and one last thing,
tell Landry to put the cost on paper and send it to my castle. I'll
make sure he's well compensated."

She nodded eagerly. "Yes, my king."

"Damn. Being the king certainly has its benefits," Leper muttered under his breath.

"Has its perks," Madislak replied with a smirk.

"What's a night kicker?" Leighth asked, curious.

"You'll see," Harmony said, resting her hand on Madislak's
arm.

A few moments later, the waitress returned with two large
oval trays, each lined with shot glasses. Leper watched as she
set them on the table, her arm trembling slightly, causing the
glasses to clink together. She kept her gaze fixed on him, and he
looked away, trying to ease her nerves.

He realized then that Madislak probably took a lot of heat
for being his brother. How did the citizens feel about their king
openly accepting a Chernzerk into their kingdom? His shoulders sagged as he thought about the turmoil he'd likely caused
for his family and friends.

If Blank Face would stop hiding behind that damn hood, at
least Leper wouldn't be alone in trying to change the course of
history. There would be two known Chernzerk proving they
could be civil, peaceful. He hated his brother, but so far, Blank
Face hadn't done anything to remind the world of his past as
an assassin. Just one more thing Leper had to keep an eye
on—along with everything else he was fighting for.

"There's like, twenty shots here, Madislak," Petrovana said,
eyeing the colorful array. "We'll never drink all those. What's
in them?"

"We'll give away the ones we don't drink," he replied, then
pointed to various shots, naming each one. Reds, blues, greens,
grays, blacks, and yellows filled the tray, adding a vibrant splash
of color to the table. His eyes locked onto Petrovana's for more

than a few seconds. *Is that longing in his eyes?* Leper pushed the thought back out of his head.

The servers placed the bottle of wine and the pitchers of beer beside the trays. "Enjoy," she said with a smile. "Your food will be out as soon as it's ready."

"Thanks," Madislak nodded to her.

Madislak held up a blue-colored shot glass. "This one's called Powerpuff. Tastes like blue, black, and raspberries mixed together." He set it back on the tray.

"What's this?" Leper picked up a black shot that looked ominous.

"Boosted," Madislak replied with a grin. "Supposed to taste like coffee with a kick. But I don't like coffee, so I've never tried it."

"Coffee!" Petrovana perked up, nearly bouncing in her seat. "Me! ME!" She squealed, snatching it from Leper's hand and downing it in one gulp. Leper couldn't help but smile at her, her cheeks puffed up as she wiped her mouth. *Goofball.*

She let out a delighted moan as the liquid went down. Her playful nature truly shone. It was one thing he completely adored about her.

"Here, try this one." Madislak held out a yellow shot, making Leper cringe. "It's a mix of maple, honey, and... something else. You can smell the maple."

Leper's eyes lit up as he took the glass, sniffing it. It had a strong maple scent. Shrugging, he threw it back. It started sweet, tasting of honey with a slight burn, then shifted to rich maple with a smoky hint—was it whiskey? Rum?

"Sweet Straw," Madislak nodded. "Straw, like animal bedding, not the kind you drink from," he clarified.

From that one shot, Leper already felt the effects and understood why the platter was called the night kicker—or maybe it was just because he hadn't eaten in a while. The smell of seasoned roasted chicken from the kitchen made his mouth water. He noticed Blank Face still hadn't touched a drink, and many patrons' eyes kept drifting toward him. They probably looked like an odd bunch, but with King Madislak present, they managed to avoid stirring up trouble.

After relentless prodding from Leighth and Petrovana, Blank Face finally grabbed a few shots and started to open up a bit.

As much as Leper loathed being near him, he decided to focus on enjoying the evening with his friends, just like Harmony and Petrovana had asked.

When the food arrived, they all dove into the roasted chicken and baked potatoes. The chicken was even better than it smelled—seasoned perfectly, juicy, and tender. The potatoes and asparagus were excellent sides, peppered just right to complement the meal.

People started to pour into the tavern as they enjoyed their meals and drinks. Even the beer was exceptional—there was a darker, richer blend and a lighter, honey-flavored one. Leper favored the heavy, full-bodied taste of the dark brew. Madislak noticed the crowd growing and ordered one of the waiters to fetch some guards and his bulwark to keep the peace.

With the plates cleared away, Leper felt ready to head back to the castle. He'd had more than his share to drink, and his gaze kept drifting to Petrovana, who returned his looks with shy, teasing smiles. But the women weren't ready to leave. They insisted on savoring the evening, claiming they might not get another chance like this anytime soon.

He wanted to enjoy the evening like anyone else, but time was ticking. He had maybe a day, two at most, before he needed to find the entrance to the trials. And right now, they were wasting precious time—time that could be spent finding another way to destroy the shard of Theora. He bit his lip, swallowing a snarky comment, just as Petrovana pressed her warm lips to his neck.

Her eyes met his, and he let out a slow, calming breath. Somehow, she always seemed to know when he was getting irritated—and what he needed to steady himself. Her breath still carried the rich scent of the coffee shots she'd been downing, and her lips tasted like it, too. She leaned in, whispering softly in his ear that they would leave soon, and a shiver ran down his arms.

His hand found the open part of her shirt, brushing against her soft skin as he leaned back in his chair, taking in the rest of the atmosphere.

A group of local bards entered, filling the air with soft string and percussion music. An older gentleman in fine maroon attire approached the table, but Madislak's guards quickly intercepted him. Madislak waved them off, allowing the man to pass.

The gentleman approached and exchanged a brief look with Leper before turning to Madislak. "I trust the atmosphere is to your liking, my king?" He gave a polite bow.

"Yes, Landry. Thank you. You'll be compensated handsomely for your hospitality, and I'd like your entire staff to receive a generous bonus," Madislak replied with a warm smile.

"Hardly necessary, my king. I think word is spreading of your presence. I've had to call in extra staff and open the second part of the tavern. We haven't seen this much business since the city was rebuilt," Landry said, gesturing toward the doors leading to the newly opened section.

"It's necessary, Landry," Madislak insisted, offering a handshake.

Landry turned to Harmony, who leaned forward. "Can you clear out some space in front of the bards for a dance area?" she asked, gesturing to an area in the corner of the tavern.

"Yes, pretty please!" Petrovana chimed in with a bright smile.

"At once, miladies," Landry replied, bowing before heading back behind the bar and barking orders to his staff.

Madislak frowned at the suggestion. "Is that really necessary?"

"Lighten up, sweetie. Tonight is about having fun and shaking off the nerves," Harmony said, batting her eyelashes at him.

"This is a great bonding opportunity for all of us," Leighth added, throwing back another shot.

Leper leaned back, taking in the lively scene and realizing he was truly enjoying himself for the first time in a long while.

The next several hours flew by as the group danced and sang, caught up in the moment. But with each passing second, the thought of Zanera and Kelindra's safety lingered at the back of his mind. No matter how much he tried to enjoy himself, he couldn't shake the worry that they might be in danger while he was here, wasting time. The shard needed to be destroyed, and he needed to get to Costin.

It was time to go.

Madislak approached his mother's grave, nestled two miles west of Lantess, with a heavy heart. The soft yellow glow of the moon Veridian lingered in the morning sky, casting a gentle light over the scene. Three days ago, his father had dropped some heavy truths and a flood of unexpected information. His head still ached a bit from all the drinking two nights ago, just from the sheer amount of stress he faced. The day they took to recuperate left Leper with ten days to enter the rain trials. Seeking clarity, he had come to sprinkle roses on his mother's grave, the headstone still glossy and pristine as the day they laid her to rest.

Wrapped in his thick black coat with fur-lined shoulders, Madislak felt the wind cut through him, sending a shiver down his spine. His new plethocyte armor, comfortable enough to wear everywhere, was hidden underneath. Spring was finally breaking, and he hoped this would be one of the last cold days before the warmth returned.

Leper, Leighth, Blank Face, and Petrovana had arrived yesterday. Madislak knew he would have to discuss the startling revelations his father had shared, including the proposal to marry Petrovana. His heart raced at the thought. Though Petrovana was stunning with her long black hair, purple eyes, and perfect curves, his heart belonged to Harmony. Her short curly hair, radiant smile, and the way she complemented him brought him immense comfort. His life, built on lies his father had spun, now felt like a betrayal.

Madislak fell to his knees, dropping roses on the cold earth. The smell of wet, muddy dirt filled his senses. It had been too long since he last visited. Crawling to the headstone, he placed a hand on the engraved name "Svetlana Idelth" and took a deep breath.

"Hello, Mother," he whispered, a tear rolling down his cheek.

Madislak's chuckle broke the silence, tinged with bitterness. "I know. You're not really there and can't hear me. I'm talking to a shaped rock with your name on it."

He leaned closer, resting his head against the headstone. "I just wish I could talk to you. One last time. I don't know what to do, who to trust, or where to seek our family's happiness. Why can't I..." His voice cracked. "Why can't I have a happy life with the ones I love most? Why must I sacrifice? I can't avenge what happened to you, and if I had known..." He slammed the ground with his fist, tears streaming down his face. "I was six. There wasn't much I could've done. But when I grew up..."

He buried his face in his hands. "I'm so lost right now. Please, whatever god is listening or cares, let me..." His sobs grew heavier. "Let me see her. One more time."

The wind blew harder, but Madislak felt no pain, no cold, only the fracture of his heart deepening. The sting of his father's revelation had worsened the ache that had haunted him for years. Maybe he would have been better off not knowing it was his own father's actions that led to his mother's death when he was so young. Now, his own children would face that same hurt, that same emptiness he had felt his entire life.

"You've grown into such a handsome, muscular man, my son."

Madislak looked up, blinking through his tears, and there she was. His head snapped back in shock, both at her presence and her appearance.

Her long dark hair fell gracefully to her shoulders, her tan face and large brown eyes radiating comfort. She was as beautiful as he remembered, taken from this world too soon. If only he could touch her. *How is she here?*

Madislak had never been a committed worshipper of any god, yet here she was. He'd heard of shrews communing with the dead, with spirits—but he was no shrew. He doubted any god truly cared about this world or the people in it. Half the time, he wasn't even sure they were real.

But she was here. He could see her.

Whatever the reason for her presence, he wouldn't waste it by questioning how or why.

Madislak rose to his feet, arms outstretched, but his mother was no more than a ghostly vision.

"Can you hear me?" he whispered.

She nodded, her blue robe flowing like water around her.

"I know what happened to you," Madislak said, his hands trembling. "Father told me. I...I kicked him out of Lantess. He lied to me my whole life. I thought I was following his example, being a noble warrior: just, kind, like a king should be. But I'm not. I'm a failure, a pawn. I murdered Goreldea's sons for Nalecht; I let them destroy Lantess and its people. I abandoned my own brother on an island to fight a dragon. I..."

"Stop, Madislak," she interrupted, her voice a soothing melody.

Madislak shook his head. "How... I am no king. I am an idiot. Worthless."

"Oh, my precious, mighty Madislak," she said, her words like a balm. "Your father and the world have not been fair to you. But don't for one second ever tell me, or anyone else, that you are worthless. The people—and you yourself—might not see it yet, but you, my son, you are the king this world needs. Now more than ever. You are better than your father, better than Nalecht, and better than Zonoh."

Madislak scoffed. "I could really use his counsel right now."

"Your father is full of lies, my son. I've come to warn you." She swayed back and forth. "Being taken from you so early was a tragedy. The gods have allowed me to answer your pleas once, and I chose this moment, right now."

Madislak shook his head again. "I don't know who to trust. I thought Father would be the one person to confide in, but he led me down a path of deceit. You're saying it's more than what he just told me?"

Her transparent head bobbed up and down, then her hand hovered over his chest. "Who do you trust in here?" she asked, then moved her other hand to his cheek. "Not up here. Realize, Madislak. Change is coming, and you will lead it."

"I can't. I don't even know what you're talking about." Madislak tried to cup her hand but felt only his own cheek. "But I will try. I will do my best to figure it out."

"Follow your heart. It is made of gold." She backed away. "Someone is coming. I must go. Never forget how much I love and am proud of you. You... and your brothers."

"I love you, Mom," Madislak whimpered as she began to fade.

He reached out, desperation tightening in his chest. "Please... don't go."

The memories of her loss lashed at his insides, as if it had just happened again. Footsteps filled his ears, accompanied by the maple scent of his non-assassin brother, Leper. Madislak finished sprinkling the roses on her grave.

Though his heart cracked once more as she faded away, he couldn't help but think she was referring to Leper. Trusting him, his blood, his family. Perhaps helping his brothers would provide the clarity he needed to push forward.

Chapter Eight

Madislak wiped the near-frozen tears from his face and turned as Leper approached, his thick black beard and glossy horns catching the dim light. The weight of telling him about Petrovana pressed heavy on Madislak's chest; he knew it could set Leper off. He wanted to be there for him, to help him understand the political side of the marriage, but he wasn't sure how.

Snowflakes drifted from the overcast sky, blurring Veridian's yellow glow. The temperature had dropped even more in the few hours Madislak had been outside. Leper's coat clung to him against the cold, his thick black pants and sturdy brown boots planted firmly in the snow.

Leper knelt by the headstone, tracing the letters with his fingers. "So this is our... your mother."

"She was your mother, too," Madislak reassured him.

Leper stood, his eyes misty. "What was she like?"

Madislak grinned through his sorrow. "She was the best mother anyone could ask for. Beautiful, kind, wouldn't hurt a fly. You would've loved her."

A tear escaped Leper's eye. "Does it ever get easier?" he asked, voice cracking.

"Not really," Madislak replied, unsure if Leper meant Rinawen or Svetlana. "It might hurt less over time, but it never goes away completely."

"I wish I could've known her. Even for just a little bit. With Rin gone..." Leper's throat bobbed. "Zanera and Kelindra are too young to face the danger I must. But I'll get that damned shard to keep them safe. Rinawen was the only one who truly looked out for me. I'd trade my life to bring her back to her kids. Not many would miss me anyway."

Madislak grasped his brother's shoulder. "I would miss you. Zanera, Kelindra, Harmony, Lillian, Petrovana—all of us would miss you. Don't say things like that again." He offered his hand. "I'm here for you. I'm sorry if you felt like you couldn't come to me."

"I know." Leper grabbed his hand. "Then we stick together, through thick and thin. Whatever happens, I've got you."

Madislak squeezed his hand. "And I've got you."

Leper turned back to the headstone as they prepared to leave and said, "Fodoxuga lo jugr aye," then bowed his head.

"What does that mean?" Madislak flicked his eyes to Leper.

"It's the Kordrarian way of saying our parting words." Leper nodded.

"Where'd you learn that language? I thought it was a dead dialect." Madislak started walking towards the city.

Leper paced beside him. "Rinawen taught me. Her parents taught her. They don't teach everyone, only the royal family. I was lucky enough to be considered part of theirs."

"What brings you out here?" Madislak asked.

The wind picked up, nearly blowing his jacket open. He longed for the warmth of his castle and fireplace, a better place to discuss Petrovana.

"Just came to check on you and see her grave." Leper sighed. "I decorated Rinawen's tree in Kordry and got curious about the funeral customs here, so I went to see a graveyard. But Nalecht burned her tree to the ground." His hands balled into fists at his sides. "I need leave to go after that shard. Harmony said Petrovana and I couldn't leave until after you shared your news, so I came to get you. I'd love to stay for a while, but I won't risk Zanera and Kelindra's safety. I need to get moving."

"Yeah. I can't believe Nalecht threatened them." Madislak cupped his chin. "We're going to need to stick together, especially if Tamara is working with him like we suspect."

"That's another thing." Leper scratched around his horns. "What you did the other day, that execution—I don't want you thinking you have to do that for me. Punish them, sure, but I feel like it's painting a bigger target on my back. And yours."

"Well, Harmony did most of the pushing for that to happen." Madislak's shoulders sagged. "If she wasn't there, I probably would've just given them a lifetime prison sentence. But she was hell-bent on executing them. However, you need to remember one thing: I'm your older brother, and it's my job to protect you."

"Okay, Mad, only by eight years." Leper winked at him, then changed the subject. What's up with you two, anyway?" Leper side-eyed his brother. "Something seems off... with everyone. I can't stand Blank Face, and Petrovana and I are constantly getting into stupid arguments like you and Harmony. It's like we're imploding as a group here."

Madislak hadn't really considered that before, but Leper had a point. They *were* falling apart, and it was about to get worse. He didn't want to tell him the real reason things felt different with Harmony just yet. And he couldn't deny what Leper was saying—he *did* have a bigger target on his back now. The entire reason they hadn't discussed this Petrovana mess was because of Leper's outburst over Blank Face, and then Harmony had only added to the conflicts. Leper was right. They were on the brink. But they weren't lost yet.

"I think we need to just clear the air, Leper." Madislak let out a dejected sigh. "All of us. Together. We need to work out our differences; I'm certain we can."

Leper shook his head. "As long as it's quick. Nalecht threatened the girls directly and slapped both of them to the ground. And if he gets both shards, Kordry and Kundry will probably be destroyed too. So, I'll get that shard and use it as leverage against him. But I can't do that if I'm stuck here talking about my feelings to everyone. I have ten days, Madislak."

"Leper, we don't even know what you'd be walking into. We need a tactical plan. Just marching into Costin and demanding the shard of Kasherri seems *too* easy; there's a reason Nalecht hasn't taken it himself. Maybe it'd be better to take a couple of days and research with Harmony?" Madislak suggested hesitantly.

Leper fixed him with a scowl. "I have *ten* days, Madislak. Did you not hear me the first time? I don't *have* time for that."

Madislak thought for a moment. Maybe there was something he could do to strengthen the bond between them, something that might help when, eventually, he had to drop the devastating news.

"Let's make one quick stop before we go to them. There's something I want to show you." He pointed toward the massive four-pointed castle looming in the distance.

Leper groaned. "Ugh. *Only* a minute. I need to get moving."

"Only a minute." Madislak clapped him on the shoulder. "I think you'll appreciate it. This is an Idelth secret. You can't tell anyone about it. Not Harmony, not Petrovana—not even my children. Only my father and I know it exists."

Leper stopped, staring at him. "And you want to share it with *me?*"

Madislak nodded. "You're an Idelth, technically. You should know. I guess Blank Face should too, but I'll show him some other time."

"Is it really that important that you *have* to show me now?" Leper crossed his arms. "I'd like to see it, but I don't want to waste time when I need to find the damned rain trials."

"I promise it won't take long. I just want you to understand that I'm here for you—no matter what happens with everyone else." He bumped Leper's arm lightly. "We'll figure this out. And if I *have* to, I'll invade Kordry myself to rescue those girls. I'll march my army against Larnadix and Nalecht if it comes to that."

Leper huffed a quiet laugh. "I appreciate that, Madislak." He nudged him back. "But I think it's best if I handle this shard thing. Marching an army in isn't exactly a discreet move."

"If it comes to that, you have Lantess's support," Madislak assured him. "But first, you have to promise, you can't tell a soul about what I'm about to show you."

Leper nodded. "I swear. I won't tell another soul."

"Follow me." Madislak motioned for him to come along.

Though nervous, Madislak felt an odd sense of trust in Leper. Maybe it was because, as a Chernzerk, Leper had kept his own existence a secret for twenty-four years. Or maybe it was the strange sense of camaraderie he felt with him—after all, Leper was his brother.

Perhaps when the time came to tell Leper about marrying Petrovana, it wouldn't be as explosive as he feared. But a lingering doubt gnawed at him. If angered, Leper might reveal the secret to *everyone*—purely out of spite.

Leper followed Madislak to the castle, a trek that took nearly two hours. Madislak was insistent on showing him something secret, something only he knew. Leper appreciated the gesture—Madislak was trusting him with a family secret—but impatience gnawed at him. Who knew how long this would take? And after that, their planning session with everyone else could drag on even longer. The sooner he heard Madislak out, the sooner he could move.

Nalecht had given him fourteen days to enter the rain trials. He only had ten left. It would take a day to get there, and then how long until he could take this oath? Or find the entrance? He didn't have time to linger.

Yesterday, he'd received a note from Zanera and Kelindra. They'd snuck out to send it, letting him know they were safe, but the chaos in Kordry was intensifying. They'd left out the details, but Leper didn't need them. He knew what had to be done. If he wanted to keep them safe, he had to get into the rain trials. It was the only leverage he had. Otherwise, Nalecht would kill them without a second thought—just like the heartless bastard he was.

Madislak led Leper through the grand castle, guiding him toward the central tower—the tallest point, unreachable and isolated as if the castle had been built around it. They descended several winding stone stairwells until they reached an underground chamber. Cave? Crypt? Leper couldn't tell. A guard stood at the door, who straightened and nodded to Madislak immediately.

"I only station elite guards down here," Madislak commented, clasping the guard's forearm.

"My King." The guard kneeled briefly, then looked up with a sneer at Leper before returning his gaze to Madislak. "What is he doing down here?"

"You will treat him with respect, soldier. He is a trusted member of the Idelth line." Madislak frowned at the guard.

The guard's expression flickered as he glanced between Madislak and Leper. "I... I will inform the others," he stammered.

Madislak cleared his throat, fixing the guard with a sharp look.

"I mean—yes, sir!" The guard straightened and saluted, performing the standard Lantess salute: hand to the weapon hilt, then fist over the heart. Madislak and Leper mirrored the salute. Though neither had a weapon at their side, they made the motion. Maka Kura rested against Leper's back, secured with a spring-loaded mechanism, while Skyrunner poked out just over Madislak's left shoulder, the three-pronged pommel hovering just above his head.

"Better," Madislak grunted, passing by.

Leper continued to follow him down the straight corridors, where glowing quartz stones placed in sconces lit the way. They stopped at a large double iron door bearing Lantess's emblem—a lion's head surrounded by intricate runic symbols. Madislak held up a hand to stop him, then approached the door, placing his hand on the lion's head.

"The soul of the lion seeks entry to the resting place of the brave lions," he intoned.

The doorway glowed blue and yellow briefly before fading back to gray.

"If you don't say that line, you'll be burned and bludgeoned to death." Madislak nodded at him.

Leper nodded back, though he still didn't understand why Madislak had chosen now to share this secret. "Is there some kind of significance to this room?"

"Every Idelth is buried here. It's where I'll be buried, and where my children will be too."

"Everyone? Since the original?" Leper furrowed his brow.

"Yes, ever since the first one. When Lantess was established over five hundred years ago, Miraslav Idelth built this crypt and protected it with magic to honor Lantess's leaders and safeguard our legacy." Madislak gestured toward the open doors, pride shining in his eyes.

Leper followed his gaze, stepping down two stairs into a large rectangular chamber. Along the walls were sarcophagi, starting on the left with Miraslav's. Each wall held two caskets, one on top of the other, with a stone bust at the front marking which sarcophagus belonged to whom. A stone tablet beside each bust offered a brief history of each person's accomplishments.

Leper read a few inscriptions, noting that Miraslav had started Lantess as a small town and built it up into the stronghold it was today. Most of the men displayed the traditional long beard, making them look like a clan of dwarves—only much taller. A few women rested here too, but Leper noticed Madislak's own mother wasn't among them, which made him wonder. Was she not an Idelth?

"So, I know Svetlana wasn't blood, but she was married into the family; wouldn't she be buried here, too?" Leper asked, sparing a glance at Madislak.

Madislak's shoulders sagged. "I'd rather not get into that. Though... I feel like she should be here—like you will be."

Leper straightened. "Oh."

He didn't know how to tell Madislak that he didn't want to be buried here; he wanted to rest beside Rin. Kordry's people, its society—those were his. And Rinawen, Zanera, Kelindra... they were his family. Not Lantess. Yet, not wanting to disappoint one of his only blood relatives, he kept silent. Another time and place would be better for that conversation. But he did have other questions.

"Well, my father isn't Nelaan, so why would I be buried here?"

Madislak grimaced slightly before turning back to the rune-covered walls. "Her blood runs in my veins, as it does yours. That's reason enough."

Leper rubbed the back of his neck. "Not to get in your business, but couldn't you bring her down here?"

Madislak huffed. "I should. My father said she was..." He stopped, glancing at Leper before lowering his gaze to the floor. "Tainted."

"Tainted?" Leper's voice echoed louder than he intended. "Because of me and Blank Face?"

Madislak gave a solemn nod.

"That's ridiculous." Heat crept up Leper's ears as he shook his head. "That's got nothing to do with her," he growled.

"Listen." Madislak fixed him with a stern glare. "Since I met you two months ago, I've realized that a lot of what's written in our history books doesn't line up with what I've seen first-hand."

"Meaning?"

Madislak stroked his beard. "You, for example. Aside from your... anger sometimes, you don't go around looking to cause chaos and destruction. You're not making everyone's lives miserable. Same goes for Blank Face."

Leper sputtered his lips. "Pfft."

"I'm serious." Madislak paced along the wall. "I know what he did wasn't right, and I get that. But since being around Leighth and the rest of our group, he's done nothing but help. Meanwhile, Nalecht is attacking the entire world and going after immense power—power that, somehow, has been completely erased from our history books."

Leper scratched his head. Good point.

If history had been altered or outright erased, like Madislak suggested, that would explain a lot. But why go through all that trouble just to eliminate one race? And why hide the existence of the talisman and shard?

"Maybe you're right." Leper rubbed his chin. "It doesn't make much sense, but someone could've changed the records."

"Exactly." Madislak exhaled sharply. "And if they're going to rewrite history, then I'll change it myself. If I want my mother down here, even though she isn't Idelth by blood, then she will be down here. Same goes for you and Blank Face."

Leper shrugged. "You're the king. That's your call."

Madislak let out an exasperated sigh. "Let me show you one more thing."

Leper caught the tension in Madislak's expression. He wanted to change the subject, and Leper couldn't blame him. It was probably a sore spot between him and his father.

As Leper looked around and took in the damp stone smell, he realized how much he appreciated Madislak bringing him here.

At first, he hadn't wanted to come down, but now he was glad he did. Technically, this was all part of his heritage, too.

Madislak approached the first sarcophagus. "We're directly beneath the center tower of the castle now."

Leper followed, raising a brow. "So if it crumbles, we'll be buried."

Madislak chuckled. "It won't. The tower is inaccessible. The outer layer is stone; inside that is banded iron, and inside that, a coating of glass."

"Glass?" Leper rocked back on his heels. "Why glass?"

Madislak smiled and pressed two stone buttons just below Miraslav's sarcophagus. "Just watch."

The grinding sound of stone against stone filled the room, then smoothed out as the roof began to separate, revealing a small four-by-four square opening like a viewing window.

Leper walked over to the center of the room with Madislak and looked up. The glass lining the iron tower shimmered, casting a spectrum of colors. He peered through the opening and saw the sky, closer than he'd ever seen it, even closer than when he flew on Ghost. A sliver of the yellow moon, Veridian, looked almost close enough to touch through the snowy clouds, as though he could reach it if he scaled the tower.

"Whoa," he mouthed, awestruck.

"Yeah." Madislak clapped him on the shoulder. "It funnels magical light down here that powers the wards, preserving the bodies, busts, and sarcophagi."

Leper felt the magic from the moon seep into his skin, warm, almost overwhelming. The scent in the air shifted, losing its damp stone aroma and taking on something unexpectedly sweet. As he glanced around, the room appeared brighter. Along the walls, faint outlines emerged—shards. All of them.

His gaze swept the walls, startled by the subtle impressions of each one: Kasherri, Ryollin, Amarook, Aisha, Hathor, Obidiah, and Theora. How? If Miraslav built this place, it would have been long before the shards were even known.

"Is there a reason the shards are on the wall?" Leper pointed at the outlines.

"They work kinda like a towel. Absorb the magic from the moons, hold it in this room. Keeps everything preserved. And if you don't say the magic phrase when you open the door—"

Madislak gestured to the large and smaller openings along the roof and walls. "—fire blasts from the ceiling, arrows fire from the walls. Least, that's what my father said, but..." He trailed off.

"Seems odd, doesn't it?" Leper traced a finger along Theora's bow shape, then touched the shard at his neck. "The shards hold immense power, and yet the first Idelth marked them here before they were even discovered from the broken talisman? Their shapes carved into this room... to hold power?"

Bzzzzzt.

The shard of Theora vibrated against his chest. Its indentation on the wall glowed a bright brown as light streamed from the ceiling, pouring into the shard around his neck.

"What the heck is happening?" Madislak rushed toward him.

"I have no idea!" Leper panicked and grabbed at the shard.

Shock ripped through him. He stumbled back as numbness rolled through his fingers. The shard rocked against his chest, sending another wave of numbing pain straight through him. His ribs ached, or maybe they just weren't there at all.

"Ouch!" He gasped. "Get this thing off me!" He clawed at the chain, trying to break it, but his fingers refused to work.

Madislak lunged forward, yanking at the chain. The moment it snapped, the shard brushed Leper's neck—another shockwave of agony surged through him. His throat seized. He tried to inhale. Nothing. He tried to exhale. Nothing.

Leper gripped his neck, but like his fingers, like his chest—numb. The shard hit the floor, but before it could settle, light waves lifted it, guiding it toward the bow-shaped indentation on the wall. A small compartment clicked open.

"What the fuck?" Madislak stammered, frantically assessing Leper.

Leper still couldn't breathe. Panic surged through him. Maybe shutting off the magic would stop it. He sprinted to the bust of Miraslav and slammed the buttons. The door groaned as it slid shut.

The magic stopped.

Air rushed back into his lungs, and he gasped, staggering forward. His fingers and chest still tingled, but at least he could breathe again.

"That sucked," Leper panted, leaning against the bust of Miraslav.

Madislak pulled a small journal from the wall. The compartment clicked shut, and the shard of Theora tinked against the stone floor. Leper looked at it, still wary that it might shock him again, or worse.

Madislak flipped through the journal. It wasn't large, maybe ten to fifteen pages, but with each turn, his eyes widened.

"What?" Leper asked, gingerly poking the shard of Theora. No agony surged through him this time.

"I know why Nalecht wants you dead so bad." Madislak handed him the journal. "I know why he wants your entire race exterminated."

Leper grabbed the book and skimmed through it. "Why?"

"Amarook built the talisman as a way to keep the evil gods in check. They didn't want to kill them outright unless they had to—it was a defense mechanism to protect mortals." Madislak flipped to a page, tapping an inscription. "Only a member of Amarook's bloodline can destroy the talisman."

Leper's eyes scanned the passage. Sure enough, only a Chernzerk could *destroy* the talisman. Anyone could break it, shattering it into the seven shards currently scattered across the world. But a Chernzerk, they could erase it completely, wiping out its power forever.

He shut his eyes briefly. Nalecht had once said he *might* let him live if he retrieved the shard of Kasherri. But now, after this revelation, Leper knew the truth: Nalecht would *never* let any of them live. His thirst for power, his obsession with the shards, had already driven him to threaten children and raze cities. He'd stop at nothing to claim them.

There wasn't a chance in this lifetime or the next that he'd leave a single Chernzerk alive.

"Mind if I give this to Harmony to study?" Madislak tapped the journal.

Leper shook his head.

"Let's get back to the others. We need to tell them what we found." Madislak clapped him on the shoulder.

"Yeah. We definitely should." Leper forced a grin.

The weight of it settled in—he *would* be hunted. *All* of them would be hunted until Nalecht was dead.

With three shards already in his grasp, Nalecht was too powerful to face. And now that Leper knew the truth, the fight wouldn't end with him—it never would. The only way to stop it was to take the shards back and *destroy* the talisman.

The problem? He had no idea how to do that.

One problem at a time, Leper.

Perhaps going alone to the rain trials was the better option. No one would slow him down, and he wouldn't have to worry about anyone else if it was dangerous. Plus, he might figure out how to destroy the dumb talisman on his own anyway.

Which sucked. He didn't want to go alone to a city of dwarves and hunt for the shard by himself, but it was likely his best choice. The others would be better off focusing their efforts on destroying the shard of Theora.

"I know that's depressing to hear." Maka Kura's voice drifted into his mind, steady, reassuring. "But Nalecht can't forge the talisman without the shard of Kasherri. If you get to it first, maybe you'll have enough strength to claim the rest. But your priority is Kasherri—Zanera and Kelindra's lives depend on it."

"You're right." Leper turned toward the door. "I'll make sure they're safe first. Then I'll worry about destroying the talisman."

They started back out of the crypt, Madislak leading the way.

Leper truly wished he had more time to spend with Madislak—his brother. Or better yet, that Madislak could come along with him. He knew King Madislak, but he wanted to know Madislak, his brother. Perhaps someday. Either way, he felt closer to him now, in a way he knew he'd never feel toward their other brother, no matter the circumstances.

Chapter Nine

L eper sat stiffly at the round table in Madislak's throne
room, arms crossed as he watched the king savor a piece
of cake. They just discovered a wealth of knowledge about the
shards and their connection to the Chernzerk, and Leper didn't
like any of it. The warmth of the fire did nothing to ease the
cold growing in his chest. The scent of burnt wood filled the
air, mixing with the sweetness of vanilla as Madislak washed
down another bite with milk. His eyes focused on Petrovana for
some reason, it made Leper feel uneasy.

*Just get through this conversation. Make a plan. Get the
shard of Kasherri and rescue Zanera and Kelindra.*

"One thing at a time, Leper." Maka Kura reminded him.

Leper reassured him he would try to focus on one task at a
time. Then took a seat at the table beside Petrovana.

Petrovana made the cake, and it was perfect. Not too dry and
not too moist, just the perfect mix of texture, and the vanilla
flavor was divine, one of his favorites.

The others hung their coats on their chairs, water pitchers
and plates set neatly before them. They chatted about the last
month, about last night's events, as if there weren't bigger things
at stake. Leper clenched his jaw. Enough of this.

"We need to get the shard of Kasherri and safeguard the shard of Theora." He yanked the shard from around his neck and placed it on the table. "I'll go after Kasherri's. With Madislak being king, Leighth queen, and Harmony the queen-to-be, I'm the only option. None of you can leave. Petrovana can come with me, but I think it might be better if she stayed here to help destroy the shard of Theora, and I went alone." He allowed himself a nod in her direction. She looked like she was about to protest.

"Actually, she can't go at all," Harmony cut in. "Coraidon and Finrod were killed. Assassinated by The Latter, in what we can only assume is an attempt to win the shrews' allegiance."

Leper's hand shot to Petrovana's shoulder as her body trembled beneath his touch.

"It's fine," she blubbered. "They kicked me out anyway. Nothin' I can do to fix that. They won't let me back in, even fer the funeral."

Leper inhaled sharply, his pulse pounding in his ears.

Madislak exchanged a glance with Harmony before turning to Petrovana. "Actually, there might be a way around that."

Petrovana's head snapped toward him. "And what is that exactly?"

"You're not going to like it," Harmony said, taking a sip of water. "None of us will."

Madislak cleared his throat. "My father suggested that Petrovana and I get married. This would restore her as a queen and potentially nullify the banishment, uniting us with the shrews instead of Nalecht."

Leper's head turned slowly to Madislak, his breath leaving him in a short, disbelieving laugh. "This is a joke, right?" He let the words hang, then scoffed. "Or is everything you just said to me not two hours ago a bunch of bullshit?"

Madislak winced. "I know, Leper, I really do, but if Nalecht adds an army of shrews to his arsenal... well, you get the point."

There had to be someone in this mess of people who didn't agree with this garbage, right? Someone who saw it for the load of crap it was.

Now it all made sense—Madislak's lingering looks at Petrovana, the way he assessed her when they first arrived.

He'd been sizing her up, judging whether she could fit the role of Lantess's queen.

Leper turned his glare to Harmony, then to Petrovana. "What do you make of this?"

Harmony flicked her hand. "I hate it."

Petrovana let out a heavy sigh. "As bad as it sucks, Leper, it makes sense. I don't see you that way, Madislak, sorry, but the union would benefit us greatly. And maybe it'll let me back into my hometown."

Leper's fingers curled into his palm, nails digging into his skin. A sharp gasp left him. "So that's it? After these last few weeks, you just up and marry Madislak?"

Petrovana reached for him, her hand brushing his arm. "No, dear, that's not what I mean. I choose you, but when the fate of the world depends on it, marrying Madislak makes sense. We're all goin' to have to make sacrifices."

Leper yanked his arm away like she'd burned him. "Get your hand off me."

She gasped, eyes widening at him.

"Hey!" Madislak barked. "Calm down. We're all on the same team here, trying to decide what's best for the future."

"Exactly. *Your* future." Leper's voice was sharp as steel. "None of you give a damn about anyone else."

It was all they ever cared about. Madislak had only been nice to him so that when he dropped this news, Leper wouldn't be as furious. And Petrovana—she was actually willing to throw away everything they'd built together just because the king suggested it?

Unbelievable.

"You're not thinking clearly, Leper," Leighth interjected. "We all care about each other, but tough decisions have to be made."

Leper let out a bitter laugh. "Really? Where's Lillian? Or did nobody care enough to find her?"

Madislak flinched, only fueling the wildfire in Leper's mind. He'd never planned on looking for her in the first place.

And as for Zanera and Kelindra—if anyone could keep them safe, it was him and him alone. Not these greedy, self-serving so-called friends.

He shoved his chair back with force, rising to his feet. "Fuck you all. I'm going after that shard." His hand slammed against the table so hard the plates rattled.

Madislak's eyes flicked to him, and for a brief second, something passed between them. Recognition. Fear. Leper saw what Madislak saw—an echo of the madman who had attacked Blank Face after Rinawen's death, and Madislak was scared of that person.

And perhaps he should be.

When he lifted his hand, the shard of Theora lay on the table.

Leper's voice was low, dangerous. "Keep that shard safe. It better be here when I get back. And Madislak," he pointed a shaking finger at him, "since what you just told me is apparently bullshit, do me one favor? Keep an eye on Zanera and Kelindra. Should something happen to me, they won't have anyone to look after them like I do."

"Actually, you might want to get them out of there," Blank Face finally spoke up.

Leper's blood boiled at the sound of his voice. "And why is that, *Ass Face?*" he snarled.

Blank Face shrugged. "I killed Larnadix for Kendra about five years ago. Whoever this is, it isn't Larnadix."

Kendra, Leighth's mother, who Nalecht murdered about a month ago. Blank Face killed Larnadix for her? He wasn't sure why he didn't really care why.

Leper's vision blurred at the edges. His head throbbed. His breaths came faster. Rage. Pain. Anguish. He felt all of it, seething inside him, clawing at his ribs.

"The kidnapping of Larnadix, his disappearance, and sudden reappearance all those years ago... Rin and I knew something was different about him." His pulse pounded as he took a step toward Blank Face. "Why didn't you say anything in the past *month?*"

Blank Face lifted a brow. "You never mentioned his kidnapping to me or anything else. I mean, I knew you were close with Rinawen and all, but it's not like we talk and know each other like brothers should."

Leper's hands balled into fists. His teeth ground together. "Whatever. Get your lanky, useless ass over there and get them out." His gaze swept across the table, his fury bubbling over.

"And mark my words. Once we stop Nalecht, I *can't wait* for the day I don't have to look at your stupid, backstabbing faces."

He grabbed his chair, lifted it, and *slammed* it to the ground, shattering it into splintered pieces.

Silence.

The only sound was Petrovana's hard, broken sobs as he stormed out of the room.

Marry Petrovana. Of course, that's the answer. Leper stomped through the castle hallways as guards quickly moved out of his way. Anytime he found something worthwhile, it got ripped away from him, just like Rinawen, just like her daughters will be if he fails again. *Marry Petrovana.* He ripped down some of the banners and decorations celebrating Harmony and Madislak's engagement. *Screw this place and these people. Marry Petrovana.* A phrase that continued to fuel his rage with every thought. Find Ghost and leave for Costin. Get that shard, get Zanera and Kelindra to safety, and get on with his life. *Marry Petrovana.*

He stomped to the landing pad of Lantess, where several flying chariots were parked. He whistled loudly for Ghost, pacing back and forth on the stone. His face heated, and his ears burned with rage. *What a joke.* Judging from Petrovana's face, she could've married Madislak right there on the spot, without even asking how he felt about it. He whistled again, growing impatient, his mind consumed by anxiety, rage, and disgust. Total burning rage. Nobody else gave a shit, why should he? *Marry Petrovana.*

"Leper, wait, don't leave like this," Harmony panted, rushing over to him.

Leper turned away. "What do you want? As soon as my bird gets here, I'm leaving. I suggest you hurry."

"You're upset, I get it. Nobody hates this idea more than I do," she pleaded.

"What do you want?" he replied dryly.

"Look, I know this might be hard to hear, but they're right about that wedding. We could use all the shrews from Terynsipple's assistance." She sighed. "Especially if Nalecht keeps attacking cities."

Leper rolled his eyes. "You know this is all bullshit, right? When all these political games are over, where does that leave people like us? Why don't you come with me to Costin? Show Madislak and Petrovana what it feels like."

Harmony sighed. "I can't exactly leave. I'm the proxy to Lantess."

Leper chuckled bitterly. "Right. So Madislak will marry Petrovana, and you'll stand by happily as the proxy, watch them have a family, raise their kids, and not resent them?"

A tear rolled down her cheek. "You can be a real asshole, you know that?" She sighed. "But you're also completely right. No, I couldn't. But..." Her eyes widened. "Leper, you are technically an Idelth. You share the same mom. You could be king, if Madislak would yield it to you."

"I'm not exactly an Idelth, Harmony. I'm his mother's son, not Nelaan's." Leper shrugged it off.

"He's the king, Leper. If any king or queen wants to yield their rulership to someone, they're allowed." She huffed, waving a hand over the city. "Leighth offered to give Kundry to Madislak or Brebian if Blank Face doesn't behave himself... remember?"

A solid point.

Leper burst out laughing. "I'm no king. The people would never follow a Chernzerk king, not in my lifetime. And Madislak would never yield this place to me anyway, why would he?"

"Leper, you don't seem to realize how many people care about you." She moved to place a hand on his shoulder, but he pulled away. "If you and Petrovana presented it to Madislak in a way that showed you care as much as he does about the future of Lantess... there's a possibility he'd do it."

"That's a long shot, Harmony." He whistled again, ears still burning. "I don't want any of this anyway... ever."

"If he would—would you do it?" Harmony placed a hand on his arm, and this time, he didn't pull away. "Even just for a little while, until Rylin is of age?"

"You want me to be king? And marry Petrovana?" Leper scoffed.

She nodded earnestly.

"Why are you even bothering to fight this so much? What I want, or what you want, doesn't even matter to these kings and queens." His gaze locked onto her sparkling blue eyes.

"You saved my life, Madislak's life, his children. You gave me this." She held up the vial hanging from her neck. "This can bring someone back to life, Leper. You trusted me from day one. We didn't show you the same respect—especially Madislak. But I believe our friendship goes beyond the others' bond. Why else would you give me something so invaluable?"

He remembered handing her that vial when they first arrived on The Talon, a desperate attempt to earn their trust. At the time, both she and Madislak still eyed him with suspicion. That was also when his hat came off, and they discovered his true identity. Whether the vial had changed Harmony's view of him after that, he didn't know. But it had earned him her approval.

Leper touched the glass with his fingertip, admiring its vibrant yellow color. "Honestly? To gain your trust. But I knew if I took it back, I'd lose part of that trust. Even though..." He trailed off, shaking his head. "Never mind. I just wanted to prove I was worth trusting. Why didn't you turn me over at the council meeting? I could tell you knew I was lying—the way you stared at me."

Her golden locks bounced as she nodded and grinned. "Because I saw how you acted with Madislak's kids. How you helped us. The rejuvenation vials. I knew how they'd react, and I knew you didn't deserve that." She grabbed his hand, squeezing it gently. "And I realized something during that meeting—when I first showed you that horn. The complete terror in your eyes, the fear on your face... You weren't scared of the Chernzerk. You were scared of *us*, of what we would do to you if we knew. And no one who's shown the kindness you have, Leper, ever deserves to feel that way among friends."

She had figured it out before he could even confirm it. It was something he would always remember.

Ghost finally appeared in the sky, soaring down towards them. She landed with magnificent grace as the cold wind that gusted past them sent a shiver down his spine. Once he got to Costin, he would probably yearn for these cooler temperatures, but he was headed to the desert. A hot, dry, miserable desert.

The dust and leaves kicked up, tickling his nose. He ran his hands down her smooth, feathered neck and atop her furry head.

"Are you ready for a long journey? Maybe we can poach some chickens along the way, your favorite." Leper rubbed Ghost's cheek.

Ghost squawked and clicked, then nestled her head into his chest as he wrapped his arms around her neck.

"You sure you're okay to travel on your own, Leper?" Harmony asked.

"Are you going to come with me?" Leper quipped.

"I can't."

He rolled his eyes at her. "Of course not. Why would anyone give two shits what happens to anyone but themselves in this group of so-called friends?"

"You don't seriously think that, we all care." She pleaded as she tried to get in his way.

He pushed past her and hopped on Ghost.

"Regardless, I don't care anymore. Don't lose that gods-forsaken shard. And get Zanera and Kelindra to safety. Because I can promise you one thing—if neither of those things is done when I get back with that shard of Kasherri, there will be hell to pay."

"Spoken like a true king," she muttered as she turned and left.

Leper hopped on Ghost and urged her east, towards Costin, towards the immense heat, as fast as she could go.

Petrovana wiped the tears from her face, squared her shoulders, and composed herself. She just watched Leper storm out of here angrily. This could've gone better, but she hadn't expected Leper to just up and leave. Her mind swirled. *Was he done with her? Was leaving his way of saying they were finished?* She didn't know. They needed to sift through the storm of problems in front of them. Did he even care that her adoptive parents had died? The people who raised her. She shook her head.

She could worry about his antics later. For now, she needed to figure out if she was needed to go after a shrew alliance, or if they wanted her to chase after Leper to get that shard.

"What's the plan, Madislak?" She leaned forward, resting her arms on the table.

Madislak ruffled through his beard. "I'm the King, I can't go chasing after him. The shards are important, but I have a kingdom to run. And I can't openly attack Kordry to get those girls out. That will incite yet another war. Blank, can you get into Kundry and get those girls out without causing any commotion?"

Blank Face nodded. "If that's what's needed. Whatever keeps the shards out of Nalecht's hands."

Leighth interrupted. "So, if Larnadix is dead, who's pretending to be him? Could it be the fourth Chernzerk we can't seem to find? The shapeshifter?"

"Yeah, Ace's sister, she's still out there somewhere." Blank Face leaned back in his seat. "My assumption was she was the one who flew in on the dragon that saved Nalecht at the battle of Tudela."

Madislak let out a dejected sigh. "That's the problem with shapeshifters, guys. You can never tell who or what they are. They could be the horse you're riding on or the person sitting next to you." He took a drink of whiskey. "We should just remain focused on keeping this shard safe and getting those girls out of Kordry. I haven't heard anything from Brebian or Theodamar either. They were supposed to seek an alliance with Goreldea, who knows what happened to them."

"Reckon it could be. What else could change forms or personalities like that?" Petrovana flicked her eyes to Leighth. "But why would a Chernzerk do that? Especially for five years?"

"Good point. I mean, Leper said he knew Larnadix, and if whoever posed as Larnadix knew Leper was a Chernzerk and they themselves were a Chernzerk, I would think they would have revealed themselves to him or Rinawen, and she would've told Leper." Leighth took a sip of water.

Harmony rejoined the table and took a shot of whiskey, glancing at Petrovana. Blank Face walked over and poured himself a shot. "When I went back to verify and saw him, he smelled... otherworldly, like sulfur and rotten eggs."

Harmony folded her hands in her lap. "Sounds demonic, honestly. But the barrier between planes would've prevented any demon or Kasherri herself from getting to the material plane. It's been in place since the first war. Three hundred years ago,"

As soon as she said it, Petrovana remembered something that had happened long ago. Something dark, something she and her companions hadn't spoken of in ages. They hadn't just dabbled in an illegal form of blood magic—they'd gone so far as to tempt fate with channeling, too.

Channeling meant stacking a shrew's power. One would cut their palm and clasp hands with another whose palm was cut, the mingled blood mixing their magical energies and amplifying each shrew's power. But it also came with extremely dangerous side effects. Overdraw, for instance, could happen when a shrew—or shrews—couldn't stop casting magic, burning themselves out until they withered and died. Or they might open a portal to another plane of existence, allowing passage to whatever lay on the other side. Other risks included going blind, losing all magical abilities, or suffering underdraw—a fate like overdraw, except the power stayed locked inside, building up until the shrew became so saturated with energy they went mad enough to end their own life. *It can't be. Can't be.*

There was also oversaturation and undersaturation, where the magical moonlight either flowed too heavily and built up until the body exploded, or didn't flow enough, causing the body to disintegrate into nothing. Many, many dangerous side effects of channeling.

"Shit... no..." Petrovana downed a shot of whiskey, the liquid burning all the way down. "Shit, shit, shit, shit."

"What!?" Madislak's deep voice boomed. Everyone glared at her.

She took a deep breath, grabbing another shot. "Do you have anythin' that depicts demonic-like creatures?"

Harmony riffled through the books on the table. "Yes, a very old one."

"About seven years ago, my adoptive parents and a couple of other shrews were testin' our limits and capabilities of blood magic with... Channelin'. We may have accidentally summoned a demon and couldn't send it back. We never spoke

of it since. We hoped it got killed or taken back to Malastion."
She downed the shot and sat back in her chair.

Everyone at the table gasped. Harmony handed Petrovana a
book, its bindings worn and barely holding together. The cover
bore an engraved depiction of a minotaur's face. Petrovana
traced her finger over it for a moment before opening it. She
sniffed a couple times, taking in the wonderful aroma of the
book.

"What kind of stupid shit goes on over there?" Madislak
didn't hide his frustration.

"So, you get a demon loose and just turn away?" Leighth
confronted her.

"Just look for it in here." Harmony stood over her shoulder
as she flipped the pages. "Were any of you aware of what can
happen with channeling? Or were you all just stupid enough to
think you had some kind of control over it?"

Petrovana looked up at her briefly. "You were never curious
about the properties of channelin'? Figured a shrew, especially
one as ambitious as you, would've at least thought about the
possibilities of what you could do with that extra power."

Harmony tilted her head, rolling her eyes. "Yeah, I'm curious,
but knowing you've got no control over the side effects is enough
to keep me away. I've got no desire to lose any part of my mind.
I've worked hard to get where I am, and I'm not risking it over
some stupid power trip."

It wasn't a power trip. She wanted to say it, but she held back.
Petrovana didn't want to get into the details—that they'd been
on The Talon, trying to subdue the protective beasts roaming
there so they could explore the mountain itself. That would
only bring more attention—negative attention—to the shrews
of Terynsipple, and she preferred to keep her beloved home out
of the spyglass. They were a peaceful people who simply enjoyed
their magic, wanting only to explore The Talon's mysteries
and uncover the secrets hidden within the massive mountain.
Perhaps if they had been successful, they would've found Ace
earlier and discovered the Chernzerk still remained, but in a
more peaceful state. Maybe they could've avoided this entire
war altogether.

Petrovana turned the pages, revealing imps, minotaurs, centaurs, and large arachnids—many variations of denizens of

Malastion, the underworld, that used to find their way to the material plane.

She froze when she saw the page. This was definitely what had emerged. There were two depictions, one with black skin and one with red. It had two-toed feet, six-inch talons for fingernails, and round, sharp, elongated teeth that retracted into its mouth. Its eyes were pitch black, and its wings stretched from its back. An iron whip tail curled behind it. She shuddered, remembering the foul stench and wicked demeanor. The protections they'd placed around themselves had kept it at bay until it finally gave up and left. But they had summoned the black-skinned one with crimson eyes, which was apparently the stronger version.

She couldn't read the lettering on the page identifying the creature.

"That's it?" Harmony said, unimpressed.

Petrovana nodded.

"You're sure? You could pick literally anything else in this book and I'd be okay with it," Harmony demanded.

"No, by Obidiah's grace, I'm positive that's it," Petrovana reiterated.

Harmony closed her eyes and let out a long, deep breath.

"Can you read that?" Blank Face pointed at the page.

"Yes, it's an old language the shrews used to use." Harmony grabbed the book and slammed it down in front of Madislak.

"Well?" He looked up at her. "What is it?"

"The short version: it's quite literally the worst thing to bring from the underworld depths. From the Loyal Order of Vermilion Deathbinders." She took another shot of whiskey.

"And the long version?" Leighth winced.

Petrovana listened intently as Harmony detailed these abominations. Seven elite warriors comprised Kasherri's most trusted, loyal, and lethal guardians. The book didn't explain how these creatures were made, but it stated they could only be killed by a legendary weapon, the talisman, or healing magic. Though Petrovana wasn't solely responsible for bringing this thing to Kalazaar, she felt the weight of it. The one caveat: they were controllable with the shard of Kasherri in your possession.

They were very resistant to magic, though capable of using it at devastating levels. *Great.* No matter what she did, everything came back to haunt her. She felt as though she could never do anything right, even when she was trying to help.

"Holy mother of Theora," Madislak muttered, rubbing his face. "I hope you and your village are proud of yourselves. Using illegal magic and ignoring the consequences. Let someone else deal with it."

"It wasn't all my fault. But for my part, I'm sorry. I won't disappear or abandon this group until this is resolved," Petrovana said earnestly. "I was young and still learnin' then."

"Still are..." Harmony sneered.

"We must get those people out, all of them..." Leighth's words were cut off by the shattering of glass at their feet.

A black smoke swirled up from the glass, and Petrovana's body started to go limp.

Smoke swirled in Petrovana's eyes as Blank Face materialized before her and snatched the shard of Theora from the table.

Chapter Ten

Petrovana's body was limp as thudding boots met the stone floor around her. She saw the eccentric mohawk man, The Latter, who had cut off Leighth's ear, materialize in front of her. Blank Face had seized the shard of Theora and vanished before the room filled with choking smoke. Beside The Latter stood another man with a catlike face and large, bulging eyes, someone she didn't recognize. *What the hell is going on here?*

The man waited for the smoke to clear, his large eyes glinting with sadistic pleasure as he leaned in front of Harmony, grinning. "Do you remember me, sweetie?"

Fear flashed in Harmony's eyes.

"Thessek, you piece of shit. What are you doing here?" Madislak barked.

Thessek was the cat-faced person Harmony had told Petrovana about—the one who kept stabbing her in the leg when they were captured. He was leading some contingent of orcs south to Xaneth Harbor, and he had taken Madislak and Harmony prisoner, torturing them for answers about Leper.

Blank Face appeared behind The Latter, slashing his side with a dagger. As he aimed for The Latter's neck, The Latter shifted into smoke, hovering around Blank Face in an attempt to incapacitate him. But Blank Face blinked away, then lunged at Thessek, slicing his arm and leg. Both men converged on Blank Face, but he fended them off with expert agility and lightning-fast parries. His movements were a blur, and the clash of steel echoed through the throne room.

"I told you fucking idiots to engulf everyone in this room with smoke!" a woman's voice bellowed. From the corner of her eye, Petrovana saw Queen Tamara sauntering through the doors. *Oh gods, no. The last person any of them wanted to see.*

Blank Face glanced toward the doors, locking eyes with Petrovana for a fleeting second before vanishing. Was that fear in his eyes? He did not return.

"Sorry, master, we had a resistant one," Thessek slinked away.

"Blank Face," The Latter growled. "Come back here. I want to show you who the true notorious assassin is, you coward." Still, Blank Face did not return.

"Can they talk? I told you I want them immobile but able to speak. Tell me you didn't screw that up, too," Tamara commanded.

"Yes, master," Thessek replied. "They can talk."

"Good." Tamara took a seat, squeezing in beside Madislak and Harmony.

Her poofy, curly brown hair reached down to her shoulders, almost matching her tan skin. Dark brown eyes bore into Petrovana. She wore the brown and yellow guard attire of Xaneth Harbor with pride. Fastened to her side was a pristine, gleaming falchion. Behind her stood a hulking brute of a man. Though Madislak was muscular, this guy was stacked to the brim—and very, very tall. Strapped to his back was a massive warhammer, which Petrovana was certain she couldn't lift even if she tried.

Petrovana's heart thundered in her chest. She couldn't move—a prisoner to dread and helplessness. Frantically, she tried to will her legs, her fingers, anything to respond, but her body refused. It was as if she were chained against a wall. It didn't hurt, but she couldn't feel anything.

"What is the meaning of this?" Madislak blurted.

Tamara grinned arrogantly. "Do I even need to ask, or are you all that stupid?"

"This is an act of war. We will unite and tear you down," Madislak threatened. "How'd you even get in here?"

Tamara scoffed, pulling a knife from her belt. She seized Harmony's hand, slammed it palm down on the table, and drove the knife through it, pinning it there. "Every time you guys lie to me, I'm going to cut more of her hand off. Now, where's the damned shard of Theora? Where are Blank Face and your horned friend, Leper?"

Harmony's eyes widened as she stared at her hand.

Madislak growled. "He's gone. Threw a fit and left on his griffin, taking the shard of Theora with him. As for Blank Face, he's around here somewhere. Why?"

Tamara looked at Petrovana for confirmation. "He speaks the truth. Leper left a while ago."

Petrovana's heart pounded so hard she thought it might explode. After Tamara's brutal display, she feared for all their lives, realizing that everything known about Tamara was true. She didn't mess around—straight to the point and ruthless. She and Nalecht made the perfect, despicable couple.

"Well, that's unfortunate. Nylor, cuff these two. And make sure to put the magical cuffs on her," Tamara ordered, pointing to Harmony. She yanked the dagger from Harmony's hand, and blood poured forth. Petrovana wished she could use her newly formed healing magic to help, but her limbs refused to respond.

"Bandage that wound too," Tamara called as she sauntered over and took a seat beside Petrovana and Leighth. Inches from Petrovana's face, she hissed. "You best get that shard to me quickly, or I'll start sending them back to you in pieces. Do you understand?"

Tears slipped from Petrovana's eyes. "Yes."

Tamara turned to Leighth. "And you. Send your precious little boyfriend to Xaneth Harbor. No..." She shook her head. "Tell him to run those damned rain trials and show up with the shard of Kasherri or... Well, I think you two dumb bitches understand what will happen."

Leighth didn't back down. "When my precious boyfriend stabs you straight through the heart, I'll be there, laughing in your face."

Tamara slammed her hand on the table, then turned and grasped Petrovana's cheeks, forcing her mouth open. She grabbed her tongue, pulling it out as far as she could, and held her knife against it, digging in slightly.

"Want to insult me again? Do it. I dare you. Push me, bitch," Tamara gritted.

When Leighth said nothing, Tamara grinned. "Thought so. I better see some results in two weeks, or you'll be getting body parts. Not sure who I'll start with, but I'm looking forward to it." She grinned at Petrovana as Nylor helped haul Madislak out of the throne room. Tamara helped The Latter carry Harmony out, and they disappeared. Petrovana's mind raced as tears streaked down her face. What were they going to do? Madislak was the King of Lantess, and Harmony was set to be queen—they led this entire group. And now, they were prisoners of Tamara. What would they tell his people?

Leper guided Ghost eastward, determined to reach Costin quickly but careful not to push her too hard. After a two-day journey, they landed on the outskirts of the city, near a cluster of sandstone statues standing openly in the blistering desert heat. Leper wished for a canopy to shield him from the relentless sun, the heat searing his skin like he was being cooked alive. But his attention snagged on the statues standing a few miles north of Costin. Were they connected to the shard of Kasherri? He had to find out. He had eight days left to find the entrance to the rain trials.

During his journey, he penned a note to Zanera and Kelindra, grateful for how they had refilled his vial case. Fortunately, they could exchange notes as well—so long as the case in his old hut remained intact, it stayed magically linked to the pouch at his side. He urged them to leave Kundry, warning them about Blank Face's revelations and advising extreme caution around him. He instructed them to find Madislak for protection or, if Blank Face appeared, to trust him only to get them out. Zanera, always composed, thanked him and mentioned that Kordry was becoming increasingly chaotic, like a war zone at times. She appreciated the direction to seek out Madislak and wished she could have accompanied him to Costin, though she understood the dangers he faced. Kelindra's little heart drawn in the bottom corner of the paper brought a smile to his lips.

As the evening sun descended, the oppressive heat began to fade. Leper turned his attention to the statues before him, mostly Chernzerk, with only two exceptions. One was human, the other an elf with a wild mohawk—The Latter. The human statue was short and stocky. Inscribed on the plaque at the marked elf's feet was the name Vickus Morth. Was this The Latter's name before the trials? What did these statues signify? Why were they here, and why were most of them his people?

Sweat trickled down his brow, his mouth dry and gritty. He licked his parched lips, regretting his lack of preparation for the desert—no water, no cool clothes, just a hasty departure on Ghost.

Marry Petrovana. What a crock of shit. She'd jumped at the offer without a second thought. And then Blank Face made everything worse, as usual. Killing Larnadix, who even was Larnadix now? Who could take on his identity so easily? Everything changed since that night six years ago. If only Blank Face had spoken up sooner. *Idiots. All of them. Lying, backstabbing idiots.*

Leper sighed, weaving through rows of statues, hundreds of them. He searched mindlessly for any clue about their purpose, the shard, or the elusive rain trials. His mind replayed his last encounter with the group. Maybe Blank Face had it right—work alone, trust no one, and avoid disappointment.

If only Rinawen were here... *Rinawen.*

"No," Maka Kura's voice broke through his thoughts. "Don't go down this path again."

"What? I should just forget about her then?" Leper grunted.

"You should focus on why you're here. It's sweltering, for you, at least. I'm fine, but linger too long and you'll die. You need to find water, shade, a place to stay for the night."

"Exactly, you're a stupid piece of metal. Now shut up and let me sulk," Leper snapped.

His clothes clung to his sweat-drenched skin, and he wiped his brow with his shirt. Ghost trailed behind, pecking at the sand.

"I hold more knowledge than you ever will. Watch your tongue, boy. I can take away as much as I give," Maka's voice was stern.

"Who you calling boy? I'll leave you on the ground again and walk away."

"Do it. It'll be your last mistake, you stubborn, insolent fool. This requires both of us, not just you," Maka retorted.

"You're a weapon. You don't understand what it's like to lose someone. You couldn't possibly grasp abandonment—by parents, by Madislak. Losing the one you love, being tossed aside like you don't matter. My brother killed the one I loved, and I have to accept it while he gets to live!" Leper yelled.

"Life is unfair, Leper, but people count on you. Zanera and Kelindra look up to you. Madislak depends on you finding this shard. The world depends on it. Please, push aside this darkness and be the other Leper. The one the world needs," Maka pleaded.

The plea in his voice was almost enough to sway his temperament. But thoughts of Rinawen flooded his mind. Madislak and Petrovana.

"No. I like this guy. He takes no shit, including yours," Leper gritted.

"You'll only lose more friends. Tell me, how will you act when you're the reason they all die?" Maka countered.

"Shut up! Shut...UP!" Leper screamed.

Visions of Rinawen's last breaths haunted him. His stupid argument with Blank Face had caused her death. *Failure.* Why hadn't he just gone with her when she asked? If he had known about Blank Face, he would have been there. *Another failure. Marry Petrovana.*

Leper's mind went dark. Rage, pure and unchecked, consumed him. He could no longer control his own actions.

He faced the Chernzerk statue and unleashed a scream, straining his throat and turning his face flush. He punched the statue, his fists bouncing off and drawing blood. Again and again, he pummeled it, switching hands until blood dripped from both. He head-butted it repeatedly, ignoring the pain. Unsheathing Maka Kura, he aimed to slam it against the statue, but his arm halted midway down to strike.

"NO! Control yourself. I will not desecrate these statues," Maka held firm.

"You will do what I command! Now hit the damn statue!" Leper roared.

He swung again, but Maka refused to strike.

"Useless," Leper mouthed, slamming Maka to the ground. Rage blinded him, but he couldn't bring himself to disrespect Maka Kura further. Ghost nuzzled him from behind, knocking him off balance. Leper glanced into the griffin's eyes as she let out a squawk and shimmied her body, as if complaining about the heat. Regaining control, he retrieved Maka Kura from the sand.

"Sorry..." Leper muttered, but his thoughts were interrupted.

"Is there a reason you're trying to destroy these statues?" A deep male voice called out.

Leper turned to see a figure standing before him in a robe. How long had he been there? The man's hood was pulled back, revealing shaggy black hair, unkempt and sweaty beneath the thick material. He was shorter than the average human, almost dwarf-like, with a round belly, much like the statue beside The Latter's. Despite his clean-shaven face, signs of age marked him, suggesting he was in his late forties or early fifties.

What really caught Leper's attention were his eyes. They were square, like glass cubes inserted into his eye sockets, with triangular blue pupils.

"Can you see with those things?" Leper waved his hand up and down.

The man waved back. "Yes, quite well, actually."

"You're not scared? Of my appearance?" Leper asked, noticing the man's calm demeanor.

The man chuckled. "Should I be? I'm more scared of how you act, not how you look."

"Who are you? You look just like that statue over there... What are these statues?" Leper's throat was hoarse from the dry air and his relentless screaming.

"These statues represent those who have run the rain trials," the man explained. "But let's take your griffin and get to a place less hot. There's someone I'd like you to meet. They've talked an awful lot about you."

"About me? Who?" Leper eyed him up and down suspiciously. But if this man could provide some food, water, and shelter, that would only help him get to Costin sooner.

"You'll see," was all the man said as he approached Leper and Ghost.

Leper followed the strange man's directions, guiding Ghost as instructed. Trusting him felt like a gamble. He reached out to Maka Kura, briefly telling the weapon to be ready, just in case he got crossed and was led into a trap. It wouldn't be the first time. Likely wouldn't be the last either. Still, the mystery gnawed at him. Who the hell was waiting for him? A nagging part of him clung to the impossible hope that Rinawen would be there. Maybe Blank Face had somehow brought Zanera and Kelindra here, or maybe Petrovana had come to resolve things. A foolish hope, but one he couldn't shake.

The sun had just vanished, but it was still hot, and he wiped his brow, taking in the landscape. Massive sand dunes stretched endlessly, with houses impossibly built into them. How? They had to be hundreds of feet high, thick enough that no structure should stand. The sandstone buildings of Costin loomed in the distance.

They landed in front of a house supported by four massive pillars, holding up a sandstone canopy. Several windows dotted the exterior wall, and a single set of double doors marked the entrance. It looked massive from the outside, and Leper wondered if the inside matched the grandeur. The sun's absence provided a much-needed respite, the temperature dropping significantly. Ghost let out a low huff of relief, stretching out by a window.

"Let's get that amazing creature some water and food. What does she like?" the man asked.

"She loves chickens, and yes, some water would be great," Leper nodded, still trying to get a read on him.

The man opened the door and called out for someone to bring water.

Moments later, a dark-haired girl with hazel eyes emerged. She wore a green sleeveless shirt, loose shorts, and sandals. Her sturdy frame suggested she could handle herself in a fight. As she passed, she barely spared him a glance—no fear, no hesitation. Anyone on Uskela would've shrieked and run for their life. What set these people apart? Were there more Chernzerk here than he knew?

"You're not afraid of me?" he asked.

She didn't answer but returned moments later with a glass of water, handing it to him. He gulped it down, savoring the crisp, refreshing taste.

"No, I ain't afraid of you." She extended her hand. "I'm Delinah. Nice to meet you."

"Leper. A pleasure." Her palms were rough and calloused.

"Any idea who he ran off to get?" Leper grinned.

"If he told you, it'd be a surprise; reckon I won't spoil it." She smirked.

"You from Terynsipple? Your accent matches two people I know from there." He tilted his head.

"Born and raised."

"What spells do you have?" He assumed that coming from a village of shrews meant she'd be one herself.

"Reckon I don't use magic like them. Miserable place—I prefer cold, hard steel." She held out her palms.

No tattoos. Interesting. Much like someone else he knew.

Heavy footsteps thundered down the stairs. Another set followed. His chest tightened. That had to be Zanera and Kelindra. But when the door opened, he wasn't ready for who he saw.

"Lillian!? What are you doing here?" he blurted. Then he caught sight of the person behind her, and his stomach twisted. "Ace."

The last time he and Ace crossed paths, they had fought in the War of Tudela. Ace had sided with Nalecht. And yet, here he stood, beside Lillian, looking more put together than before—hair trimmed, clothes clean, not a hint of garbage clinging to him. A change, sure, but did it mean anything?

Most of Leper wanted to start swinging right then and there. Last time they spoke, Ace had threatened to make him watch while he killed Petrovana. That thought alone should've been enough to make his blood boil. And yet... he couldn't deny some-

thing about Ace's shameless indifference was almost refreshing.

"What happened to you? Were you attacked?" Lillian asked,
eyeing the dried blood on his hands and face.

The glass-eyed man behind them approached, his gaze unreadable. When he opened his lids, the blue shield in his glass
cube shifted into a yellow swirl. It reminded Leper of the markings on Petrovana's arm when she gained the ability to heal.
The man let out a deep chuckle. "I've never seen anyone get beat
up by a statue before. It was rather... amusing."

Lillian shook her head, then grinned wide. "Let me guess. The
tramp strikes again."

Rage flared through Leper like a torch thrown into dry
brush. His hands clenched, nails biting into his palms. Of all
the things she could've said, that was where she started? Not
"How are you?" Not "What happened?" Straight to the insults.
Straight to gutting him where she knew it'd hurt.

He stepped back, forcing the anger down. "Thanks for your
hospitality and for healing me, but never mind. I'll see myself
out."

"Hey! Leper!" Lillian called after him, but he was already
heading for Ghost. "Get back here!"

He ignored her, patting Ghost's feathery neck. Both buckets of
water Delinah had brought were gone. "C'mon, girl. We'll find
no respite here."

Ghost let out an irritated squawk and moved to her feet, but
before Leper could mount her, Lillian's calloused hand grabbed
his arm and yanked him back down.

"Excuse me, you moody fuckin' baby. What in tarnation is yer
problem?" Her vibrant green eyes burned into him.

Leper scoffed. "Don't pretend you care now."

"I was just screwin' around earlier because the Leper I know
would've found that funny. Not thrown a tantrum and walked
out like a toddler."

"Well, the Lillian I know wouldn't run away and hide at the
first sign of adversity, especially not straight into the enemy's
bed," he bit out.

Crack.

She punched him right on the cheek. Pain rippled through his
face as his ears heated.

"How dare you!" she yelled. "You selfish, self-loathin', fuckin' prick. You don't know a godsdamned thing about why he's here or why I'm here. You chose that tramp over me, remember? It ain't yer fuckin' business what I do. Why are you bein' such an asshole?"

Leper grabbed her wrists before she could strike again. "Then what's Ace doing here?"

"He left Nalecht and Tamara after they got Voldahyl killed by you and Madislak. He's hidin' here until we're ready to fight back."

Leper snickered. "He's hiding. I'm happy for you—sounds like you're made for each other."

Silence stretched between them, thick and bitter. When he finally let go, she didn't move—just glared at him, her stare sharp enough to cut.

Like she was seeing right through him. Like she was daring him to say something else.

And damn if he wasn't tempted.

Chapter Eleven

After the paralyzing smoke wore off, Petrovana stood up from her chair in the throne room, stretching her stiff muscles. The taste of Tamara's grime lingered in her mouth. She spat out blood and wiped her tongue with her cotton shirt. Pacing back and forth, she watched as Leighth walked over to the whiskey and took a shot. Anxiety churned in her mind. How were they going to get Madislak and Harmony back without sacrificing the shard? She hoped Tamara wouldn't go on a manhunt for Leper now that they told her he wasn't here and that he had the shard in his possession. Damn, probably not the best idea to tell her that; he will be pissed if she somehow tracks him down because of them. *What a mess.* An absolute disaster, especially with the two girls in Kordry, oblivious to the danger.

What were they going to do? Give them the shard for their release? That didn't seem like a good idea, but neither did letting them suffer Tamara's torturous whims. She casually jabbed a hole into Harmony's hand. Tamara was unhinged, demonic. Blank Face had endured her cruelty and was permanently scarred. A shudder ran down Petrovana's spine. Moments later, Blank Face reappeared.

"What are we going to do?" Leighth asked, breaking the silence.

Blank Face set the shard back on the table. "I won't be responsible for this. Also, I don't know about you two, but I'm going after Madislak and Harmony."

"What about Zanera and Kelindra?" Leighth countered.

"We know where they are. We don't know where they're taking Madislak and Harmony, and the longer we screw around, the farther away they get. Not only that, if we don't get moving right now, not only will we lose the trail on Madislak and Harmony, but we won't be back in time to get Zanera and Kelindra either. Leper said Nalecht gave him two weeks to enter the trials; they'll be safe until then," Blank Face muttered.

"I can go get those two. Leper will be uncontrollable if something happens to them," Petrovana said, taking another shot of whiskey. "Besides, if Larnadix is a Deathbinder, I played a part in bringing him here."

"Maybe... We have time. Larnadix doesn't know what we know, so he'll be very unsuspecting of anything," Blank Face said, stroking the back of his neck. "We don't know if Larnadix is a Deathbinder or if he's the fourth Chernzerk. It's still a mystery. We know for sure Madislak and Harmony are in direct danger, and that has to take precedence. And... I mean no offense, but you kind of grab a man's attention when you walk by," Blank Face argued.

Was he subtly flirting? No, assassins didn't flirt; they didn't have feelings. A pang of curiosity flickered within her. *No. You're with someone.* This is why you and Lillian are no longer friends. Yet, the desire flickered within her, these constantly changing feelings, these whims. Why was she like this? It happened when Lillian was with Alzen, then when she heard about her with Leper. Anything she couldn't have, she was drawn to, and she hated it.

Here stood an assassin, Leper's brother, scarred and marked all over. But if you looked past the scarred visage, you'd find a handsome man slender with a strong jawline and deep brown eyes. She shook her head, breaking her trance. They had more important things to worry about. *Get it together!*

"I can go to Kordry," Leighth offered. "I'm the queen now."

"Leighth, if everythin' Harmony said is true and that's who he is, we need to be together when we confront him. Not that you can't handle yourself, but we'll need fighters to face it." Petrovana reached for the shard of Theora on the table.

Leighth snorted. "I know. I'm not a fighter, and ever since Borlden... I don't think I will be. I just don't have it in me to end people's lives like that."

She didn't want to risk anything happening to Zanera and Kelindra; Leper would be furious. But Lantess missing its king and future queen? Her heart galloped in her chest at the choices before her. Neither one was a good option.

"I don't think I can take on Tamara, Nylor, The Latter, and Thessek by myself, guys," Blank Face interrupted. "If we leave now, we can hurry up and get them out of Tamara's custody, then go get Zanera and Kelindra. I will make sure it's done."

"That's pretty risky." Leighth sipped her drink. "What if you don't get back in time? What if they capture you, too? What if they kill you?"

"They won't." Blank Face spat quickly. "I'll never be stuck in Xaneth Harbor's dungeons ever again."

"Blank and I are gonna go get Madislak and Harmony back, hopefully while keepin' the shard of Theora in our possession." Petrovana sighed. "Then we'll rush back here and get to Kordry as soon as possible. Leper had two weeks to enter the trials, right? So they will be safe for that long at least."

"You keep this place running while we get their rightful rulers back. Try not to instill fear or panic among the people. Tell them Madislak and Harmony had to leave abruptly. Be the queen of Lantess until we return with their king," Blank Face commanded.

"Right, how am I supposed to do that? I don't know any of his chain of command or bulwarks, and he just kicked his father out of this place," Leighth muttered, taking another shot.

Blank Face grabbed her wrists. "Talk to Rylin and Alissia. We're going to need a safe harbor. Plus, if Zanera and Kelindra leave on their own, they will likely come here because they know Madislak is Leper's brother, and they trust him."

Leighth stomped her foot. "And what do I do if Leper returns and he is... unreasonable?"

"Turn his attention to the enemy, even if you have to lie, and point him in their direction. Then wait for the fireworks," Blank Face said, giving a half grin.

"That could get him killed," Leighth spat.

"Could also win us a war," Petrovana quipped with a smile.

Petrovana placed the shard of Theora around her neck and tucked it under her shirt. She would need to change into a less revealing shirt to conceal it. Time to put the girls away and get to work.

Lillian looked into Leper's hazel eyes, those large, round, beautiful hazel eyes. But the person looking back at her seemed hollow and angry, missing the glint, the spark that used to be there. His gaze was blanketed with sorrow and grief. *He looks broken.* What happened in the weeks since they last parted that had reduced him to this? What did that bitch do to him? Maybe it was something else entirely—maybe he was still reeling from Rinawen's death, or had Blank Face done something to make things worse?

He's clearly dealing with enough in that tall, muscular frame and wondrous face and the beard. Though it looked good on him, she preferred the goatee he used to have. But she wasn't about to bring that up right now. He didn't need any more surprises, not right now. She would do anything to snap him out of this trance.

She grabbed his hand. "Why don't we take this bird and fly, and you can tell me about it?"

"About what? I'm here to get the shard of Kasherri. So, unless you know where it's at, I'd rather not waste my time. Plus, won't your boyfriend get jealous?" Leper retorted.

"He's not my gods-damned boyfriend," she spat, her tone sharp with truth. "Alright, you stubborn ass. Come with me. Talk to me a bit about what's goin' on, and I'll tell me everythin' I know about the shard."

Leper nodded curtly. "Let's make this quick. I'm on a sched-ule."

Lillian led Leper back through the doors and formally in-troduced him to The Former, explaining his reasons for being there. The Former sought the shard of Kasherri to end his curse and his ties to the evil goddess herself. Somehow, he had become connected to her during the rain trials, though his memory, like The Latter's, had been wiped clean upon their escape from the dangerous trials. Anything related to the trials had been erased from his mind—the dangers within, escape routes, the shard's location. All he remembered was owing Kasherri his life and being bound to her, a situation that unsettled him deeply.

She led him upstairs to her room, where the bed was cov-ered in green and brown blankets and sheets, still in disarray. Lillian should have tidied up—picked up the clutter and clothes littering the floor and dresser, or at least put away her collection of belts and perfumes.

"Place is a mess," Leper quipped.

Lillian smacked his shoulder, momentarily surprised by how taut his muscles felt. "Shut up and sit."

Leper settled cross-legged in front of her, pulling his legs close. "What?" he said dryly.

"What happened while I was gone?" She rested her hands in her lap. "Tell me everythin'."

He let out a long, dejected sigh. "Well, we had Rin's funeral, which I couldn't attend. That was awesome. Then, when I visited her tree they chose for her remembrance, not a damn soul—other than her kids—did anything to decorate it. It's like the entire village, her husband, none of them gave a shit. And then." His throat bobbed as he paused to get the next part out. "Nalecht burnt it to a crisp in front of Zanera and Kelindra."

He took a deep breath through his nose. "Come to find out, Blank Face killed Larnadix, so her husband isn't really her husband; someone's impersonating him. And to top it all off, Madislak is apparently going to marry Petrovana."

Lillian choked on her spit. "What!? Why?"

Leper eyed her up and down. "You must not have heard. The Latter assassinated Coraidon and Finrod. They assume it's a move by Nalecht to win the shrew's allegiance. So Nelaan, Madislak's father, suggested Madislak and Petrovana marry.

That would challenge the banishment placed on her and also make her an acting queen, likely restoring her status as heir to Terynsipple."

Leper placed his calloused hands on her arm. "I'm sorry."

"Well, fuck me sideways," Lillian spat.

"Is that an offer or...?" Leper grinned.

There he is.

Lillian burst out laughing. There's that spark, that glint of happiness. He just needed someone to vent to, someone to listen to his long list of problems. His maple scent wafted up her nose, and she soaked it all in. Perhaps he just needed someone he could trust, someone who understood him. Someone she'd been looking for her entire life since her father died. He probably felt betrayed by all of them, and that was a feeling she knew all too well. And they just let him run off on his own to get this shard, to face the insurmountable dangers of the rain trials alone, in this state of mind. *Assholes.*

For the first time in the two days since he left Lantess, Leper's mind felt clear. But he was left with only eight days to enter the rain trials from the oath room, wherever that was. The constant nagging anxiety, anger, and mental fog dissipated. Relief, sweet relief. Lillian sat across from him, her brilliant, radiant grin lighting up her freckled face. She smelled like steel and black pepper, and something about the scent just seemed to fit her. With his mind finally clear and at ease, he remembered why he had come here in the first place.

"So...the shard of Kasherri? I need it, Lillian, and I don't have much time. Zanera and Kelindra are in danger. I have to get back to them. I don't trust Blank Face to get them out without screwing something up." He lay back, feeling the weight of exhaustion as his head connected with the cool, soft comfort of the pillow.

"It's locked within the rain trials. There's a reason it hasn't been discovered yet." She lay down beside him.

"What's the reason?"

"Well, you saw the statues of The Former, the glass-eyed man who found you, and The Latter. Nobody survives the rain trials." She huffed.

"They survived. Can't they just tell us?" Leper rolled to his side to face her.

"No. Before you enter, you have to take a blood oath in Costin. It erases any memory of the rain trials—probably to stop anyone from actually gettin' the shard. So even if The Former wanted to tell us, he can't. He has no recollection of anythin' from his time in there. Trust me, I've asked a thousand different times in a thousand different ways."

Leper rubbed his face. *Nalecht had said he needed to take the oath as well to enter, but had left out the details of where to take this oath.*

There had to be a way. A way in, a way out. And he needed to do it quickly. There was no time to dwell on how or why.

"Where do you take this oath?" he blurted.

Lillian sat up and glared at him. "Don't you even think about it. You'll die... There is no way out. We're tryin' to find a way to get the shard without goin' in."

"Zanera and Kelindra's lives depend on it, Lillian, so whether or not I'll survive isn't a question. I'm going in there." Leper flicked her arm playfully.

She flicked him right back on the cheek. "You got eight days left until you have to go in there; all I'm askin' fer is two days. It's more of a sacrifice than anythin' else, Leper. The dwarves have some sort of long-standin' deal with Kasherri to sacrifice the Chernzerk to her in the trials. Apparently, their magical abilities feed her power more than a normal human or elf."

"That makes no sense to me." Leper snorted. "Regardless, whether it's a sacrifice or whatever you want to call it, I'm going in there, Lillian, end of story. There's nothing you can say or do to stop me."

"C'mon. Give us two days!" She pleaded, resting her calloused hand on his cheek.

He took a deep breath in, relishing her peppered scent.

"You and The Former?" He rolled to his side.

"And Ace." She stood up from the bed. "Let's go get a drink; you look like crap."

"You really trust Ace? After all he did?" Leper followed her back down the stairs to the kitchen, already missing the comfy pillow.

She grabbed some vegetables from the chill box and a loaf of freshly baked bread. Ace walked in and sat down at the same table with them. Lillian told Leper she'd just let Ace explain himself. So he did.

For the next hour, Ace recounted how he had spiraled after Voldahyl's death, growing distant from Nalecht—especially after discovering Nalecht had lied about the power within the well on The Talon. Nalecht had led him to believe that if he eliminated the other Chernzerk connected to the well, he would absorb their power once it was distributed. The substance Tamara had given him only amplified this belief and his desperation to claim that strength. But in truth, the power was always shared—it could never belong to just one person. And the power from the well, that they received when they all finally visited it, was only for them; any other Chernzerk would get their magic from the moons like everyone else.

Then he started talking about how Tamara had been feeding him a toxin, an amplifier that preyed on the festering anger and despair all Chernzerk faced, keeping him in a constant state of rage that Leper had just escaped. Lastly, he informed Leper that he had never killed their fathers in the cave. When they first met, he thought Leper had killed them, which was why he was so furious and attacked him in the first place.

After Leper clarified he didn't kill their fathers either, they surmised it might have been Tamara while Ace was looking for the shard of Amarook within the mountain. Ace also let Leper know he would be willing to aid them when the time came, along with his new dragon, Peridona the Tempest. Leper still wasn't sure he could trust him, but Ace's words and body language seemed sincere enough.

Ace didn't know what had happened to his twin sister when they were younger. The last he had heard, she was in Xaneth Harbor with their father, Oubank—but that was years ago. Leper wanted desperately to ask more about their fathers, what they were like, what they had done, but he couldn't afford to dwell on his past or his heritage. Time was not on their side. All he knew was that both Oubank, Ace's father, and Samaja, the father of Leper and Blank Face, had sired two sets of twins and died when the power from the well was released.

He bit down on some fresh carrots and cucumbers. The crisp, cool flavor was refreshing. After the lengthy discussion, Lillian led Leper to the living room, which had several plush couches. The place was huge for four people to live in. The high ceilings were majestically crafted with dwarven design. Candles lined the walls, providing light, which was nice, especially since darkness had crept in from outside. The Former, Ace, and Delinah joined them, with Delinah holding a baby dressed in a blue shirt and pants with a sun hat on.

"A baby!?" Leper bellowed.

Lillian glanced quickly at Leper, then at the baby as she picked him up. "This little boy is Artemis." She set him in Leper's lap.

When Artemis opened his large, round eyes, the vibrant green color was so pure. He had short, dark black, fluffy hair that peeked out from under the hat, more than any baby Leper had ever seen.

Leper glanced at Delinah, noticing her dark hair. "Is he yours?"

Delinah flicked her hazel eyes to Lillian, then back to Leper. "No. He got abandoned in Xaneth Harbor when I was there. I took pity on the poor child and scooped him up. We're raisin' him on goat milk and keepin' him safe. I have no idea who the parents are, but they just left him."

"What were you doing in Xaneth Harbor?" Leper asked, poking the baby's nose.

"Trainin' and makin' gold. Not that I need to explain myself to you," she snapped.

Weird. She got extremely defensive for no reason.

Leper shrugged. "Sorry to pry."

Lillian put a calming hand on Delinah's arm. "It's okay. I'll take care of it."

He glanced back at Lillian, who was staring at him with that look in her eye, that longing. "Here, take him back." He held the baby out. "So where do you take this blood oath again?"

Lillian hollered before anyone answered him. "Don't tell him! He's fixin' to go in there regardless of the consequences."

Ace finally spoke up. "You'll die; there's no way out."

"How do you know if he can't remember, and nobody's gone in?" Leper barked, pointing at The Former. "I need that shard. I'll find a way."

Leper glanced around the room as they looked dumbfounded at him. It was like there was something they weren't exactly telling him about these rain trials.

"No, you won't," Lillian growled, handing Artemis back to Delinah. "Give us two days. I promise if we don't have it in two days, you can go in."

Like always, I'll just have to do everything by myself.

"Any of you know anyone named Xartazza?" Leper asked. Finding the place to take the oath was a bust; might as well try and find out more about this Xartazza character.

"He used to hang around Xaneth Harbor last I knew." Delinah playfully jostled the baby. "He was the only person to ever go undefeated in Tamara's arena. Five full years and he never lost one match."

"Really?" Leper tilted his head. "Any idea where I could find him? Or what happened to him?"

Delinah shook her head no. "He disappeared about five years ago. Accordin' to my guard buddies at the time, him and Tamara had some sort of misunderstandin'; nobody's seen him since."

"What do you want with him?" Lillian interrupted.

"Nothing major." Leper leaned back on the couch. "Nalecht wants him to run the rain trials. I'm just trying to figure out who he is and why he wants him to run the trials."

Ace and The Former shook their heads as well, offering no more insight on the man. With all of them agreeing not to tell Leper where to take the oath, Leper decided he'd have to get some sleep, then go find it himself. He didn't truly expect them to help him find it; no one around him ever had before. Why would they start now?

The nighttime chill seeped through the windows, a glorious relief from the relentless daytime heat. The cold breeze raised goosebumps on Leper's arms, and he shivered as he contemplated Lillian's words. *Do I have two days? Do Zanera and Kelindra have two days?* He quickly checked his pouch for any notes from them. No notes, but a full pack of healing, revival, and a bluish protection vial. He must get those incredible young ladies to safety as quickly as possible. At any cost.

Leper ended up sleeping on the couch, while Lillian, still apparently concerned and not entirely trusting him, slept on the couch across from him. She'd offered her bed, but with how things were left between him and Petrovana, he didn't want to be considered disloyal or unfaithful. Quite frankly, there was definitely something about Lillian that tugged at his heart. He decided to take no chances and avoid doing anything stupid. He still had very strong feelings for Petrovana and found himself missing her company, her purple eyes, her warmth, her soft, radiant skin. As the noise settled and he wrapped himself in a brown blanket, it didn't take long to fall asleep, even though the night was still early.

When he awoke, darkness still greeted him from the outside, and Lillian lay fast asleep across from him. Checking his pouch again, he quietly grabbed his boots and snuck out the front door.

The cool night air was refreshing, clearing his mind. He couldn't wait two days. There was too much at stake.

Chapter Twelve

T he heat of the sun filtered through the windows, landing on Lillian's face. Her eyes popped open, and she immediately looked at the couch across from her. *Gone. You son of a bitch.* She jumped up, threw on her boots, and brushed her hair quickly with her hand as she headed for the door.

"Where ya headed?" Ace called from behind her.

She quickly turned to him, wearing a sleeveless brown shirt and black shorts. "Leper left. I'm pretty sure I know where he went."

"Want me to come with you?" he asked.

"No. Just stick to the plan. If I don't come back, The Former knows what to do," she ordered.

Ace nodded, and she bolted for the door. Under the baking sun, it took her an hour to reach Costin. Wiping sweat from her brow, she clenched her teeth, rage settling deeper with each step. *Idiot.* He better not have taken that oath.

They told him the dwarves used it as a sacrifice to bring rain to the desert, that they were trying to commune with Kasherri to obtain the shard, but hadn't found a safe way to do so. The Former was working on a boundary spell to keep demons and underworld beings at bay, but there was no way to test if it would be strong enough to hold her. She hadn't told him that part; she didn't need him getting all pissy about summoning the deity of the underworld here.

Kasherri only accepted Chernzerk as a sacrifice, which was why The Former and The Latter had been rejected. If he was truly willing to throw his life into the very danger they warned him about, then he was more broken than she thought.

Yet she completely understood why. Feeling that there was no one who had your back was something she had felt her entire life. She could easily relate to that, still searching for the person with whom she could share that connection, that tether... Maybe.

She wanted it to be Leper, but, for once in her life, became increasingly scared to broach the subject with him. Especially after his reaction to Rinawen and whatever he went through with that tramp, clearly affected his mood swings. She would have to keep him from killing himself first.

The construction of Costin always captivated her. The research and magical development building, an upside-down triangular structure, sank its tip deep into the ground for support. She still didn't understand how it could stay upright. The houses, in peak condition, spread throughout to serve as both dwellings and sources of shade. Large cloth canopies extended from house to house, providing shade from the relentless sun. Two other buildings quickly caught outsiders' attention. The towering rectangular figure reached skyward, and the farming quarters, another rectangular building, stretched for miles, farther than the eye could see.

She made a beeline for the tall rectangular building where royalty and important community members resided. It was also where anyone running the rain trials took the blood oath. Her footsteps quickened. Hopefully, she wasn't too late.

Odig Noblespine stood guard at the door, his thick, long beard resting over his broad chest. Beady black eyes peered up at her beneath heavy brows, and his brown hair flowed past his sturdy shoulders.

He had helped her find her way around when she first arrived. Dwarves didn't like outsiders, especially ones who looked as aggressive as she did. Delinah, the woman who had trained her since childhood, and The Former had found Lillian in the desert. The dwarves had accepted her into their solitude on their word alone.

But that wasn't why she was here. She shook her head. *No time to dwell on the past. Find Leper before he does something stupid.*

"Hey, Odig," she barked. "Have you seen a tall, handsome, horned man come through here today?"

Odig's eyes narrowed slightly as he scrutinized her face. "Aye, you mean Leper? He came by a little while ago, looking like he had a death wish."

"Son of a bitch," Lillian muttered under her breath. "Yes."

"He's inside. With Shpockten." Odig opened the door.

Not good.

Lillian sprinted through the hallway and headed straight for the oath room, where the statue of Kasherri, the goddess worshiped in Costin, stood.

She barged through the doors. The ever-present up-side-down candles greeted her. These candles, connected to the rain trials, hung inverted and burned eternally. They only dripped wax when the water reserves were being used. When the bowl under the candle was nearly full, it meant the water was almost gone, and someone needed to undertake the rain trials—the sacrifice—to refill the water. If the dwarves didn't use any water for a year, the bowl wouldn't fill, and the candle wouldn't drip wax, though it would continue to burn. When the rain trials were completed, they brought a monumental amount of rain, and the candle grew longer with wax as the bowl emptied. She didn't understand how it all worked, but she had dedicated the last few weeks to learning everything she could about these trials and the sacrifice, all in an effort to get the shard of Kasherri and keep it from Nalecht.

She moved past the candles, her gaze drawn to the center of the room where the statue of Kasherri stood. There he was, slicing his hand and dripping his blood onto the statue.

"NO!" she hollered.

Madislak stared straight ahead at Harmony. Bound and caged
with him once more, they rattled through Stragglers Forest in
the back of a horse-drawn wagon. Bushy branches scraped
against the rickety frame, showering them with a spray of
leaves. The stench of Thessek clung to the air like a curse as he
flanked their left, while Nylor's imposing form mirrored him
on the right. Behind them, Tamara rode, her sneer a constant
reminder of their predicament. The shard of Aisha pulsed orange around her neck, a constant temptation just out of reach.
If only he could get close enough...

Escape. The singular thought hammered in his head. Nylor
might be a mountain of a man, muscles straining the seams
of his jerkin, but fear was a stranger to Madislak. He'd faced a
dragon and lived—a victory he shared with his brother, Leper,
of course. But this? This cage, this indignity, was an insult that
demanded vengeance.

Frustration gnawed at him. *A king. Caged.* Tamara, wielding
a shard that shouldn't be hers, a shard that pulsed with an
unnatural orange light. The whooshing of shimmering blue
wings in the evening soared overhead. How is it she can control
this particular dragon? *Dragons answered only to the Chernzerk, or so the legends claimed. Were those legends wrong, too?*

The rhythmic creak of the wheels grated on his nerves. Cold
seeped through the gaps in the wood, a mockery of the spring
that stubbornly refused to arrive. *Where were Brebian and
Theodamar?* They were supposed to meet him in Lantess a
week ago, yet they vanished like smoke on a summer breeze.
Now, the sky was bruised with approaching clouds, threatening
rain or snow on top of everything else. This entire situation left
a bitter taste in his mouth.

They were heading to the Bay of Disdain. *Fantastic.* The
bone-chilling air would soon morph into a suffocating wall
of humidity. Madislak flicked his gaze between Harmony and
Tamara, then back to Harmony. He held her gaze for several
moments, a chance to snatch the shard if the opportunity arose.

Harmony's subtle head shake and a catlike hiss were her
response. *Be wary of Thessek,* he interpreted.

Harmony leaned towards the bars, her voice tight. "Where's
Nalecht?"

Tamara's smile widened, a cruel twist of her lips. "Wouldn't you love to know."

Madislak ran his fingers along the steel cuffs, searching for a weakness, a hidden mechanism. "Still nursing his wounds after that pathetic display in Tudela?" he taunted, unable to resist a dig.

Tamara snatched the whip hanging at her side and lashed it against the bars.

Crack.

"Watch your tongue, Mighty Madislak. I don't fuck around." She hung the whip back along her side.

Madislak flinched at the sharp crack of the whip. Harmony recoiled, her eyes wide.

"Who gets the glorious talisman once it's reforged, huh?" Harmony pressed, her voice regaining its edge.

"That's hardly your concern, Lantess lapdog," Tamara mocked.

"No, it's not my concern. Perhaps it should be yours. Only one talisman, two claimants. Simple arithmetic, wouldn't you say? Or are you naive enough to believe Nalecht will share with you?" Harmony countered, her voice laced with a dangerous amusement.

Tamara scrunched her face. "Are you trying to insult me?"

Harmony smiled mockingly. "Never. Only asking what your plans are once Nalecht has the talisman. I'm sure he has no plans of sharing... so? What will the Queen of Xaneth Harbor do?"

"Maybe just go back to your silent language before you cross a line there, bitch," Tamara creased her brow.

Madislak nudged Harmony with his foot, trying to get her to stop provoking Tamara. They were still prisoners of ruthless people. Toying with them could only lead to suffering.

"Ahhh... didn't think that far ahead. Not surprising," Harmony piled on.

Tamara let out a menacing laugh. "You're not very smart, are you?"

Tamara nodded to Thessek, who climbed into the cage with them. Retrieving his needle-like blade, he asked, "Do you remember our game?" He giggled.

Still reeking of vile garbage, maybe even worse than the last time their paths crossed, Madislak dry heaved at the stench.

He remembered their game all too well; he jabbed Harmony ten times with that small, needle-like blade. She nearly died from the blood loss.

"Don't you dare touch her," Madislak threatened.

Thessek's grin widened as Harmony's entire body started to tremble.

Thessek dragged the blade down her arm, pressing just hard enough to leave a red line. A wicked grin crawled across his feline face. He could nearly smell the fear on her. Her eyes wide, pleading, and Madislak couldn't stand the thought of this sick bastard harming her again. Rage took over.

Madislak kicked Thessek as hard as he could, then slid his cuffs down under his feet. Perhaps this is what Harmony was going for the whole time.

"Help me!" Thessek squealed.

Madislak grabbed Thessek's arm and slammed it into the wooden plank of the wagon again and again until he dropped the blade. Then he grabbed Thessek by the throat and squeezed, slamming him against the cage.

"Let her go, and I'll stop," Madislak growled. "I won't fight anymore. Just let her go."

Black smoke filled the cage, then materialized into the wild mohawk man. Madislak felt a searing pain lance up his side as The Latter plunged his dagger into him. He rocked his head back and collided with The Latter's face. Using Thessek, he barged through the unlatched gate, throwing him to the ground and launching himself at Tamara. Managing to get his hands on the shard of Aisha, he ripped it from her neck.

Madislak gripped the shard of Aisha tightly in his hand, the mace-like trinket humming to life, its glow now a bright orange as it healed his stab wound from The Latter. Wrestling Tamara in a chokehold, Nylor swiftly intervened, landing a massive blow to Madislak's side with his warhammer. Again, he used the shard to mend the damage, but his weapon, Skyrunner, lay on the carriage's bench.

Dodging Nylor's lumbering attacks, Madislak noted the slow but powerful strikes of the massive warhammer, each blow resonating heavily and leaving deep imprints in the ground. Tamara circled him with her pristine falchion in hand.

"Stand down, King Madislak, or she dies," The Latter called, his knife drawing blood from Harmony's neck.

Fingin swooped in, his frosty pale blue scales shimmering even in the evening's light. Platelets ran down his back and along his tail, which ended in a whip-like formation. Clusters of spikes covered his head and face as he roared defiantly at the king, chilling the air with every frosty exhale.

Madislak glanced from Harmony to Tamara, who wore a wicked grin. *Shit.* He was cornered; he could free himself, but it would cost Harmony her life—a price he refused to pay... ever.

Where the hell is Blank Face when you need him?

Madislak desperately wished for one more ally to aid their escape, but the realization of their failed attempt weighed heavily on his spirit. He lacked familiarity with the shard's abilities to leverage it effectively in this dire situation. Could he summon the sun, as someone had done to save Nalecht during the War of Tudela? He noticed a redheaded woman atop the dragon.

Surrounded by trees, a potential cover for escape loomed as they neared the open, dry plains of the Bay of Disdain, where warmth awaited. Yet, with Fingin's chilling presence and the sun sinking behind the trees, the cold only intensified as dusk approached. Madislak turned the shard of Aisha in his hand, debating his options, his heart pounding in his temples not for himself, but for Harmony's safety—aware that their captors knew his affection for her and would exploit it. He tossed the shard back on the ground, a failed attempt to grab it and escape.

Before Madislak could move any farther, Nylor's fist connected with his nose.

Crack.

Blood filled his mouth as pain shot through him. Tasting iron and feeling his nose tingle. *This guy can hit.*

"Time to return you to your cage," Nylor declared in his deep voice.

Tamara swiftly took the shard of Aisha from the ground.

"Oh no. We're not making that mistake again." Tamara's flat tone interjected as Nylor dragged him towards the cage.

Petrovana urged her horse to its limits, racing to keep pace with Blank Face, who was relentlessly tracking Madislak and Harmony. Wrapped in a thick turtleneck shirt, she concealed the shard dangling around her neck, its powerful hum barely muffled. Her attire, a dark green shirt under a coat with thick black pants, was chosen for practicality during their hurried departure from Lantess. They'd been tracking them and avoiding the overhead dragon as quickly and efficiently as they could. She'd never used any of these shards before and wasn't even certain she could, but she could definitely feel the power running through her.

Navigating Stragglers Forest, they avoided the main paths to evade detection, pushing their horses to the brink. Upon reaching the Bay of Disdain, weather would cease to be an obstacle. Leighth remained in Lantess to prevent panic in the king-less city, while they opted for horses over a flying chariot due to Fingin, the Arctic Tyrant, patrolling the skies. Blank Face set a relentless pace, their journey now entering the eighth day since Madislak and Harmony were taken—time critical as they finally closed in on their target. Leaving them with only six more days to free Madislak and Harmony, then race back to Kordry and help Zanera and Kelindra.

To distract herself, Petrovana focused on the mission, pushing thoughts of Leper and his safety aside. *Was he safe? Did he reach Costin? Was he closer to the shard of Kasherri?* If only she could send him a magical note and ask. His swift departure after her potential marriage to Madislak had left their relationship uncertain.

Despite missing his tall, rugged frame—the beard, muscles, and intense eyes—they rode on in silence while Petrovana let her thoughts wander. As the day began to wane, she was startled by Blank Face snapping his fingers in front of her face.

"Hey!" he snapped, readjusting his hood. "Did you hear anything I just said?"

Petrovana looked up, shaking her head. "What?"

"They're just up ahead," Blank Face informed her curtly. "Looks like they're setting up camp. We should sneak in tonight and free them. But you need to focus. What are you doing?" His tone was cold and demanding.

"I'm here. I'm ready," she replied, rolling her shoulders.

Blank Face scoffed. "No, you're not. If I were one of them, I could've stabbed you in the face, and you wouldn't have seen it coming. I'm not here to babysit you, got it?"

Pushy bastard.

"I don't need yer babysittin'. How are we gonna get them out?" Petrovana hardened her expression.

"First, we find Madislak's sword and get those anti-magic cuffs off Harmony," Blank Face said, taking a breath. "The quicker we arm them, the better chance we have at escaping. Once they're free, we fight our way out, but watch out for Tamara."

She clutched her right forearm, glaring at it, panic coursing through her. White-hot pain rippled through her arm as she turned away from Blank Face. She spared a glance at her forearm, and another tattoo was forming, a brain tattoo. She quickly covered it back up with her hand.

"What's going on with you?" Blank Face shook her shoulders from behind.

How could she answer that question? Tell him she's some kind of abomination? She's some kind of freak that not only has three spells but now four and has no clue how she got them?

"I... I don't know," she panted, the agony intensifying as she tried to hang her arm by her side.

"What's wrong with your arm?" Blank Face turned her to face him.

"I don't know!" Petrovana hollered, tears welling in her eyes. "I don't know what kind of abomination I am, okay!?"

Blank Face grabbed her shoulders forcefully. "Stop screaming, you'll give us away!"

"Dick," she blurted out in frustration.

"You're not an abomination. No one as pretty as you could be an abomination," he murmured, barely above a whisper.

There it was again... Was he flirting? No. Assassins didn't flirt. This man had killed Leper's only friend. Yet as she glanced at his deep brown eyes, a swirl of conflicting emotions churned in her gut. *Curse me.* Why... why must I always be so conflict-ed? Lillian is right. *I'm nothing but a useless tramp.*

"Stop doin' that!" she snapped.

"Doing what?" Blank Face recoiled, puzzled.

"Flirtin'. Tellin' me I catch others' attention and callin' me pretty," she growled.

Blank Face chuckled dryly. "I'm not flirting with you. Har-mony is pretty; Leighth is pretty. Get over yourself. Can we get back to the problem at hand?"

Petrovana glanced over his tall, lanky figure. Beneath those scars, she imagined, would be an undeniably handsome man, with his large brown eyes and the scent of pine that wafted off him—different from Leper's maple, but still alluring. She shook her head forcefully. No distractions.

"Let's," she agreed, refocusing. She rubbed her arm where the new tattoo had formed—hopefully, he didn't notice.

Was she becoming a monster? She possessed nearly all forms of magic, lacking only vitalis magic. Terynsipple would be in an uproar; healing had been a dwarven specialty for years. Why the sudden change now?

Blank Face outlined a detailed plan and contributed backup plan after backup plan. Either he knew their enemy well or feared them deeply. She was too focused on her new tattoo and how to use the shard effectively to even hear what he was babbling on about.

Thankfully, they were out of the cold climates, creeping to-wards their enemies under cover of night. The crackling fire and the scent of smoke and cooked meat drifted into her nos-trils. It didn't take long to locate Madislak and Harmony.

Petrovana's heart plummeted to her stomach. In the flick-ering light of the crackling fire, Madislak and Harmony were bound to the wagon, their hands cuffed above their heads and secured tightly. Their torsos and legs were immobilized, ren-dering them completely helpless. Bruises marred Madislak's face, and Harmony's exposed torso bore a fresh gash that promised to scar. Petrovana shuddered with revulsion. These were truly despicable people.

She fought to steady the trembling in her arms. They could do this. They had Blank Face; the shard would help them...

right? She possessed four types of magic. They could do this, she repeated to herself like a mantra.

A toxic black smoke filled her senses, its medicinal scent reminiscent of rubbing alcohol. Then, The Latter materialized before them.

"Welcome. Did you come to join us?" he cackled mockingly.

Chapter Thirteen

I n a flash, Blank Face's weapons were in his hands, and he stabbed The Latter right in the gut.

"Fucking bastard!" The Latter growled, caught off guard.

Nylor, Tamara, and Thessek scrambled to their feet and rushed towards them. Petrovana quickly summoned the shard of Theora. It glowed a faint brown, and a couple of plants moved and swayed, but nothing major happened. Shit.

She could rely on her typical means of battle. She conjured a massive wall of fire in front of them and made it circle around them by twisting her hand in the air.

"I'll get them free. You handle him," she nodded towards The Latter and bolted for the wagon.

"Don't forget the plan," Blank Face growled as she hurried away.

She couldn't remember *the plan*, she didn't even hear *the plan*. It was him, rambling on for about an hour. She was way too busy trying to figure out what kind of freak she was.

She threw her hand up in mock acknowledgment and kept running. As she reached the wagon, she saw Madislak's eyes widen with relief, but Harmony was shaking, fear-stricken. The poor girl.

"Skyrunner's on the bench. Tamara has the keys to the cuffs," Madislak relayed quickly.

Petrovana didn't think; she only acted. She hopped to the front seat and tossed Skyrunner onto the wagon, then darted towards Tamara, who managed to put out a small path of fire to free herself.

Petrovana raised her other hand, and ice shackles latched around Tamara's legs and arms, then locked themselves around the closest tree.

Their eyes locked briefly, and Tamara's were filled with rage. "You dumb fucking bitch. You will all suffer."

"Shut yer trap," Petrovana spat. She tried to use her new magic to paralyze her, but she didn't feel any energy leave her body.

No time. She hustled over to Tamara and rifled through her pockets, her hands shaking, and found a key. Rushing back to the wagon, she hopped up and immediately unshackled Madislak, then moved to Harmony as Madislak cut the rest of his bonds with Skyrunner. Harmony was visibly trembling.

"It's okay; we got you," Petrovana tried to calm her friend, her voice steady despite her own fear.

Harmony didn't respond. What had they done to her? Besides the gash across her stomach and the bruises on her face, there might've been other unseen horrors. As Petrovana unlocked her cuffs, she heard the unmistakable whoosh of wings. Fingin plowed into the cart with his massive shoulder, tearing it to pieces, then exhaled a frosty breath on her ring of fire, snuffing out the flames.

Petrovana was thrown through the air, colliding with The Latter. He transformed into smoke, reemerging moments later, crouching over her. She quickly launched a shard of ice, forcing him back off her as he formed into smoke again. Fingin roared defiantly, drawing in a deep breath. Oh shit.

His throat glowed bright blue as he opened his maw toward Petrovana. Frost and blue steam spilled from his mouth, but before he could unleash his frost breath—

"No!" Tamara yelled at the dragon, halting him. "I want that one alive."

Madislak, thirty feet away, wobbled as he got to his feet, trying to finish freeing Harmony. Nylor charged at Petrovana, but before she could react, Blank Face intercepted, stabbing Nylor's torso and thighs before blinking away. Fingin's tail whipped Petrovana out of nowhere, leaving a massive bleeding welt on her torso.

Pain seared through her, but she forced herself to stand. They had to escape. They had to survive. This was their only chance. This isn't going as planned. Petrovana pressed her hand over the wound briefly, wincing at the sting. She glanced back to see Madislak lying unconscious, a dart protruding from his neck—and Harmony's.

She called to her new brain tattoo again and tried to use the magic to paralyze them all at once, but nothing happened. They came into this battle arrogant, and now they were completely screwed.

"Surrender," Tamara barked.

Blank Face grabbed hold of Harmony and tried to blink—their last resort. He had only ever managed to blink with inanimate objects—a pillow, a cup, a chair—but he had never attempted to move a person. Still, this was their last-ditch effort. He would blink them both away and find a place to hide. But he only flickered in and out of transparency.

Petrovana glanced around desperately. Seconds later, Blank Face reappeared beside Tamara, aiming for her throat. She narrowly avoided his swipe, but he persisted, putting a dagger to her neck. She quickly refocused on the shard of Theora and tried to call down the trees to crush them. But they just wobbled and swayed as if a tornado was blowing through.

"Give us the king and proxy back, and we'll leave," he commanded.

Tamara's eyes twinkled maliciously as she chuckled in the face of death. "Do it. I dare you. You'll never see your friends again. Give us that shard, and we'll let you live."

"Let them go," Petrovana demanded.

Blank Face yanked the shard of Aisha off Tamara's neck. "We'll be taking this too."

Nylor hurled his massive warhammer, and it collided with Blank Face, sending him flying back and knocking him away from Tamara—an impressively accurate throw. Blank Face blinked, clutching his shoulder as Tamara closed in. He evaded each strike, rolling, dodging, blinking.

Petrovana summoned ice and slammed Nylor in the chest, knocking him to the ground. Overhead, the dragon bellowed, unable to land as the wind howled and trees swayed wildly.

Nylor charged at Petrovana again, fists raised. She unleashed a blast of fire, but he muscled through it, ramming into her at full speed. She seized his arm and immediately sent a surge of frost through it, the ice thick enough to make him let go. Scrambling to her feet, she sprinted toward Blank Face—only to find Tamara's sword pressed against his neck.

Petrovana's heart raced, fear and adrenaline surging through her veins. This wasn't just a battle—it was a nightmare. She had to keep fighting, had to keep them all alive. They were running out of options, but surrender wasn't one of them. She could taste the blood on her lips now.

"Enough!" The Latter bellowed, his hand gripping Harmony's arm and a knife to her neck.

Her breathing was frantic; her shoulders rose and fell quickly. Petrovana noticed bruises around Harmony's neck and shoulders. Thessek moved over and pressed a knife right through Harmony's knee. Her shoulders moved even faster.

"Drop the damn shards now, or I put this all the way through," he demanded.

Tears streaked down Harmony's pale face, her blond curly hair dirty and frizzled. Agonizing sorrow pierced through Petrovana. Harmony had already been through so much, and they were making it worse. Petrovana could feel Harmony's pain—the bruises, the gash across her stomach. Her heart jumped. They failed. They weren't getting out of this. Soon she would be restrained like Harmony, poked and prodded. This was what Blank Face had gone through. He knew. That's why he was so scared of facing them. These people were ruthless. Now, they were going to lose even more time to go get Zanera and Kelindra.

Petrovana took off the shard and tossed it on the ground in front of her. "Take it, and me. Let them go."

Thessek glanced at Tamara, who sneered and nodded. He removed his dagger and tossed the shard to Tamara as she stood beside Harmony.

"Where's my other one?" she demanded.

Blank Face blinked away from Tamara's sword and beside Petrovana, then tossed it on the ground. Petrovana discreetly floated healing magic onto Harmony, a dim yellow light shimmering around her. Maybe it would offer a little relief. She didn't seem to notice.

Tamara picked up the shard of Aisha from the ground. "Now... this is how this is going to go."

"What do you want?" Petrovana asked, her voice trembling.

"Lucky for you idiots, I have a proposition, one that I'm sure you'll be thrilled to accept," Tamara mocked. She placed the shard of Aisha beside Harmony and said, "Is that paralyzing poison still holding you back, beautiful?"

Using the shard, Tamara withdrew the poison from Harmony. A brown light swirled around her as she gagged, then spat out the toxin from the dart. She rolled her shoulders and arms around, allowing her to move again. But why? What was Tamara about to do? Petrovana's heart thundered in her chest, echoing in her ears. She closed her eyes, dreading whatever would happen next, knowing it was her fault. Nalecht was bad enough, but at least he was direct. Tamara... she took wickedness to another level.

"Either of you move and she dies, as does King Madislak." Tamara's voice took on an even more chilling edge. "You're going to get that shard of Kasherri for me, regardless of where it's at, and you're going to bring it to me without saying a god-damned thing to Nalecht. But if you do..." She grinned maliciously. "You can expect more of this."

Tamara slammed Harmony to the ground, took out a knife, and started digging into Harmony's face. Harmony's pained screams echoed through the forest. Tears streamed down Petrovana's face, unable to stop them. She was humiliating her, mutilating her, and there was nothing they could do. How would Harmony react if they ever got free, her face carved up, knowing they were standing there, doing nothing? But what choice did they have? If they moved, Harmony would die. They would all die.

Blank Face's grunts and growls pulled Petrovana from her harrowing thoughts. She glanced over to him as he looked away, apparently unable to bear any more of it.

Moments later, Tamara stood up and tossed something their way. Blank Face caught it, then opened his palm to show Petrovana. It was Harmony's eye. Wicked... ruthless... disgusting. Petrovana's anger surged, her face flushed with heat. She wanted to light Tamara's ugly, poofy hair on fire right there. Blank Face set a hand on her arm. She would pay for this.

"Well, it looks like Blank Face caught your eye, doesn't it, proxy of Lantess?" Tamara chuckled, pure evil. "I better have that fucking shard in my possession in two weeks, or you can expect more body parts. Do we understand each other?" Tamara barked, aiming the knife at them.

Petrovana nodded, her body trembling. "You will have it. Don't hurt them anymore."

"I see either of you again without that shard, and you better believe I will continue what I started here. Now, get your useless asses out of here and get to it. I hate waiting," Tamara sneered in their direction.

What a terrible queen.

"Wait," The Latter called, aiming his own dagger at Blank Face. "When this is over, when we have the shard, I want you. Me and you, no abilities, no magic, a duel to the death. So I can prove that I am the master assassin, not some boy from nowhere."

Blank Face slightly cocked his head back. "I'll accept on one condition."

"And!?" Impatience laced The Latter's voice.

"No harm to them for these two weeks," Blank Face demanded, his tone deep and authoritative.

The Latter glanced to Tamara, who smirked, then said, "No promises on that end as these are my prisoners, not his. But I will try and refrain."

"Fine." Blank Face gritted his teeth. "Make sure you pick your headstone; you're going to need it in two weeks."

The Latter scoffed. "Please, I'm hundreds of years old. I will decimate you piece by slithering piece."

Petrovana grabbed Blank Face's cloak, and they hustled back the way they came. Because of them, Harmony lost her eye. Her eye! They were in a much worse situation than before now because of them. Gods, I suck. Hopefully, Leper had some luck in Costin. She glanced at Blank Face's unreadable, empty face. The moments this poor man must be reliving inside that brain of his—he was in this wicked bitch's control for six long years. They had to get them free. They had to get that shard of Kasherri, even if it meant taking it from Leper. Whatever it took, she would right this.

As they moved deeper into the woods, Petrovana's mind raced. Every step felt heavier, burdened with the weight of their failure. The memory of Harmony's scream and the sight of her mutilated face haunted her, fueling a fire of determination mixed with guilt and anger. They couldn't fail again. They wouldn't fail again.

"Keep your focus," Blank Face said, his voice a low growl. "We have a job to do."

Petrovana nodded, swallowing hard. "I know. Let's get movin'. We got a shard to find."

"She seemed set on not telling Nalecht we're after the shard of Kasherri for her. Hopefully, that means she's willing to double-cross him," Blank Face muttered, keeping pace. "Wouldn't surprise me; she's always been about herself."

"Yeah, reckon it does. But we don't got much time, and we just lost another day. What about Zanera and Kelindra?" Petrovana shook her head. There was no way they had time to go after them now—not if they were going to get the shard Leper was after. That would have to come later. For now, their best bet was pitting Nalecht against Tamara if things went south.

"We'll get them, okay?" Blank Face rubbed his neck. "Right now, we focus on them—getting the shard back and freeing them. They're in deep, deep shit, and I will not let what happened to me happen to my brother."

"What about Kasherri's shard?" Petrovana's head snapped toward Blank Face. "She said if we don't get it in two weeks she's goin' to cut them apart."

"Leper's already after that. We don't have the time to track it down, free them, try to get Theora's shard back, and then go after Zanera and Kelindra. It's too much. We focus on getting them free, and we have two weeks to do just that."

Petrovana rubbed her arm, uneasy. There was also the fact that she had new magic she couldn't use right, but his words made sense. They had to focus on one thing at a time. First, free Madislak and Harmony. Then, they could worry about the rest. And Blank Face was hell-bent on making sure they didn't suffer Tamara's vicious ways. Maybe they could get in and out completely unnoticed.

Leper sliced his hand and let the blood drip onto the wicked-looking statue. His eyes narrowed as he observed the strange figure before him. She was otherworldly, her black hair resembling eight long tendrils flowing down to her belly button. Her face was devoid of a nose, featuring two large human eyes and a third eye on her forehead. Her arms bore spikes, and her fingers extended into six-inch-long fingernail talons, while her tail coiled around her legs and terminated in a trident-shaped end. Her skin was yellow, and her clothes were a vibrant green. A triangular-shaped mouth, filled with hundreds of cylindrical teeth, formed an unsettling, spiked vortex.

Ignoring Lillian's protest, Leper quickly turned to Shpockten. "Where's the entrance?"

Shpockten's brown eyes sparkled. "At the southern edge of town. Thank you, sonny."

Leper nodded but noticed Lillian staring at him in contempt. "What are ya doin', ya idiot? Yer goin' to die."

"It's okay, sweetie. He wanted to go in, said so multiple times." Shpockten winked at her.

"Like hell. Shpockten, you shouldn't just let anyone enter the damn trials." Lillian roared.

Shpockten's head snapped to Lillian. "Quiet, girl! I'll not have you tell me how to run my kingdom!"

"Why are you trying to stop me from keeping Zanera and Kelindra safe? Why are you so hell-bent on letting them die?

They have seven days left, Lillian... SEVEN!" Leper glanced back and forth between them, the anger and fog returning to his once-clear mind.

"We're tryin' to find a way to summon Kasherri to the material plane and get the shard that way. We just needed a couple more days to figure out the holding spells." Lillian said.

The darkness took over within Leper. "I don't give a shit what you need. I'm sick and tired of everyone else always getting what they want and taking advantage of me. Fuck you, Lillian; go summon the goddess of death to your doorstep—maybe she'll get rid of you for me."

"Excuse me, asshole?" Lillian rubbed her temples. "Do you even know what yer sayin', you worthless prick? We're tryin' to help you, but yer runnin' around on some stupid warpath because what? Nalecht? You still have time before you go in, dipshit! Use it!"

Leper chuckled darkly. "Honestly, at this point, I don't care. Why would anyone I know be honest or care about me? Why don't you just do me a favor, Lillian, and fuck right off? The oath is apparently only my problem now. What do you care?"

Lillian gaped. "You mouthy, ignorant ass. What would yer precious Rinawen think of who you are, Leper? How you act? I guess that doesn't matter, does it? She's dead! Because of you!" She jabbed her finger at him.

Leper was taken aback by her comment. He tried to fight against the darkness, the red vision taking over, but he couldn't manage to get a hold of himself. Her bringing Rinawen up and the fact that he was a massive failure when it came to her turned him into something else entirely, and he couldn't control it.

"Bitch." Leper gritted his teeth, his cheeks burning with heat and his ears ringing with fury.

He snatched Maka Kura from its sheath and bolted for Lillian, who unsheathed her scimitars. He swiped at her, and she deflected, then she elbowed him in the nose. White-hot pain rippled through him for a brief second before he grabbed her wrist and threw her on the ground.

"I will kill you!" He roared.

Shpockten motioned for the dwarven guards to interfere, and in a flash, thirty of the stocky, bearded men filled the room. Unsheathing their various weapons, Shpockten held up his finger and got between them.

His bushy white hair and eyebrows peered up at Leper. "This is sacred ground. Take your squabbles outside." He pointed his chubby finger at the door.

"I was leaving anyway," Leper spat. "To go die."

He glared at Lillian. The guilt gnawed at him, but he deflected it onto her. It wasn't his fault; it was hers. Stupid bitch. Another liar just like the rest. There was truly no one in this world he could trust. The only person he could trust... maybe he would be reunited with her soon. *Marry Petrovana...* He squeezed the handles of Maka so hard his knuckles turned white, feeling as if he might break the weapon.

Leper turned back to Lillian before leaving the room. "When I die in these trials, at least I'll be with someone who has my back. Someone I can call mine and mean it. At least I'm not some low-life coward that runs away from everything."

Lillian's face twisted in regret and frustration. "Just go, Leper. Just go."

Leper marched out into the baking sun, his mouth parched and a breeze blowing stray grains of sand into his face. He whistled for Ghost once more, and she squawked from around the building, where she was resting in the shade. Together, they flew south, and just as Shpockten had described, they found the underground cave entrance.

"I know what you're doing, Leper," Maka Kura said sternly as they approached the cave. "Stop lying to yourself and everyone else. You want to die so you don't have to face the pain of loss. You complain that nobody loves you, pretend that nobody loves you, when they do. You have friends—you just need to wake up and see them."

"So? At least I won't have to listen to you anymore. Or anyone else," Leper quipped bitterly.

A shuffle sounded beside him, and he knew exactly who it was without looking.

"I'm going in, asshole. They better be safe." He glanced over his shoulder.

Nalecht's white hair blew sideways in the wind. "They're safe. Don't forget to bring that shard directly to me when you get it... if you get it."

"I'm assuming you didn't find your precious Xartazza?"

"Not yet. If you manage to surprise me, though, I won't need him," Nalecht retorted with a throaty chuckle.

If he didn't have Zanera and Kelindra in his custody right now, Leper wouldn't hesitate to attack. But he didn't offer so much as a goodbye or even a flick of the head as he stormed towards the entrance.

Maka Kura didn't relent. "Once you stop blaming and hating yourself for what happened, you'll start to heal. You'll feel like your normal self again. Everyone makes mistakes. Everyone faces despair. The great names in history fight through that despair. They don't give up."

"I'm no great name from the past. I'm Leper. The failure that was, is, and always will be," he muttered as he walked into the cave without a second's hesitation.

Chapter Fourteen

M oments after walking through the doorway, the stairs
gave way to a tunnel about ten feet long, which then
opened up to a larger chamber. Leper scanned the area, and it
was nothing like he had imagined. He found himself standing
at the edge of an endless ravine, where there was no visible
floor, just jagged rocks and numerous tunnels he couldn't figure
out how to reach. The trials were unlike any cavern or terrain
he had encountered before. The rocks were not merely shiny
surfaces; they were covered in live vegetation, lush with grass,
and adorned with unusual flowers—deep purples, browns, and
blacks—emitting an otherworldly purple smoke.

He examined the edge of the tunnel, knowing the doors behind him were sealing shut. A pungent odor of death and iron
hung in the air. The doors slammed shut, but the cave remained
illuminated by the soft glow of quartz scattered among the
rocks. As he turned back to inspect the entry steps, he heard
a rustling noise. Fear gripped him. "Who's there?" he called
out, his eyes darting in all directions. Then, he saw Lillian
descending the steps.

"Lillian!" Leper stammered. "Why are you in here?"

He needed to do whatever it took to get her to leave. He did not trust her right now, nor did he want to be responsible for her life in here.

"Yer a reckless idiot. Yer a complete disaster, you know that?" She furrowed her brow.

Leper narrowed his gaze at her. "Go away. All of you. Madislak, Petrovana, Blank Face, Ace. Everyone. I don't want to see any of your faces again. Just leave me alone."

Lillian shook her head as a sigh escaped. "Leper, yer hurtin'. I get it. I'm sorry fer what I said. Now, please, calm down so we can try and make it out of here."

Leper glared at her. She followed him here. Why? Why would she follow him here? His endless turmoil swirled in his head, trying to decide what to do. Most of him wanted to walk away and just jump off the cliff edge to get it over with. Now he felt responsible for Lillian's life. And he was the selfish one?

Because of you! The words rang out in his head. Marry Petrovana. These were the people he associated himself with: liars, backstabbers. He shook off the negativity building within his mind—except Lillian's words. *Because of you!* The last words Lillian had spoken to him in Costin were the truth; Rinawen was dead because of him.

She was right. He should've gone with Rinawen. Shouldn't have argued with Blank Face and gone straight for the vial. Idiot. Useless idiot. Soon enough, he would be sacrificed anyway. Why worry now?

Lillian grabbed his hand, then put her calloused palm on his cheek. "Please. Let me help you through this."

"You don't know what I'm going through," Leper gritted. "I don't want you here. Turn around and go back to Ace and The Former."

Just then, a plunging sound echoed from the ravine. Leper's head swiveled toward the noise, but he couldn't discern its source. The wall opposite where they stood began to recede, distancing itself. The tunnel floor extended while countless tentacles sprouted from every conceivable spot on the walls outside and inside the tunnel.

One of the tentacles snaked around Leper's waist, yanked him backward, and hurled him into the air. Time seemed to slow down as he was launched upward, hanging suspended before beginning a slow descent. He glimpsed Lillian still standing in the tunnel, determination etched across her face, as she sprinted toward him in a desperate bid to outrun the tunnel's relentless extension. Leper watched as she pumped her legs as fast as she could, but soon he could no longer see her, only the ever-expanding tunnel that separated them.

Moments later, Leper watched in awe as Lillian performed a swan dive over the expanding edge and extended her arms to gain speed, heading straight for him. This is it; we're both going to die, and we didn't even last ten minutes. His body felt weightless as he plunged toward the rocky ravine floor, his stomach lurching into his throat with the dizzying descent. In one fluid motion, Lillian spread her arms, executed a graceful 360-degree spin, and transformed into a majestic griffin. The creature had a ghostly presence, with a fiery red mane that left Leper utterly speechless.

If there were a floor beneath him, his jaw would have met it as he plummeted towards the jagged rock floor. Incredibly, she swooped down and snatched him in her pawed talons, gliding skillfully through the treacherous underground, with tentacles swiping at them and the surroundings shifting to halt their advance. Their journey led them to yet another opening, this one featuring a circular platform in the center resembling a field of hay. The platform spanned a hundred-foot radius, anchored by a solitary rock pillar for support. As they touched down on the platform, Lillian reverted to her human form.

Leper landed heavily, staggering to regain his balance. He stared at Lillian, his mind whirling with questions. "What...how did you...?"

It suddenly dawned on Leper. The connection he felt with Lillian made sense now. She was comfortable to be with, and he finally understood why. She was the other twin from his visions on The Talon—Ace's sister, the shapeshifter they'd been searching for. The clues had been in front of him the entire time, but he hadn't pieced them together. The red hair, just like Ace's. The way she felt at ease around him, even knowing he was a Chernzerk. The freckles dusting her nose, the same as their father's. The same as Ace's.

"You're Ace's sister!" he declared, his emotions a tangled mix of anger, happiness, and confusion. "Show me your true form, horns and all!"

Lillian let out a huff, stepping back a few paces. Her expression hardened, and her tone left no room for argument. "You ain't breathin' a word to anyone about this if we survive."

Leper observed her closely. Everything about her appearance remained nearly the same, except for the two ivory-white horns that gracefully curved from her temples and met near the back of her head.

"Beautiful," Leper muttered, still in awe.

Blushing, Lillian twirled a strand of her hair with her finger. "Thank you."

He stared at her, still reeling from the shock. But now that he knew the truth—her real heritage—maybe she was exactly who he needed to get through the rain trials. With two Chernzerk down here, maybe they had a chance. Maybe they could make it out alive. There had to be a way.

Leper narrowed his eyes. "I don't understand. Why wouldn't you want me to know?"

Lillian glanced at Leper, his hollowed eyes flickering with a kaleidoscope of emotions—sadness, anger, depression, joy. They had just landed on the circular platform, and the tentacles that had sprouted from the walls vanished and went back to wherever they came from. His handsome face was a puzzle she couldn't piece together. His gaze questioned her, lingering mostly on the horns and her face. The sting of tears threatened, but she pushed them back; she didn't cry anymore, not since...

"I've lost someone that meant the world to me, too," she said, looking down and brushing back the tears. "You're not the only one." Her voice was strained.

As much as it pained her to remember her father and relive what happened to him, she realized it might be the only way to save Leper from himself. If he let this anger consume him, driving his every action, he would be lost to his own rage forever. And if that happened, the Leper she knew would be gone—along with any hope of stopping Nalecht or making it out of the rain trials alive.

It was the most painful thing she'd ever faced, but it was time to show him who she was and tell him about her father—and his. He needed to know before he became like Samaja, consumed by greed and hatred, lost to himself forever.

"Your father..." Leper took a step back, his demeanor softening. "I..." He sputtered.

"I lost my father long before he died on The Talon a few months ago," she said, the words pushing out of her.

Surprisingly, he took her hand in his. "I'm so sorry, Lillian. I didn't know. What happened?"

She glanced at Leper's glossy black horns, which started near the front of his head, arced backwards, before curving outward for a bit, and then back up and to a point. It reminded her of how mighty her own father's horns were the last time she saw him.

As she finally opened up, her mind flooded back to Xaneth Harbor when she was eleven years old.

Oubank, her father, had called her to the table. This would be her last meal with him. She sat across from him, her hair in black pigtails. Oubank's glossy black horns extended from his temples, arching up about four inches; the same center mass curved down roughly to his chin, forming a semi-circle on the side of his face. His red hair was buzzed short, and his freckled face glimmered in the sunlight pouring through the windows. He had a large nose, wide at both the tip and base.

Lillian took a bite of churnak soup—her favorite dish he made. She didn't know everything that went into it, but her father had told her it was a Chernzerk specialty from before their downfall. Everyone had loved churnak soup. Churnak was the name of the cow-like animal the Chernzerk raised for its rich, tender meat, perfect for stews. Whatever he put in it was incredible—the blend of veggies and churnak steak in the beefy broth was perfectly cooked and tender.

"What's the problem today?" His deep voice resonated.

Lillian huffed. "I miss Petrovana! Why'd you have to take me from Terynsipple? And why can't I just be myself? We've been here for a month, and my friends would understand! I asked them what they thought of the Chernzerk, and they were fine with it." She babbled on.

"No!" He slammed the table. "Don't you dare, Lillian."

"Why? I like shiftin'. They don't care, Dad. I promise." She pleaded. "They would be so impressed if I showed them what I can do."

"No, they won't. You keep hidden! Do you hear me? Don't you ever—ever—reveal yourself to anyone! You are the only heir to the Chernzerk line." He commanded.

"I'll show you then." Lillian stopped eating. "I told Cylandra you were a shifter, and she was excited to see you shift. She even said her family would come back to see it later."

"You did... what?" His eyes went wide. "Lillian, you—" He stiffened. "You didn't tell them I was your father, did you?"

"No," she said quickly.

He let out a long, dejected sigh. "Don't you dare tell them or change to your natural hair color. Keep your hair black until you go back to Terynsipple. And if anyone asks, you are simply here for training and learning history. Then get out of here as soon as possible, do you hear me? Get out and go back to Petrovana."

Oubank closed the journal he'd been writing in and placed it in a hidden compartment on the top left cupboard, closing it tight.

"Dad, I don't understand. What are you talkin' about?" She pleaded, looking up at him.

Oubank shifted back to his human form, putting the horns away for now.

A knock on the door broke her concentration on his disappointed face. She'd never seen his blue eyes look so sad, so angry.

Oubank rubbed his face. "This is going to hurt you more than it'll hurt me. Lillian, make sure you go back to Terynsipple. Find Petrovana; her parents will make sure you're taken care of." He walked over and kissed her on the top of the head. "And don't you ever forget how much I love you, me and your mother both."

Lillian started crying, confused and scared. "Daddy, what are you sayin'? Who is my mom?"

He forced her to look him in the eye. "Shhh! Don't say that word with me. Don't call me that anymore. Your mother's name doesn't matter. She was beautiful, sweet, kind—just like you. That's all you need to know."

The pounding on the door intensified, and Lillian's heart raced. What had she done? Why was he being so cryptic?

"Come out, or we'll come in and drag you out!" Voices shouted from the other side of the door.

"I'm scared. What's happenin'?" Lillian bawled.

He knelt down and squeezed her tightly. His tears dripped onto her arm. "Da...Oubank, what's goin' on?"

The door burst open. "There he is! Get him."

Cylandra's father, Nylor, charged through—a hulking, massive brute of a man in his late twenties. Twenty-nine, if she remembered Cylandra's words correctly. His cropped brown hair was shaggy around the ears, and his massive frame was packed with unusually large muscles. His piercing blue eyes locked onto Oubank as he grabbed him by the shoulders and shoved him out the door and into the streets, where a crowd had gathered, waiting.

"Hey! Stop it!" Lillian bellowed.

Nylor grabbed Lillian by the shirt. "Is it true? Is he a shapeshifter...a Chernzerk?"

Her heart raced, fear gripping her every instinct as her stomach coiled. She started bawling again, unable to respond to his demands.

"Has he hurt you? Did he threaten you to keep quiet about his true form?" he demanded.

Lillian shook her head no, unable to produce words.

"Show us your true form, Cherno!" Nylor tossed her to the ground.

Her knee connected with the rough gravel. People began emerging from their run-down, beat-up dwellings in this residential district of Xaneth Harbor. All of them looked dirty, ragged, and malnourished.

Oubank shifted to his Chernzerk form. The people gathered around gasped in disbelief. Lillian scanned the crowd for Cylandra but couldn't find her. Her father had brought her here for something regarding a shard and her brother, but she hadn't paid attention to the details. She just wanted to go back home to Terynsipple and Petrovana. She would give anything to be there right now.

Several men and women began beating Oubank with sticks, throwing rocks at him, and when he fell, they kicked him. She heard every single thud of the boots against his bones, the deafening cracks, and his pained groans. They didn't stop.

Thud, thud, thud.

"Hey! Stop it! He's nice!" Lillian hollered.

She couldn't stop the tears, and no one listened to the pained, insignificant cries of an eleven-year-old girl as they continued their ruthlessness.

"Go!" Oubank looked her directly in the eye and pointed toward the gates.

She'd never seen that look in his eyes, the agony, the disappointment. In her. But she couldn't go. She caused this. It was all her fault, and if she found Cylandra again, she would punch the ever-living shit out of her face. She wasn't supposed to tell anyone other than her family.

They brought out a wooden cross and slammed Oubank up against it.

"No, please," Lillian begged. "Stop it."

The first hammer pounded the nail through his wrist. She would never forget that sound. Or the pained scream that erupted from him. The tang of blood burned her nose as it poured from the sensitive spot. But they persisted, pounding another nail into his other wrist.

Whack.

Whack.

Whack.

That was all she could hear, along with his grunts as he tried to hold back his agony... for her. They put nails all the way up his arms, then started on his legs.

"Stop!" She pushed forward. "Please!" Tears flowed like a river as she fell to her knees.

There was nothing she could do to stop the wild band of people nailing her father to the cross. Each cry he let out became weaker and weaker as the life drained from him. Then they left him hanging in the hot, bright sun to die. Because of her. What an idiot. What a complete fool. She did this to her own father, betrayed him. Cylandra. Her eyes burned with rage and tears. Her face was hot with utter fury.

She slumped at the cross after they finished and tried to pull the nails out, but she wasn't strong enough. They were large nails, embedded deep.

"You don't realize the threat he was to this world. It's for the best," Nylor's deep voice called out. "Now you'll have to join the orphans of Xaneth Harbor or go back to where he brought you from."

Lillian didn't answer. She just buried her face in her hands and cried, cried until there was nothing left. She stayed there all night and eventually went back to their old house.

She barged into her father's bedroom, snatching up his scimitars and testing their weight in her hands. But they were too heavy—too unwieldy for her to swing with any real precision. She wiped away the last of her tears. Anger burned in her chest, and she was ready for blood.

Rage clouded her mind as she stormed toward the door, but before she could step through, thick hands seized her. She twisted, glancing back—and there he was. Samaja. The crazy one. Leper and Blank Face's father.

Samaja and Oubank had been best friends. It was Oubank's job to keep Samaja focused, though he'd never shared the details with her. But it hadn't mattered in the end. Samaja had lost himself, like so many Chernzerk before him. His downfall hadn't been one thing but a storm of them—his own greed, his rage, and the blood magic that had consumed him.

His black beard was thick, covering most of his cheeks and neck. He looked ragged and pissed, like she'd pulled him from something so important he couldn't be bothered to help, even with his own friend's life on the line.

"Stupid girl," he accused. "You have any idea how bad it hurts when we die? You foolish idiot." He mocked.

Yeah. I know. She didn't say anything.

"He told me to come get you before you do anything reckless down here. Now put those away and come with me, or are you going to have to learn another lesson the hard way?" He grabbed her arm.

Lillian dropped the scimitars to her side, not having a sheath, and nodded. That would be the last time she cried, and it sure as hell would be the last time she was a helpless little girl. They killed him just because of who he was. She wouldn't show her true self again. She wouldn't let the world have the pleasure of knowing what a delight her father and her kind were. No to all of it.

NEVER AGAIN.

Lillian's mind returned from the vivid memory. The salty taste of her own tears brought her back to the present as Leper held her closer than she realized. His musky, maple scent filled her nose, and his taut muscles against her told her she would be alright. But they needed to get moving; she had already wasted enough time recounting this memory to him.

"Yer father told me repeatedly how worthless and stupid I was on the way back. But I haven't shed a tear since that day. I picked up my father's scimitars and told myself I'd never change again. That I'd train and become the fiercest fighter so that no one ever has to go through somethin' like that again. And I will go to Xaneth Harbor, find Nylor and Cylandra, and kill them both for their part in his tortured death," she gritted.

"My father..." Leper muttered through clenched teeth. "So he was a complete asshole?"

"Yeah, I didn't know him terribly well. Oubank made me keep my distance. He lost himself, Leper—much like you could, if you keep actin' how you act. He became uncontrollable, which was the only thing my father wanted to prevent—keepin' him from doin' somethin' destructive."

"Doesn't surprise me. The piece of shit just left me and my...brother, if you can call him that, in the ocean and ran off to be a crazy bastard," Leper added.

"Oubank said he used to be a good man, though, Leper, that he wasn't always like that. Somethin' in him changed."

Lillian leaned into him.

"Didn't your father come back because of the well?" Leper held her at arm's length now.

The well on The Talon had indeed kept their fathers alive—at least until all four of them were born and visited the shrine. It had held their magic in reserve, keeping it from them until they were old enough to wield it with respect.

But once they all claimed their abilities, the well would no longer shield Oubank and Samaja from death. And then, Lillian, Ace, Leper, and Blank Face would be the last Chernzerk to walk the planet—unless they could convince the world they weren't evil. Unless they could persuade the masses to let them live.

Lillian sighed. "Yes. But we had rules. He said it was too risky for him to be seen again after bein' dead. So, he didn't leave The Talon after that. I think it was his third time dyin'? I don't know." She shook her head. "But he said if it happens too many times, people will get suspicious, and they need to stay off The Talon for now. Then I swore off ever shape-shiftin' again."

Leper nodded. "I see. That's terrible. I... I don't know what to say. I'm sorry for how I've acted. I can't... I can't control it, and it's getting worse. But the worst part is, I kind of like it."

Honesty. Wow.

"I can help you. It's not as difficult as it seems, but I will try and help you control it. We dealt with it as kids, so we kind of have a better understandin'. And it's easier at a younger age, but I will be there for you, just like Rinawen was." Lillian set her hand on his cheek.

"Thank you, Lillian." Leper wrapped his arms around her. "I'm sorry about those ignorant assholes. I want to be there with you when you show them."

Lillian nodded. "Would be my pleasure, Lep."

Leper took a step back and looked at her. "That's what Rin used to call me."

"I'm sorry, I won't say it again." She recoiled.

"It's okay. I... I need..." He sputtered. "Never mind. Let's move on."

Lillian glanced into his sad eyes and felt a wave of sympathy wash over her. This man is broken. But they had to move forward. He was in no emotional state to be here, doing this, but they sent him anyway. Assholes. According to Leper, Zanera and Kelindra were in trouble, and they needed this shard to stop Nalecht's plans. But for now, he was in a good place, even if only doom awaited them. As they scanned the platform, it became clear—there was no way down. Trapped on this dizzying height, their only options were grim. She could shift into a griffin again, but she refused. Or they could take the narrow, crumbling pathway that looked ready to collapse at any moment.

After multiple protests, Lillian finally convinced Leper to take the unstable path. She wasn't shifting again—ever. She'd only done it to save his life.

Hopefully, they were heading in the right direction. Maybe now that Leper knew the truth about her, he'd be less volatile. Maybe he'd finally start to control it—especially knowing his father had lost himself to the same affliction.

It was their responsibility to carry on the Chernzerk lineage, but that felt nearly impossible when only she and Ace remained—all the other Chernzerk she knew of were lost.

They wound through twisting tunnels choked with jagged vegetation, each step shaking loose dust from the ceiling. The ground trembled beneath them. When they finally stepped onto solid rock in a well-lit, oval-shaped chamber, the air turned sharp with cold. A sickly scent of decay clung to the space.

Then, all the exits slammed shut.

A massive black shade panther slipped inside just before the way was sealed.

Chapter Fifteen

Petrovana followed Blank Face down the dirt path leading to Xaneth Harbor. It had taken them a week to get here—the city they needed to reach, yet the last place they wanted to be. If anyone spotted them, word would surely reach Queen Tamara.

Xaneth Harbor was the most dangerous and lawless city in all of Kalazaar, a place ruled by Tamara's iron grip. A tyrant in her own right, she commanded the streets through fear, and no one crossed her without consequence. The city, located on the southeastern edge of Uskela, was the largest trading hub, with numerous docks for ships and accessibility by land and sky. Despite the muggy and uncomfortable weather, the hot sun was partially hidden by clouds, offering some relief. The ground was parched and cracked, a testament to the scarcity of rain in the desolate Bay of Disdain. But they needed to go, to get into Xaneth Harbor and somehow find Madislak and Harmony.

They'd argued for hours in a heated debate on whether to seek the shard of Kasherri or attempt to free their friends. Neither of them had a particular plan in place. That would come later; for now, get in and find information on their whereabouts. They decided against taking the time to get to Costin and help Leper with the shard of Kasherri. They had to hold out faith that he would somehow get it and return; they needed to free the king. For now, they had to find where Tamara was keeping Madislak and Harmony and get them out, unnoticed, with any luck.

While Petrovana had never been to Xaneth Harbor before, Blank Face appeared familiar with the place. She sensed a similar unease in him, mirrored in his body language. The desolation around them extended for miles, devoid of any greenery, trees, or mountains. Blank Face led her to an open, dry area roughly fifty feet from the city. He knelt down, muttered some words, and the ground beneath them washed away, revealing a hole with a ladder descending into a dark tunnel.

Petrovana followed him down the ladder and into the dimly lit underground tunnel. The unmistakable scent of damp mushrooms filled her senses. The tunnels were approximately five feet wide and six feet high, supported by thick wooden beams.

Blank Face, always concealed under his hood, mentioned, "I have a reputation to keep up if this is going to be successful."

Petrovana, remembering the cut-off horns under his hood, was reminded of something she had meant to discuss earlier. "By the way, if you ever want to regrow those horns, I think I can help you with that." She wasn't exactly sure about her healing powers' limits, but it was something she would like to test out.

"Is there anything you can't do?" Blank Face asked.

She replied with a smile, "Plenty. Forgive Lillian. Take out Nalecht. Rescue Madislak and Harmony. Find my real parents."

"Your real parents? How do you not know them?" He stopped and looked around a corner, checking for anyone else who might be in these tunnels.

"No, Zonoh told me he'd tell me on my thirtieth birthday, but... He's dead, and I'll be thirty soon, so... Guess I'll just never know." She sighed.

He placed a comforting hand on her shoulder for just a second, then got back to his hunter personality.

Blank Face led them through the tunnels, eventually emerging in a run-down safe house. The house was in shambles, with walls badly damaged, broken furniture, and debris strewn everywhere. The sight was irksome and sent a shiver down Petrovana's spine. She briefly closed her eyes to rid her mind of the image. She absolutely hated clutter and garbage every-where. For another week, they chased down every lead until Petrovana broke through his obsessive, bloodhound-like focus.

"So, what's yer plan exactly?" Petrovana inquired, fixing her attention on Blank Face.

He turned to her, his eyes serious. "First, we need to establish if they're actually here. Then find out where and a way to get to them. It's already been two weeks, so we need to hurry and hope she hasn't started mutilating them. After we get them out, we head straight to Kordry for Zanera and Kelindra."

Petrovana draped a hooded cloak over her shoulders. "I'll try and blend in. Where are we goin' first?"

Blank Face peered out of the broken window. "We need to get to the Pinnacle Bar. It's an underground trafficking and bounty hunter hangout with only the most prestigious and dangerous contracts. The owner of that place will surely know what's going on within the city. He has ties to Tamara and her right-hand man, Nylor."

Petrovana steeled her gaze. "And yer sure this guy won't run right to Tamara and tell her we're here?"

"No. This is a criminal town, and like I said, I have a reputation here. They wouldn't dare turn me over to her; I've made them way too much gold." Blank Face corrected, then walked out the door.

She followed Blank Face out of the house, venturing onto the streets of Xaneth Harbor, which looked like slums. Torn canopies adorned houses, broken windows, and shattered doors. The residents were in rags, appearing battle-worn and desperate. The air was thick with the smell of trash and filth, pity sinking in her stomach at the conditions these people had to live in.

Blank Face walked so quickly he nearly left her behind before barging through the double doors of a bar. Upon entering, Petrovana noticed the tavern's patrons, about ten in total, scattered across tables, booths, and the bar. All eyes turned to examine the newcomers as they found seats at the bar. Blank Face signaled for two shots of rum, placing two gold pieces on the bar.

The barkeep nodded and brought over the drinks. Petrovana didn't immediately drink hers, inspecting the murky liquid. "Is that dirt?" she inquired.

"I don't know or care. Drink it or not, don't matter to me," came the barkeep's uninterested response.

The barkeep was a large, rotund man with thinning brown hair, a mustache beneath his narrow nose, and brown eyes.

Blank Face shot a disapproving look at Petrovana. "Never mind her. I need some information, Jenkins."

Just then, someone slammed a paper down on the bar to Blank Face's right, causing Petrovana to jump slightly.

Blank Face remained unflinching and turned his head to face the intruder. "I'm going to warn you to get out of my face right now."

The intruder, a toothless man, sneered. "This is a hit on you—twenty-thousand payout. I'm willing to let it go for one night with your little side piece." He leered at Petrovana.

Petrovana felt uneasy as the toothless man's eyes roamed her body. She glared back at him and retorted, "Excuse me?"

Blank Face raised his hand to silence Petrovana. He addressed the intruder, his tone warning, "I don't know who you are, nor do I care. I'm giving you one opportunity to walk away right now. Whatever's on your mind isn't going to happen, and you need to leave."

Petrovana became aware of shuffling behind her, a disconcerting sign that they were surrounded by dubious characters.

"You plan on taking all of us? We're taking your girlfriend with us, Blank Face. You're outnumbered," one of the attackers called out from behind.

Petrovana's throat tightened with anxiety. She had faith in Blank Face's abilities and her own, but they were severely outnumbered, and the nature of these people remained a mystery to her.

Blank Face seized the moment, setting his glass down with a quip, "I warned you." He disappeared and reappeared behind the man, executing a swift and precise series of stabs to the side, leg, and arm, causing the man to slump to the ground.

Petrovana spun around to confront a group of unsavory thieves who eyed her uncomfortably. Their filthy appearance, gnarled teeth, and sinister glances made her shudder. She channeled her energy into creating an ice shard, sending it hurtling into the chest of one assailant, then another. Blank Face continued his swift movements around the room, dispatching the others in the blink of an eye.

In no time, the battle had concluded, leaving Blank Face standing amongst the carnage. He addressed the defeated bandits, "Anyone else got something they want to try?"

"C'mon, quit gloating. Someone could've seen us." Petrovana grabbed his arm and pulled him towards the bar. "Let's go get whatever information you think he has and disappear before the guards or someone else gets curious."

"We'll be fine," he barked.

She slapped his shoulder. "Now who's the one losin' focus?"

He nodded back. "You're right. I am losing focus. I got comfortable. We can't get comfortable here, and we can't lose sight of the objective: get in, get the shard, get our friends, and get out."

A solemn silence hung over the tavern, broken only by the labored groans and whimpers of the disoriented bandits attempting to regain their footing.

"I see you haven't lost your touch," Jenkins called from behind the bar.

Blank Face reclined in his seat, a smirk crossing his face. "No, I haven't. Now about that information?"

Jenkins signaled his staff to clean up the chaotic aftermath. "Tell me what you want to know, and I'll tell you what it'll cost."

"I need to know where King Madislak and his proxy are being kept prisoner." Blank Face glared directly at him.

Jenkins let out a chuckle. "I'm going to pretend you weren't dumb enough to just ask that question."

Just then, another hooded person slammed the same paper the first one did on the table: the contract for Blank Face's head. This is going to take forever with all the interruptions. A girl's voice emanated from beyond the hood and caught Petrovana by surprise. "How about if I ask about collecting this bounty?"

The girl was very petite. She couldn't be taller than five—maybe five foot two—about seven inches shorter than Petrovana. Beyond the hood, she caught a glimpse of deep hazel eyes and a few licks of dark black hair with flecks of red and green fluttering out from the front of the hooded robe.

"Intiva," Blank Face snarled. "What do you want?"

"The money for this contract." She giggled, then pulled her hood back a little and locked eyes with Petrovana. "And who is this slut you brought with you?" Her voice went from high to low in an instant. And was that... jealousy in her eyes?

Petrovana glanced from Blank Face back to Intiva, trying to make sense of her presence here and how he knew her.

"Well, unless you plan on killing me, you won't get that money. And who she is doesn't concern you," Blank Face retorted, motioning for Jenkins to pour them another shot.

"Oh, trust me, I've given up on killing you. Or even trying to compete with you, ever since you used me to..." Her response was cut off by Blank Face grabbing her throat.

A brief wave of fear and pleasure flew across her eyes. She even moaned a bit. What a weirdo.

"Unless you have some useful information, then pack your things and get the fuck back out of here," Blank Face gritted, then released his grip.

Intiva rubbed her neck. "Just like old times. If only." She looked at Petrovana. "Never mind. Wouldn't want your pretty girlfriend to get scared off now."

Blank Face grunted. "Again. Out with it or on with it."

"Fine. I know where you can find your precious friends, but it's going to cost you." Intiva flicked her hair back into her hood. "But why don't we discuss this somewhere else?"

After a grunt, Blank Face nodded at Intiva to lead the way.

Petrovana followed them out of the establishment, keeping a cautious eye on Blank Face as he led them back to the destroyed safe house. The remnants of their first encounter loomed like silent witnesses to their return. Blank Face settled into a creaky chair at the three-legged table, the wood groaning under his weight. Petrovana took the seat across from him, with Intiva occupying the last chair.

Unease prickled at Petrovana's senses. Who is this girl? Her obvious attraction to Blank Face was unsettling. The memory of the girl's twisted enjoyment when he squeezed her throat prickled Petrovana's spine. There was something she needed to clarify about this strange dynamic and the familiarity the girl seemed to have with him. Jealousy? Petrovana shook her head. No, I'm in a relationship. Why would I be jealous?

"What will it take?" Petrovana demanded, settling her gaze on Intiva.

The girl lowered her hood, revealing jet-black hair streaked with red and green, worn in ponytails—left tipped with green, right with red. Her face stole Petrovana's breath with its perfect beauty.

"Mostly gold," Intiva replied softly, her button nose twitching adorably.

Blank Face leaned back in his chair. "How much gold?"

"At least half of the twenty thousand offered for your capture," Intiva smirked arrogantly.

Petrovana's eyes widened. "We don't have that kind of money."

Blank Face shot Petrovana a glare. "You don't." He flicked his eyes back to Intiva. "Done. Where are they?"

Petrovana stared at Blank Face, wondering where he would get this kind of gold. What else did this assassin-turned-ally hide from everyone? Intiva rocked back in her chair, an unsettling grin spreading across her face.

Leper circled the panther. Lillian twirled her scimitars skillfully. The panther lunged at her, but she rolled away smoothly, and Leper seized the opportunity to strike, his weapons connecting with the beast's shoulder. He hoped defeating it would open the tunnels so they could continue toward the shard and, hopefully, find an exit.

Maka Kura sliced through with remarkable ease. The panther roared in pain and recoiled, but its spiked mace tail caught Leper off guard, slamming into his chest and sending him crashing into the wall. Blood seeped through his green shirt, stealing his breath.

"Leper!" Lillian's voice cut through the chaos as she rolled in front of him, hacking at the beast with her scimitars, though they couldn't pierce its tough hide.

"Need Idelthian steel or stab through the roof of the mouth," Maka's voice echoed in Leper's mind.

Gasping for air, Leper relayed the information to Lillian. She absorbed it quickly, circling the beast. In his pack, he found a yellow vial and poured it onto the open wound. The burning sensation was excruciating, coursing through his torso, but he gritted his teeth against the pain.

Lillian continued to deflect the panther's attacks, her focus unwavering. As it lunged at her again, she sidestepped deftly, driving her scimitar straight up through the roof of its mouth. The panther collapsed to the floor, lifeless.

She is incredible.

Leper's mind briefly drifted back to Petrovana as the creature emitted its final gurgle. He felt a pang of guilt for leaving her, everything unresolved as she cried her eyes out. I'm such a jerk. He shook his head, pushing thoughts of Petrovana aside. Not now.

They needed to escape this room so he could retrieve the shard of Kasherri, and then... Leper glanced around, taking in the runes and writings etched onto the smooth rock walls, along with scattered books and papers on a small oval table in the center. Some writings were in an old runic language he couldn't decipher, while others were in Kordrarian. Why Kordrarian here?

"What now?" Lillian's voice broke his reverie as she surveyed the room.

Leper shrugged, his gaze fixed on the pictures and runes on the wall, mostly depicting demonic beasts—imps, centaurs, minotaurs, and winged figures with red skin, commanding them with whips. He ran his hand over the rock, feeling its jagged texture and the familiar scent of stone. The pain in his chest was beginning to ease as he explored the oval-shaped room.

As he glanced around, his eyes caught a drawing on the wall that resembled the shard of Theora. Evenly spaced around the room were depictions of all the shards: Hathor, Obidiah, Kasherri, Aisha, Amarook, and Ryollin.

Leper pointed out the shard to Lillian, whose eyes followed his finger around the room until she looked up and pointed out something etched on the ceiling—a pristine, magnificent sword beaming with shards embedded into its hilt and pommel.

"Is that the..." Lillian trailed off.

"Talisman," Leper finished.

Lillian cupped her chin, contemplating. "I think it is. So, it's not just a talisman, but an actual weapon? I thought you only gained the powers of all the shards with the talisman."

"Seems like it," Leper said, scratching his head. "But what does it all mean?"

Lillian shrugged.

Her captivating green eyes met his, filled with wonder.

"I can't read any of this ancient stuff. We need Harmony. Or..." Lillian paused. "Never mind, we need Harmony."

Leper grunted. "It's okay to say her name. I may have handled things poorly with Petrovana."

Lillian grinned. "Didn't want you to get all pissy."

"You're the one with the attitude problem," Leper chuckled.

"Like this here," Lillian handed Leper a paper. "What's all this gibberish?"

Leper glanced at it. "It's Kordrarian, some kind of poem or riddle."

He read it aloud to Lillian:

Synchronized beneath the moonlit pledge.
Where whispers bind the gleaming edge.
The heart alone must thread the seam.
Through shadows deep and dreams that teem.
Not by magic nor by might.
But through a gift given to night.
Only then the shackle shatters.
As destiny awakens and darkness scatters.

"What the fuck does that mean?" Lillian blurted out.

Leper stared at the riddle a moment longer. "I have no idea. Maybe it's a riddle to get out of here." He shifted his thoughts to Maka Kura. "Any insights you care to share?"

"I've never seen or heard of this before. You might be onto something, though. Could be a way out, or something else entirely," Maka responded.

"Wow, awesome. Hundreds of years old with all the books and knowledge of everything, and the one thing I need help with," Leper chuckled inwardly.

"Careful, asshole," Maka retorted.

Leper folded the paper and tucked it into his pocket. If he couldn't figure out what it meant, he knew someone who could. Glancing around the room again, he noticed Kalazaar's four moons painted between some of the shards, each marked with its respective colors.

The deep purple glow of the Mortis Nightshade, Veridian's bright yellow, Serenula's green, and the deep ocean blue of Luna Novara littered the wall. All of them looked identical except for the Mortis Nightshade, which had lines or bars through it. Beside it was what appeared to be a page from a book, covered in runes and symbols.

He waved Lillian over, and she traced her hand along the carved book on the wall. Nothing happened, and she stood there with her mouth slightly open.

"Honestly, it looks like the page is missing or someone intentionally ruined it," she murmured.

Leper opened his mouth, closed it, then opened it again. "No way."

"What?" Lillian's head snapped in his direction.

Leper quickly rifled through his pack, praying that the book Rin had given him was still there. After a few moments of searching, he found it and opened it to the relevant page. Holding it beside the rock carving, he saw that they matched. But what did it mean? How did someone get this out of the trials if the only way out was death? Leper inched closer, hoping proximity might reveal the secret. He folded the book back and placed the page directly over the carving, examining any differences. As soon as all the corners aligned, the image changed. Leper yanked it away and looked at Lillian.

"Did you see that?" He scanned her face.

She nodded, her eyes widened. "Yes. Put it back there."

Leper placed it back over the carving in the wall, and it changed again—different letters, different runes, different symbols.

"That looks like a... God language," Maka murmured in his head.

"God language. Who built this place? Where did it come from?" Leper prodded.

"I don't know. The only thing I remember about the rain trials is to stay away from them. Most texts I've absorbed warned against entering, saying those who entered don't come out," Maka relayed.

Leper shook his head. "Can you read it?"

"No, no one except the gods can read god language," Maka Kura told him.

Leper tried to move the paper closer to the wall, and as soon as it touched, it got sucked into the wall, as if the page carving was absorbed by it. The Mortis Nightshade's color grew in intensity, and the wall started changing, coming alive. Miniature figures depicting the gods themselves appeared: Ryollin the minotaur and Aisha the dwarf, standing over what must have been thousands of people bowing to them. The gods incinerated the people with magic and power, reducing them to ashes in one blast.

Then another figure emerged: Eden Sarsnip, the first wielder of the talisman, who stabbed Ryollin and Aisha, causing them to fall. Amarook, the Chernzerk, picked up the talisman and used it to push the fallen gods away until they vanished from sight. The Mortis Nightshade, in its purple hue, reappeared, showing the bodies and chains wrapping around the moon. The chains grew thicker, threatening to break the moon, and the last chain's lock clicked beneath the final two links.

Amarook slid the talisman into the lock, turned it, and removed the lock. He then shattered the talisman into seven lesser pieces. Leper's heart raced, panic flooding his mind. What did it all mean? The shards meld the talisman, but was it more than that? Were those gods actually locked inside... a moon? They couldn't be, there was no way. They were dead. Right? Or were they just subdued and locked in the moon until... someone opened it? His mouth hung open.

Lillian's voice cut through his thoughts. "Leper, what's happening? What does it mean?"

Leper struggled to piece it together. "I think... the shards are more than just parts of the talisman. They might be keys or fragments of a larger whole that can unlock something—or someone—sealed away."

"You're saying the gods might still be alive, trapped inside the moon?" Lillian's eyes widened with realization and fear.

"Maybe. Or their power is. Either way, we need to find Harmony and figure this out. We can't let anyone get their hands on the complete talisman without knowing what it truly is."

Lillian nodded. "We need to move quickly. Nalecht is after the shards; he might know more than we do. And that makes him even more dangerous."

The only god that wasn't in that depiction on the wall... Kasherri. Where was she during all this? Was she uninvolved or scheming in the shadows? As the Mortis Nightshade returned to its original glow, the shard of Amarook alighted, followed by Kasherri's scythe glowing purple. Then the red spear of Ryollin, the green axe of Obidiah, the brown bow of Theora, the blue trident of Hathor, and finally the orange mace of Aisha.

"What the fuck did you just do?" Lillian blurted.

"Gained the knowledge that gets memories erased in this place or people killed," Leper retorted.

The talisman on the ceiling alighted and floated down, transparent, hovering over the table. Then, slowly, it glided over to the Mortis Nightshade, sinking into the lock and turning the opposite way. The chains fell off, the bars retreated, and what emerged sent shudders of fear down Leper's spine. Either the dead gods themselves or their extracted power ripped from the moon—a dark swirl enveloping Kalazaar with raw, evil, deadly force.

Lillian's face turned white as a ghost, and Leper was certain his did the same as he felt the blood drain from it. This revealed the final piece of information they needed: the talisman was not some tool for ultimate destruction. Whatever lay in the contents of that moon was the absolute destruction. The world would be doomed if Nalecht got his hands on that power. Worse, it wasn't just Nalecht. Anyone who knew the truth could seize that power.

After the smoke cleared, there was nothing but desolation, destruction, and misery.

Fuck me.

Lillian stepped closer to him, her eyes still wide with shock. "We have to stop this. We can't let anyone get the talisman."

Small openings formed in the top corners of the room, and smoke started billowing in, black, suffocating smoke.

"Not good," Maka's voice tinged with urgency. "That's toxic smoke meant to paralyze or kill! Get out, Leper! Get out now!"

"How?" Leper screamed in his head. "The doors are all shut."

"Figure it out... quickly!" Maka bellowed back.

Leper glanced around nervously. "Lillian, we need to get out of here, now!"

"What do ya think I'm lookin' fer?" she barked back.

Leper moved the chairs and the table, looking for any sort of button, latch, or hidden mechanism. He frantically paced the room, his heart pounding in his chest. Lillian ran her hands along the walls, pushing and touching everything she could reach. She circled the entirety of the room until she touched the shard of Amarook. It glowed white for a couple of seconds, then dissipated. She touched it again. Nothing. She touched the shard of Obidiah, and it alighted green. Both the shard of Amarook and the shard of Obidiah glowed and then dissipated. The smoke's density increased, blasting faster through the newly formed vents.

"Fuck!" she screamed. "What did I do?"

Leper could now smell the toxic smoke. Its pungent odor seeped into his nostrils, leaving a very sour taste on his tongue. He pulled his shirt up over his mouth, trying not to breathe in too much of it. We're going to die, we're going to die—the phrase repeated in his head, but he pushed it away. He didn't want to die, not now. That was the other Leper, the dark Leper. This Leper wanted to live, to survive, to see Zanera and Kelindra to safety.

"The order! Touch them in the order in which they glowed, Leper!" Maka growled.

"Touch them in order, Lillian!" Leper hollered out.

Lillian looked at him, incredulously, "I don't remember the godsdamned order, Lep!"

She ran back and touched Amarook again. It lit up, and she glanced back at him with a mixture of relief and frustration.

"You remembered which was first, didn't you?" Leper said, the corner of his lips tilting upward.

He ran over and touched the shard of Kasherri. It alighted purple and then faded. Right choice.

"What's next, smart ass?" Lillian called.

Leper tried to recall the specific order. "I think it was white, purple, red, green, brown...then...I don't remember."

Lillian ran over and touched the shard of Ryollin. The spear glowed red and dissipated. Leper touched the shard of Obidiah. The axe lit up green and then faded. Lillian was closest to the shard of Theora. She touched the bow, and it glowed briefly before disappearing.

Leper cupped his chin, his anxiety mounting. "Two more left. Was it the trident or the mace?"

The smoke was now so thick he couldn't see across the room. It invaded his personal space, making it hard to breathe. His heart pounded against his rib cage as the smoke continued to threaten their lives.

"Leper!" Maka's voice echoed in his mind, refusing to leave him alone.

Lillian shrugged, looking equally lost.

The taste of rotten eggs filled his mouth, disgusting him. He spat into his shirt several times, trying to keep the poison at bay. His vision blurred, and he could hear Lillian say something, but the words were unintelligible.

"Blue! Try blue!" Maka Kura demanded loudly, bringing him back to the present moment.

But Lillian was already heading for the mace, the shard that would glow orange.

"No!" he hollered. "Not yet." But she kept going, either making a last-ditch effort or unable to hear him due to the poison's effects.

"Go, Leper! Push yourself! Get to the trident before she gets to that mace! RUN!" Maka demanded.

Leper willed his legs to move as fast as they could, aiming for the shard of Hathor. Lillian was nearly upon the shard of Aisha, reaching out to touch it.

Leper dove with outstretched arms and hit the shard a half second before Lillian got to the wall. He saw the shard light up and then disappear. That was all he saw before he collided with the wall and collapsed to the ground, as darkness overtook him.

Chapter Sixteen

L eper woke up to Lillian yanking on his arms, her head right
above his. Sweat dripped down the sides of her cheeks, and
her fiery red hair tickled his nose. He batted the strands of hair
away.

"Finally." She panted. "How much do you weigh, you fuckin'
moose?"

Leper let out a chuckle as he sat up. "Apparently, just enough
to piss you off. How long was I out?"

She tilted her head to the side. "Thirty minutes or so longer
than me."

"Were you able to get anything useful from that room, or
did you have to get out quickly?" Leper brushed debris off his
shoulders.

Lillian bumped into him. "Had to get out. Smoke kept comin'
in, but with the doors open, it wasn't thick enough to knock us
out."

"Thank the gods," Leper muttered. "What do you make of it
all—everything we just saw?"

"That there's some serious power. Some serious evil we need
to make sure never reaches the surface." She rubbed her cheek.

"Yeah." Leper poked at a few flowers as they walked past. "We need to get rid of it all. I can't let that happen. We have to get this shard of Kasherri, and we have to keep anyone and everyone from unlocking that moon."

"How're we goin' to do that... exactly?" Lillian shot him a scowl.

"I don't quite know yet." He shrugged. "But I'll figure something out."

So many thoughts raced through his mind—the gods' battle, the shards, the talisman acting as a key to unlock the moon and unleash... what? A vast, dark oblivion? The power of the gods themselves? The thought sent prickles up his arms.

But first, they had to get out of here. And how, exactly, was that supposed to happen? He wasn't any closer to finding a way out than he had been the day before. He didn't even know where to start.

What was worse, he couldn't be entirely sure how long they'd been down here, though he knew it had been quite some time. They were running low on food rations and had to resort to eating only as needed. Every day, he felt weaker and weaker. Fatigue gnawed at him even though they had just slept for who knows how long, and the toxic smoke lingered in his system. They continued walking through the tunnels, not even knowing if they were headed in the right direction. His body was weary, an ache in his chest, ankles, and knees. Everything throbbed from sleeping on hard surfaces, and then just walking and exploring until exhaustion took over, and they slept. He wished the plants down here produced berries or anything edible for them.

Leper called out to Maka Kura. "Any idea how long we've been down here?"

"Two weeks since you arrived in Costin," Maka informed him. Then he added, "You both slept for three days from that toxin—though it would've been forever had you not stopped the smoke and opened the pathways."

"Awww. Were you afraid to lose me, Maka?" Leper teased.

"Shut up. Get us out of this darkness," Maka replied sarcastically.

Leper chuckled to himself and focused on the path ahead.

Lillian snapped her head to Leper. "Just what in the hells is so funny?"

"Oh, just talking with Maka. He was afraid we died. Said he couldn't stand the thought of having to watch you decay." Leper grinned at her.

"What?!" Lillian furrowed her brow. "That's not creepy at all. That thing has feelin's?"

Maka Kura made a resonating noise in Leper's head that made him cover his ears. "Keep pushing me, Leper."

Leper chuckled again. "Yes. Apparently, even though it's a piece of metal."

The tunnels seemed to take on an otherworldly edge. The vegetation now morphed together awkwardly, and the color changed from purple and black to orange and green. Weird. But the plants remained the same types: brushes, grass, weeds, some flowers. Each of the longer plants swayed back and forth as if there were a breeze blowing through the tunnels. A soft, gentle breeze, but Leper felt no air. The only air he felt was the damp, pungent underground smell he'd suffered through for weeks now.

He left a note in his pack for Zanera and Kelindra, explaining they were still stuck down here and low on food. He asked if they could please pack some in the metal case they had and inquired how things were going on the surface. Then he closed his vial pack and opened up his other one, tossing Lillian a piece of jerky and some cheese.

"I think... I think the reason people don't get out of here is because they have to face Kasherri herself to get out. To claim the shard," Leper said through bites.

The smoky meat flavor of the jerky was as good as it could be after being down here for so long—but the cheese? Gross. He grew tired of eating jerky and cheese every day for the last week. But that was all they had, and the cheese wasn't even kept chilled.

"I agree," Maka interrupted. "It's the only logical explanation. Find Kasherri and find a way out."

"You don't exactly kill a deity, Lep." Lillian tossed her cheese on the ground.

"I know, but we have to find her regardless. I'm pretty sure it's the only way out," he argued.

"What makes you so sure it's her, though? Couldn't it be one of the other gods?" She got to her feet and picked at her teeth.

He pointed down one of the tunnels. "Look at this place." He started walking down the tunnel. "It's got that otherworldly aura to it. We're not in Kalazaar anymore, and I'm certain Blissoria wouldn't have shade panthers and toxic smoke in it. Plus, Mount Harbinger and The Talon are somewhat known to be in her territory, and look at what lives in those places, the same stuff that's down here."

"You have a point." She looked around at the walls and touched a couple of plants. "If that's the case, then we'll need to keep an eye out for her. Don't let her get the surprise attack on us. We're already at a disadvantage goin' against a deity; no need to make it worse."

Leper nodded. "I agree. Let's find her before she finds us—and get that damned shard."

Leper looked at Lillian; her eyes showed unending focus as they plodded along. Not once did she yell at him for his involvement in her being down here. He was a stubborn, reckless idiot, but his goal remained the same: get the shard or die. Nothing would stop him. Most of the time, he preferred the second option, but right now, in her company, with her companionship, he started to sway back to making it out. For now.

"Thank you." He side-eyed her.

Lillian was taken aback. "Fer what?"

"You didn't have to come down here. You came down here for me. I just wanted to say thank you. Regardless of what happens in here, it means a lot to me." He lifted the corner of his lips.

The damp air took on a moldy smell as they passed through yet another room and picked a tunnel to continue walking down. Without a map or any sense of direction, they could only choose a tunnel and hope for the best. At least the temperature was comfortable, and there wasn't any threat of rain, snow, or any sort of storm to add to their misery.

"Yer welcome. I'm sorry... Fer what I said about Rinawen. Lep, it's not yer fault she died. She is not dead because of you, and you need to know that." She squeezed his arm.

Leper's chest burned and ached, but he pushed down the surging anger and dread and was left with a wincing pain as he said, "It's the truth, whether you think so or not. And it's a regret I will take to my tree."

"Can I ask you a question? Reckon since I told you about my dad, maybe you can answer one fer me?" Lillian beckoned, her smile radiating.

"Fine." Leper sighed. "I owe you that much."

"What..." She tapped her chin. "What was the deal with you and Rinawen? Because when I asked her if she loved you, in the carriage, she got all red-faced and distant. Quite pissy, actually." Her beautiful green eyes met his.

Leper let out an actual laugh. "Well, that is certainly the way she would've reacted to that question. She had a very thick shell, but I'm telling you, once you got past that exterior, she was wonderful. Beautiful, funny, amazing." He stopped and gazed down at the ground, choking back the lump in his throat. "The type of person you only come across once in a lifetime."

Lillian set her hand on his shoulder. "Must be hard. I...I've never felt that with anyone."

Leper let out a long sigh. "It is. But to answer your question, yes, there was something there at one point. Then it changed, end of story."

Lillian erupted in laughter. "Jackass."

Leper bumped into her shoulder. "For the longest time, we were the greatest of friends, did everything together. Grew up together, made so, so many memories. Then, a little after I turned eighteen, I really started to see her in a different way. Zanera was nine, and Kelindra was three, and I wanted something like that for myself, but given the horns and all... well... you know how it goes."

"You mean like a family and shit? Or just her?" Lillian kept staring at him with a look he couldn't decipher. Was that longing? Jealousy? Leper shook his head.

"Both. Any of it. Not that she wasn't enough, but she had a family, kingdom, a life."

Lillian nodded.

"Anyway, it was around that time Larnadix was mysteriously taken for two days or so, then returned, a totally transformed man. Rin said he completely forgot about me. So, she left me out of their conversations." He took a breath. "After another year, we were walking on the beaches of Kordry, laughing, talking, and I put my arm around her like this." Leper snaked his arm around Lillian's waist and squeezed her body close to his. Their eyes connected, and he almost leaned in, but no, he was still with Petrovana, and he was not a man without honor. So, he pulled his face back. "Then a magical feeling overtook me, and we drew closer together. It was the first time we kissed, and it was utterly spellbinding, and I... I knew she was the one."

"I remember something similar with someone similar." Lillian grinned as she leaned back into him, tempting him with her curves, her soulful eyes, and that radiant smile. "Did you guys... you know?"

Leper nodded. "Unfortunately."

"That bad, huh?" Lillian chuckled.

"Gods, no. We didn't want to stop, but it made me an adulterer and her a cheater. She was still married and the queen. We both knew it. I felt so bad for putting her in that position. Again, all my fault. I must've caused her so much grief." Leper hung his head.

"That's unfortunate. Reckon I know how Larnadix would've felt. But my situation was different. Only good thing about Alzen was his looks." Lillian sighed as she leaned in closer.

Leper stopped her. "Lillian, I can't. I'm not that type of person anymore, and I don't even know where Petrovana and I stand at the moment, but I won't be the one to break her trust. I will never do that again."

Lillian sighed as she stepped back. "I'm sorry. I know. I don't want to be like... Never mind. I'll respect yer space. But that don't mean I won't stop tryin'."

Leper grinned. "Thank you. You're truly a gem." He sighed. "But to finish the story, we knew we could never make it work because of who I am and who she was. We would be executed, or at least I would be. We didn't talk for several months, then Zanera, bless her heart, got us together, and we became like brother and sister ever since."

Silently, they walked on. Leper kept stealing glances at Lillian, captivated by her fierce nature and spunky attitude—a stark contrast from Petrovana. Once again, he felt torn between them. No, he decided firmly. His heart belonged to Petrovana. Despite her actions that often left him bewildered and infuriated, he loved her. Her whimsical charm, so endearing, was the same quality that almost led her to agree to marry Madislak on a whim.

As they entered another room, he wondered if they were in a different room or perhaps the same one from before. Were they walking in circles? As they paused to choose a tunnel, he glanced up, noticing the shard of Hathor glowing brightly on the ceiling. Had all the rooms been adorned like this, and he simply hadn't noticed?

Before he could ponder further, a figure rushed towards them. But this was no ordinary threat—not another shade panther. This was far worse. The creature had yellow skin, eight tentacles flailing from her head, a triangular face, and a mouth lined with cylindrical teeth. The face had a third eye on its forehead, and sharp spikes protruded from its arms. This wasn't a mere enemy they could face and kill, not at all. This was the Goddess Kasherri herself.

Petrovana narrowed her gaze at the petite, painfully beautiful woman sitting arrogantly beside her. What is it about her that makes the heat rise from my stomach? What power or charm does she hold over this meeting? Even her blueberry scent, wild and infuriatingly beautiful, added to Petrovana's agitation. Perhaps Blank Face liked his women wild, but there was clearly more to their relationship. Once Intiva was gone, she would grill him about it.

They remained seated in a smuggler's safehouse, a place ripe with garbage and chaos, the stench of neglect hanging thick in the air. Intiva had promised to help them find Madislak and Harmony for ten thousand gold.

For the past thirty minutes, they'd done nothing but silently battle it out, neither side willing to budge.

"So, you going to cough up the gold, or are we just going to stare at each other all day?" she quipped, impatience lining her voice.

Time stretched thin, with neither party willing to give up their leverage. Tamara had given them two weeks to bring the shard of Kasherri, and it had already been two weeks. Almost a month had passed since she'd heard anything from Leper. Hopefully, he was still alive, had the shard, and was on his way back to Lantess.

Petrovana inhaled sharply. "Well, Blank, you goin' to tell her where this pile of gold you got is, or what? We're wastin' time."

Blank Face ran his thumb and finger along his chin. "Perhaps, unless you're interested in a more valuable target?" He turned his gaze to Intiva.

A perfect smile crawled across her face. "Right, a target as big as you? Surely the great and masterful Blank Face could just collect the bounty himself and line his pockets even more."

A low chuckle escaped Blank Face. "I have no interest in money. There's more at stake than money, Intiva." His glare intensified. "All this gold will be meaningless if the world is destroyed in the process."

"Just say the name so I can consider," she purred sensually.

Blank Face shifted uncomfortably, readjusting his hood. "Xartazza."

Shock crossed Intiva's features. She rocked back in her chair. "Are you insane?" She mocked. "I'll take the money. Even you have to admit that's a fight you'd struggle to win, though I'd like to see the confrontation."

Petrovana interjected, "Who's Xartazza? And why are you so scared of him?" She motioned towards Intiva.

"I would've thought you could at least tell her a little about the history of where you're heading," Intiva chided before turning to Petrovana with a calculating gaze. "Xartazza was, is, and always will be the best fighter the arena's ever seen. Never lost a single battle, never got bested by any warrior, beast, or bulwark."

Petrovana listened intently before asking, "What happened to him, then? Why y'all lookin' for him?"

"Someone with that kind of skill doesn't just disappear, you dumb bitch." Intiva huffed. "He's out there somewhere. He could do... anything. Somehow, Tamara let him escape five years ago. Nobody's seen him since. Some folks even say he was a god walking among us; he was that good."

"A god... Right," Blank Face muttered. "But fine. You want the gold." He reached into his pockets, producing a small piece of paper. "You can recover it from this location. Watch out for the traps." He slid it to Intiva.

She looked it over. "And how do I know it's there?"

"Because we value our friends' lives over gold," Petrovana replied, narrowing her gaze at Intiva.

"You don't understand how hard it is to trust this one, you stupid wench. Is that all you're good for—looks and being pretty? Or do you not realize you're running around with the most ruthless, heartless soul of a human being?" Intiva's gaze pierced Petrovana, sending a wave of agitation through her.

Petrovana's eyes flared. "Jealous, are we, street filth?"

Intiva produced a dagger so quickly it was a blur, pressing it to Petrovana's neck before she or Blank Face could react. "Call me street filth again, you ignorant prude. I hold a level of respect for that man that you will never reach. He's ten times the fighter any of us are, but you? You're nothing but a worthless bystander. And believe me, this war is not one any of you will win. But with gold, I can get off this doomed continent and sail south, leaving you all to rot."

Blank Face snarled. "This is exactly why I work alone. I don't give a shit what you do with the money. Where the fuck are our friends? And get that gods-damned dagger off her neck before I rip you apart."

She couldn't deny how good it felt for him to defend her; it caught her off guard. She glanced at Blank Face. His features remained inscrutable, but his hands moved under his cloak, readying to strike.

Intiva grinned, pressing harder. "Go ahead, try and strike me, Blank. I will make this bitch bleed quicker than you can kill me." She jabbed the dagger into her shoulder, then yanked it back out and pressed it to her neck.

Petrovana let out a scream of agony. "What is wrong with you!?" she hollered.

Petrovana's heart pounded, panic gripping her soul. This unhinged assassin could be the one to end her life. This small, crazy part of Blank Face's past could be where it all ended abruptly.

"What more do you want? I told you where to find the money," Blank Face slammed his hand on the table.

"I need assurances. I'm not about to let you walk out of here before I have any of it in my hands, Blank. You know that."

"I don't have the time to take you there right now. I need to get them free," he said, anger rising in his voice.

"You better figure something out quicker than that old lover," Intiva smiled as she pressed harder.

Petrovana shot her a sidelong glance. "I will not work with this unhinged tiny bitch."

"Fine. I'll give you two thousand right now to get your damn dagger off her neck," Blank Face spat, then reached under his robe and tossed a small pouch that clinked onto the table.

As soon as the dagger left her neck, Blank Face blinked over to Petrovana's side, grabbed Intiva's wrist, and pushed her arm away so quickly that the pommel of her dagger hit her in the face. Intiva smiled, blood forming around her teeth, then wiped her mouth using her arm.

He slammed his fist on the table. "Never in my life did I think I'd be the voice of reason, but she's going with us, Petrovana. She's extremely skilled and will help us in their rescue. And Intiva, you don't touch or threaten her again. Do you understand?"

Petrovana looked at him, rage fueling her vision. But she couldn't discern what made her angrier—the fact that Intiva was coming along or the way Intiva looked at Blank Face with desire and longing. But there was something else in those perfect hazel eyes—a sense of knowing. She arched a brow at him.

"Where did you learn to do that?" Intiva smiled. She quickly reached for his hood.

Blank Face's hands moved in a blur, grabbing her wrist and forcing her hand back, making her drop to her knees. He moved his face inches from hers.

"You follow and shut your mouth, or it will be the last time you say anything," he gritted through clenched teeth.

Another pleasurable grin crossed her features. "As you wish."

What the hell is going on here? Who is this bitch, and what's with all the innuendos and secrecy? And who the hell is Xartazza? Petrovana let out a long, deep sigh.

Assassins.

Intiva revealed where Madislak and Harmony were being kept within Tamara's fortress dungeon. As she recounted the exact location of their cells, Petrovana realized this was going to be far more difficult than anticipated. Madislak was in a high-security cell with only one way in and out. Harmony was held a floor or two above, with the same setup, her cell guarded by the behemoth Nylor. There were no windows, trap doors, or secret entrances to either of their prisons.

Petrovana nudged Blank Face. "You sure she's not leadin' us into some trap?"

"I highly doubt that. She loves her money way too much," he countered.

"How can you be sure? How does she know all this? Doesn't it seem a bit convenient?" Petrovana chided.

"Because you, pretty buffoon," Intiva cooed. "Look at me—I'm small, and if I wear dark clothes in low-lit places, I can be very hard to detect. How do you think Blank and I mapped out half the places we robbed?"

"So you are a thief?" Petrovana turned to Blank Face.

"It's in the past," he growled. "She knows what she's doing. Like I said before, she is highly skilled."

They were going to have to do this the hard way—either get disguises and sneak in or launch a full assault. Who knew what Blank Face or Intiva were planning at this point?

Petrovana had practiced her psyrenth magic a few times. She'd told Blank Face about it, and he hadn't seemed to mind her having more than one spell, much like Leper. But when she admitted she couldn't quite control it yet, he'd offered to be her guinea pig, saying he'd rather suffer now so she could master it before their next fight.

So she practiced. And practiced. And practiced.

Until it was time.

Time to get into position. She rolled her shoulders. "Let's go get the king back to his people."

Chapter Seventeen

Petrovana ducked through the first door, avoiding eye contact with the guards as they snuck by in their ragged Xaneth Harbor guard attire. Intiva led them to the private rotation rooms, where guards would rest, eat, or relax.

Intiva would join them later; she had gone ahead to sneak farther into the dungeons and count how many guards were on each level. Though Petrovana hated to admit it, she knew Intiva's small size and quick steps made her perfect for the task. She reminded her of a badger—small, feisty, and very deadly.

They'd been preparing this assault for five hours now, in the middle of the night.

"Well, what do you say?" she inquired.

Blank Face let out a sigh. "Right now? As much as I'd like to regrow them and help Leper out on his little quest to change everyone's perceptions, it might cause a few problems. I'll have to lose the hood, my reputation, and then everyone will be after me for my race, not my past." He swallowed hard, his eyes betraying his unease.

"Are you..." Petrovana scrutinized him closely. "Nervous?"

His eyes darted around, unable to meet her gaze at first. Then, with a deep breath, they locked onto hers. "No... maybe... you'll never understand. Maybe after we leave here... maybe."

Petrovana placed her hand on his arm, offering reassurance. "They wouldn't grow back instantly. And yer right about one thing; it certainly would go a long way fer you to gain Leper's approval. If that's what yer after."

"I'm not after his approval," Blank Face spat back angrily. "I just want him to see me as a brother like he sees Madislak. I know I messed up in the past, but I'm not that same person. He chooses not to see it."

"Maybe if you started growin' out yer horns, he'd respect you more. It wouldn't hurt. I know Leper, and that is definitely somethin' he would respect." She sighed. "It's one of the biggest reasons we ended up with each other, because I accepted who he was even when his hat came off."

Blank Face's stare lingered on her, pondering her words. "You're sure about that? Because if I wake up tomorrow and they're fully regrown, we might have some complications on this mission."

"I promise they won't regrow overnight," she replied with a burst of laughter.

"You're certain it will help him forgive me for the terrible things... the thing I've done?" He gestured towards his heart.

"I mean, I can't say for complete certainty he will forgive you, but I know it will only help yer case," she countered.

Blank Face sighed, a hint of vulnerability in his eyes. "I'm taking a big risk and trusting you right now. But if it will lead to him possibly forgiving me, what could it hurt?"

Petrovana's face lit up with excitement. "Turn around, close your eyes, and look down. No peeking."

He complied, and Petrovana knelt on the bench behind him, ensuring she had easy access to his head. She placed her forearm, just above her elbow, on his truncated horns. As she rubbed the area in a circular motion, the swirl tattoo on her arm faded to a dull gray. Her magic drained into the process, a part of her she couldn't explain.

Somehow, she possessed the capacity to access more than two spells—a rare ability among shrews. It was an intricate part of her she had yet to fathom. She still couldn't believe she had four spells now. *Four*. Nobody ever got more than two. And to make it more confusing, she could heal.

A dwarf specialty—no, a dwarf *restriction*. Only dwarves could heal. Perhaps she was half dwarf? If only she knew who her real parents were. Why'd they abandon her? Was she supposed to be a member of royalty—or just a random commoner?

Their enigmatic pasts intrigued her, pushing her to uncover more about him. The sole discrepancy was that he knew his origin and why he possessed such extraordinary capabilities. In contrast, Petrovana remained adrift, unable to comprehend why she could utilize four spell types and who her real parents were, bequeathing her these astonishing powers. But somehow, there seemed to be a softer side of Blank Face that only she could reach. It was this soft, subtle gentleness of a man she never expected. Even though they were all in Kundry at one point together, they never took the time to really get to know one another; again, Leper had a lot to do with that as well.

Would she ever unearth the truth about herself, about who she truly was? Would she remain a wanderer, forever in the dark? The idea of revealing her abilities to others was tinged with fear. Her firsthand experience of how Brebian had treated Leper left her dreading a similar fate. She couldn't help but wonder if her fate might be even more severe.

Once Petrovana had depleted her magical reserves, she could feel the blood running from her nose and eyes.

Petrovana tapped Blank Face on the shoulder, her voice soft and reassuring. "Okay. You should start to see or feel a difference in a day or two."

Blank Face raised an eyebrow, a hint of uncertainty in his voice as he rubbed the back of his head. "That's it?"

She settled back beside him, a mix of emotions stirring within her. "Yeah, that's it. Now it'll start to get rid of the old dry patch and slowly begin to grow little nubs, eventually returning to how they were before. I hope."

"Good, Intiva should be back any minute now." He turned to face her.

Petrovana let out an audible huff. "How can you be so sure about her? What exactly did y'all do together before this?"

"We were partners at one point in time. Lovers, even. But I betrayed her and left her..." Blank Face shook his head. "It disgusts me what I did to her, okay? I don't want to talk about it right now."

"It's funny. In that entire explanation, in no part did I hear any reason we should trust the little bitch," Petrovana chided.

"She won't betray us, Petrovana." Blank Face's jaw ticked.

She glared at him. "Yer mouth is movin', but I hear no good reasons yet."

As their eyes locked, an electric tension crackled in the air, and a complex swirl of emotions coursed through Petrovana. Butterflies danced in her stomach, but a gnawing pit of guilt churned alongside. In an impulsive moment, their heads drew closer, their lips met in a passionate kiss that seemed to stretch on for an eternity.

But then, she abruptly pulled away, a pit of guilt burrowing in her stomach. "This is wrong," she murmured, shaking her head in disgust at herself.

"These things happen. I'm sorry, I shouldn't have got that close." He laid his hand on her shoulder.

The door flew open, and Blank Face immediately disappeared, then reappeared with his hood back on, covering his head.

"What the hell is going on in here?" Intiva shot Petrovana a hateful glare.

Petrovana wiped her nose and eyes. "That's not yer business."

"Well, if you're both done fucking around," Intiva enunciated each word sharply, "they have both of them in the same cell and are interrogating them. Tamara is there with the shard of Theora. Now would be a good time to catch them off guard."

Blank Face smoothed his robe. "Let's go." He marched toward the door.

Petrovana grabbed a cloth and cleaned her face. Of course, now it was time to leave. I just used a bunch of my magic to help him out, and now we're going to attempt this crazy rescue. She noticed Intiva didn't move to follow along.

"What are you waitin' fer? Scared?" Petrovana quipped.

"Oh, I'm not going in there. I told you I'd help, but I'm not putting my life on the line for your friends." Intiva smiled.

Petrovana let out a sigh as her shoulders sagged. "Should've known an assassin only cares for themselves."

Intiva shrugged. "Call it what you wish. I'll be waiting when you're done."

Blank Face stopped abruptly and turned to her. "Just remember. If we die, you'll never find that gold."

Intiva's face scrunched in rage. "I knew you were lying to me, you piece of shit."

Blank Face grinned. "You know better than to compete with me. Thought you would've learned that on our last mission together."

She pointed a finger at him. "Yeah, when you seduced me into thinking you—"

Her words were cut short as he blinked over and covered her mouth with his hand. "I said to follow and shut the fuck up, remember?" he demanded.

She nodded.

"Enough!" Petrovana bellowed. "We have more important matters than yer previous love life to figure out here. Let's go get the king and his proxy out of captivity already."

"Fine." Intiva huffed. "I'll help you free them."

Utterly infuriating. Yet Blank Face seemed to hold some kind of control over her, some way of getting or making her do exactly as he said. She readjusted her guard armor to look as good as it could and marched out the door.

Lillian immediately withdrew her scimitars, twirling them in her hands to reaffirm her grip. She had practiced with these incredible blades every day since her father died. The stench of Kasherri filled her nostrils, a dank mildew smell that sent a shiver down her spine.

She began to understand why no one made it out—if you didn't die from hunger, you would likely die at the hands of this hideous goddess, Kasherri, who stood before them, black spit dripping from her triangular mouth as she grinned hungrily.

"Well, look what we have here," Kasherri's ethereal voice hissed around the room, filling it with unease.

Lillian spread her feet apart, preparing. "If yer just another test, we'll run right through you too."

Kasherri cackled loudly, the sound reverberating off the walls. "I am a god, you cannot defeat me." Her grin widened.

"According to that little history display on the walls, with the right weapon, we can," Leper snapped, narrowing his gaze.

All three of Kasherri's eyes snapped onto Leper, examining him from head to toe. "I'd watch my tongue if I were you, boy. You're in my world down here." She let out a long, dejected sigh. "But lucky for you, I cannot attack you here; it is outside the... barrier. But I'm here to offer you what you seek—a way out."

"Really? And why is that?" Lillian cocked her head to the side.

A way out? Why would she offer a way out? And what would be the price?

Kasherri's annoying cackle permeated the space. "Well, you took the blood oath on my statue, remember?" Saliva dripped from her mouth. "Or did they forget to inform you that in doing so, it gives me and my armies your scent, your blood scent? I can find you, wherever you go."

Lillian's heart ticked. She has our blood scent? She and her entire underworld would hunt us endlessly down here. This was really what they said it was: a sacrifice. Trapped down here in these winding tunnels, and the very evil, very corrupt goddess of Malastion has our scent. Fantastic.

"Or," Kasherri continued, "agree to become a Deathbinder like The Former and The Latter, and I'll whisk you right back to the surface. And you will be loyal to me!"

Leper's face turned red, a hollow shell of anger filling his eyes. "I'll be loyal to myself and only myself."

Kasherri erupted with laughter. "Yes! Yes! That is exactly the type of positive thinking I'm looking for."

"Lep, calm yerself," Lillian glared at him. "And what if we refuse?"

Kasherri spun around, walking away from them. "Then I still have your scent, and in the very unlikely event that you somehow survive down here, I will hunt you endlessly, ruthlessly. And should I get my talons in you..." She whirled back around, holding up one of her very sharp talons, a grin curled up her face.

"So, we can get out then?" Lillian retorted. "I think we'll pass on yer pathetic offer."

Kasherri's grin disappeared. "You'd pass on being immortal? On having immeasurable power? For what?"

Leper had been eerily quiet for the better part of this conversation—until he wasn't.

"I didn't say I'd pass," Leper blurted out.

Lillian rolled her eyes. The audacity. It felt like she wasn't only fighting Kasherri, but also this stubborn, uncontrollable, broken man intent on making everything as difficult as possible. It was like constantly babysitting a toddler. A big, beautiful, nearly perfect toddler.

"Hey, dipshit," Lillian snapped her fingers in Leper's direction. "What about yer precious Petrovana? What would Rinawen think? C'mon."

There had to be a better way to snap him out of this. He needed to find his anchor—whoever or whatever it was—and ground himself better than he did now. Otherwise, he could lose himself entirely and become this other version of himself that Lillian hated, forever.

Leper glanced at Lillian. "I'll worry about that. Mind your own business. I'm not asking you to join me."

Lillian huffed. "Idiot." Then turned to Kasherri. "So yer sayin' all them other statues in the sand out there said no? Except The Former and The Latter?"

Kasherri nodded. "Only two smart ones out of how many?"

"Or two cowards. How do we get out of here otherwise?" Lillian narrowed her eyes at the ugly goddess.

Again, a cackle. "Defeat me. Take the shard. But then you open yourself to the other... consequence."

"What consequence?" Leper barked, finally unsheathing his weapons. "And just to make sure I have this clear, if we defeat you, we get the shard? If we become Deathbinders, we don't get the shard?"

Again, Kasherri nodded. "Nobody ever defeats me; nobody ever made it that far. But you two... have come the farthest. For the right person, I will gladly give up the shard."

What kind of twisted, nonsensical game is this? She'd give up the shard for the right person? Who is the right person? She seems scared, worried that we might be the two to get out of here, to defeat her, but she's a god. You can't kill a god, not with a normal weapon anyway.

"What is the consequence?" Lillian said through clenched teeth, steeling her gaze on Kasherri.

Kasherri made a couple of clicking noises with her mouth. "To remove the shard is to remove the boundaries for healing magic to the dwarves, and the ever-present magical wards separating Kalazaar from Malastion."

Holy shit. Lillian's heart rate spiked. The barriers that kept the underworld, Malastion, the pits of hell themselves, from Kalazaar. Unleashing who knows what kind of chaos and misery on the entire world. But it would also open up healing magic to other people, not just dwarves. A small kernel of relief flickered in her core. Maybe Harmony could switch, or Petrovana, or any number of others could now become healers. Healers that would be absolutely paramount in the coming battles should they bring down these walls. Was the risk of endangering the entire planet worth the reward of opening the use of healing magic to everyone? Nalecht was already making the surface world insufferable. This would give him an opportunity to get the shard of Kasherri from them, unleash whatever was in that moon, along with the underworld creatures. It was too much. Way too much to put on the citizens of Kalazaar to defend against. Panic coursed through her veins. Lillian didn't want to accept the truth of what they had to do down here, the truth of what all those statues knew they would have to do.

"Why not just let someone take the shard then? If it frees your minions or whatever dumb shit you want to call them? Why not let any one of the previous sacrifices just take the shard?" Lillian inquired.

Kasherri narrowed her gaze. "Because, like you insufferable mortals, I also have a dilemma. If I give the shard to someone, I also give your idiotic races the last piece they need to build the only weapon in the world that can kill me. And if that person isn't aligned with me and my goals, then... well, you should surely get the point by now."

"Bring Rinawen back. I'll be your Deathbinder," Leper offered.

"No!" Lillian shouted at him. "You will not do that."

Kasherri's eyes narrowed on Leper. "Will you now? And why, you horned freak, would I do that?"

Leper shrugged. "Maybe because I have the most powerful weapon at my call? Maybe because I can kill dragons? Or perhaps because I'd simply be the best damn Deathbinder you'll ever have."

Lillian couldn't believe her ears. Idiot. How could he be so blindly enraged that easily? He'd throw it all away to get her back. He wouldn't even be able to be with her; he'd be a Deathbinder, her enemy. He'd be a bigger, more uncontrollable monster than he already was. She had to get him off this path, off this constant drive to either get himself killed or trade his life for Rinawen's. How... how can I make him see it?

"You pose a tempting offer. But I cannot bring those from the dead back. Her spirit is not in Malastion, but in Blissoria, a place I cannot reach," Kasherri cupped her chin.

"Useless," Leper fumed as he swung Maka Kura at Kasherri.

Thank the gods.

Kasherri's form dissipated into nothing as her transparent visage wafted around his blade.

"Sometimes, Leper, you can be dumber than that tramp girl-friend of yers," Lillian gritted.

Chapter Eighteen

According to Maka Kura, two weeks had passed since they were knocked out by the poison, and they had already been down here for two weeks before that. In two more weeks, it would be an entire month. Thank the gods, Zanera and Kelindra had put fresh food in Leper's metal container, or they would have starved.

"There you go again, running that stupid mouth of yours!" Leper bellowed.

They needed to find the location of the shard. Leper looked Lillian up and down, her face beet red, veins bulging in her neck. Her lips opened, then closed. Always putting Petrovana down, constantly. It was annoying. Sure, Petrovana irritated him at times, too, but never enough to overlook her forgivable mistakes. If only Lillian took the time to realize how smart and fun Petrovana could be. He knew he wasn't perfect either, having made his fair share of stupid decisions, but Petrovana always forgave him. For whatever reason, she forgave him. Her compassion, charm, and whimsy more than made up for her mistakes, and her intellect was second to none—well, maybe Harmony's, but that wasn't the point.

Leper glanced around the room, where more books lay on the oval table and runes adorned the walls. He tried to refrain from saying anything else to make it worse. They were still trapped down here together, and he needed to find a way to calm himself. His mind slipped into the never-ending anxiety and anger. It didn't take long for him to remember, and subsequently question, why he was defending Petrovana in the first place when she would toss him aside to marry Madislak and be the queen...goodbye. And Blank Face. He frowned. His supposed brother. Murderer of Rinawen, killer of Larnadix, and someone who put Zanera and Kelindra in potentially more danger than any of them realized. There was nothing for him to swing at, nothing to take his boiling rage out on except...

"And to think, there was a time I couldn't decide between you and her. You make that decision easier every day!" he lied.

Lillian punched him right on the cheek. "How dare you! You fuckin' asshole." She spat on the ground. "The *only* reason yer with that bitch is because yer tryin' to cover up that black fuckin' hole in yer chest left by Rinawen! Always cryin' like a baby, 'poor me, poor me, Rinawen's gone.' Grow the fuck up. You ain't the only one in this world that's lost someone they love, you bitch." She stormed off down the tunnel. "And you can forget anythin' ever happenin' between us again, cuz I'm fuckin' tired of bein' the only one that's willin' to be vulnerable."

The sting of the punch jolted him out of his angry trance. *I deserved that.*

He felt an unexplained wave of affection wash over him towards her. She was the only one who stood up to him. Well, her and Madislak. The only one who wasn't completely afraid to say exactly what she thought, right to his face.

Perhaps it was her defiance, or her brutal honesty, that drew him to her. She often acted how he wanted to, but it just wasn't in his nature to be that blunt or aggressive.

"Keep walking away; it's what you do best!" Leper shouted down the hallway, immediately regretting it. *Why, why did I just say that?*

"Just wanted you to know, you are a stupid ass." Maka popped into his head.

Leper rolled his eyes. "You again. Why are you always slandering me?"

"It's not slander. It's truth."

"Who made you? If they're still alive, maybe I'll have them remove your voice," Leper gritted.

Maka's response was swift and caught Leper entirely off guard. "Samaja."

Leper braced his arms on the table to keep from falling over. "Samaja as in..."

"Yes."

Samaja, his father, made these remarkable weapons.

"How the hell did you know of him?" Leper's eyes bored a hole into the table.

"He made my voice—my personality—when he crafted me, so yeah, I kind of have to know him." Maka countered. His voice sounded arrogant.

"Bullshit," Leper muttered angrily. "You're this massive wealth of information, except for when I need you to have a wealth of information, you jackass. You knew nothing about the talisman. How can you be so damned smart and know everything and not actually know anything?"

"I'm a combined history of texts, consciousness, and recounted histories. He put as much knowledge in me as possible, but he couldn't jam every single detail of every single text into my consciousness," Maka countered quickly.

"I swear, if you're lying to me, I will leave you the fuck down here with all the shit smells," Leper threatened.

"The way you're acting lately is just like him. I can tell you're his son. But let's get the hell out of here," Maka responded gracefully. "And go find Lillian."

In a sense, Maka spoke the truth. He was angry, uncontrollable, and wanted to hurt anyone around him—physically or emotionally—when this fog entered his mind. The consequences didn't matter; he had to let out whatever he was feeling.

His mind churned with relentless angst over everything he had just remembered—Petrovana, Blank Face, Lillian. His eyes drifted over the cave markings, scanning without truly seeing.

Two hours passed as he combed through the scattered papers on the oval table. Then, finally, his gaze landed on a map—a network of caves. At its center stood a model pedestal, a scythe-shaped trinket resting atop it.

He let out a sigh of relief. The shard of Kasherri was marked on the map, hidden somewhere within the network of tunnels. At least he had a location. Now, he just had to find it.

"Can you direct me through this maze?" Leper asked Maka Kura.

"Only if you go find Lillian," Maka demanded, leaving no room for argument.

Leper glared at the weapons. "Fine."

"Wait, you were going to leave her down here?" Maka countered angrily.

Another sigh escaped Leper's lips. "Not exactly."

"Just take on Kasherri... Selfish dick." Maka went completely silent after that.

He checked the bag of vials real quick, thankful for its small size and the way it anchored to the belt on his right side. Zanera had left him a note.

Leper. It's almost been a month, and you're still down there? It's summer again. Are you ever getting out? We need you. Kordry is becoming a crime city. Larnadix opened a brothel here. He hit me. HIT ME! I snuck out on the roof and listened in on one of his meetings with Nalecht. King Madislak and Harmony were taken prisoner by Tamara and are now demanding the shard you're after for their release. They also said Blank Face and Petrovana tried to free them, and now Tamara might have the shard of Theora, but they were unsure. He also said that if they don't get the shard in the next week, Tamara will start cutting them to pieces and sending them to Blank Face and Petrovana until they have the shard. They need you! We need you. We are in trouble, and I don't know what to do.

Love, Zee.

Leper slammed the table in front of him multiple times. "Son of a bitch!" he yelled.

She wasn't just putting herself in danger—his so-called friends were turning their mission into an absolute shit show.

"Maka, no more bullshit. I need you to take me to that god-damned shard, and if we find Lillian along the way, we find her. But no more fucking games," he declared angrily.

Madislak lay on the grimy bench in his holding cell in Xaneth Harbor. Two weeks had gone by since their capture in Lantess, and any time now, depending on Tamara's mood, they would start cutting pieces off and sending them to Blank Face and Petrovana, urging them to get the last shard faster. Now wasn't the time to think about that. He'd spent a week in here already, discerning any possible weaknesses for escape. The only problem was he had no idea where they kept Harmony. Sure, maybe he could get out, but he wasn't leaving without her. To make matters worse, Tamara now had the shard of Theora, a shard they had promised Leper they would keep safe. A shard they had to get back at any cost.

He glanced down at his missing pinky and ring fingers. The bandaged nubs were still red, sore, and tingly as he wiggled them around. They called to hold the power of his sword, Skyrunner, and the new shield Leper had gifted him. But he didn't know where those were either.

He pushed down the pain that writhed in his fingers. Whatever he was going through paled in comparison to Harmony's torture. Gods. What were they doing to her now? How else were they going to mutilate that poor girl, his future queen? In the week since being here, screams had woken him during the night, but he could only hope they weren't hers. All he was sure of were these damned bars holding him back. Since Leper's angered departure, this had been nothing but pure hell. He hoped Leper might somehow have gotten the shard and was on his way to rescue them. He shook his head as he ran his hands over the sturdy metal bars, none of them loose. No one was coming for them.

Blank Face and Petrovana hadn't so much as made an appearance yet, and why would they? Tamara had the shard of Theora now. They had no leverage. Maybe losing the shard of Theora would be a good thing if Leper did show up. Maybe it'd piss him off enough to rip her head right off and take it back. No. Madislak jiggled the door. That's not how he should think. That was ruthless—like Tamara herself—and he was not Tamara. They should have acted sooner, he and Zonoh both.

Footsteps echoed down the hall. His prison cell, secluded and the only one in his section of this underground dungeon, had only one hallway and door leading out. The approaching guard wore the leather armor of Xaneth Harbor, the brown and yellow colors, and a metal helmet. Though he couldn't see his hair, he recognized the guard as one of the nicer ones who brought food. Most would throw it on the ground, watching as he tried to salvage what he could from the nasty, mildewy floor. This guy would actually hand it to him.

The scent of gruel permeated the cell as soon as he handed it through the horizontal slot on the door. Madislak had noticed something else—the way they treated this guard differently from the others, as if he weren't part of the cool group.

"What's your name?" Madislak asked, connecting with his large blue eyes.

The guard glanced around nervously. "We're not supposed to talk to the prisoners."

"I just have one question. Please," Madislak begged.

He scrutinized the guard's face, etching it into his memory. He was young, maybe late twenties or early thirties, like him. Blond stubble decorated his neck and cheeks.

"And that is?" the guard glared at Madislak.

"Is she okay? Did they hurt her more?" he pleaded.

The guard's eyes grew sad and drooped. "She's alive. They... broke some bones. She has more bruises, but nothing's been cut off yet."

Those had to be her screams then. Rage filled Madislak's chest. What kind of animals were these people? Tears rolled down his face at his utter helplessness. He slammed his fist on the bench so hard it nearly came apart.

"You're all animals," Madislak growled, his voice rough.

"I'm sorry, King Madislak." He placed a hand on the bars. "But I do know what you're going through. Tamara did this to my sister. The rest of my family left after she did, but Tamara cornered me. She and those stupid guards have kept me here ever since."

Madislak eyed the guard, sizing him up. Maybe he could use this to his advantage. He'd find a way out for himself one way or another, but if this guard could help him get Harmony out, that would make things a hell of a lot easier.

"Please. Get her out. Tell them it was me. Please. I'll take whatever the punishment is. You can come to Lantess; I'll make you a noble. Hell, I'll make you the proxy. I will protect you." Madislak fell to his knees.

"Even if I wanted to, she's too strong. Her army's too ruthless. She has the shards of Aisha and Theora, not to mention Nalecht and his four shards as well... I couldn't." His eyes fell to the floor.

"Just consider it, please. Blank Face and Petrovana would help you." Madislak grabbed the food and took a bite. Gross.

"Nethlen," the guard said as he turned to walk away.

"Thank you, Nethlen," Madislak called out.

Madislak didn't get another bite down before the door flew open, and Nylor and Tamara barged through. His heart plummeted to his stomach as he saw Nylor dragging Harmony by the leg along the rough stone floor, headed straight for their cell.

Madislak's cell doors flew open as Tamara and Nylor marched past Nethlen, Tamara commanding him to follow. Nylor tossed Harmony on the floor in front of him, then he flung Madislak against the bars, his massive hands making quick work of securing him. The cold metal bit into Madislak's wrists as he was cuffed to the bars, his heart hammering in his chest. What were they going to do? Were they going to hurt Harmony to make him talk? He didn't know anything more than they did, or worse, would they hurt her just to make him suffer? Blank Face had warned him about Tamara's cruelty.

Tamara kicked Harmony as she writhed on the floor, her face a bruised mess, a patch covering her missing left eye. Scars marred her arms and legs, her tattered clothes soaked in blood. They had used her as a punching bag, a brutalized girl who was meant to be his queen. Rage surged through Madislak, igniting a fire in his gut that spread to every nerve ending. He strained his muscles, pulling, yanking, and pushing on the bars, the veins in his arms bulging as he summoned every ounce of strength in him. The cuffs holding him in place dug into his wrists, but he pulled against them anyway. Ignoring Tamara's command to cease, the bars began to bend under his raw power. Even as his wrists bled from the strain and his arms ached, his chest ached more for Harmony. He would keep going until he could hold her and tell her everything would be alright.

Nylor clubbed him with a massive, rock-hard fist, the blow connecting with a loud crack on his cheek. Agony roared through Madislak's face—his jaw likely broken—but he didn't care. He continued his assault on the cage, determined to break the bars or the cuffs and beat the ever-living daylights out of both of them. Nylor punched him again, this time in the back of the head, and his vision went blurry as he stumbled against the cold bars. Nylor removed the cuffs, then grabbed a second pair from his waist and secured Madislak's hands apart from each other as far as they could go.

"Are you done?" Tamara taunted, her voice dripping with mockery. "With your little tantrum?"

"Why are you like this? What is wrong with you people? She's a twenty-three-year-old girl, soon to be queen. You cannot treat us like this!" Madislak bellowed.

Tamara let out a long sigh. "And you're an idiot. Law and order won't save you, Madislak. Law and order are dead. Fear, brutality, and discipline—that's how you lead."

Madislak didn't respond. His gaze was locked on Harmony, who was on her knees, supporting herself with her hands, not even trying to fight back. They had beaten the will right out of her, broken her spirit.

"Anyway," Tamara continued, "our normal means of aggressive interrogation don't seem to be working too well, so we're going to try a different tactic." She sauntered over to Harmony, yanking her head back by her blood-soaked hair. "I need to know what this talisman does. Other than providing power, but your stupid bitch won't tell me."

"She doesn't know! None of us do. That's a question for your stupid boyfriend, Nalecht," Madislak jerked on the cuffs, his voice laced with frustration.

Tamara's lips curled into an evil grin. "I think little Miss Precious here hasn't been entirely honest with you at all, mighty Madislak. Or perhaps I should call you *misled* Madislak."

Madislak scrutinized Harmony's face, but her eye showed too many emotions to discern what he was looking for: fear, disappointment, sadness, exhaustion—he couldn't figure out what she was going through.

"Why don't you go ahead and tell him one of your many mysteries, little Miss Princess?" Tamara barked, shoving Harmony's head forward.

Harmony didn't grunt, just took it.

"You're a princess?" Madislak asked. Harmony shook her head.

Tamara rolled her eyes. "No, you buffoon. She definitely isn't a princess. Or would you rather I tell him for you?" She flicked Harmony's hair. Tears fell from Harmony's right eye, but she said nothing.

A new anger rose within Madislak's chest. Had she been lying to him all this time, too? Was she just like his father? No, this was a tactic. She was trying to get something from them, but what? Was the talisman more than just power? He yearned for a moment alone with Harmony, just five minutes. There was no way Tamara had anything on them. No way.

Tamara used the pommel of her sword to hit Madislak in the chest. "Well!? I'm not going to wait forever for you to talk, bitch. Or should I get Thessek down here?"

Harmony recoiled and shook her head vigorously, whimpering. Searing pain rolled through Madislak's chest. She hit him right under the ribs, and it took him a minute to catch his breath.

Tamara yanked Harmony's head back by the hair again. "Let's start with your last name," she gritted her teeth. "Her last name is—"

"No!" Harmony's weak voice strained as she finally spoke.

"Her last name is Burtaugh." Madislak grinned. "She's already told me."

A look of regret washed over Harmony's face as she frowned and looked at the ground.

Tamara released her head again, flicking it forward. "No, it's not."

Madislak flicked his eyes to Tamara, then back to Harmony. "Your last name is Burtaugh, right?"

Harmony kept her head down, and Madislak knew immediately she had lied to him. Why would she lie about her last name? It didn't matter; he still loved her. The pain in his chest was sharp, but he knew he would ask her about it someday. Right now, he loved her regardless.

Madislak narrowed his gaze on Tamara. "It doesn't matter. I love her all the same."

Harmony peered up at Madislak, forcing a smile.

"How noble, how utterly heroic. Yet how completely disgusting. Go ahead, Harmony, why don't you tell him about the Deathbinders and the talisman? See if he can figure it out for himself," Tamara taunted.

Harmony could barely hold herself up. Her arms wobbled, and her legs shook as she tried to stay propped up. Nylor shot forward, grabbed Madislak's finger, and broke it sideways. Madislak hollered in agony as white-hot pain rippled through his hand and up his arm.

"Tell him, bitch!" Nylor growled.

Nethlen shifted uncomfortably. Then Tamara kicked Harmony on the shoulder, and she fell to the ground, groaning.

Tamara sneered. "Stubborn bitch, aren't you? The Deathbinders are Kasherri's force to get the shards and keep them separate because they're scared of the talisman for some reason. However, they are not all born yet—the Deathbinders, that is. I know how dull you can be. That's why the shard of Kasherri hasn't been claimed yet. The bitch goddess won't give it away until all her elite are born."

"How are they born?" Madislak asked through gritted teeth.

Tamara grinned. "They accept the role as a mortal, and when the mortal body dies, they turn into black smoke and flutter off to Malastion, where they take their true shape and gain their true power."

Madislak's mind whirled in a chaotic mix. Did she tell her about Larnadix? They thought he was one but weren't sure. But he shouldn't even be on the surface, on the material plane. Who else could be a Deathbinder? No.

"Borlden," Madislak mouthed. "Borlden and who else?"

Tamara kicked Harmony down again just as she managed to prop herself back up. "The Former, The Latter. When they die, they will become one. There's already one running around. That means she still needs three more. And wouldn't you know who agreed to be one of them?" Tamara's gaze fell on Harmony.

"No," Madislak whispered.

He searched Harmony's face for anything—any sign she hadn't made that deal. But she just lay there, looking up at him, then broke into a sob. She was going to be a Deathbinder. She didn't have a last name. She was going to be an agent of the devil Goddess Kasherri herself. What in Amarook's gods-forsaken name had he gotten himself into with her?

The sting of betrayal rocked him to his core, completely forgetting about the throbbing finger angled to the side on his hand. How? How could she do something like that and keep it from me? Am I just some kind of stepping-stone for all these games? A puppet for everyone to manipulate? Not anymore.

"Why?" he mouthed in a whisper. "Why would you do that?"

Finally, she lifted her head. "Mad... I... I wasn't supposed to... love you."

"You weren't supposed to..." Madislak trailed off, looking down at the floor, then snapped his head back to Harmony. "You weren't supposed to love me? What the fuck does that mean?"

Rage burned deep within him, his heart cracking. The rolling beat of his heart echoed in his temples. She wasn't supposed to love him? What exactly was her plan? Was she going to... No, she couldn't—wouldn't. She was too nice a person. She wouldn't use him to get close just to take the shards or talisman once they had them. She'd had her chance.

"The wheels are turning, I see," Tamara cackled in front of Madislak. "Let me answer that burning question for you, Madislak. Yes. The only reason she wanted to be with you was simply to remain close, just to pluck that talisman from you if you got it."

"Get her out of my sight," Madislak barked.

"Mad... N... No," Harmony whimpered, sobbed.

Tamara huffed a laugh. "I'll make you a deal, King Madislak. She found the talisman's true purpose in her research but refuses to cough it up. I'll let you go, free and clear. Return to Lantess, take Thessek with you, and give him whatever books she was studying. But she stays here. I'll even start by healing your broken finger right now."

Tamara put his finger back in place. It should've hurt a lot more than it did, but he was numb to the pain. Then she handed him a healing vial. Madislak mulled it over, tired of being manipulated, tired of being used as everyone's pawn for their twisted endgames. Thank the gods they never got married. No wonder she had pushed so hard in recent months. Bitch. Lying, scandalous bitch. No more. No more ruling with kindness, no more being a pushover, no more trusting anyone. Perhaps Leper and Blank Face had figured it out sooner. Trust no one—not your father, not anyone, not even your own damned fiancée.

"Deal," he mouthed, pinning Harmony with a glare of hatred.

Her face mirrored his hurt, the betrayal, and regret he was feeling. The shame. Good.

"I... I'm sorry," she pleaded as Nylor dragged her beside him out of the cell.

"What's her last name?" Madislak asked Tamara.

"I'll let you figure that out, or come back and let her tell you herself. I want to see the look on your face. And if you think about it hard enough, Madislak, even you could figure it out," Tamara grinned, sauntering out of the cell.

"Wait," Madislak called after her.

She spun, fixing him with an unimpressed glare.

"If I bring the shard of Kasherri, will you overthrow Nalecht and make me an Anyth?" He fixed her with a death glare.

A fire sparked in her eyes. "Well, holy shit, King Madislak, I didn't think you had it in you." She pursed her lips. "Absolutely."

Perfect. He hadn't planned on doing that at all, but at least he now knew for certain that even though Nalecht and Tamara were allies, he could find a way to pit them against each other. Nethlen started unlocking his cuffs. He rubbed his wrists and gingerly touched his fixed finger, a fresh wave of pain rippling through him.

Madislak had barely risen to his feet when he locked eyes with Nethlen, his gaze completely cold, entirely dead. Then he noticed Blank Face's hood coming into view behind him.

Chapter Nineteen

Petrovana barged through the door into the hallway where Madislak's cell was located, immediately noticing that Blank Face had already incapacitated the guard inside. Step one. She swiftly extended her hand, holding Nylor and Tamara in place with her spell. She knew it wouldn't last long—she was still learning how to use it—they had to act fast. Tamara's eyes blazed with rage, her tanned face turning shades of red.

"Surprise," Petrovana taunted as she maintained the spell.

Intiva rushed past her in the wide stone hallway, grabbing ropes and swiftly binding Tamara's arms and legs. Blank Face blinked at Nylor and began the same process.

Madislak strode over to Harmony, grabbed her roughly by her clothes, and, instead of assisting her, tossed her into the cell and slammed the door shut.

"What the fuck, Madislak?" Blank Face growled, momentarily halting.

"She's not who we thought she was. She knows something about the talisman that she didn't disclose, and she's bound to become a Deathbinder, loyal to Kasherri, when she dies," Madislak seethed. "So, she stays here."

"She wouldn't do that. Get her out of that cell right now; I can't hold them for much longer," Petrovana retorted.

Madislak's eyes locked with Petrovana's, and she saw the sting of betrayal, shame, and disgust in his gaze. The pain, the anguish—it mirrored the look Leper had given her before flying off to Costin in a huff, right after she had considered marrying Madislak.

"No," he said, his voice low, leaving no room for argument.

Pain erupted in Petrovana's head, a piercing stabbing pain, very intense. It thudded at the front of her skull, forcing her to lose focus. She grabbed her forehead and dropped to her knees. It was like the agonizing pain that made her arm go limp in the forest. *Am I getting a tattoo on my forehead now?*

Her vision blurred as Petrovana opened her eyes. The cobblestone walkway was strewn with dirt and clutter, as if it hadn't been cleaned in ages, much like the rest of the place. In Harmony's cell, the bars were bent, and the floor bore blood stains, the bench covered in moss and mildew. The torches burning cast a smoky scent, a welcome relief from the stench of garbage and decay outside.

Tamara and Nylor were free of the magical bonds, though Tamara remained restrained thanks to Intiva's quick skills. Nylor ripped himself free of Blank Face's binds and lunged to choke him, but Blank Face vanished. Intiva rushed to Blank Face's aid, sprinting towards Nylor, vaulting off the wall, and anchoring herself to his back by jabbing her dagger into his massive shoulder. She pulled herself up, trying to wrap her arms around his neck to choke him out.

Nylor reached over his head, grabbing her hooded cloak and flinging her over his shoulder like a sack of feathers. She landed on her feet and dodged his incoming grasp, evading the first two swipes before he caught her on the third attempt. His massive hands closed around her neck, squeezing tight. But Blank Face reappeared instantly, ramming daggers into each of Nylor's vein-covered forearms. Nylor released his grip, and Intiva gracefully landed back on her feet. *Damn, she wasn't going to die today.*

She moved with the lethal grace of Blank Face, fatal finesse guiding their deadly dance as they circled Nylor. Their gazes locked on the target, focused and unyielding.

Madislak seized Tamara's restraints and dragged her up the hallway towards the ongoing fight.

"Enough!" he bellowed.

Blank Face scoffed, continuing to circle Nylor with Intiva at his side, their guard unwavering. "I'll back off when we're out of here," he shot back, refusing to yield to Madislak's command.

The torchlight flickered down the hallway lined with brown and yellow banners as Petrovana stumbled to get back to her feet, using the wall as a brace to hold herself up.

"I command you to stand down now." Madislak pointed a demanding finger at Blank Face.

Blank Face rolled his neck. "I am not your subject. You are not my king. I came down here to get you both out, so unless you plan on unlocking that door and leaving with Harmony, then you can fuck right off."

Petrovana wobbled over, pushing past Intiva. "What are you doin', Madislak? We risked everythin' to free you both. Let's get Harmony and get out of here."

Madislak glanced at Petrovana. "I am already free to go. They were just letting me out, then you three screwed it up."

Tamara let out a cackle. "Trouble in paradise already, King Madislak? And aren't you two supposed to be in Costin?"

"Fuck you," Blank Face gritted through clenched teeth.

Madislak's jaw ticked. "We are people. We are fighting a battle against the Anyth. Surely, we can find a way to work together."

"What?" Petrovana's mouth hung open.

Surely he wasn't suggesting they work with Tamara, ally with this ruthless woman. Her pulse quickened, and anger swelled within her chest. There was no way they were aligning themselves with her—her city was in shambles, with no reasonable law and order, as evidenced by their trip through it. She gave a sidelong glance at Blank Face. Tamara had caused the scars that marred his face and tortured him when he was a child. Then she turned to Harmony, bruised and broken, lying on the floor. Perhaps imprisonment had taken its toll on Madislak's mental capacity. Or maybe, she pondered, maybe this was some kind of ruse to get them all out and then never come back. She tried to glean some insight as she turned her head back to Madislak.

But there was nothing there except hollow eyes, hollow angry eyes.

"Well, well, well. Look at you, King Madislak." Tamara grinned. "Nylor, stand down. Let's see what Madislak has in mind. I'm not against being civil."

"Like hell," Blank Face spat, getting right up in Madislak's face. "I will not work with or for her. I will not do a damn thing you say to help her." He pointed at Tamara. "The only thing I came here for was to get you two out of captivity. So unlock that cage, and we will be on our way. I'll have no part in this. Whatever this is."

Petrovana saw the white knuckles on Blank Face's hands gripping his dagger. If she didn't know any better, she'd say he was beyond pissed. It threatened to unravel everything—again. Madislak was on thin ice with both of them, risking the loss of two valuable allies. She didn't care much for Intiva, whichever side she fell on, but it seemed she would side with Blank Face. If Petrovana had the money she sought, she would give it to Intiva now just to be rid of her. Crazy witch.

Madislak's face remained unreadable. "She's been hiding things from us. She stays caged, at least until we decide how to move forward. But I need to know everything before we make any decisions."

Blank Face glanced at the cage behind Madislak, then pinned him with a cold, calculating gaze that sent a shudder down Petrovana's spine. "You don't speak for me, brother."

Tamara's face twisted in shock, but she quickly composed herself. "Well, looks like we could all learn some things from each other. Let's have this conversation in a more comfortable setting."

Petrovana struggled to distance herself from the agony roaring in her head, grappling with the shocking revelation of what had just transpired. Of all the warnings about Tamara and Nalecht, forming an alliance with them was the last thing Petrovana expected from Madislak. Even if Harmony was destined to become a Deathbinder, what difference did it make? She had served Madislak faithfully for four years, or so he had told her. Perhaps Harmony had no choice but to agree to being a Deathbinder. Despite everything, she had remained loyal to them this long.

Rather than blindly accepting Tamara's accusations, they should have freed Harmony and held this discussion in private. Alienating the poor girl seemed unjustified. Yet here they were, navigating a maze of snakes, apparently.

Oddly enough, the only one of the group she felt she could trust was likely the last person anyone would trust: an assassin. Of all people, Blank Face seemed to be the only sane one. She chuckled inwardly at the thought; he murdered people for a living. But as she came to know him more, it was out of a need for survival, not a mere desire to kill people for the sake of doing so. Not like The Latter, who did it for the fame and recognition. Her mind raced as they conceded for now, agreeing to meet in a more civil manner, but Petrovana didn't trust it.

She didn't trust Madislak right now, nor did she trust Intiva or Tamara. But for the sake of Harmony's safety and well-being, she would at least hear them out.

They refused Tamara's offer for a place to stay and instead chose one of Blank Face's old dwellings from his time in the city.

Intiva had apparently kept the place serviceable—surprisingly clean compared to the rest of the town. It was a rare quality Petrovana could actually respect from the untrustworthy assassin.

What manner of betrayal awaited them there? Petrovana, Blank Face, and Intiva vowed to take turns visiting Harmony's cell, ensuring no harm befell her until they could secure her release and return to safety.

Gods, Madislak. What are you doing? We're all going to end up dead in Xaneth Harbor.

Lillian stomped through the tunnel, leaving Leper in the room to wallow in self-pity. *Asshole.* She was sick and tired of babysitting a twenty-four-year-old grown man. If he wanted to wander this place to his death? *Fine. Go kill yourself. You'll be with your precious Rinawen, you selfish jackass. I'd pick her over you.*

The darkness within her rose to an uncontrollable level, something she hadn't experienced in years. Many, many years. He could still get under her skin in a way she couldn't explain. Lillian closed her eyes, picturing him, the old him, smiling, joking, his large hazel eyes glinting, the beard that was now scraggly. That glint. The bubbling darkness vanished in an instant.

If only she could find a way to get him to see his anchor—that person or thing so dear it kept the flickering rage and darkness at bay. A way for him to control this rage on his own before he lost himself completely to it. He was bad enough now; she could only imagine what he'd be like if he lost total control.

Unfortunately, she thought Rinawen was his anchor. He didn't become explosive when she was alive. But that didn't matter now. She was gone. Now what? Lillian sat with her back against the wall, resting her head on her knees. *You make my decision easier every day.* His face, when he said it, replayed in her head endlessly. Tears started to fall, and she wiped them away immediately. She didn't cry—not for him, not for anyone. But she couldn't stop them.

She was alone again. She'd never have anyone she could truly rely on. Someone to have her back and fully believe they would be there for her. He was far too broken for that—impossible, stubborn ass. The only person she'd ever had like that was her dad, and she got him killed. *Maybe no one likes me because I'm too confrontational? Too rough around the edges?* She shook her head as she listened to the light humming coming from the darkened tunnel in front of her. The cold, damp smell of mold filled the air. It didn't matter how hard she tried; he continually pushed her away. Why? Was she that repulsive, that ugly? That brazen?

Perhaps she shouldn't have said what she did about him and Petrovana. He was clearly angry enough about their situation and Rinawen's death; she only added to his angst. The quartz flickered, casting shadows around the dim, rocky tunnels. At least there was still some live vegetation on the walls and not just solid, ugly rock. If they ever got out of here, she'd never visit another cave or mountain again.

Footsteps... *ugh.*

She didn't want to look at his stupid face right now, the person who caused her so much misery at times, but the person she was hopelessly in love with. Such a gentle, considerate, muscled giant. Then a total prick. Not to mention a dumbass. He chose that tramp over her in the first place.

"I know where the shard of Kasherri is. Let's get it and get the hell out of here," Leper said flatly as he walked by.

No apology... Okay.

"You should really try to control yourself a little better." Lillian reached for his wrist, but he yanked it away.

He shook his arm as if shaking her off entirely. "I don't need you to tell me what to do. I'm fine."

"Sometimes I don't even know why I bother," she huffed. "Yer father acted the same damn way. Yer gonna be just like him, you know?"

Leper stopped dead in his tracks. "You're the second person to say that to me. Maybe people like you and your father should stop being assholes to people like me."

"Like you and yer father, you mean?"

"No. He was an asshole—like you." Leper turned and started walking again.

This is getting way out of hand.

"Look, Lep, I just wanna help you, is all," she said, softer this time. She wasn't sure who else had told him he acted like his dad, but she wasn't about to ask. Not now. "Yer father lost himself, and I don't want the same thing to happen to you."

Leper spun on her, eyes sharp. "What do you mean, lost himself?"

She sighed. "He went past the point of no return. Did too much blood magic, stayed in this constant state of anger and hatred until he couldn't turn back into a regular person." She lowered her head. "My father, Oubank, was supposed to keep him from doin' that, but somethin' changed when Samaja started usin' blood magic."

"I'll never be like him," Leper roared. "I will never be like that rapist piece of shit who abandons his own children."

Lillian shoved his shoulder. "You sure got u funny way of not bein' like him."

Leper barely reacted to the shove. His nostrils flared, his fists clenched at his sides, but he didn't lash out. Not physically, anyway.

"I am nothing like him," he growled. "I don't abandon the people I care about."

Lillian let out a bitter laugh. "No? What do ya call pushin' everyone away, then? Huh? What do ya call tellin' me, Madislak, Petrovana that we don't matter? Sounds an awful lot like abandonment to me."

His jaw tightened. "I'm keeping them safe—keeping you safe—the only way I know how."

"By bein' a damn monster?"

"If that's what it takes." He turned sharply, stalking down the tunnel. "I don't need your help, Lillian. I don't need saving."

Lillian sighed, rubbing a hand down her face before following. "Everybody needs savin' sometimes, dumbass."

He didn't respond, didn't even slow down. Her chest heaved. She was losing him. Maybe she already had.

The tunnel stretched ahead, twisting and narrowing, the damp air growing colder. The flickering quartz light barely illuminated their path, and Lillian could feel the weight of the mountain above them, suffocating.

She swallowed hard and tried again. "Look, I get it. Yer mad. You got every right to be. But you ain't thinkin' straight."

Leper let out a low, humorless chuckle. "And what exactly do you think I should do, Lillian? Bury it? Pretend like everything's fine?"

"No. But you don't gotta let it eat you alive neither."

He stopped so suddenly she almost ran into him. He turned, and for a split second, she thought she saw something raw in his eyes—pain, exhaustion, something deeper than rage. But it was gone just as fast, swallowed up by the familiar fury.

"I don't have time for this," he said, his voice colder than before. "The shard is close. That's the only thing that matters right now."

Lillian exhaled sharply. He wasn't listening. Maybe he never would.

She glanced at the tunnel ahead, then back at him. "Fine. Let's just get this over with."

Neither of them spoke as they pushed forward, their footsteps echoing through the cavern. The shard of Kasherri awaited. And so did whatever hell lay ahead.

Leper plodded along in silence, brushing against flowers and weeds sprouting from the tunnels without a care. Maka Kura navigated the maze of tunnels for him, his focus locked on the shard of Kasherri, his only concern. His mind swirled with anxiety, darkness, and rage. Lillian's feelings, Petrovana's, anyone's—they didn't matter right now. He cared about getting the shard, escaping this hellhole, and leveling Larnadix for touching Zanera. To make matters worse, his idiot companions lost Rin's shard and got the King and Harmony captured.

Apparently, he'd have to do everything himself. They'd been down here for nearly a month! He was tired of the decay smell and other pungent odors. Sick of the taste of bread, cheese, and meat sticks. He continued to barge through the maze at break-neck pace, paying attention only to Maka's directions. Lillian lagged several feet behind him.

"You better slow yer ass down, yer goin' to spring a trap or get us killed," she barked.

"We'll be fine," he replied, not slowing.

Lillian let out a sigh. "*Gods*, yer exhaustin'. Stop, gods-damnit!"

Leper halted and turned on his heel. "What!?"

"We've been on a warpath for hours. You can't ignore the implications if we get this shard," she spat.

Leper pointed at his chest with his thumb. "What happens when I get this shard is I'm freeing Madislak and Harmony, then getting Zanera and Kelindra to safety. Then I will reclaim the shard of Theora, kill Nalecht, and put an end to this bull-shit."

Lillian's eyes widened. "Madislak and Harmony are captured? Nalecht got the other shard?"

Leper nodded. "Yes. Zanera said in a letter. She also said Larnadix hit her, and Kordry is falling apart. So, to answer your question about the implications, the only thing I care about is them. They kept us both alive."

Lillian palmed her forehead. "That's not what I fuckin' mean. Kasherri said if we take the shard, it breaks the barrier to the underworld. Don't ya think that's kind of a problem too?"

Leper jabbed a finger at her. "What exactly are we going to do, Lillian!? Just die down here and say screw the world? I'd rather get the shard and deal with the consequences later."

"So, yer totally fine with unleashin' the demonic and dark forces of Malastion on the world? Fer them to deal with at the same time? Or are ya forgettin' the Deathbinders are part of that too? They will be unleashed as well."

Leper threw his hands up. "I don't know! Who's to say that Xartazza, whoever the fuck that is, doesn't come down here and get the damned shard after we die anyway? They could come down here and get it for Nalecht and break the damn barriers anyway."

Lillian's fists clenched at her sides. "Damn it, Lep. It feels like we're rushin' into this without considerin' the risks. At least if we don't do anythin', we won't die alone. We have each other. We look fer another way out!"

"There is no other way out. The blood oath we took to get in ensures that, Lillian. We may be underground on Kalazaar, but we're not in Kalazaar. We're in a sealed section of this world and not of this world. Do you understand?" Leper snarled. "What I do know for certain is chaos is erupting on the surface. Zanera and Kelindra are in trouble. I may have failed Rinawen, but I will not..." He enunciated each word. "WILL NOT fail her daughters." Leper turned and started walking again.

"Even if it means puttin' them in more danger?" She followed. "Even if it means they might have a few more years of peace before someone else tries to get this shard? Nobody even knows where Xartazza is. Them magically findin' him at a moment's notice seems far-fetched, you jackass."

"I swear, if you weren't a woman, I'd punch you right now." Leper slammed his hand against the rock wall. "I don't give a shit about anyone that isn't Zanera and Kelindra. Do you understand that? I don't care about you. I don't care about

Madislak. I don't care about Petrovana. The only things that matter are myself and their safety."

"Wow. Real surprising, Leper." She jabbed him in the ribs. "Go ahead, hit me. I fuckin' dare you."

She clenched her fists as she walked beside him, goading him to swing.

Leper didn't have time to respond. As he took his next step, the rock floor sank—a trap. A spear came hurtling down the tunnel. Instinct took over. He turned, grabbed Lillian, and yanked her out of harm's way.

They hit the ground hard, tumbling together. Her warmth pressed against him, her body against his. That familiar comfort surfaced again, almost enough to push the anger away. Almost.

When they came to a stop, Lillian landed on top of him. Their eyes met, and she searched his face, her gaze flicking back and forth as if diving into his soul, reaching for some part of him.

"Are you alright?" he asked, his voice softer now.

She nodded.

"Let's keep moving. Every second we stand still is another second I can't get back." He helped her to her feet.

His body was fatigued from not eating well while they were down here, and sore. Every ounce of him wanted nothing more than to wash the weeks' worth of grime off himself and sleep for a week, maybe a month. Maybe more. And shave. The constant struggle in his mind added to the raging anxiety and fog in his brain that he couldn't get rid of. He wanted to push it away, but didn't know how, torn between his feelings for Petrovana and the beauty with him now.

This witty, fiery, take-no-prisoners, amazing person was with him. The only one who would stand up to him face-to-face and not tiptoe around him. The same person he took for granted. She didn't have to come in here with him, but she did it—for him. The swirling anxiety slowly backed down and vanished.

"How do you do it?" He stopped, tapping his temple. "How do you keep the darkness at bay so well?"

Lillian glanced at the ground, then back at him. "You find an anchor, someone or something that clears the fog. Something so beautiful, so wholesome, it overpowers the negativity and the anger."

"And what's your anchor?" he asked bluntly.

She scowled. "At first, it was my father... then Petrovana. Now..." She flicked her eyes to him.

I'm an asshole.

"This whole time?" he gasped.

"Since we... You know, in the mountain."

It was him. Her anchor was him. *Is she mine, then? Is that the feeling?*

They resumed walking, slower and more carefully—carefully picking his path through the brush and weeds that sprang out from the wall. If something looked uncertain, he would gingerly step around the area before proceeding.

Regret washed over his entire body. He shuddered. *Gods,* he had been such a jerk from the moment they reconnected. This whole time, he never realized that every time he slipped into his anger-filled darkness, it was she who pulled him out. She who broke that trance, yet he blamed her constantly for it and ridiculed her endlessly. A total idiot.

Leper turned as Maka instructed him, and there it sat on a pedestal, the scythe-shaped shard of Kasherri. Right in front of... Rinawen?

Chapter Twenty

Leper's knees buckled as he stumbled forward. Lillian quickly stabilized him. He could see the scythe-shaped trinket on the pedestal as Rinawen walked in front of it. She was just as beautiful as she had been in life. Her golden hair hung straight, resting gracefully midway down her back. Her twinkling green eyes still emanated their familiar sparkle. She wore a green V-neck shirt with leaf and vine patterns and brown pants that fit her curves perfectly, just as he remembered.

The large room around them spanned hundreds of feet, and all the exits, as seemed typical in this place, slammed shut once they entered. Two large, jagged rock columns were evenly placed in the room, shaped and formed like some kind of battle arena. The quartz on the extremely high ceiling glowed brighter here, providing more light than any other part of their journey down. What caught his attention the most was the scent. Lilacs. His lips curled upward. How he missed that scent, her scent.

"Rin..." He reached his hand towards her.

She backed away. "Lep. I don't have long in this place. I'm here by the grace of Theora and her alone. The other gods are angry with Kasherri; she is interfering with the mortal world, so they've allowed me a small amount of time to be here, physically and mentally."

"So, you're back for now? Or just in this moment?" Leper tilted his head to the side.

"No, I'm not back for long, only briefly, Leper, to help you and the others." She motioned her hand towards the shard. "The talisman, the shards—all of it—is far more powerful than any of the gods intended it to be. So some of them have allowed our souls to guide the ones we love, but only briefly; I can't linger. And if that moon gets unlocked, none of the other gods can return. You can't fail. So they've allowed several of our souls to pass back through, briefly, to help those that need it most."

"Then trade places with me. You deserve your life. I've been pathetic. Useless... A failure to everyone." He glanced toward Lillian.

Rinawen's smile was radiant. "Lep, you're young and never experienced anything this world has to offer, including its cruelties. I sheltered you from that. I didn't prepare you, and now you're experiencing it all at once." A tear slid down her cheek. "And I'm not there to guide you."

Leper couldn't hold himself back. He ran to her and threw his arms around her neck. "I'm so sorry, Rin. I'm so, so sorry. It's all my fault."

"How is it your fault?" She wrapped her arms around him.

"If I went with you when you asked me to. If I... if I ran for that vial instead of arguing with Blank Face, I would've saved you. If..." He couldn't hold back the burst of tears.

"Lep, stop it. Stop blaming yourself right now," she demanded, wiping his face. "I knew when I first saw you and Blank Face in that boat that you two would be the ones to change this world. Forever. What I didn't know was the amazing people your magnetism would pull together to help you." She glanced at Lillian with a smile.

"I wanted you to be a part of that world, Rin! It means nothing without you in it." He put his hand on the side of her soft neck.

"I know it's difficult, Lep. It's hard for me too. Zanera and Kelindra will grow up motherless—and now, fatherless. They are in trouble, and you're the only one they can trust enough to help. Your friends are in trouble, and they need you. The world needs you. It needs you and Lillian, and Blank Face, and even

Ace to lead the fight against the evil that spreads and to put a rest to the old biases against the Chernzerk." Rinawen cupped his hand that rested on her neck.

Her hands were so soft. He moved his hands up to her beautiful face, taking it in, etching it into his memory. Just in case this was the last time he would ever see her.

He felt her warmth, smelled the lilacs. "I'll never forget you, Rinawen. I'll never stop missing you, stop loving you."

She smiled back at him, bringing the most serene, comforting feeling across his chest.

"Our love was before its time. I will love you forever. Cherish those memories, those times we spent together. The times we had when Zanera was little, and when Kelindra joined us. Those were good times. Don't let those moments be a source of anger and despair, for when you do, the enemy wins." She pressed her soft lips against his.

"Do you remember that walk on the beach? When you put your arm around me? The first time we kissed?"

Leper nodded as a couple more tears fell down his face. How could he forget?

"That will always be my most cherished memory of ours. In that moment, I couldn't have been any happier." She smiled.

Rinawen's visage fluttered as Kasherri began to take form behind the shard.

"What should I do, Rin? You know what happens if I take the shard. What happens if I don't?" Leper grabbed her hands.

Rinawen shrugged. "I wouldn't trust anyone else to keep my girls safe more than you." A wide grin spread across her face as she winked at him, then nodded toward Lillian. "You and she are part of the original four Chernzerk—born to destroy the talisman and rebuild this world."

What!?

His mind spun with questions. The original four Chernzerk? Did Rinawen know about them before they were even born? Had she always known he'd have to deal with this mess—the shards, the talisman, all of it?

He didn't have time to contemplate it all. Rinawen faded away.

Kasherri's echoing cackle bounced off the jagged rock walls, which no longer had vegetation growing on them. The scent of lilacs was replaced with a damp, pungent odor. Leper gave Lillian a sidelong glance and, with a smirk, walked straight toward the goddess of the underworld.

"Alright, you ugly bitch." He unsheathed Maka Kura. "I don't give a damn that you're an all-powerful god. I am taking that shard and I am saving my friends."

Kasherri flashed her wicked teeth as black ooze dripped from her mouth. "You can certainly try," she hissed.

Petrovana's thoughts raced as she prepared herself for anything to happen. She made sure to rest and not expend any magical energy during the time Tamara allowed them to clean up and compose themselves before they were to gather in a room together. Petrovana wasted no time. Blank Face stayed in Petrovana's room with her, while Intiva occupied the room beside them, though Intiva spent most of her time here. Luckily, it was her turn to wait by Harmony's cell, and so far, Tamara had kept her word about not harming her anymore. Blank Face did anything but relax, pacing back and forth constantly, cursing Madislak and vowing to rescue Harmony and escape, which Intiva naturally seconded. Petrovana wanted the same thing but also saw an opportunity to gather information from Tamara about Nalecht, the shards, and the talisman—as long as she could focus through the pounding headache. She didn't agree with this situation, but if they were required to be in Tamara's presence, they might as well gain some useful information.

Ever since she used that binding spell in the hallway, the consistent agony in her head wasn't severe enough to bring her to her knees, but it was there—ever-present. It mirrored the pain she experienced when the new tattoos formed on her arms.

The safe house they stayed in was surprisingly tidy, thanks to Intiva's upkeep. She would never dare say it out loud to the little witch, but she definitely appreciated not feeling like she might catch some kind of disease—or a flesh-eating parasite—from simply sitting down.

The morning sun finally broke through two days after their attempt, but those two days had felt more like two years.

Petrovana dressed in leather, the full rush of her magic surging through her. She didn't bother sheathing any daggers—she didn't need to. Confidence burned in her veins, stronger than ever. She hadn't yet mastered psyrenth magic, but she improved with it every day. Even without it, she had fire, ice, and healing magic at her command, well-practiced and deadly when needed.

Tamara, wielding the shard of Aisha and Theora, posed a real threat, but beyond her, Petrovana hadn't seen any other shrews in this town. As far as she could tell, Tamara had no shrews working under her employ.

She made sure to wear well-fitting leather, something that hugged her curves tightly and perfectly. Something that would typically catch a man's attention or make them gawk, just in case she needed to be a distraction. Today was the day they'd meet with her and Madislak—the king they had only seen once since the attempted rescue. Even then, he seemed very distant, as if he'd changed dramatically. Perhaps it was the prolonged capture or the fact that he was missing two of his fingers. Maybe the sheer brutality of it all had altered his entire demeanor. Or perhaps it was the fact that Harmony—the shrew who had stood by his side for four years, the woman who was supposed to be his wife—had knowingly kept the truth about the talisman from him. Or the fact that she had agreed to become one of Kasherri's Deathbinders.

Blank Face paced alongside her as they walked through the nobles' district. This area was slightly more stable than the rest of the city, with moderately nice houses and buildings. However, many of the houses had guards at the doors, resembling a crime-lord city ruled by gangs.

Her heartbeat raced at the sight of the gangly men and women standing in front of the houses, hoping they wouldn't attack for no reason. She didn't dare make eye contact with the mercenaries who glanced their way. They were still in enemy territory, and much hinged on whatever they were about to discuss. Harmony remained locked in a cell. Petrovana wasn't sure what to make of the whole situation.

Harmony becoming a Deathbinder and keeping secrets from them had driven a thorn into what had once been an unshaken bond. Had she been working for the enemy all along? If so, why hadn't she taken the shard of Theora when she had the chance?

The questions circled in Petrovana's mind, but no answers came. With a frustrated shake of her head, she pushed the thoughts away.

She needed to maintain her mental acuity. Petrovana glanced around, noticing Intiva hadn't joined them.

She gave a sidelong glance at Blank Face. "Where's Intiva?"

"She is not of royal bloodline or caught up in this mess. She did her part," Blank Face replied in a monotone voice.

"So she's gone? Just like that?" Petrovana made a vanishing motion with her hand.

Blank Face nodded.

Apparently, he didn't want to elaborate. Thirty more minutes passed before they reached Tamara's manor. It was clearly the nicest building in this dump of a city, though it still lacked regal splendor. If Petrovana ever discovered her lineage and became the queen of Terynsipple, her castle would be nothing short of glorious—nothing like this. She imagined large gardens, trees, and shrubbery with bundles of decorations, fine cutlery, colored drapes, furniture, statues, vases, and pictures inside. She'd have it all, including her family tree, if she found one. But her mind momentarily drifted back to Leper as they plodded along—nope, later.

The inside of Tamara's manor wasn't any better than the outside. It lacked everything she had just envisioned. The walls were bare, painted in that ugly brown and yellow. Dust and trash littered many of the hallways, with not a single picture or scent of a flower. Instead, it smelled like dust and dirt. She cringed.

Finally, they reached the conference room, where she locked eyes with Madislak. Tamara and Nylor sat eerily quiet at a large round marble table—the nicest thing in this city—with a jug of water, glasses, and biscuits with butter or jam placed at the center.

Petrovana had already decided not to eat or drink anything they offered. If Blank Face didn't trust it, neither did she. He specifically warned her not to touch or ingest anything.

"Thanks for showing up," Tamara quipped with her snide attitude. "Let's get this negotiation underway, shall we?" She gestured towards the empty seats.

Petrovana took a seat. "What will it take to get Harmony free?"

Madislak held up a hand. "No. Let me tell you about our dear friend Harmony before we start down that path."

So, he did. Petrovana listened intently as he explained she would become a Deathbinder when she died, binding her servitude to Kasherri. He claimed she held secret knowledge about the talisman, refusing to reveal it, even to him. He also mentioned that besides her, The Former, The Latter, and Larnadix were Deathbinders, and when their human forms died, they dissipated into black smoke.

Petrovana narrowed her gaze. "You mean like Borlden?"

Madislak nodded. "Exactly like Borlden."

He stiffened, eyes locking on Petrovana before turning to Tamara. "That's why she joined the Deathbinders, isn't it? Her last name's Gruzca. She's Borlden's sister."

Tamara clapped her hands slowly. "Congratulations. You're not as dumb as you look."

Madislak let out a disgusted sigh. "I should've known. They're both powerful shrews. That puts one from each family on opposite sides of the talisman business. If Nalecht got it, Borlden could take it. If I got it, Harmony could take it. She was going to use me—just like everyone else."

Petrovana couldn't believe her ears. Her mouth opened, closed, then opened again. "That's crazy. They look nothin' alike. They act nothin' alike. Madislak, she is *not* evil like Borlden!"

"It doesn't matter." He scoffed. "How many Deathbinders are there total?"

Tamara wore an arrogant grin. "She'll have seven in all—one Deathbinder for each shard."

Blank Face growled. "How do you know this?"

"Let's just say, since The Latter is going to someday be one, he has ties to Kasherri herself. She doesn't want the talisman reforged. But I don't give a shit what that goddess wants. I want to know what Nalecht knows. Something Harmony has figured out, but I can't get her to talk, no matter how many bones we break." Tamara shoved a biscuit in her mouth.

"Yer breakin' her bones, you ruthless bitch!?" Petrovana started to rise from the table, but Blank Face's hand caught her arm and held her back. Enemy or not, torture was not the way to treat anyone.

"We told her she could be free if she just told us what we need to know." Tamara smirked. "For being so smart, she's pretty stupid, if you ask me."

"And yer certain Harmony is tellin' the truth?" Petrovana pushed her jet-black hair over her shoulder.

Madislak's throat bobbed. "She never denied it when they exposed her in front of me. I could tell by the look on her face."

"She is the future queen! Madislak, you love her. How can you just leave her in there?" Petrovana pinned a gaze on Madislak.

"Not anymore." Madislak stroked his beard. "You are. She will be banished from Lantess and stripped of her duties as proxy. I've known that girl for five years. If someone loves you, they don't hide things like this, especially when we're trying to get the shards Deathbinders are sworn to protect. She was using me to get to them; I know it."

Blank Face shifted in his seat. "She had the opportunity to get one when Leper left it lying in front of us in Lantess. Your royal, sheltered upbringing clouds your judgment. You don't know why she made that deal. Did you ask her?"

Madislak leveled a stare at Tamara. "Well?"

Tamara shrugged. "Speaking of the horned freak, where is he? And how is it you two are brothers... exactly?"

Petrovana flinched at the mention of Leper, readying her palms under the table. "What concern of it is yours where he's at?"

Tamara chuckled. "Should be all of your concerns. Ace is no longer aligned with us. They could be plotting to bring an army of dragons down on us." She turned to Madislak. "Well? How is this man your brother?" She pointed at Blank Face.

"We share the same mother. Different fathers. It's not something I like to talk about, so drop it," Madislak answered curtly.

Tamara's head slowly turned to Blank Face, then back to Madislak. "Nalecht forced Ventessa into submission as well. Took their entire army and people as slaves, if my sources are to be believed. Kundry will be cutting food supplies soon, and Brebian will ally with him to keep his people alive. So, if you're going to do something, I'd make it quick."

Madislak rubbed his face, muscles flexing with each movement. "He's growing his numbers, crossing too many lines, and attacking anyone who refuses to follow him. If we're going to stop him, we'll need your army and mine, and that might not be enough. He has four shards; we have two."

"I have two," Tamara corrected. "Nalecht thinks these shards are his at his call. And make no mistake, I will help you against him, but if my life is jeopardized, then I will give him my support."

"So, basically, you'll stand against him as long as we win?" Petrovana pinched the bridge of her nose. "That's not loyalty."

This whole meeting sucked. But so far, they'd managed to gather very useful information from Tamara on the Deathbinders and Nalecht's movements. If they could just figure out his next moves, they could put an end to this and get out of this crap city.

"She doesn't know what loyalty means," Blank Face spat.

Madislak let out a defeated sigh. "Fine. What are you asking for, Tamara? What is it that you want?"

Her grin sent a shudder down Petrovana's spine as she explained. "Well, it's simple. We decimate Nalecht. I'll tell you where he'll be, and you attack the strongholds he's acquired while he's away. We'll weaken him piece by piece. I'd start with Kirilick or Tudela. He believes they can stand on their own. Then I need what's in your precious girlfriend's head. I need to know what they know. And I need to know where your horned friend Leper is and what he is doing."

Madislak arched a brow. "Fine. In return, you don't attack Lantess. You may keep Harmony prisoner, but no more torture. When we wear him down, we retake the shards and split them up amongst us. Each of us in this room gets one."

Tamara sat back, wearing that stupid, arrogant grin. "I get to choose which shards I keep first."

Madislak nodded. "Actually, we'll have to have that conversation later. I'm sure Leper will not part with the shard of Theora, especially since he's the one tracking down the shard of Kasherri right now."

Tamara's eyes went wide. "Then you might as well dig him a grave right now. Nobody gets out of the rain trials."

"The rain trials?" Petrovana's heart fell to her stomach.

"That's where the shard is kept. Three hundred years, and no one's ever made it out alive. Except for The Former and The Latter, but, well, look at them. Why do you think Nalecht doesn't have it yet?" Tamara rolled her neck.

The blood drained from Petrovana's face, and a comforting, calloused hand rested on top of hers. The last time she saw him, he was so mad at her for not asking his thoughts on marrying Madislak. He looked at her like he hated her, and she let him march off in a heap of anger, right to his doom. A tear rolled down her cheek as the unnerving truth settled in the pit of her stomach. She glanced at Blank Face, who seemed to try for a comforting grin, but it looked more creepy than anything. *Gods*, Leper, she gave months of her life, her body, to him, and relished every minute of it. Grief swelled within her, and she lost all focus. The last few days might not have been as great as the first few weeks, but she didn't want him to die.

"If anyone can make it out, it's him," Blank Face broke the silence, squeezing her hand. It was the softest voice she'd ever heard from him.

"He's a dead man. Get over it." Tamara sneered.

Petrovana's heart pounded in her chest, heat boiling in her blood. Who the hell was she to tell her to get over his death? There was no proof he was even dead yet.

Madislak glanced at Petrovana. "Petrovana and I will get married. Then we'll get the shrews of Terynsipple to fight with us too."

Tamara pursed her fingers together. "Perfect. Nalecht already pursued them. I haven't heard the outcome."

Petrovana narrowed her gaze. "What about Leper?" she gritted through clenched teeth.

"Fuck him. He's a grown man. I won't coddle him like Rinawen did. He'll accept it for the peace treaty it is, if he's alive, and we will spare this world from whatever horror Nalecht has planned with that talisman." Madislak made a dismissive gesture.

She wasn't a consolation prize to be handed back and forth. And she would not stand by and let Madislak start demanding what was going to happen now. He might be the eldest of the group and a king, but he had another thing coming if he thought he could order her around like she was some useless whore.

Petrovana squared her shoulders and glared right into Madislak's deep brown eyes. "I'll think about marryin' you, but first I'm goin' to see if I can get a note to Leper. I'm not against the union if it saves the world, but I will not be ordered around like I'm someone's fuckin' whore."

Madislak rose to his feet. "This meeting is over. You will do what is best for the group." He started towards the door, but a quick knock gave him pause, and he looked over his shoulder at Petrovana. "Actually, we'll just get married here and now. Then you can take the news to Terynsipple and tell them to join us."

Incredulous man. Whatever had happened between Lantess and now had certainly taken its toll on his mental capacity and kindness. She wasn't sure she wanted to marry him anymore, even if it was for the good of the world. He was being a dick.

A guard burst through the door and ran to Tamara, cupping his hand over her ear.

Her eyes went wide. "Where's your tiny, black-haired friend?"

All eyes moved to Blank Face as he grinned.

Chapter Twenty-One

Seconds went by, and leather straps ratcheted around Petrovana and Blank Face's arms on the chair. Tiny metal spikes lining the leather straps dug into her skin, sending a pinching pain up her arm. Panic surged through her veins, her heart pounding against her ribcage as she turned a worried glance to Blank Face. He tried to blink, but only flickered in and out of transparency. Petrovana tried to launch an ice shard at Tamara, but her magic wouldn't respond, remaining trapped within her. *Great.* Anti-magic cuffs, just like the ones they used on Harmony. Were they going to treat them like they did Harmony, too? Blank Face frantically rocked in his chair. Of course, the only solid furniture that wasn't about to fall apart would be in this room.

"Nylor, go make sure Harmony's secured," Tamara barked an order.

Nylor disappeared immediately. Madislak pointed at Blank Face. "What did you do?"

"What you should've done." He shot back, glaring at the king.

Petrovana looked at Blank Face. Cold, calculating death emanated from those eyes. His gaze was so intense she shuddered. "You sent her to free Harmony?"

That was why she was missing. Not because she did her part.

Blank Face nodded. "She's safer out of here. Nobody deserves the type of abuse that goes on in this shit-hole."

"Well, this alliance is off to a good start." Tamara glared at Madislak, then slowly walked over to Blank Face. "But let's take off this hood, you look familiar, and I want to know who I'm dealing with."

Tamara grabbed Blank Face's hood, and he ducked his head into his robes. Then he yanked his head back up and started rocking the chair vigorously. He really didn't want her to see his true form—probably for the best. Good thing his horns didn't grow back faster. Still, Petrovana needed to help him keep that hood on so Tamara didn't discover what he was. They've seen what she does to normal humans. Imagine what kind of torturous whims she would unleash on a Chernzerk.

Petrovana tried swaying back and forth to tip her and Blank Face's chair over, but couldn't get it to fall. Tamara clutched at Blank Face's throat to stop him from shaking, and then he bit her arm. The sound of a glass vial breaking emanated from his mouth.

The scent immediately hit her. A pungent medicinal odor akin to cleaning supplies, like orange or lemon mixed with rubbing alcohol. It was foreign to her. He bit again, and she finally recoiled her arm.

"What the fuck?" she bellowed.

A sinister grin crawled across his face. "They call it a thousand ways to die. It's a poison that can take hold in many different ways, but you'll need a healer or the antidote to live."

Tamara grinned. "Clever man, I like you. But you just sealed your fate as well."

Blank Face rolled his neck. "I don't care, as long as you are dead too. You better hurry to your best healer, that poison doesn't take long to fill your veins."

Did he just sacrifice his own life to kill her? Petrovana assessed Blank Face's demeanor.

Tamara immediately bolted out of the room. Blank Face stuck his head back into his robes and moments later began munching on glass again. Then he spat out the small pea-sized glass container that he broke apart in his mouth. Blood red colored his teeth.

"Are you insane? Yer goin' to kill yerself." She nodded towards him.

"I have my own antidote; she didn't need to know that I was just buying us time." He countered.

Petrovana struggled against the bindings, trying to loosen them, then looked to Madislak. "C'mon, get us out of these chairs! Let's go! Intiva's got Harmony, we need to move now!"

Madislak rolled his shoulders and glanced at the door, then back to them, then back to the door, as if caught between two worlds. "We need this alliance, you idiots. Tamara has two shards, and if Leper's dead, we lose another powerful ally. We need this to work!"

"We can worry about that later!" Petrovana begged.

Nylor came back in. "Where's Tamara?" His deep voice echoed.

"She had to run out for a minute. Take them to the dungeons. No harm, no torture," Madislak ordered.

Nylor looked Madislak up and down briefly, then strode forward and released them from the chairs. The anti-magic cuffs remained. A few minutes passed, and Tamara sauntered through the door again.

"I will rip you both apart piece by piece," she seethed, pointing at them.

Madislak slammed the table. "No harm. Put them in the dungeon. But no fucking torture. Get someone to marry us, and we will get those shrews to help us. But if you harm either of them—or hurt Harmony anymore—I'll burn those gods-damned books."

The rage simmering in Tamara's eyes made Petrovana's own skin heat. She clenched her fists at her side as she said, "Fine. No fucking harm. You have one week after this makeshift wedding to get both the shrews and those books down here, or I swear to Amarook, you will all die a slow, painful death."

Was Madislak turning on them? Had he completely lost his mind? They just gave him a golden opportunity to get out of Xaneth Harbor, away from Tamara, and he let it pass for a possible alliance with someone who held no loyalty towards them. Every time they tried to escape, they met massive failure. Every plan ended in disaster, thinning the line of trust between them all.

"What the hell is wrong with you, Madislak?" Petrovana shot angrily. "I will not marry you. You don't put yer damned queen in a dungeon! This is not how you treat people—wake yer ass up!"

"I am sick and tired of being lied to and used as everyone's puppet in their hunger for power. I will not sit back and take it anymore. Whether you like it or not, we are getting married. Terynsipple will fight for us, as will both of you, Harmony, and whoever else I order to fight for me. I am getting these shards, I am becoming Anyth, and once I do, you can all thank me for saving your lives. Because if it was up to Tamara, you would both be dead." He gritted.

"I won't marry you." She shot back again.

"Then enjoy your stay in Xaneth Harbor. Because that's your only option now." Madislak stomped out of the room, and guards entered, escorting them to their new prison.

Panic ran rampant through Petrovana as they were escorted through the dark dungeons. She prayed Harmony somehow got out with Intiva. Someone needed to talk sense into Madislak. This alliance with Tamara might look good on the surface—her army was definitely the best in the world—but her loyalty was not. She would turn on them the second the odds didn't favor her, and that was not someone you wanted in an alliance. Soon, it wouldn't even matter. Soon, Kalazaar would be destroyed by all these tyrants competing for power.

The ground trembled beneath their feet. Leper stumbled and fell onto the grass that lined the large room's floor. Standing before them, towering at about seven feet tall, was Kasherri, the goddess of the underworld. Her appearance mirrored the statue from Costin, now animated with wide-open eyes, emanating a deep blend of purple and black. Eight tentacles writhed atop her head, moving at her command, while her trident tail swayed menacingly. Kasherri's presence was utterly terrifying. They were face-to-face with the embodiment of corruption, fear, and chaos.

Drawing closer, Kasherri's menacing presence enveloped Leper and Lillian. An eerie hiss escaped her lips as she spoke, malevolent delight coloring her words. "Welcome to your final resting place."

Leper struggled to his feet, his voice quivering as he addressed the dreadful deity. "Kasherri, what do you want?" he inquired.

"Mortal fools," Kasherri sneered, her voice dripping with malice. "You will merely be added to the many who suffer these trials. An eternity of torment, agony, and pain await you," she cackled. The hair on the back of his neck stood on end.

Lillian remained unyielding, offering a challenge of her own. "The Former does not agree with you."

Kasherri's amusement came to an abrupt halt. Her eyes narrowed, a grotesque visage contorted with rage. "How dare you mention that name in here!" she snapped.

Leper shot a worried glance at Lillian. "Stop pissing her off," he warned.

But it seemed Kasherri's fury couldn't be easily quelled. Her smile disappeared quickly, replaced by a menacing scowl. With a sudden, violent motion, she lunged at Leper. He drew Maka Kura, preparing for a confrontation against a god, fully aware that one could not kill a deity.

Leper nimbly evaded Kasherri's lunging attacks as her jaws snapped rapidly. Her head tendrils swatted at him, sending him sprawling to the ground. In response, Lillian sprang into action, her scimitars gleaming as she unleashed a flurry of stabs and slices aimed at Kasherri's chest. One of her strikes connected, drawing a spurt of dark blood.

Kasherri hissed in pain and retaliated by thrusting her trident tail toward Lillian in an attempt to impale her. Lillian adeptly parried the assault, using both scimitars to fling the tail aside. Lillian continued her offensive, slashing twice more at Kasherri. However, Kasherri displayed her proficiency, expertly using her tendrils to fend off Lillian's attacks. Leper joined the fray, beating back the tendrils and tail. Lillian seized the opportunity and landed a precise strike across Kasherri's neck. Black blood oozed from her body onto her yellow skin, and she crumpled to the floor, dissipating into black smoke.

"She's a lot weaker than I thought," Lillian grinned.

Leper glanced back at the pedestal with the shard of Kasherri still atop it. "It can't be that easy."

An echoing cackle filled the room, reverberating off the walls and pounding into Leper's head. He covered his ears, the ringing so intense that he nearly fell to one knee, his head filled with fuzziness.

With a stomp of her powerful leg, Kasherri sent a shockwave racing through the ground, propelling Leper and Lillian backward.

Kasherri swooped in quickly, getting right in front of their faces. "You cannot kill a god!" she screeched.

Panic surged through Leper as he scrambled away from Kasherri's incoming piercing tendrils, which slammed into the ground beside him. One nicked his side, drawing blood immediately. He couldn't stop, with more attacks on their way. Rolling onto his back, he swatted with Maka Kura, desperately blocking the onslaught.

Lillian quickly got to her feet and ran towards Leper, closing the distance, but Kasherri's power was overwhelming. She launched herself at Lillian, covering the twenty-foot gap in a single leap. Lillian, taken aback by the sudden assault, backpedaled against Kasherri's vicious attacks with her talons, hands, and tail.

Regaining his footing, Leper unleashed his chakrams, aiming once more for Kasherri. One found its mark on her arm, while the other pierced into her chest, striking her dark heart. Black blood flowed freely as she fell and dissipated into black smoke once again. Maybe that was the final blow, but it still seemed too easy; something was missing.

Leper rushed over to Lillian, checking her for injuries as he helped her to her feet.

"Yer hurt," she pointed at his side.

"It's okay. I'll fix that real quick," Leper grinned.

He retrieved a healing vial from his bag, a dull yellow one, and poured it over the wound. It stung for a few seconds before starting to heal and close. The echoing cackle returned, louder and more intense this time, dropping them both to their knees.

Kasherri swooped in once more, unleashing a powerful wave of force that sent Leper flying backward, crashing onto the grass that sprouted from the stone floor, knocking the breath out of him as he gasped for air. Lillian, better prepared this time, landed on her feet and immediately resumed the attack as Kasherri reappeared. Her blades became a blur as she launched a furious assault, aiming to exploit any opening.

Kasherri's tendrils moved with astonishing speed and precision, expertly blocking each of Lillian's strikes. Lillian pressed on, weaving in and out with rapid, calculated movements. Their exchange of blows created a breathtaking display of combat, each move executed with skill as the pangs of steel thudding against the leathery material of her tendrils.

Kasherri taunted Lillian with a hiss, "Is that all you've got, mortal scum?"

Lillian responded defiantly, "Just a warm-up, deity bitch."

Leper regained his breath and hurled Maka Kura at Kasherri, but she deflected them with her tendrils. Now both attacking in unison, Leper and Lillian coordinated their strikes with unparalleled precision. When Leper swung high, Lillian struck low, and vice versa, increasing their attack speed and driving the goddess back into a corner.

With a low growl, Kasherri bared her large, saliva-covered teeth. Despite her resistance, Lillian managed to sink her scimitar into the goddess's neck and heart once more. Kasherri dissolved into black smoke yet again, but Leper still didn't believe she would stay down. There was no loud cackle this time as the floor vibrated and shook, and they both placed a hand on the wall to steady themselves. A strip of blackness ripped upward from the ground and then materialized into Kasherri as the shaking stopped. She swatted Lillian aside with one hand, gashing across her torso. Her scimitars clattered across the hard, grassy floor as she rolled.

Leper rolled his shoulders and launched his attack, feinting in and out to catch Kasherri off guard. However, her defenses were formidable, providing numerous ways to deflect and counter. He focused on severing some of her tendrils, her tail, or her hands, knowing it would improve his chances of delivering a decisive blow to end her completely. His heart thundered in his chest like a stampede of buffalo fleeing a predator.

"Slam me together," Maka Kura's voice echoed in his mind.

"What? How will that help? You're distracting me," Leper retorted, struggling to stay focused on Kasherri's movements.

She pressed her relentless assault, jabbing him in the shoulder and leg with a tendril, forcing him to stumble back and create space. Leper squared his shoulders and prepared for the next round.

"DO IT!" Maka yelled.

Trusting in his legendary weapons, Leper swung his arms in a sweeping arc, bringing Maka Kura together just as Kasherri rushed towards him. A loud clang reverberated, and a yellow wave of force burst forth from the connection, hurling the goddess back about fifteen feet.

"What the hell?" Leper exclaimed.

"Our bond and power are growing," Maka cooed.

Lillian managed to get to her feet, clutching her wound, but Leper knew he needed to eliminate Kasherri quickly to ensure their escape. Ignoring his pain, he hurled Maka Kura at Kasherri, severing three of her head tendrils, which writhed and slithered back towards the goddess as she cried out in agony.

Meanwhile, Lillian entered a trance-like state, her strikes becoming stronger, faster, and more precise as she aimed to wear down her opponent. She sliced off the tips of two more of Kasherri's tendrils, prompting a grimace and hiss of pain from the goddess. In retaliation, Kasherri unleashed a powerful attack, her tendrils and tail flailing as she leaped and landed with brutal force. The ground cracked beneath her, and a yellow force wave sent Lillian flying backward with a sickening thud, followed by cries of agony. Rage boiled in his blood as he heard her screams and pressed the attack, ignoring his shoulder and leg screaming at him to slow down. He didn't care; he would not let her die down here. He sliced off the remaining tendril and then rammed his shoulder into her chest. As she stumbled backwards, he swung Maka Kura with all his might, cutting deep into her neck. Again, she floated away in black smoke.

If nothing else, it would buy a little time. Leper rushed over to Lillian and grabbed two more healing vials from his bag, one a bright yellow and the other a duller hue. He quickly put the bright yellow one on Lillian's wounds and the dull one on his.

"She keeps comin' back stronger and stronger, Lep. We're missin' somethin'," Lillian said, getting to her feet.

Leper checked his vials. One more bright yellow, one neon yellow for emergencies, and the blue one. *Can't keep this pace up, we have to end her.* "I know. But how do we defeat her? I tried to take her head off, and still she floated into smoke."

Lillian sighed as she glanced around nervously. "I don't know, but get ready, I feel like she's comin' back again. Lep, I don't think we can actually kill her."

"I was thinking the same thing." Leper looked around again until his eyes landed on the pedestal. Then it hit him. "The shard!"

Leper sprinted towards the pedestal, recalling the book's guidance that the shard held the key to breaking the barriers and escaping, not necessarily defeating Kasherri. Perhaps removing it would end this endless battle. Just as he neared the pedestal, Kasherri slammed into him with tremendous force, sending him hurtling across the room. Lillian rushed to his defense, swiping her scimitars at the goddess. Kasherri backhanded Lillian and sent her back to the ground.

That must be the answer. Why else would she defend the pedestal?

Leper leveled his gaze on Kasherri and stared squarely at the malevolent deity before them. With a sinister grin, Kasherri raised her left arm, gesturing towards her left. The ground quaked and undulated like a turbulent sea, but only on Leper's side. Waves of rock surged, pushing him away from Lillian, once again separating them. At the rear of the room, a rock wall emerged from the floor and started ascending towards the ceiling, threatening to further divide them.

On Lillian's side, the ground trembled as she struggled to rise, swaying unsteadily. She steadied herself and gripped her scimitars tightly, preparing for the impending confrontation. Kasherri advanced menacingly towards the vulnerable Lillian, while the wall continued to rise, narrowing their connection. The effort to keep Leper and Lillian apart was palpable.

Kasherri lunged at Lillian, her trident tail slashing wildly. Lillian's defense faltered momentarily, but she managed to block the tail's attacks. Two of Kasherri's tendrils ensnared Lillian's arm, pinning it in place, while the others tightened their grip, pulling her arms apart, and her scimitars clanged to the ground. One tendril forced its way into Lillian's mouth.

Leper refused to surrender. He couldn't bear to watch another friend die at Kasherri's hands. Seeing Lillian being manipulated drove his inner animal to action. Though the healing concoction had sealed his wound, his shoulder and leg still throbbed with pain. Gathering his resolve, he leaped three feet at a time, bounding from one wave crest to the next, all the while a rising pillar threatened to divide them. He felt like a gazelle racing across the sea, except the waves were unforgiving rock, and any misstep would result in serious injury. His heart hammered endlessly in his rib cage.

"Maka, get ready for something reckless," he instructed his weapon.

"I am at your command, no matter how daring," Maka responded.

"Prepare for the agility of a cat," Leper grinned.

The closing wall now approached within twenty feet of the ceiling, obscuring Lillian from his view. Pushing through the agony, he propelled Maka Kura in a sweeping arc. Using his control over the weapon, he swung it, using it as a stepping-stone to elevate himself. He repeated the process, propelling himself higher until he only needed one more swing, one more step. But on the final swing, he misjudged, landing on the blade instead of the center.

"Shit," he bellowed, scrambling to regain his footing.

His chest slammed into the rising rock wall. Desperately, he reached up and barely managed to grip the top but found no purchase. Ten feet to the ceiling. He clawed and pulled, searching for anything to hold onto. Panic surged through him. A fall from this height would be fatal. His heart pounded, his shoulder searing in agony as his hands shredded against the jagged rocks.

"I'm screwed, I'm screwed, I'm screwed," he repeated, straining to find a grip.

Six feet to closure. If he didn't make it through the gap, he would either plummet to his death or be crushed. *This is it. This is how I die.* His hands began to slip. He stopped straining, resigned. At least he would soon see Rinawen again. He glanced down and took a deep sigh. *I'm sorry, Zanera. I'm sorry, Kelindra. I have failed you, too.* A tear rolled down his cheek as he let go, four feet from closure.

A searing white light flickered into the gap and grabbed his hand.

"You do not die down here. My daughters need you. Now get your ass over there and find your way out! That is an order!" Rinawen's sweet voice barked.

She pulled him up, smiled, then nodded towards Lillian. Leper returned the smile and nod, then crawled the remaining four feet to the other side as Maka Kura swooped by. He descended as swiftly as he ascended, using his weapon as stepping-stones.

Kasherri had all eight tendrils restraining Lillian by this point. Leper swiftly regathered his chakrams and flung them at Kasherri. Seeing Leper's rapid approach, Kasherri extended her tail to block him. Leper expertly hurdled over the tail, catching Maka Kura in both hands mid-air. With a spinning motion, he severed all eight tendrils at once.

Landing forcefully, Leper steadied himself with a hand and slammed Maka Kura onto the ground. A yellow wave of force erupted, sending Kasherri careening out of control. He immediately turned to Lillian, noting the shriveled tendrils that had fallen from her head, gasping for air. She coughed several times, and the last one slithered out of her mouth. She grabbed her neck and rubbed it.

He needed to get her moving. If she focused too much on what just happened, they'd lose this opportunity to attack.

He grabbed under her arm and hoisted her up. "C'mon, first one to grab the shard wins."

Her hands stopped moving on her neck as she snapped her head to his. "Oh, yer on!" her voice squeaked as the words came out.

Kasherri writhed in agony, letting out a deafening screech as her severed tentacles slithered back and reattached. Leper and Lillian pressed their assault, moving with flawless coordination. They struck as one, weaving around each other with precision, breaking through Kasherri's defenses at every turn. She was the only thing standing between them and the shard, which rested on a pedestal just before the newly risen wall.

Leper slashed at her legs, drawing black blood that quickly healed. Simultaneously, Lillian stabbed at her abdomen, eliciting the same rapid regeneration. Amidst Kasherri's agonized recoil, a brief opening emerged. Leper seized the opportunity, thrusting Maka Kura into her chest. With swift precision, he plucked the shard of Kasherri from the pedestal, securing the necklace around his neck and tucking the shard beneath his shirt.

"Nooooo!!" Kasherri hissed, her voice filled with despair. "Nooooo! I will not go back!"

As the rocks sealing the tunnels crumbled, revealing the exits once more, a group of imp-like beings materialized and whisked Kasherri away against her will. She shouted as she was taken, "Mark my words, mortals. You will pay for this!"

Leper shuddered.

Chapter Twenty-Two

Petrovana held back the urge to retch as the putrid smell of rotten garbage and old food filled her senses. For two days, they had been left in the deepest, darkest part of Tamara's dungeons. So far down, the faint glow of quartz provided just a sliver of light. Neither Madislak nor Intiva bothered to visit, though she hadn't expected Intiva to. If she had a magical note, she would have sent it to Leighth, pleading for help. At least they weren't being brutalized by Tamara's guards or Thessek. She and Blank Face were confined together, while Harmony was in the adjacent cell. Intiva failed to get her out.

For the past two days, Petrovana had tried endlessly to get Harmony to talk, hoping to extract any information that might offer them leverage to escape. The only sounds from Harmony were sobs, whimpers, and the occasional scream from a nightmare. Most of the time, she hugged her knees and stared into nothingness, her body still bruised and struggling to move. If Petrovana ever got these cuffs off, she would heal the poor girl and talk with her. She clearly knew something about the shards or the talisman—something Tamara considered important. If they survived and got out of here, knowing what that was could give them an advantage.

The guards had taken all their clothes and weapons—except for Blank Face. He had threatened to bite them, warning that the same fatal poison he used on Tamara was still in his system.

After they were thrown in the cells, he explained that the poison was stored in a single glass vial, with the antidote kept separately in another—just for situations like this. Working alone, trusting no one but himself, he always had contingency plans. If escape wasn't an option, he'd rather die on his own terms.

Harmony and Petrovana were dressed in simple cloth garbs, and the guards had derived perverse amusement from watching them change.

The dungeon was dimly lit, with benches attached to the rock walls for seating, as if the place had been carved out of stone. The floor was cobblestone, the walls jagged rock, and the cell bars were thick and unyielding under any pressure. The cell was so far down that they used a rope pulley elevator system to get there. Thankfully, it hadn't broken; perhaps next time, she would insist on the stairs. Blank Face lay motionless on the bench as usual, while Petrovana sat at his feet, admiring his long, narrow frame.

"Do you think Leper's dead?" Petrovana broke the silence.

Blank Face lowered one leg to the floor. "Maybe. I don't know."

"How long does it take to run the damn rain trials?" Petrovana muttered, noticing Harmony's gaze snap to hers.

"Considerin' how quickly he learned some crisp fightin' tactics, I assumed he'd survive, but it's been almost six weeks now. A full month. Not that I don't have faith in him, but with no food supply down there... one has to wonder if he's alive." She dropped her gaze to the ground.

Petrovana's eyes burned as a tear escaped. "Ugh. I'm a terrible person. He went down there feelin' betrayed by me, and unloved." She sniffled. "I sent him to his death, and the person that should've sent him with encouragement... Instead, he went off, angry and confused because of me."

Blank Face sat up. "He went off on his own accord to get the shard and burn the world down. You didn't send him anywhere. And you are not a terrible person. You're trying to protect people. He's just too blind to see it."

"No, it was before that, too. We argued the day he went to Rinawen's grave. I told him he was bein' stupid goin' alone. Then I told him he needed to get off yer back and stop treatin' you like shit all the time." She admitted. "That just made it worse."

"You." Blank Face locked his gaze on Petrovana. "You defended me? To him? ... Behind my back?"

His face softened, showing a tenderness she'd never seen before. He looked... compassionate? Empathetic? Something in those piercing brown eyes flashed, and it was... beautiful.

She tore her eyes away to break the connection. "Yes. All the time. He hates it, but he needs to forgive you. Yer the only family each other has. I'd kill to know who my parents are. If I have any siblin's, to not be alone."

"We're not alone. You have him, and all the rest of us. He may still hate me, and I don't blame him. I took away something more dear to him than I can fathom. To be honest, I'm more jealous of what he had with Rinawen; it's more than I've had my entire life." He inhaled sharply. "But my point is, each breath we take could be our last. I know my past is beyond reconciliation, but over these last few weeks, being with Leighth, you, and even though he hates me, Leper. I've started to experience what happiness could feel like. If you'll have me as a friend, I'd be glad to call you one, because if anything, you are not a terrible person, Petrovana."

Petrovana's mouth fell open. Hearing her name on his lips sent a wave of heat through her. So much for a soulless assassin. She couldn't resist looking over his rippled jawline and blond stubble that decorated his face. She wanted to touch his face, to assure him she was his friend. Her stomach churned. She shouldn't be craving his attention. But she was.

Harmony made some hand motions, and Blank Face snapped his head toward her, responding in kind.

"What was that?" Petrovana walked over to Harmony's cell and put her hand through the bars. "Are you ready to talk?"

Harmony shook her head no, then signaled something else with her hands.

Blank Face sat fully up on the bench. "She knows hand code."

"What's hand code?" Petrovana tilted her head.

"A secret language taught in the assassins' underground safe harbors so they can converse quietly," Blank Face muttered.

Harmony sighed again.

"I told him I was sorry! What more do you want from me?!" Blank Face spat angrily, and the soft, gentle expression vanished. His face slackened, and he glanced at the ground.

"What did she say?" Petrovana eagerly rushed back to him.

"First, she said I was full of shit. Then she said I needed to make it up to him, and that's when I yelled." He sighed. "Then she just spelled out Zanera and Kelindra's names. I never got them to safety like I told him I would."

"We were tryin' to save yer ass!" Petrovana snapped at Harmony.

Blank Face interpreted her response. "She said they are adults; those kids are more important, and we should've gotten them first."

Good point.

"Yer..." Petrovana blinked a few times.

Harmony was right. She had failed Leper—epically failed him. She had never once put his needs above her own, yet he had always kept her secrets, always stood by her. He had even promised to track down her parents, no matter what it took. And she couldn't even promise to help the kids he cared for most?

"I have failed him," she mouthed. "Yer right, Harmony."

"You haven't failed anybody," Blank Face reiterated.

"Yes, I have." She leaned her head against the bars. "I never stopped to consider his feelin's or what was important to him. I only made things harder fer him, and now..." She trailed off.

I'm in love with his brother.

She wanted to say it. The words pressed against her throat, but she couldn't force them out. She was a terrible person—always had been, always would be.

"And now what?" Blank Face set a hand on her shoulder.

"Nothin'," she mouthed quickly. "It's nothin'."

She couldn't even look Blank Face in the eyes. She and Leper had grown apart, and she couldn't keep denying her feelings. She did love Blank Face. But she still cared deeply for Leper as a friend and wanted to stand by him—for the shards, for whatever else they needed to face together.

It only took a few more exchanges for them to discern that Harmony didn't want to talk about the talisman. She didn't want to implicate them or risk them going through what she had endured. Besides, she didn't trust that they could withhold the information if put in a similar situation.

"I think yer all too focused on the talisman, seekin' answers fer that. I think the answers lie in what happened with Pasileveo and the Chernzerk," Petrovana said. Harmony lifted her head off her knees.

Blank Face cupped his hand to Petrovana's ear and whispered, "She thinks you're on to something and never thought about that herself. But yelled at me to not speak anything above a whisper."

They all moved closer together, with only the cell bars separating them. Petrovana sat on the disgusting, grime-covered cold stone floor. "If you tell me what you know, we could probably figure this out together."

Harmony studied her for a bit, then signaled, and Blank Face translated. "She said she wants to tell us, but we can't give up the leverage. If any of us break under interrogation, we all die."

Petrovana nodded. "I swear on my life."

Blank Face nodded and repeated the sentiment.

With a sigh, Harmony signed. "I don't want to be a Deathbinder. I was forced to agree or die. I've been looking for a way out. Madislak wouldn't understand. But the purpose behind seven Deathbinders is to keep the shards separated. Kasherri doesn't want the talisman reforged. It holds the power to kill the gods."

Petrovana's heart pounded, her pulse quickening. What would Nalecht do with that kind of power? What would anyone do with the ability to kill a god? If the talisman could slay a god, just how powerful was it? The thought of anyone wielding such a thing sent chills down her spine. The hairs on the back of her neck stood on end.

She softly spoke through the bars. "But how do we get rid of it? How do we destroy it or the shards and eliminate that sort of threat?"

Harmony shrugged and made some motions with her hands.

"The shards are indestructible." Blank Face interpreted. "They tried to destroy them in Lantess and couldn't."

Petrovana sighed. "Where did you find this information?"

Harmony signaled, and Blank Face continued to translate, clearly growing irritated. "She says she found a series of personal scrolls—accounts penned by Enoch and Ghendala's own chroniclers. Most of them recounted their lineage and their dragons, especially Eluvae the Wicked. He was the largest, most deadly dragon ever. She didn't have enough information, but hoped the Ruby Tip Tower in Ambrosia would hold the rest. It houses the largest library and the biggest collection of historical records. Nalecht wouldn't let her inside."

"And yer lookin' fer their accounts, or are there history books that tell the stories?" Petrovana asked.

"She says most of them cover the Bay of Disdain's downfall and history. But the most puzzling thing she found is that before Enoch and Ghendala met Pasileveo, they were good people. Something changed."

Petrovana cupped her chin. "Hmm... That would match. Most accounts of Chernzerk history in our lands say they were farmers, crafters, and enchanters. Not violent or aggressive." She shifted against the bars. "I mean, before they met Pasileveo, Enoch and Ghendala were known as kind rulers of the south, with the most powerful dragons ever. Why would they suddenly shift their allegiances and want to rule the entire world when they could've done that at any point after bonding their super-strong dragons?"

"Precisely. They could've started their tyranny at any time, but it didn't start until they formed an alliance with Pasileveo... It's frustratingly convenient." Harmony frantically signaled. "Again... She says she went over every city's past recount of Chernzerk activity, and each one, going back a hundred and fifty years, labeled them as evil. But, the similarities in how it's worded are too convenient—like the same person wrote all of it. And then there's the idea that the shards somehow affect or control them, but that doesn't make sense either."

Petrovana took a minute to think about what she'd just discussed with Harmony. But another thought began to take root. Sure, Harmony was helping them right now, but the lingering fact remained: she was still a Deathbinder, which meant she had to follow someone's command, right?

As if he could read her mind, Blank Face leveled a stare at Harmony. "Harmony." He said in a flat tone. "Is what Madislak said true? Were you with him just to get the shards when the opportunity arose, and is Borlden your brother?"

Harmony snapped her head to Blank Face, and tears rolled from her eye. She nodded yes, then buried her face in her knees and sobbed. She signaled, her head still shoved down as she cried.

"What did she say?" Petrovana turned her attention to Blank Face.

He let out a long sigh. "She said she's sorry for everything. She fell in love with Madislak and couldn't keep up the façade anymore. She wants to stop Nalecht and do whatever it takes to help Madislak. That's all she cares about. But she fears it's too late... that Madislak will never take her back. She's even more scared now that she's going to make an enemy of Borlden. He's just as bad as Tamara and just as powerful as Nalecht."

"Is he still the one you answer to? Do you think we can take him?" Petrovana asked. "I don't suppose there's any possibility he would join us?"

Blank Face grunted as he started to translate again. "She said no. There's no possible reason he would switch allegiances; he's not even aligned with Nalecht, he's after the talisman for himself, for us both to take over rulership. At first, yes, it sounded nice to be a queen and rule a city, but not like this. Not by force."

Petrovana wondered if she'd ever be able to talk again after what she went through and being a Deathbinder, at the beck and call of Kasherri for a lifetime of servitude. She shuddered. It still didn't quite explain why she wouldn't just tell all of this to Madislak before everything happened. Perhaps she was scared he'd leave her? Send her off on her own? Something she would definitely inquire about later.

"Maybe we pushed too far," Petrovana offered softly. "Let's give her a minute, Blank."

She stood up and brushed herself off.

"So..." Blank Face stood beside her. "What do we need to find out now? Where are we at here?"

"Well." Petrovana let out a breath. "We need to understand how Pasileveo turned Enoch and Ghendala into murderous tyrants—and why he wanted the talisman protected so fiercely. If it's so powerful, wouldn't he just be able to kill anything or anyone himself with the damn thing anyway?"

"Right." Blank Face rubbed the back of his neck. "Maybe we can find out how to stop him, too."

Petrovana forced a smile. "Yeah. Reckon we should dig into Axeladdle's histories. Might find somethin' there."

Harmony's eye widened in shock, and her head snapped up at Petrovana.

She signaled, and Blank Face grumbled. "She said she looked into every city's past—Lantess, Ambrosia, Tudela, Wen-Tath, Xaneth Harbor—but never thought to check Axeladdle. All their books were burned, wiped from the libraries."

Petrovana's grin faded from fake to real. "Then I reckon we got some research to do."

If Harmony had studied each city's past dealings and reached the same conclusion—that the Chernzerk were peaceful—then maybe the real answers had been buried in the one place no one thought to look. Axeladdle. The city that had been destroyed.

Perhaps that was where the truth had been kept.

What happened to Enoch and Ghendala? Where had Pasileveo or Nalecht learned what they knew about the shards or the talisman that everyone else was chasing?

Blank Face chuckled. "Suddenly, she feels threatened as the smartest person in the room. But she says one of the books also mentioned it being a key for something."

"A key," Petrovana mouthed. "Regardless, when we get out of here, you and I are goin' to do some diggin'. There's got to be a way to end this charade. And startin' with Axeladdle would be the best place. That's Pasileveo's old stronghold and was Nalecht's until Brebian destroyed it."

Blank Face added, "It'd make sense for Nalecht or Pasileveo to cover that up, then rewrite history to make people focus on a false problem. And if they painted the Chernzerk as evil, the world would turn against them, wiping out the biggest threat to the talisman. If the Chernzerk are the only ones who can truly destroy it, the easiest way to eliminate them is to make the entire world hunt them down."

Petrovana's eyes widened, her heart racing. "That's it! I bet between Axeladdle's unexplained downfall as one of the greatest cities and what's hidden in The Talon, we would find somethin'."

She didn't have long in her musings as the cell started shaking, vibrating like an earthquake. Dust and debris fell from the ceiling, little chunks of rock raining down. Her lungs constricted, her pulse pounding in her temples. After all this, they would get buried at the bottom of Tamara's dungeons. She was certain this place was going to collapse under her feet.

The thrum of energy from Kasherri's shard pulsed against Leper's chest. Dark energy rolled through him, tempting him to let it control his mind, but he wouldn't give in. He closed his eyes and pushed it away, focusing on Lillian's freckled face, her vibrant green eyes, and her radiant smile. The memory of their night at the inn in Wen-Tath calmed him. When he opened his eyes, Lillian was studying him cautiously, her tattered clothes and sweaty brow furrowed.

"Are you good?" she asked, tactical and wary.

Leper's lips curled upward. "I'm fine. I'm me. We need to get moving before things get worse on the surface."

His shoulder still pulsed with pain, and his leg barked at him. He debated using one of the last two healing vials and splitting it between them. As he opened the pack, a crumpled note lay on top of the vials. He quickly retrieved it, unfolding the paper to read Zanera's shaky handwriting.

Leper,

Leper hurry back oh no they're here they're coming in they found out Larnadix isn't who he says he is we need hel—

The last word, "help," trailed off as if someone had grabbed her while she was writing. She must have crumpled it and tossed it into the metal container as they carried her away.

"What is it?" Lillian asked, grabbing the paper from his shaking hands.

The heat of rage burned through his core, an unquenchable fire. The shard pressed against his mind like a jagged splinter, forcing its way deeper, clawing for control. A searing pressure built behind his eyes, a tide of foreign will crashing against his own. Whispers slithered through his mind, voices not his own, their murmurs threading between his thoughts, insidious and unshakable. His lungs constricted, and his heart thrummed in response. Panic surged through him, flooding his every thought. *No! No! I will not give in to despair.* He repeated the mantra in his mind.

"We..." he growled. "We need to go right now."

"Leper," Lillian said, setting her hand on his back as he stumbled forward, fighting the endless assault.

Lillian gripped his shoulders and steadied him, forcing him to face her. She put her hand on his face. "Look at me."

Leper opened his eyes and gazed into the never-ending depths of her soulful, soft, comforting gaze. It helped. It helped a lot.

"We will get to them. Together," she spoke softly, in a tone she only ever used around him, that he noticed anyway. "Whatever it takes."

Leper nodded. "Whatever it takes. We have to save them."

Lillian pointed towards the tunnel exits. "Which one?"

"Maka, quick, which one do we take?" Leper called frantically.

After a short pause, "Take the middle path," Maka instructed.

Leper immediately bolted for the middle path, and Lillian followed closely behind him. As soon as they left the room, the entirety of the underground labyrinth began to shake uncontrollably. A huge wave of transparent energy burst from the center of the room, and the pedestal shattered into tiny rocks. Leper and Lillian were sent flying through the tunnel, bouncing off the rocky surfaces, with no grass or vegetation to soften the blows as they careened onward. The shaking continued, and a large rock slammed into the ground beside them. Leper spared a quick glance up. More rocks had broken off and were falling their way.

"Oh shit, I think it's goin' to collapse, Lep. We need to go!" Lillian hollered, picking herself up slowly.

Loud yips and yaps emanated from all around—the sounds of imps, kobolds, and the grunts of minotaurs and centaurs. Thundering footsteps echoed all around them. Large, half-horse, half-human creatures, centaurs, thundered through the tunnel in the distance, pouring out in a stampede. Behind them came walking cows, minotaurs, and strange, winged rat-like creatures with wings and a beak—Shriekers. Imps and kobolds, though small, swarmed in overwhelming numbers, emerging from the tunnels and crevices of the cave, their presence just as dangerous as the larger beasts. The underworld army.

"They're coming. They've been unleashed," Leper groaned as he got up.

"Leper! RUN!" Maka screamed in his head—and that tone wasn't concern. No, it was pure fear.

Leper motioned onward, then put his hands on Lillian, aiming her in the right direction. They ran, as fast as they could possibly go, the tunnel caving in behind them, the sound of the massive army forming a knot in his throat. What had they just done?

Chapter
Twenty-Three

L illian pressed forward, sprinting despite the searing gashes across her stomach that protested with every step. The
breached barriers meant the army would soon swarm out,
racing towards them. They hadn't eaten in days, and fatigue
strained every muscle. Ignoring the ache and exhaustion, she
pushed onward through the collapsing tunnel toward a clearing just ahead. Glancing back, she saw Leper hobbling behind.

"C'mon, Leper! It's gonna swallow you whole if you don't run
faster!" She frantically waved her arm in a quick circle.

"I'm trying!" his voice came out panicked and shaky.

Breaking into the clearing, Lillian looked up at a towering ravine, seemingly insurmountable, before their pursuers
caught up. Amidst the stench of decay that had plagued them for
weeks, she caught a hint of fresh air. Just as the cave collapsed,
Leper barreled out and collided with her, sending them both
sprawling.

"Sorry," he groaned, untangling himself. "I couldn't stop."

"It's fine. How do we get out? What does Maka say?" Lillian
brushed herself off.

"He says we need to climb up there. Any progress upward has to be the right direction," Leper pointed to the towering expanse above them.

"Fuck me," Lillian muttered. "I should've known."

"Is that an offer again? Or..." Leper grinned.

"Seriously? Now?" Lillian chuckled.

Leper rummaged through his bag of vials as Lillian eyed the ridge line of the ravine they now faced. She knew a quick way up there but kept it to herself. Shifting into a griffin would get them out fast. Fear crept in—she hadn't shifted in years, honoring a promise to her dying father never to do it again. Her pulse pounded in her ears, urging action she wasn't ready for. Panic seized her, chest heaving as she struggled to control her breathing. Leper reached out, steadying her before she could collapse.

"Are you alright?" Leper asked, concerned.

"I'm fine," Lillian snapped. "Don't worry about it."

He handed her a vial. "It's for recovery. It'll help with the exhaustion a bit, but the others were destroyed. This is the last one."

"You should take it," she insisted.

"No, you need it more," he replied firmly, pressing it into her hand.

"Why do I need it more than you? Yer the one who got yer ass kicked by Kasherri," she teased, trying to lighten the mood.

"Because you're going to fly us up there," Leper said, rubbing her back reassuringly.

"I can't," Lillian argued.

"You can," he countered. "You have to."

"Leper, you don't understand. Every time I think about shifting, I see his face, I hear the beatings, the sound of the nails going into his hands. I can't do it. I just can't."

"Can't or won't?" Leper pressed gently.

The thundering footsteps grew nearer, the yapping sounds louder. Her head throbbed with turmoil. Shift again or run? When Leper's life was at stake, she hadn't thought about it. But now, they had a choice.

"Lillian, please," Leper pleaded, gripping her shoulders and turning her to face him. "If we don't escape in time to save

Zanera and Kelindra, it'll be because you're too scared to be who you're supposed to be... Shift!"

"Don't lay that on me! It's not fair," Lillian shot back, her voice rising. "We wouldn't be in this mess if yer stubborn ass had listened to me. We'd be on the surface, able to reach them!"

"I know. And I'm sorry I've put you in this position. But do this to save them, and I'll never ask you to shift again. I'll never tell another soul as long as we live," Leper promised, his gaze unwavering.

She saw the sincerity in his eyes, his deep concern for their friends. His gaze held determination, not sadness or despair, but the fierce hazel fire of resolve. His connection to those girls was admirable and cute. One of the many things she adored about him, loved about him. Maybe one day he would feel that way about her, too. *Oh,* how she yearned for him to look at her like that.

Her fingers tightened around the vial, heart pounding against her ribcage. With a flick of her thumb, she popped the cork and downed its contents. Relief flooded through her, banishing the exhaustion that had weighed her down. Though the gashes on her stomach still pained her, she felt revitalized, no longer on the brink of collapse.

"Now, turn into a griffin and I will..." Leper's grin widened mischievously. "Mount you."

"Yer a fuckin' idiot," she burst out laughing.

As Lillian focused her thoughts on Ghost, Leper's griffin, a strange pull twisted through her body, like invisible threads unraveling and weaving her into something new. A deep, aching heat spread through her limbs, bones grinding and reshaping beneath her skin. Her fingers curled inward, hardening into powerful lion's paws tipped with razor-sharp talons. A sudden weight pressed against her back, muscles stretching and straining as wings burst free, unfurling to their full span. The rush of air against them sent a shudder through her, every fiber of her being caught between human and beast. In this form, she felt an unshakable connection to nature, as if every living thing around her whispered its presence into her mind—the rustling of plants, the steady pulse of unseen creatures, their emotions surging through her like a second heartbeat.

Right now, all she sensed was hatred. Rage boiled in the air, thick and suffocating, driven by an insatiable thirst for blood.

From every tunnel, imps, kobolds, minotaurs, and centaurs poured in—too many to fight.

She felt Leper scramble onto her back. Instinct took over. She crouched low, muscles coiling with raw power, then launched herself into the air.

Madislak trudged through the coliseum, determined to uncover the source of the recent quake or surge of power that had erupted. He suspected Tamara's ally, Nalecht, might be involved. If not, he could use the event to instill fear and perhaps coerce Tamara into returning a shard. It had been three days since Petrovana, Blank Face, and Harmony were imprisoned in the deepest dungeons. Securing them there ensured they wouldn't reach the surface if they somehow escaped.

Inside the coliseum, wedding decorations were being hastily put up. Cheap replicas of daisies adorned the walls, and a central archway awaited his wedding with Petrovana tomorrow, where they would exchange vows. Sacrificing his own happiness for someone he barely knew stung, though he admitted knowing more about Petrovana than he had about Gwen when they married. What would he tell Rylin and Alissia? They adored Harmony.

Pushing guilt aside, Madislak boxed and buried it deep within himself. Too long had he been a pawn, fulfilling others' debts and defending those he cared for, only to be betrayed. From now on, his word would be law—he was the damned king, and he would act like one, heeding no one's advice. Memories of Harmony's gentle touch flooded his mind. They were perfect together, she the brain, he the brawn. After her silent confession and his rash actions, going through with this felt easier.

But Harmony made her choice. Not only would she become a Deathbinder, but she also kept vital information from him. Why? Perhaps she spent too much time with his wretched father. It felt like he didn't know anyone for who they truly were. At least Leper always told him exactly what he was thinking—more than anyone else ever did.

Madislak knew they would be angry with him for the betrayal, for imprisoning them, but it had to be done. Lantess stood alone against all other kingdoms, and the slim hope that Tamara would support him with her ruthless army was worth the risk. Lantess couldn't stand alone against Tudela and Kirilick, let alone Ambrosia, Wen-Tath, and Xaneth Harbor. They would be overrun before they had a chance to defend themselves.

Adding to the turmoil was the likely loss of Leper, who, if he survived, would be furious, probably launching into another unending fit of rage. Maybe even lose himself entirely.

But like everyone else, he'd have to deal with it. Time to man up or shut up. Madislak clung to a sliver of hope that his brother would survive, but knew he couldn't dwell on it. He had to plan for the possibility that Leper wouldn't make it. And where was Lillian? Had she bailed for good?

Madislak nearly missed the steps to the dais where Tamara stood barking orders. The moans and groans of her beasts filled the coliseum. He took the steps two at a time, and Tamara offered him a cup of tea, which he accepted cautiously. Remembering Blank Face's warning about her cunning, he gingerly sipped. It was black tea with a wickedly strong aftertaste. Not trusting it, he dumped the entire cup on the floor, and Tamara's mouth fell open in shock.

"You really can be an asshole, can't you?" Tamara grinned. "I like this new Madislak. I think he and I will get along just fine."

"Let me try yours," he demanded.

She held her cup out to him. He shoved it back. "No, you drink first."

Smiling, she took a large sip. "Happy?"

"Almost." He grabbed the cup and drank. Black tea, with no disgusting aftertaste.

"Alright, what was in mine?" he asked, setting her tea on the table.

"Truth serum," she shrugged. "Have to make sure you don't lie to me."

"Fine." Madislak took a chair and sat.

Like hell.

If she had truth serum, she would've used it on Harmony to extract whatever information she'd been trying to beat out of her for days. So much for an alliance based on trust. Madislak was prepared to play whatever card he needed to get himself and his friends to safety, though he still wasn't sure if that included Harmony. Either way, he would do anything to rid himself of these shards and the surrounding tyranny. But the real question for now was, what the hell was in that tea?

Tamara's poofy brown hair fluttered in the breeze before settling back into place. The breeze offered a welcome reprieve from the constant, intense humidity that plagued the area. It was like being in Malastion. Making him yearn for the spring temperatures that lingered in Lantess. Summer would now be in full force in Lantess, hopefully still standing under Leighth's guidance. The mere act of walking out here had him sweating in his light tunic and pants.

"That quake, that something your boyfriend did? Or your dragon?" Madislak didn't mince words.

Tamara took a chair. "I don't know."

Just the look on her face was enough to make him want to jump across this table and punch her. He instinctively started to rise, but caught himself.

What the hell?

He was never impulsive before, but suddenly he couldn't control himself.

Madislak drummed his fingers on the table in agitation. "He didn't reforge the talisman, did he?"

"You can't be that dumb." She placed a finger under her necklace, pulling out the shard of Aisha and Theora from under her brown shirt.

"Well, if it's some kind of threat, we should be ready to face it," Madislak glared at her.

Tamara scoffed. "We're prepared. I'm always prepared."

He tried to get her to offer more, but if she wasn't going to take the bait, he'd just see how this played out.

Madislak pinned her with a gaze. "I think it would be smart to split those up, at least until we know what the talisman's power truly is. That'll keep Nalecht from getting all of them and give me another weapon if that quake meant anything."

Tamara matched his intensity. "Careful, Madislak. I gave you back your precious sword and shield. That should be defense enough for you. Or are you forgetting that Nalecht now thinks I have them both? What would I tell him if he comes calling?"

"Any word on where Nalecht is lately? His absence every-where is concerning. You shouldn't take it lightly." Madislak leaned back, genuinely curious.

"No. He might still be in Ambrosia, where he rules. He recent-ly conquered Ventessa, so he's probably either out conquering Wen-Tath or Tudela or securing their allegiances. That's my best guess." She smirked arrogantly.

Madislak's expression darkened. "What kind of queen guess-es? How do you have no idea where he is?" His fist slammed against the table.

Holy shit. That poison had some serious side effects from one sip.

Tamara burst out laughing. "What's the matter, Madislak? Having trouble controlling your anger?"

"Yeah. Some fucking truth serum you have," he shot back.

Her smirk disappeared. Exactly like he thought it would. He'd doubted what she put in his tea. Now he knew it wasn't just truth serum.

"You ready to let me have Blank Face as my prisoner yet?" She leaned back, shifting the subject.

Madislak bounced his leg with restless force. "Why do you want him so bad?"

Her arrogant grin returned. "It's not easy to waltz into Ventessa and kill King Zonoh. I swoon over someone who can eliminate people with the kind of ease he does."

"So you want him as a murder weapon?" Madislak ran his fingers through his beard.

"He reminds me of someone I used to know." She looked away.

"And that is?" Madislak pressed.

"Xartazza." She leaned forward, resting her arms on the table. "He was, is, and always will be the best fighter—no." She shook her head. "The best killer this world has ever seen. I kept him hidden, away from the public eye. Wherever I sent him, whatever the target, he won. How do you think I took over

Xaneth Harbor and earned their respect so quickly? Nylor is good, but Xartazza... he put me on this throne."

Madislak stood. "Make sure everything is ready for tomorrow. I don't want any disturbances. And consider what I said about splitting the shards. Both of us wielding one is stronger than one of us wielding two. And whatever caused that earthquake, be ready."

Tamara's eyes flared with anger. "Do not talk down to me. Lest you forget, I still have both your potential future brides in custody."

Madislak grinned. "Threaten me again. Maybe I'll whisk this magical note to Nalecht. The one I've pre-written with everything you're plotting against him."

Tamara threw her chair back, the legs scraping harshly against the wooden dais. "You dare?"

Madislak whirled, slamming both hands on the table. "You're the one who tried to poison me. I took the liberty of telling your shrews that if I die, you wanted to make sure this letter got to Nalecht. Told them it contained information about the talisman I couldn't share, so they linked it to my life force. If I die, it'll be sent directly to him."

He held out his hand. "A shard, please."

Tamara's face turned so red he thought she might combust. "You fucking—" She was so angry she couldn't even form words. He had caught her off guard.

He kept his hand steady, waiting. His heart pounded in his ears, but he didn't let it show. This was a bold move, even for him, and if he miscalculated her fear of Nalecht, it would go badly.

"I'll give you Blank Face as a prisoner as well," he offered. "Now give me that fucking shard."

Her face shifted from fury to something calmer. Then, a malicious grin crept across her lips. Slowly, she unclasped the shard of Theora from her necklace and handed it to him.

Outside, he kept his stride steady, cool, and collected as he swaggered down the stairs. Inside, his gut churned with anxiety.

Petrovana walked through a field of wildflowers, a cup of coffee in her hands. She inhaled sharply, savoring the scent of the blossoms brushing against her ankles. Did she die from rotten food? Was she in Blissoria? She glanced up and saw a dirt path leading to a large castle—her castle. Made of elegant stone, smooth and glossy, the walls were painted a light purple with hints of light blue and green trimming. Sunlight reflected off the walls. She walked up to the double doors bearing Terynsipple's crest, a purple sword piercing the sun, and pushed them open.

Everything was neatly arranged. Each surface glistened, from the marble tabletop to the fine china in the glass cupboards. She sipped her coffee, its sweet vanilla flavor just how she liked it. Everything was just how she liked it. She walked up the stairs to the second level, her bare feet feeling the plush purple carpeting. She entered the queen's quarters, which held two armoires—one with a glass door housing the finest jewelry and makeup. Hoops, studs, trinkets, rings, necklaces, perfumes, and various lip colors, eyeliners, and blushes—everything she could dream of, all neatly placed.

She tried on a few pieces, brushing her glossy black hair back to look at herself in the mirror.

The sun disappeared, replaced by a loud boom of thunder, followed by a massive bolt of lightning that shattered the window closest to her. The breeze shot through the room, flinging the blue curtains wildly and rustling the purple bedcovers. The stone charred from the strike, and then she heard it—a hissing, gurgling noise behind her. She hung her head as a sense of dread washed over her. *Not in Blissoria.*

She slowly turned around and saw the scary, nasty visage of Kasherri, her decaying underworld scent overpowering all other smells.

"Hello, child," Kasherri hissed. "Sorry to interrupt your... fantasies."

"Where am I?" Petrovana backed up slowly.

Kasherri's feet clicked against the stone as she approached. "Currently with me. I must say, you keep good company." Her toothy grin grew.

"Wh... what do you want?" Petrovana's arms trembled as she braced herself against the window.

"You, dear. You are powerful. Like Harmony, The Former, The Latter, and Borlden. Join my loyal order." She made a beckoning motion with her finger.

Petrovana started sliding along the wall towards the bed, her pulse thrumming through her temples. "No... never. I won't let you shackle me like you did Harmony."

Kasherri's yellow skin glistened as another bolt of lightning struck close to the same window. "I have something I can give you," Kasherri taunted. "Something you crave."

"What is that?" Petrovana sneered, grabbing her wrist to stop the shaking.

Please don't say my parents, please don't say my parents.

"Exactly," Kasherri cackled. "I'll tell you all the secrets you seek."

"Genova, Brebian's shrew, knows. I'll make her tell me," Petrovana shot back.

The tendrils on Kasherri's head wiggled. "She doesn't know. Only Zonoh knew, and he's deceased."

No. No. No. No. Godsdamnit. There had to be someone. Some way to find out. She refused to live her life in this constant pursuit. But last time she had this offer, she turned it down to save Leper's life. Luckily, too, if Genova didn't know, then she would've done it for nothing.

With a defeated sigh, Petrovana responded, "Then I guess I'll go to the grave not knowin'." She bluffed.

"That would be a waste of a strong bloodline. The likes of yours, you have so much... potential." Kasherri swiftly clicked across the floor to the bed.

"Who! Who is it!?" Petrovana yelled.

"Agree," Kasherri demanded.

"No! Tell me!" Petrovana held her ground.

"Is that a verbal agreement that if I tell you, you become a Deathbinder?" Kasherri grinned, dripping black saliva onto the clean purple sheets.

"No, stop tryin' to trick me. Just tell me!" Petrovana screamed.

Why was it always her? She'd spend the rest of her miserable life searching, wandering. Why was there always a cost she wasn't willing to pay? First, it was Leper's life, which, thank Hathor, she didn't sacrifice. Now she'd have to give up her afterlife to a never-ending servitude to the evil goddess. Nothing ever came easy in this world. Nothing.

She glanced at Kasherri, her three eyes locked on her, roaming up and down. The black and purple hues in her eyes held nothing but pure evil and malice. She wanted to. She wanted to do it so badly it hurt in her chest. Just to know. Just once.

She and Harmony could figure a way out of it together if she accepted. But if they didn't, if they didn't find a way out, what would happen to her? She looked at the tendrils wobbling on Kasherri's head, then back to the floor. Would she look like that, too, if she became a Deathbinder? Or like the red-skinned beasts she saw in that book?

"Last chance," Kasherri hissed.

A tear slid down her cheek. She shook her head no, dooming herself to never knowing who she was. She would spend whatever years she had left roaming namelessly before she died. Just a nomad walking Kalazaar, an empty shell.

Kasherri flicked her six-inch sharp fingernails out, then yanked Petrovana's head back, exposing her neck. Slowly, making sure Petrovana felt every inch of the incision, she ran her sharp nail across her neck.

Petrovana gasped awake, screaming, grabbing her neck in fear. Her pulse pounded wildly through her veins. Her chest felt heavy as she panted, like someone had put a vice on it and kept squeezing. Her head stung in piercing agony, her vision blurred, and she could hear Blank Face saying something to her. She felt his hand on her back as he stroked up and down, but it did nothing to stop the gripping fear, the grief, and the unrelenting headache that refused to cease. It hurt so badly that tears rolled down her cheeks, and she cupped her face.

Finally, it started to subside, and she glanced up at Harmony, sitting on her bench, her hand covering her mouth in shock and terror. She felt a surge of power, like a tingling in the back of her head. Something had changed. She wasn't just stronger. She was *more*.

Powerful?

She'd been feeling more confident lately, but now... now she felt unstoppable.

The magical tattoos on her body glowed, their potency increasing before her very eyes. Had she just ascended another pinnacle? Was whatever she was becoming still growing stronger—what was she truly capable of now?

What kind of magical abomination *was* she?

"What?" Petrovana's voice was gruff.

Even Blank Face looked something akin to shocked. It was the first she'd ever seen that look cross his stoic, brooding face.

Petrovana slammed her hands down on the bench beneath her. "What, godsdamnit!" she frantically felt around her neck.

Was she bleeding? Was she that ugly or transformed? What happened that was so shocking they couldn't even speak?

Blank Face grabbed her hands and guided them to her forehead.

She stopped cold as soon as she felt little nubs on her forehead. *What the fuck!*

Chapter Twenty-Four

"Please tell me those aren't what I think they are." Petrovana swallowed hard, feeling two protrusions at the top of her forehead.

Blank Face's mouth fell open. "Well, they aren't spikes or nails if that's what you're talking about."

"Seriously? Jokes now? I'm not in the mood, asshole." Petrovana sneered.

"One more hour until the wedding. Eat up and be ready, we're taking the hooded one and the purple-eyed bitch!" A guard hollered down the steps.

"They're going to see me for the freak I am." Petrovana paced back and forth, her arms and hands trembling. "Why does he want to push this marriage so quickly! Why right now?"

She glanced at the dress they brought her and the tray of food. She couldn't eat right now; nausea ripped through her core. Anything she ate would come back up. Her nerves were shot. What was she? Chernzerk? Some kind of ultra-powerful shrew? She didn't know. She regretted not taking Kasherri's deal; at least she'd know what she was.

Blank Face grabbed the dress off the hanger. "They're horns, Petrovana. You're Ace's sister, the fourth one. But..." He trailed off.

Which was completely true—they still hadn't found Ace's sister, the fourth Chernzerk. Probably because she was *here*... and she didn't even know it.

She was still confused, though. All the other Chernzerk—Leper, Blank Face, and Ace—had always known what they were because of their horns. So why had *hers* been hidden from her until now?

She pinched the bridge of her nose, trying to calm herself. "They're goin' to kill me. I'm goin' to die today. Fuckin' great. I finally find out what I am, and I'm gonna die."

"Wait." Blank Face rubbed his neck. "The shrine on The Talon. The magic was supposed to be released when all four of us visited it, touched it. Did you go to the shrine?"

"Yes. I was there with Leper when he stepped on the platform. He said he heard a voice telling him to step up." She threw her hands up, shrugging. "Then, when he saw his memories, he told me everything. He saw that he had a twin brother—and that there were two other Chernzerk out there, a boy and a girl. Which one was obviously Ace, but we never found the other one, just knew it was a girl."

"It should've shown you your past. Our fathers' and mothers' memories were locked in there. Did it call to you?"

"No. Just him." She shot back quickly.

"That doesn't make any sense. That well of magic wouldn't be released unless you touched your statue. It's not about proximity, it's about touch." Blank Face turned to Harmony, still holding the dress.

She tried to speak, her voice coming out as more of a mouse squeak. Then she sighed resignedly and signaled to Blank Face.

"She said she thought Chernzerk couldn't do magic. That it drove them crazy," Blank Face mouthed, then turned back to Petrovana. "That's true. My father, Leper's and mine, was like that. He kept using blood magic, and it drove him insane. It got so bad he completely lost himself, couldn't shake the affliction. Do you feel... crazy?"

"No, I still feel like myself. Just pissed. Why now? What..." she trailed off, going still.

She would be thirty in a week or two. She had lost track of time since they arrived, but it was close. If Madislak hadn't locked them down here for days on end, she might actually know when her birthday was. Zonoh had promised to reveal her parents on her thirtieth birthday. Was this the reason? Did he cast some kind of cloaking spell on her so she wouldn't change until now? *Gods*, she wished he was still alive. She turned, fixing Blank Face with a gaze, and attempted to slap him.

He jumped back, easily avoiding the strike without dropping the dress. "What did I do?" he said, raising his hands.

"Well," she poked his chest, "you killed Zonoh. He would've told me what I am on my thirtieth birthday, and that's not far off."

"Petrovana, I'm sorry." He finally set the dress back down and took her hands. "I was a different person then. I wanted to find Leper and thought the only way was to get Borlden to track him."

"I know... it just sucks not knowin'." She locked eyes with him, then glanced at the dress. "Maybe we can cut off some fabric from the dress and wrap it around my head, like a bandanna to cover the horns."

"We'll figure something out. You better get dressed." Blank Face picked the dress back off the bars and handed it to her.

Blank Face averted his gaze respectfully as she changed. Yesterday, the guards had brought down the dress and changed their restraints from linked cuffs to a single anti-magic cuff on each wrist. It was both a show of trust and to make the process easier. Except for Harmony—she still had linked cuffs on her hands. She snarled as she put the gown on. Marrying Madislak was the last thing she wanted to do; there were so many more pressing matters. He'd become one of the biggest jerks she'd ever met, and that list of jerks included both Blank Face and Brebian. Her pulse quickened. This wasn't how she'd anticipated her life would be. Not at all. As the gown flowed over, she imagined Leper having that stupid, large grin on his face and making some flirtatious comment, and a smile tugged her lips.

The gown was surprisingly comfortable and very elegant, dropping just past her knees. The neckline formed a V-shape

down to her navel, clinging to her curves as if it were meant
for her. The back was open halfway down, with streamers
hanging from the sleeves that draped just beyond the elbows.
The ocean blue color blended to a green with some slivers of
purple, and the streamers on the sleeves alternated between all
three colors.

"Well, how do I look?" She twirled in front of Harmony and
Blank Face.

Harmony gave her a broad smile and two thumbs up.

"Wow, you look completely stunning," Blank Face said, his
mouth slightly hanging open.

Their eyes met, and she saw the longing in his gaze, the desire.
But he blinked and it vanished, just like that.

"Let's cover up those horns, Cherno." He ripped some of the
streamers off.

A bubble of laughter rolled up Petrovana's throat, and she let
out a genuine giggle. "Maybe it's not so bad."

Carefully, he intertwined the blue and purple streamers and
gently wrapped them around her head, tucking the little horns
between the weaves. His hands made quick work of the weaving.

"There. All covered up." His hand grazed the side of her cheek.

She quickly grabbed his hand and held it there for a moment,
comforting and relaxing. His touch nearly sent a fire through
her, heating her blood as she gazed into his deep, piercing brown
eyes. *Gods,* why was he suddenly so desirable to her? His gaze
fell to her lips and then back to her eyes, causing her cheeks to
flush even more.

She had to know. She had to know, undoubtedly, if there was
something there before she made another monumental mistake. She grabbed the back of his neck and pulled him in, and
he kissed her so gently. He pulled away and mouthed Leper's
name.

"Don't talk. We'll cross that bridge when we get there. Just
kiss me like you mean it," she begged.

He locked gazes for a moment, then grabbed her by the neck
and pulled her in. Their tongues brushed, igniting a fire. Pure,
hot fire, just like Alzen. Everything blurred in her mind. They
were in their own little world, nothing else mattered, and she

couldn't get enough. The answer to the burning question she'd been avoiding for so long, she just knew.

Lillian beat her wings as fast and hard as she could on takeoff. The centaurs raised their bows and fired arrows. Her pulse leaped as she angled and dodged, but she rammed into the unforgiving rock wall.

"I'd prefer not to die on the way up!" Leper shouted. She responded with a scree.

Maka Kura zipped in front of her, deflecting several incoming arrows. The ravine was incredibly narrow at the bottom, leaving little room for error. One accidental tilt, one shift in momentum, and they would fall into the swarms of enemies gathered below. The walls were jagged rock, without the soft vegetation that covered the other walls and floors throughout the rain trials. A perfect lift-off was crucial. She had to be perfect.

Lillian angled her four lion's paws towards the wall, banking and gripping a few protruding rocks before vaulting herself upward, soaring farther and farther towards the top.

"Yes!" Leper hollered, and she could picture him smiling his goofy ass smile. "Yeaaaasssss."

They climbed higher and higher, the scent of fresh air growing sweeter as they inched towards the surface, towards sunlight and freedom. After several minutes of flying, they finally reached the ridge at the top. She landed gracefully and shook her body, trying to get Leper off her back before shifting back to human form. But she could see from the shrinking size of the tunnels that there was no way her griffin form would fit through any of them.

Thudding boots beside her confirmed his dismount, and she changed.

"You did it!" he grabbed her, picking her off her feet and squeezing her tightly.

"We did it." She enunciated each word.

He set her down, his hands cupping her cheeks. Her skin heated at his touch, waves of desire coursing through her. She looked straight into his large hazel eyes. Since they met, she had never been shy about what she wanted, and she wasn't about to start now. She could see the uncertainty in his eyes, practically feel the tension in his palm.

"I..." he stuttered.

"I know." She interrupted him. "I told ya I'd respect yer space."

"I don't even know what to do anymore. I'm tired of being so conflicted..." Leper's shoulders sagged. "I still don't know what to feel. I feel so... dirty, even looking at you like that."

"She wouldn't bother with consideration." Lillian fired back. "She has before, and she didn't feel dirty. But I admire yer respect, yer loyalty." *It only adds to the fire.*

"I don't think she would. We have something special. She is special to me," he insisted.

Barf. She was probably cheating on him right now.

"She's special, alright." Lillian chuckled.

She looked around at the three tunnels, yet again, another option where they had no idea which one to take. *Should I tell him about Artemis being his son now? No. Not yet. They're not out alive yet, and he needs to love me for me. Not because they have a child together.* Then, she'd tell him.

The yips and yaps were distant, but the constant thudding and pounding of footsteps and hooves told her they needed to move. Linger too long, and they would catch up, losing the precious distance they had created. The thought of actual food made her heart jump. Sinking her teeth into a nice juicy steak, or a fish kabob with fresh veggies and tender succulent fish. She placed her hand over her stomach as it growled at her.

"When we get out of here, I..." She trailed off briefly as her shoulders fell. "Don't take this the wrong way, but I ain't watchin' you and her together. I won't be around."

"What about Nalecht and the shards? We need your help, Lillian." He started walking towards the middle tunnel.

Lillian followed closely behind him. "Reckon I'll help with that. I'm just lettin' ya know, if you choose her again, I'm leavin' fer good."

"You're giving me an ultimatum?" Leper paused briefly on the steps. "So, we can't be friends?"

"Don't make this hard." She pushed past him, leading the way out.

He sounded frustrated. "I'm not making this difficult; you are. I care for you, Lillian. End of story."

Lillian sighed. "Never mind, let's just get the fuck out of here."

She heard his footsteps halt behind her and turned to face him.

"What?" she snapped. "I'll drop it. Let's go."

"Shhhh." He pursed his fingers to his lips. "Maka is rambling on about some bullshit."

Leper plodded up the steps, already arguing with Lillian about Petrovana, and they hadn't even made it past the first section of steps yet. He considered her valid point about not wanting to watch them together; it was the same thing he had said to Harmony before he left for this cursed place. Maka Kura interrupted his thoughts, saying he had to tell Leper something, while Lillian continued yammering on about their conversation. All he wanted was to get out of this hellhole, to the sunlight and fresh air. Fresh food and water—he licked his lips.

The stairs and tunnels were more refined in this section of the rain trials, as if someone had taken the time to carve out all the steps. Leper estimated that the task would take years; the stairs seemed never-ending. There was no railing on the walls—only jagged rock and faintly glowing quartz to light the way.

"What's so important, Maka?" Leper called after Lillian stopped talking to him.

"I promised Rinawen I would be honest with you. It was me who reached out to her—to Theora— at the wall, when you were about to give up and fall."

Leper grinned. "Okay, well, thank you for that. Why would that be so important?"

"I wish that thing could just talk out loud because your face is all over the place," Lillian blurted.

Leper arched a brow at her.

"That's not what I need to be honest with you about," Maka Kura clarified.

"Then what is it?" Leper snapped, impatience sharpening his words.

"It's actually two things. One is what it cost to get her to intervene. The other is something else." Maka paused. "Being a sentient being, I can reach other planes of existence. I can communicate with the gods. When I asked Theora to send Rinawen back down one last time, she told me there would be a price."

Leper's jaw tensed. "What's the price, Maka?" His voice was low, edged with warning.

Maka let out what sounded like a sigh in his head. "When this is over—if you manage to defeat Nalecht and claim the talisman—you'll have to choose. Me or Ghost."

Leper scowled, slamming his fist against the rock wall. "So..." He exhaled sharply. "You're telling me that if I somehow pull this off, I'll have to give up either you or Ghost? Why the hell would you do that?"

"It was that, or you die, Leper. And I don't want you to die."

Leper clenched his teeth. "Sometimes you really piss me off, Maka." He really didn't want to think about choosing between his weapon and his companion right now. Shaking his head, he muttered, "What other bullshit do you have to tell me?"

Maka's voice barely rose above a whisper. "Remember when I told you about my origins? That Samaja made me?"

"Yes," Leper said flatly.

"And when you asked about how I know Samaja?"

Leper frowned, a cold dread creeping into his chest. "Yeah. Where are you going with this?"

Maka spoke quickly. "I lied."

Leper's pulse pounded in his ears. His temples throbbed as he waited, already certain of what was coming but needing to hear it from his own weapon.

"Damn it, Maka Kura, I don't have time for this bullshit right now. Spit. It. Out."

Maka's voice came steady, absolute.

"I'm not just made by Samaja. I *am* Samaja, son."

And there it was.

Rage ignited in his veins, burning through every fiber of his being. His hands tightened around his weapons, his knuckles white with the force of his grip.

Then, without a word, he let go.

Maka Kura clattered down the steps, bouncing off the stone before coming to rest near the bottom.

"No." He spat.

"Please. Listen to me. I know you aren't ready for this. I know how you must feel, and I'm sorry," Maka pleaded.

"Shut up! Shut up!" Leper screamed out loud, not just in his head.

"Leper, you don't understand," Maka reasoned.

Lillian grabbed his arm. "What's the matter?"

He didn't bother to keep the rest of the communication between just him and Maka Kura; he wanted everyone to know what a useless liar his own bonded weapon was. The sting of betrayal raced through him all over again. He didn't care what the cost was at all; he was too blinded by rage to even bother asking.

He shouted down the steps at the weapon lying on the ground. "No, Maka, you don't understand! But you are about to find out what years of abandonment feel like, asshole."

"You have no idea what I've sacrificed!" Maka Kura's voice roared through Leper's mind, so loud it sent a spike of pain through his skull. He clamped his hands over his ears, but it did nothing to shut him out.

"I gave my soul! I gave up being with my children to create that well—to give you all a chance! I knew I would lose my mind, but blood magic was the only way to preserve what we had. And if I could have..." Maka's voice wavered, raw with something Leper couldn't name.

"I would've destroyed the talisman for you."

Leper bellowed down the stairs. "What *you* sacrificed?" He said slowly. "You killed Svetlana! Madislak's mother—he was a seven-year-old boy when you did horrible things to her! And then...and then..." He panted, trying to control his breathing. "You just ship me and Blank Face off to wherever, never bothering to care if we're alive or alright, just ditch us like the garbage we are!"

His chest heaved, like a snake had found its way around his lungs, squeezing, squeezing, squeezing. Sucking the life right out of whatever he had left to give. They were exhausted. Everything hurt. And now this stupid weapon was going to lay this on him.

He strained his voice as he hollered as loudly as he could, his face heating. "I fucking HATE you!"

"Lep. Calm down, yer freakin' me out here. What is goin' on?" Lillian placed her hand on his back and started rubbing.

The anger, the darkness returned tenfold, threatening to take over his mind once more. The shard of Kasherri pressed through his mind, the pressure almost unbearable. He pushed back, trying to clear the fog, the creeping anxiety that clouded his every thought. *No.* He didn't want to lose control now that they were so close to making it out, so close to Zanera and Kelindra. He fell to a knee, shoving against the pressure that crushed through his mind, but it relentlessly shoved back, reaching for a hold, grabbing for anything to latch onto in his consciousness. Tempting him. "Give in. Give in." A ghostly voice whispered.

He shook his head, then felt two warm, calloused palms cup his face. "Look at me!" the voice commanded.

Leper opened his eyes and immediately found Lillian's green eyes staring back at him, holding his face in her hands. "You got it! Push it away. I am with you. We beat Kasherri; you can beat this."

His head began to pound, a thudding headache in the back of his neck, and he grabbed her hand on his cheek and squeezed it.

"Don't let go," he mouthed through ragged breaths.

"I will never let go of you." She smiled warmly. "I'm with you."

Another wave of anguish, dark energy plunged its way into his mind, and he pushed back again, squeezing Lillian's hand for dear life. It wanted him to cave, to give in to the agonizing pain that erupted in the back of his head. To surrender to the dark pulses and temptations flooding his mind. He would not give in; he would not let it corrupt him again. He shoved and shoved until he collapsed on the stones, everything going black.

Chapter Twenty-Five

L eper slowly opened his eyes and was immediately met with Lillian's gaze, cradling his head in her lap and running her fingers through his dark hair. His head still throbbed from the intense battle within, but he forced himself up and looked down at the bottom of the steps where he had tossed Maka Kura. Still there. *Good. Let him rot.* Lillian set her hand on his beard.

"How long was I out?" Leper asked.

"I don't know. Maybe seven hours? I have no way to tell time, but I dozed off too." Lillian ran her hand down his neck. Damn, that felt good.

"It's been thirteen hours," Maka interjected in Leper's mind.

"Shut the fuck up. Get out of my head. Go away and never come back." Leper's words dripped with venom as he replied mentally.

"We have to go," Leper said as he rose and offered a hand to Lillian.

His stomach growled in protest at not having eaten in a while—days, maybe. Fatigue still plagued his body, which continued to ache and protest as they started climbing again.

"Wait, yer not goin' to grab yer chakrams?" Lillian pointed back down. "What's goin' on?"

"Like most people in my life I meet, Maka Kura is nothing but a liar and a snake," Leper gritted.

"Yer goin' to have to explain how. What did he say that was so bad?"

"For starters, his name is Samaja. Samaja fucking Tes'thorean," Leper enunciated each syllable.

"Oh..." Lillian's gaze dropped, her eyes flashing with anger.

"I know. It's disappointing," Leper said. "So I'm going to abandon him down here, like he did to Blank Face and me twenty-four years ago."

Lillian let out a sigh. "Lep, as much as I hate to say this, you can't deny he did save yer ass and mine multiple times down there and directed us out."

"Oh, I should take him with me then?" Leper growled.

Lillian threw her hands up. "I'm not sayin' you gotta talk to him. But you can't deny the fact that he's the most legendary weapon ever created. The pinnacle of weapon craft. He'll cut through dragon scales, shade panthers—hell, you can control his flight. That's invaluable. So, I'm just askin' you to hear him out. Fer me."

Of course, she had to add "for me." He didn't want to talk to or take those stupid weapons anywhere, not after how Maka Kura treated people in general—especially Svetlana and his own children. Not to mention the ridiculous things he said to Lillian, an eleven-year-old child, after what happened with her father. He had absolutely zero intentions of taking Maka Kura anywhere, and he sure as shit wouldn't be calling him dad or Samaja.

The only thing he'd be losing was an irritating voice in his head—one that grated on his nerves now. Though if he was being honest, Maka Kura had never irritated him before. Back then, he'd been playful. Helpful, even.

Leper shook his head. *No.* Maybe Maka had been useful, but in the end, he was just like everyone else—a liar. A deceitful wretch.

Of all the people in the world, *he* had to be Samaja?

A flicker of curiosity stirred in him, but it was drowned beneath disgust. How could he possibly listen to anything that bastard had to say? A man who abandoned his own children, made life hell for Oubank—Lillian's father—raped women.

A monster.

There was nothing—*nothing*—Samaja could say that would ever change his mind. At least, not now, probably not ever.

Leper held his hand out and floated Maka Kura back to his waiting palm.

"I am doing this for her and for her alone. Do not talk unless I ask you something. I don't want your damaged excuses or your damned whining. You are a weapon. My weapon. You fight for me, and that is it. I am not your son, and you'll never refer to me as that again. You are not my father. You will continue to be known only as Maka Kura. Agree, or I drop you right now."

"Yes. I agree," Maka responded and immediately ceased talking.

At least he could follow directions.

"We were out for thirteen hours, but we need to get a move on. I'm sure that army behind us made some ground. I'm starving, we're beat to hell, and I'm absolutely sick of all the nonsense," Leper muttered.

"Then let's get movin'," Lillian perked up.

The stairs seemed completely endless as they climbed for the next two hours.

But the higher they climbed, the denser the fresh air from the surface crawled up his nose. Leper could barely contain his excitement as he hurried up the steps, his legs throbbing from the wounds sustained down there. Their clothes were torn and tattered, making them look like they'd been through bulwark training. Lillian's face was covered with grime and dirt, but he could still see her wonderfully freckled, beautiful face. And the smell of them, woof.

Eventually, they came to a large expanse and a door. A door. Thank the gods. Leper had never before imagined just how bone-jarringly thankful he would be to see something as simple as a door. Nor did he ever expect to be this excited to get back to the hot, miserable, sweltering desert. But he was. He would welcome it all with open arms and hug the sand once they saw the light of day again.

With a quick glance at Lillian, they rushed towards the door. The large, cavernous area wasn't a natural rock formation like most of the rain trials. The floor was carved out and flattened, and even though there wasn't any furniture or anything from the surface, it seemed crafted by human or dwarven hands. Along the perimeter of the wall, carved into the stone itself, stood giant statues.

Leper immediately recognized them as the gods. He took a moment and eyed each one, awestruck. Amarook, the Chernzerk, holding a young girl in his arms. She looked maybe five or six years old. The horns drifted back from his temples, then curved upward. He sneered at the carving of Kasherri, her three eyes and tendrils draping down in solid stone. He continued to take in all of them: Ryollin the minotaur, Aisha the dwarf, Hathor the orc, Obidiah the human. Then his eyes spotted Theora, the elf. Vines flowed from her head, and tree bark had been carved for her legs.

He knelt down by her carving and placed a hand upon her foot. After a moment's silence, he rose, turned back to Lillian, and together they made their way to the door. Leper's mouth fell open. Skeletons littered the space in front of the door—tons of them, bones everywhere, not just a few, but thousands.

"What is this place?" Lillian muttered.

Leper resisted the urge to ask Maka.

"I don't know. Let's just get out of here." Leper turned the door handle, but it broke off. He stuck his finger in the hole and pulled back. The door squeaked as it opened. Lillian stepped up beside him, setting her hand on his shoulder as they eagerly peered through the doorway.

Leper's shoulders sagged, and Lillian's did the same. Steps. Thousands of them.

"Fuck me," Lillian muttered.

Leper gave her a sidelong glance.

"Don't you dare say it," she smiled.

The morning of the wedding, Madislak paced back and forth in his guest room, brushing by the brown and yellow plaid sheets on the large bed. The dresser, once a rich chestnut brown, had worn down with use. He glanced at the doorway leading to the hall inside Tamara's manor. Madislak remembered that Tamara planned a fighting tournament after the wedding, giving him the perfect opportunity to check her chambers beforehand. She would be too busy catering to that to notice. This would be the opportunity he'd been waiting for to sneak into her room and see what kinds of poisons she kept there. About the only thing she was good for was training bulwarks. Many of the bulwarks would participate in these tournaments to make a name for themselves, then they would start to challenge more prominent fighters until they could reach the rank of bulwark. Perhaps he'd get lucky and find other, more valuable information or the shards.

He couldn't be entirely sure, but deep down, he knew she hadn't used a truth serum on him. It wouldn't make any sense. As the King of Lantess, his father had exposed him to truth serums before they were used in interrogations, replacing the cruel torture methods Tamara favored. They had a distinct minty taste, unlike the garbage she put in his tea.

Madislak donned his freshly washed and polished plethocyte armor, fixing the cuffs on his sleeves before opening the door. He had instructed a tailor to add a patch of Lantess on his left shoulder—a lion's head with an open maw, shaded yellow and outlined in blue, the colors of Lantess. He had debated changing both the insignia and the colors to dishonor his father, whose actions had led to his mother's death. But didn't feel like explaining to his children or his people why the sudden change occurred, so he left it alone. The rest of the armor was black with red linings on the seams, buttoned down the front with a V-shaped collar. It fit snugly against his large muscles, moving with them as he flexed.

He had also sent a magical note he purchased from a shrew to Leighth to check on his beloved children and city. So far, they were fine, and he let out a sigh of relief. However, Leighth mentioned something that needed to be discussed upon his return—it would have to wait.

He finished straightening his long sleeves, made of a mesh-like material that offered little breathability. Instead of wearing a comfortable sleeveless shirt and shorts, he had to endure this hot, sticky, long-sleeve, and black pants ensemble that would roast him all day. He opened the door to the hallway, still fuming that Tamara would try to poison him and lie about it.

He needed to refocus on the present. After fixing his attire, he nonchalantly made his way toward her chambers, paying close attention to the guard detail.

Several guards patrolled the area, their armor clinking softly in the dimly lit hallway. For the most part, they paid him no heed as he strode forward with purpose. He reached Tamara's large double doors, their pristine, shimmering dragon-face handles gleaming under the torchlight. The keyhole sat at the center of the open maw.

Shit. I hope it's not locked.

Glancing over his shoulder, he checked the empty corridor before gripping the handle. Locked. Of course. But he had come prepared. He pulled out a hairpin, recalling what Harmony had taught him about the delicate mechanisms inside a lock.

He worked fast, slipping the hairpin into the keyhole, wiggling it to manipulate the pins. His fingers were too large for this kind of precision work, and frustration pricked at the back of his mind. He counted the seconds in his head. The nearest guard was still walking away, but he had maybe forty-five seconds before they turned back around.

Fifteen seconds.

The lock refused to give. Maybe if he just forced it—

Thirty seconds.

He shoved the hairpin harder than he should have. It jammed. Neither budging forward nor coming free. *Wonderful.*

The sound of footsteps grew louder.

"Hey! What are you doing?" a voice barked.

Madislak froze, then let out a slow breath and turned around, schooling his face into an easy smirk. Two guards approached, hands resting on their weapons.

"Nothing you need to worry about," he said casually, stepping back from the door as if it didn't matter.

One of the guards narrowed his eyes. "You don't belong here. Leave."

Madislak feigned offense, throwing up his hands. "Fine, fine. I was just looking for a quiet place to think. No need to get all worked up."

The guards didn't budge. One gave a sharp tilt of his head toward the end of the hall. "Go. Now."

With a slow nod, Madislak turned on his heel and started walking. He kept his pace easy, measured—no sudden movements. He could feel their eyes burning into his back, ensuring he obeyed. *Damn it. I'm losing precious time to get answers. And now I have to find another way in.*

Only when he rounded a corner, out of their line of sight, did he spot movement in the shadows. A red-haired girl. She stood just inside an alcove, one finger pressed to her lips. Then, without a word, she motioned for him to follow.

Madislak wasted no time. Slipping into the shadows beside her, he let her lead him through the winding halls, his pulse pounding. He wasn't sure he could trust her, but she was hiding him from Tamara's guards; he had no other option but to follow. Whatever she had planned, he could only hope it got him into Tamara's room.

She led him through another doorway to Tamara's room, and it was not at all what he expected. It was immaculate. Every surface glistened in the sunlight streaming in. The yellow and brown bed sheets were neatly made. The floor was spotless. The dresser was neatly organized, its large mirror mounted on the back, not a single streak or speck. *Holy shit. Why isn't the rest of the town this clean?*

Above the mirror, a horn—the exact same one Harmony and he had found at that abandoned house—was mounted like a trophy. Was that horn from the same person? His gaze lingered on the horn as he glared at it and then swallowed hard... Did Tamara cut Blank Face's horns off!?

"Why are you trying to get in here, King Madislak?" the woman asked.

Madislak looked her over. A striking redhead woman. Her ivory nightgown clung to her figure, leaving little to the imagination.

"I, uhhh..." Madislak stammered, searching for the right words. "Got lost. This place is a maze."

"No, it's not." She held up her palms, showing him both her spells: lightning and a shield. It wasn't often you saw vitalis magic. "Don't worry. I won't say anything. I know how my sister can be."

"Tamara has a sister?" Madislak's mouth fell open.

"Standing right here." She smirked.

"What's your name?" Madislak's shoulders eased slightly. Any relation to Tamara might be just as wicked, or worse. And how was it she's never been spoken of or even heard of all this time? She looked like she was in her mid-thirties. Younger than Tamara, but obviously an adult.

"I could call the guards right now or send this note to Tamara." She held up a small piece of paper inscribed with runes around its edges.

Oh shit. Oh shit, I'm so screwed.

"I just want you to understand, this is my gesture of trust to you. Whatever is said in this room is not repeated. Do you understand?"

Wait...what!?

Madislak looked her up and down, assessing her body language, her stance, her face. She seemed normal, maybe a little scared—probably just because of his presence. Her nose was slightly elongated, and cute freckles dotted her cheeks and neck. Her eyes were a striking shade of blue.

Madislak ran his hands through his dark brown hair. "Does that go both ways?"

She nodded cautiously, her curly chin-length hair bouncing forward. "My name is Jocelyn Remmy. And I'd like your help."

"My help? Lady, before now, I didn't even know you existed." Madislak crossed his arms. This was either a genuine plea or another sadistic plan by Tamara to test his true intentions. But she did just help him get into her room.

"You must have wanted in here for a reason, no? I can still call the guards." She wrapped a lock of hair around her finger.

Madislak studied her again as she moved over to the armoire, opened it, and grabbed a bottle and two glasses from the bottom half. Could he trust this woman? Sure, she didn't call the guards and didn't send that note, but exactly how far was Tamara willing to go to weed out anyone not loyal to her? From what he'd noticed, everyone close to her was very loyal.

Blank Face would likely kill this woman and run. But he was not Blank Face. How many other secrets did Tamara have?

"How do I know you're not going to run to Tamara the second I say something and have me thrown in prison with the other three?" Madislak watched every move she made.

She poured two glasses. "Fine. I'll start then, and you tell me. I'm nothing like my sister. She is cruel and arrogant, and she's going to get us all killed. She keeps me hidden from the world, doesn't let me out of this room, and makes me do...unspeakable things with her and that brute bodyguard of hers."

Madislak's eyes widened as he realized who she was. "You're the one who saved Nalecht. On that dragon, last year. We had him beat, and you saved him! You're exactly like her!"

She winced. "And I paid dearly for my tardiness."

She turned around and dropped the ivory nightgown to just above her waist. Horizontal scars, eight of them, crossed her back—scars made by a whip. She pulled the nightgown back over them and turned back to Madislak. "I want out of this place."

Madislak knew Tamara was capable of wicked things, but whipping her own family and the other things Jocelyn mentioned? This couldn't be some kind of ploy...right? He rubbed his temples, then stroked his beard. *What did I get myself into?* He still had leverage with the note, and maybe he could use this as more leverage against Tamara. She would have no idea he knew about Jocelyn if what he was being told was true.

"Just whiskey," Jocelyn said, taking a sip.

After a good sniff, Madislak took a sip. "So, you want out of here?"

She nodded. "Now, what did you come in here for?"

If this was some kind of setup, he would never forgive himself, but the only risks that never pay off were the ones you never took. He inhaled sharply through his nose.

"Fine. I came in here to see what poisons Tamara has. She attempted to poison me yesterday. I didn't recognize it, and when she told me it was truth serum... Let's just say I know it's not truth serum. So, what poison does she have that tastes like shit?" Madislak pinned her with a glare.

Her cheeks reflected the color of her hair, and she finished her entire glass. "Do I have your word you'll help me escape? And that nothing we say will leave this gods-damned room?"

Madislak nodded. Her nervous reaction eased his mind just a little about this encounter.

"Say it!" she demanded, gritting her teeth.

"Alright. You have my word. I will get you out of here. Me or someone else I know who's good at this sort of thing," he promised, tipping his head to her.

"And?" She stomped a foot down.

"I will not repeat anything." He took another shot.

"Good." She sighed. "How much of it did you drink?"

Jocelyn poured herself another drink, then grabbed a different bottle from the armoire—a black liquid that looked like death in a bottle. "And did it smell like this?"

Madislak wiggled the cork off the black liquid bottle and gingerly put his nose over it. The smell overtook him; it was strong, thick, and unlike anything he'd smelled before, like burnt rock or charred earth.

"Taste it. Just a small sip. It won't kill you," she promised.

Madislak eyed her cautiously, then dumped a little bit on his hand, licked it, and swallowed. The nasty aftertaste matched the tea he had the other day. He grimaced.

"Yes, that's it." He quickly washed it down with the rest of his whiskey.

She put the cork back on the nasty black liquid and placed it back exactly where it came from.

"What is it?" Madislak poured another glass of whiskey.

"It doesn't have a name. She just calls it Kasherri venom. It's found in the deepest, darkest caves in Kalazaar. They say it's so deep it nears the underworld barriers. It has higher concentrations in Mount Harbinger and The Talon," Jocelyn said, taking a seat on the immaculate bed with a post at each corner.

"What does it do? And how does she get it?"

Jocelyn patted the spot beside her. "Well, she got a bunch from the orcs last year, from the north. It's what..." she trailed off.

Madislak sat beside her, placing a hand on her shoulder. She moved away from the touch initially, then relaxed.

Jocelyn inhaled sharply through her nose. "It's what Nalecht's grandfather used. It's corruption liquid. It amplifies feelings of greed, anger, hate, resentment, and control."

"That changes... everything." Madislak mouthed as his eyes went wide.

"It definitely changes the story of Enoch and Ghendala." Jocelyn's shoulders sagged. "If they were given this venom, and their madness came from Pasileveo's doing, then they weren't tyrants at all."

"Ho...ly...shit." Madislak's mouth fell open. "The caravan Harmony and I encountered. They were transporting it back here. It wasn't an army to add to her forces like we thought; it was a trade caravan."

His hands curled into fists at his own incompetence. He slammed his hand against the bed, then snatched the whiskey from the nightstand and took a deep swig. The smoky, burning liquid did little to dull the shame gnawing at him—for missing the clues, for running off when he should have taken a moment to take control, to demand answers.

They were so eager to escape and focused on what was happening in Tudela. Was that all a ruse? Did Tamara intentionally let Nalecht's plans of war unfold to keep that caravan, this venom, a secret while it got transported and distributed? How much did they have, and how were they going to distribute it? His mind raced at the possible chaos and destruction this venom could cause.

Jocelyn's red curls bounced forward as she nodded enthusiastically. "Selfishly, I hoped they'd bring you and her back here. I was going to seek you out then—tell you that if I freed you, you'd have to take me with you."

"Why me?" The bottle of whiskey thudded against the nightstand as he set it down with force.

"I mean... You're King Madislak. The mighty Madislak. You felled Goreldea's three sons. You slayed that dragon. Your reputation is well known, and you have the fastest learning shrew in history at your side." She smiled. "So, how are you going to get me out?"

Good question. *How am I going to get her out?* Madislak glanced out the window, weighing his options. The sun hung in a hazy glare, its heat pressing down on the city. Outside, Xaneth Harbor bustled with movement—some heading to the coliseum for the wedding, others busy with their daily crimes.

His best option was locked away in a dungeon with his future wife right now. He didn't know his way around this place or how to sneak in and sneak out. He preferred a loud and proud beat-down-the-front-door approach. But he would find a way to help her get out; she was a shrew and another person they could add to the ever-thinning ally list. If nothing else, she would owe him a life debt, and having any leverage against Tamara would always be advantageous.

"I don't know about all that. How did she discover this stuff? If it's so far underground?" Madislak shrugged.

He needed to get moving. He'd spent an hour in here with Jocelyn already, leaving only two more hours until this wedding that he suddenly wasn't so sure about. He also needed to figure out how to get Jocelyn out of her sister's grasp, discreetly. Just another thing to add to the growing list of complications that came with these shards. Taking Jocelyn out of here posed a huge threat to this alliance if Tamara knew Madislak was behind it. It would absolutely shatter the already-thinning trust between them. Maybe it wasn't worth the risk, but the thought of leaving an innocent, decent person in this hellhole of a town didn't sit right with him. In just an hour, Jocelyn seemed like the only sane person he'd met. The rest were thieves, liars, and a backstabbing queen.

It could also offer them some very valuable information if he could get her out of here, where they could continue this conversation without the hassle of having to hide it.

"She didn't discover it. Pasileveo did. She read about it in his journal that she found in the ruins of Axeladdle."

Madislak's eyes widened. "His journal! Do you have it?"

Jocelyn shook her head, the scent of peaches drifting from her hair. "No. That one she keeps hidden—locked away somewhere or on her at all times. I've only seen it once."

"Your sister is a damned liar." Madislak seethed.

"I know. So, can you help me or not?" She set her hand on his arm. Her hands were soft and delicate, like Harmony's.

As her soft hand brushed his arm, Harmony's face flashed in his mind—her bright smile, her perfectly white teeth. The scent of her pond lily shampoo, the one she always used. But most of all, the delicate touch of her hand.

He may have failed Harmony, may have screwed things up too badly to fix. But Jocelyn was delicate like Harmony. A shrew like Harmony. Smart like Harmony.

He wouldn't let Tamara treat people this way anymore. He would get Jocelyn out, even if it meant beating down Tamara's front door and dragging her out by force.

"I need a bit of time to figure out the logistics. After this wedding, I will get Blank Face or his little assassin friend to get you out. They know how to get in and out without being seen." Madislak pushed her hand off him.

"You're going to send assassins to get me out?" She furrowed her brow.

Madislak narrowed his gaze. "He is my brother. Not exactly an assassin anymore. The other one..." Madislak rolled his eyes. "Never mind. It'll be Blank Face or me."

"Please don't abandon me here. I'll help in whatever way I can. I can't handle the monstrous nature of Tamara or her big-ass boyfriend anymore." She pleaded.

Madislak offered her a bow. "I will get you out of here, one way or another. I gave you my word, and you shall be freed."

Though he wasn't entirely sure how he was going to get her out, he would figure it out. He'd plead with Blank Face if he had to, though Blank Face certainly didn't owe him any favors right now—none of them did. If worst came to worst, he would simply charge in here and take her with him when the time came. Consequences be damned.

Chapter Twenty-Six

M adislak entered the coliseum, the heat already forming sweat on his brow. The long-sleeve black shirt and pants didn't do much to help either. The cheap floral decorations along the ten-foot-high walls of the coliseum looked hazy, casting a surreal atmosphere over the arena. Flowers were scattered across the dirt floor beneath his feet, leading to an archway at the center of the space. Two more hours. Two more hours and he'd be married again, to another person he didn't exactly want to marry, all for the sake of peace. Though he wasn't sure that he wanted to marry Harmony anymore either. Perhaps it would be best to remain single for the rest of his life and just enjoy his kids and help them learn and grow. Teach them not to be as gullible or naïve as he'd been. Teach them to run the kingdom the right way and to be loyal to each other. Be people they could truly trust and depend on.

He marched straight for the shaded dais where Tamara already sat at the table. She hadn't even bothered to dress up or try to look nice for the occasion, still wearing her dirty brown and yellow leather ensemble. He felt the thrum of the shard of Theora around his neck. He'd tried to practice with it the other day, but couldn't get it to do much other than move some dirt around and talk to a few plants. He didn't know how to utilize it to its fullest extent; he never really messed with magic or magical items before, so his knowledge of working them was minimal.

He squared his shoulders. If he could get Tamara to surrender the other shard—the shard of Aisha—that would give him two shards and the means to march out of here with Jocelyn, provided he could figure out how to use them. Maybe they could all just use this wedding as a distraction, and he could slip them to Petrovana. She seemed to have at least some grasp of their capabilities.

He tapped his left pectoral, where he had tucked the magical note that would go to Nalecht should he die, just to make sure it was still there. His mind whirled at the discussion he just had with Jocelyn. Before now, he didn't even know Tamara had a sister. Did she hide her on purpose? And what was that purpose? Should he use that knowledge as leverage or keep it to himself? Certainly, anything she knew would be useful for their predicament. She knew about this venom. What else did she have tucked in that brain of hers? He wished he had more time to talk to Jocelyn.

He needed to stay the course, gather as much information as possible on the venom, then find a way to pull off a grand escape during the wedding. It was a daring plan, but Tamara would never truly ally with them—she only ever allied with herself.

They needed answers. They needed to get out of here.

And that journal—Harmony would unlock all its secrets.

Provided they could get their hands on it.

Harmony... Would she even help him at this point? Would any of them? *Gods*, what had he done? His life was a mess, treading a thin line with the enemy, and how long until they considered *him* the enemy? *Focus.* He shook his head as he approached Tamara. Wedding first, then figure out the rest of this mess.

"Well, don't you look ravishing," Tamara grinned seductively at him, her hair still in its typical poofy style.

"Thanks, I guess." *You lying bitch*, he wanted to say. "I have another proposition for you."

"We'll get to that," Tamara leveled him with a glare. "Congratulations on your big win."

"What big win?" Madislak mouthed.

"You haven't heard? Your precious Lantess was attacked by Kirilick's forces, led by Nalecht himself," Tamara grinned.

His heart stopped. The pressure in his chest coiled tightly as a cold sweat formed on his brow. The overwhelming pit of fear took root deep within him. Did Leighth lie to him when he asked her? Was she a prisoner, and had they forced her to craft that response? Damn it. Now he had to get back to Lantess as soon as possible to see what was happening there. His pulse raced through his veins. Were Alissia and Rylin alright?

"What's the matter, King Madislak? You look a little worse for wear over there," Tamara chuckled. Nylor, standing guard behind her, shuffled closer, his grin stretching wider at the sight of his misery.

"You're an asshole. What happened? Are my children alright? How do you know?" Madislak stared directly into her brown eyes.

She handed him a missive from one of her spies or correspondents in Lantess. First order of business when he returned would be to eliminate any and all of her spies. He opened the letter.

My Queen,

Kirilick forces showed up in Lantess today. I will hide in the woods outside the city. Nalecht led the charge. Young Queen Leighth led the battle valiantly, but the overwhelming numbers of Kirilick began to breach the walls of Lantess.

Madislak's heart jumped, but the letter continued.

Something unnerving happened once they reached the walls. A green dragon came to their defense, and another man shot lightning from his eyes. He made stone rain down on them from the sky. The Cherno on the green dragon saved them, and Kirilick was forced to retreat, with most of their forces destroyed. Nalecht retreated with them. He did not look happy, and he murdered Queen Goreldea of Kirilick before riding off to the south. Will post up in a new location once the chaos dies down.

A sigh of relief escaped his lips. Thank the gods they never got in. Why was it always Lantess? What did these people want with his city so much? Why did Ace and this other guy come to the rescue, and how did they even know? Regardless, he owed them both his thanks when he eventually returned home.

"So, how did you get Ace to come to your defense?" Tamara sat back in her chair, her earrings reflecting the sunlight.

Madislak shrugged. "I honestly have no idea. I haven't seen him since Tudela."

"How does a nineteen-year-old girl defend against Kirilick and Nalecht?" Tamara gritted her teeth.

"Wow, Tamara, you seem quite angry over the fact that Lantess didn't fall again. Any particular reason why?" Madislak clenched his fists at his sides.

She chuckled arrogantly, clearly deflecting. "No, not at all. I'm more impressed by the resilience you and your comrades seem to have. I'm sure that victory did nothing more than light a fire under Nalecht's ass. He doesn't take lightly to losing."

Madislak arched a brow at her. "Not to mention it weakens him a little. Now that I know, perhaps this alliance will benefit you more. After all, Ace seems to have brought the dragons to our side of this... war."

Tamara's nostrils flared, her tanned face turning red. "Neither of us knows what side of this war Ace falls on," she spat.

Her need for the upper hand, for control that she currently didn't possess, irritated her. Madislak could tell, and he couldn't keep his lips from curling upward. For once, he had the upper hand if Ace truly did switch sides. If Leper were dead, this would be the type of tide-turning alliance they needed to fight back, especially if the shrews fought with them. For once, everything seemed to be going Madislak's way, and there was no better time to push for more control in his favor.

"Either way, with their help, my army, and myself, we've proven we can contend with Nalecht—as shown by the outcome of that battle. So why don't you show me you're truly committed to this alliance? Hand over that other shard or send me troops to replenish what was lost."

Madislak's toes curled in his boots. *This is it.*

Tamara sneered. "Why don't you go fuck yourself, you arrogant prick?"

Madislak tapped his tunic, where his note to Nalecht remained intact. Nylor reached his massive hands over his shoulder to the large warhammer strapped across his back.

Madislak glanced up at the giant, beads of sweat escaping the lines of his buzz-cut hair. "Go ahead, you overgrown brute. Kill me. See how much that helps your precious queen."

Nylor bared his ugly teeth. "One day, I will show you who the true mighty one is, Madislak. It might not be today, but one day I will get my chance to pummel you to the ground."

Madislak sat back arrogantly. "Careful, old man. Many have tried and many have failed. Don't forget you were struggling to beat that petite little assassin. Isn't forty a little old to be challenging the best?"

Madislak didn't doubt his abilities, but missing a pinky and a ring finger against a man of Nylor's size, he didn't know if he'd come out alive. But he'd never back down from a challenge in his life, and he certainly wasn't about to start.

Nylor's mouth spread into a grin, his goatee stretching. "Let me have him right now in the arena. My queen, give me the opportunity to put this asshole in Malastion where he belongs."

Tamara held up her hand. "We don't kill our allies, Nylor. But after this wedding, it'll be your turn to finally provide something for this alliance. Don't forget I want those books, and I want them quickly—one week." She held up her finger.

"The shard?" Madislak asked again. "With the dragons and the shrews, I think you'll have enough backing to tell Nalecht where to shove it."

Tamara never took her eyes off Madislak as she let out an audible sigh and reached for the necklace under her brown shirt. She unhooked the shard of Aisha from the necklace and set it on the table. The sun reflected off the mace-shaped shard. Madislak's heart pounded. He was really getting it this time; all it took was a little reach across the table. They'd have two shards now. If he could get them to Petrovana or Leighth, who actually knew how to use them, it would go a long way in leveling the playing field. He almost jumped out of his seat to grab it, but kept his wits, realizing that would only make him seem desperate. Tamara started to push it over the center of the table, and black smoke filled the space between her and Nylor, materializing into The Latter.

"What's going on here?" His wild mohawk was now green in color.

"Indeed." A deep voice behind Nylor emanated.

The color drained from Tamara's face, and Madislak felt his heart leap into a gallop. They were so incredibly screwed.

"Nalecht?" Tamara asked, her voice barely above a whisper.

"Wha... What are you doing here?" Tamara muttered.

Oh, this is an absolute disaster. This would surely end with all of their deaths. He had no leverage with him, no angle, nothing. They were doomed. *Should've known he would head straight here after that defeat at Lantess.*

"Well, after suffering the surprising turn of events at Lantess, I told Brebian to attack from the north and thought I'd ask my second in command to attack from the south. But imagine my complete shock to see the king sitting here, planning what appears to be some kind of union." Nalecht's voice was incredibly low and calm as he motioned out towards the arena.

Panic roared through Madislak's veins. What did they say to that? If they told him Madislak was about to marry Petrovana, he would know the reason why. His mind whirled with anxiety, searching for a reason, any reason. Judging from the shocked look on Tamara's face, she had no good answers either. Madislak wished he had that glass of whiskey with him right now.

"Maybe I changed my mind." Madislak kept his hands under the table so Nalecht couldn't see them trembling.

"About?" Nalecht tilted his head back, his beady black eyes glaring at Madislak.

"Which side of this war I'm on," Madislak lied.

Nalecht let out a throaty chuckle. "One of you has definitely changed which side you're on, but the question remains, which one?" He glanced at Tamara. "Seeing as she's sliding my shard to you..." He let his words drop off.

"It still remains yours when you want it," Madislak lied, not meaning a single word of it.

He desperately wanted to grab it now. Grab it and use it against Nalecht. But there were too many variables in that plan, one being the new alliance he had just struck with Tamara.

He felt the thrum of power from the shard of Theora hanging on his neck, then glanced at Nalecht, whose necklace proudly displayed the shards of Ryollin, Hathor, Obidiah, and Amarook. Nalecht flicked his silky white hair over his shoulders, his elven ears poking out as he took a seat at the table.

"Why don't we catch up on what exactly is going on behind my back here? Starting with where your precious friends are. That horned abomination that helped you kill my dragon and cost me my dragon riders' alliance? Have you heard from him by chance?" Nalecht rested his arms on the table.

Nalecht's demeanor rivaled that of Borlden—he would kill or crush anyone in his path to get what he wanted. With the shards hanging around his neck, his already formidable skill with a falchion had only grown sharper. He had always been a masterful swordsman, but the shards amplified his abilities beyond mortal limits. Yet the shard of Amarook glowed with a softer white light than usual.

More importantly, he had just confirmed Brebian's allegiance, stating they would attack from the north. That meant King Theodamar of Wen-Tath wouldn't oppose him either. With those two armies added to his ranks, he now commanded the forces of Ambrosia, Tudela, Wen-Tath, Ventessa, Kordry, and Xaneth Harbor. Nearly every army in the world bent to his will—save for Lantess, Terynsipple, and Kundry. His power had grown tenfold. Madislak feared that Nalecht's power had grown beyond anything they could hope to defeat.

Madislak's throat bobbed. "Haven't seen him for a month. Why do you hate him so much?"

Nalecht's grin was anything but comforting. "Wouldn't you hate the son of a man who killed your wife?"

Killed his wife? Leper's father killed Adalyn, too?

"Leper had nothing to do with that. How did his father even kill Adalyn?" Madislak asked, bouncing his leg under the table.

"Killed her in cold blood like the raging lunatic all of them are. They shouldn't be allowed to live." Nalecht's voice was sincere as he slammed the table with his hand.

"You let Ace live," Madislak blurted, then immediately wished he'd kept his mouth shut.

Nalecht slowly, slowly, turned his head to meet Madislak's gaze. "Because he was serving a purpose for me." His toothpick nose twitched. "I'm not the one answering questions. Where the hell is he?"

Tamara finally spoke up. "He attempted to retrieve the shard of Kasherri. In the rain trials. The king here hasn't heard from him in a month, so he is probably... dead."

"That's how you answer a question," Nalecht sighed.

Madislak already knew why Nalecht wanted all the Chernzerk dead, but he wanted to see if Nalecht would still lie about it—and he did. Maybe. Madislak wasn't entirely sure how Samaja was connected to Adalyn's death, but he knew one thing for certain: only a Chernzerk could completely destroy the talisman. And that was what Nalecht couldn't allow.

"What about that redheaded bitch who shredded my army and the purple-eyed one who assisted her? The potential queen of Terynsipple. And where is that annoying ice shard-throwing bitch of yours?" Nalecht growled.

Madislak's blood boiled at the insult. Why? He had cut off his feelings for Harmony when she lied to him, betrayed him, hid the fact that she knew something important about the talisman, and was a Deathbinder. He couldn't quell the rage that flowed through every pore in his body; he couldn't deny it. Hearing him call her a bitch, he started to see red.

"Locked in a prison cell. They attempted to thwart my efforts to establish this peace treaty," he gritted through clenched teeth. "So, I imprisoned them."

Nalecht pursed his fingers together. "I'd very much like to speak to them. What prison?"

"I need your assurance that you will stay away from Lantess and my children," Madislak leveled a stare at Nalecht. He didn't care how powerful he was; he was done allowing himself to be intimidated.

"You'll tell me, or I'll beat it out of you." Nalecht pointed his slender finger at Madislak.

"Meh. You could." Madislak sat back in his chair arrogantly, his pulse pounding with anticipation as he tried to maintain a composed demeanor." Lay a finger on me, and not only will I refuse to tell you where they are—I'll make sure everyone knows the real reason you want the Chernzerk dead, you lying prick."

Nalecht's head snapped back in shock. His beady black eyes raked over every inch of Madislak before settling back on his face, a crooked grin spreading across his lips.

"What are you playing at?" he asked calmly.

"I play at nothing, *Anyth*." Madislak pointed at Tamara. "Does she know? Did you tell her what the Chernzerk can do with the talisman—what no one else in the world can? Or am I the only one who knows?" Panic crept into his chest. He was digging himself into a deep, deadly hole.

Nalecht's face darkened to crimson. "I will kill you right here, *King of Lantess*. Whatever you think you know about the talisman, you don't. So quit while you still can, or this will get very bloody, very fast. I won't warn you again."

"Fine." Madislak's heart pounded. "I'm willing to share information. I've struck a deal with Tamara—I'd negotiate with you as well, *Anyth*—but I want to know where you've been. And why does that shard look dimmer than before?" He gestured to the sword-shaped shard of Amarook.

"Oh, this?" Nalecht's grin widened as he tapped the shard. "It's been used recently, that's why. A little present I plan to show Ace and his entire pack of dragons on The Talon... once the beast is well enough to move and fly again."

"What beast?" Tamara's worried gaze flicked between Madislak and Nalecht.

"Eluvae the Wicked," Nalecht mouthed.

Cold sweat broke out on Madislak's brow. "*Eluvae?* Enoch's dragon? The largest and fiercest dragon that ever lived?"

"The only dragon that couldn't be opposed," Tamara murmured, jaw slackening in awe.

Eluvae—the dragon Enoch had bonded with—was one of the first dragons born, and by far the largest ever recorded in history. He had been just as wicked as Nalecht, devouring everything in his path—people, livestock—while reducing entire landscapes to cinders with his massive columns of fire. He was the most feared dragon to ever live... until a dragonslayer finally killed him—at the cost of their own life.

"Exactly." Nalecht chuckled. "Brought back from the dead and bonded to me. I'd love to see you try and kill an *undead* dragon, mighty Madislak."

Madislak swallowed hard. "How do you even kill an undead dragon?"

"You don't," Tamara snapped. "It's *undead*."

"Now," Nalecht gestured toward the table, "let's get back to business. Either of you dipshits manage to find Xartazza or Blank Face for the rain trials?"

"Blank Face is his *brother*," Tamara said, jabbing a finger at Madislak.

Madislak almost jumped across the table and punched her straight in the face. *Stupid, useless bitch.* That was the last thing he wanted Nalecht to know. Damn Blank Face for telling her about that. Nalecht's face rocked back, his brow furrowed, his whole face scrunching together. Then he grinned and flicked his gaze between Tamara and Madislak. She had apparently made her allegiances perfectly clear now.

Nalecht's eyes settled on Tamara. "Did you know that Leper, the horned freak, is also Madislak's brother?"

Tamara's eyes widened, realization dawning on her face as she gasped aloud.

"I fucking knew it!" she exclaimed. "All this time."

Nalecht nodded. "You know what that means?"

"I know exactly what that means," Tamara sneered, shooting a glare at Madislak. "I'll take you to Blank Face myself."

Madislak's pulse pounded in his temples. What just happened? Why did she suddenly turn on him like that? What did Blank Face being a Chernzerk change or have to do with them? Did they truly despise them that much? Madislak's mind raced, desperately searching for something to say to defuse the situation, but the revelation had completely shifted the conversation's dynamics. They both glared at him, a thirst for vengeance evident in their eyes.

Madislak tapped the note on his body, glaring back at Tamara. A desperate last-ditch effort to regain some leverage among these powerful giants.

"Go ahead. Tell him about my dealings. He knows who I am, and you've just given us what we needed." Tamara glowered, snatching the shard from the table once again.

Nalecht grabbed her arm and yanked the shard out of her grasp. "My fucking shard now."

Fuck me.

He knew he shouldn't, but his leverage was dwindling to mere scraps now. Whatever they had just discovered had changed everything.

Tamara began sauntering away, her arrogant walk simmering his blood.

"Even if I tell him about that venom? You know, the one you tried to use on me? The one you discovered with Pasileveo's journal?" Madislak called out loudly, and she stopped dead in her tracks.

Nalecht's head snapped in her direction. Tamara turned to face Madislak slowly, and if looks could kill, he would be dead.

"I don't know what you're talking about, King Madislak," she enunciated each word slowly.

"Sit your ass back down," Nalecht commanded, pointing at the chair.

Her nostrils flared as she stomped back to the chair.

The shard of Ryollin glowed red on Nalecht's chest, and he moved in a blur, grabbing Madislak's arm and wrenching it onto the wooden table. Agony ripped through Madislak's hand and arm as Nalecht drove a dagger straight through his hand, anchoring it to the table. Blood immediately pooled around his hand and onto the table. Nalecht repeated the action with Tamara, and she screamed in pain.

Nalecht casually sat back down in his chair. "Now, we're going to tell the whole fucking truth about what the fuck is happening here."

Leper took each step as quickly as he could, pushing aside the anger that surged through his system. They'd been at this for half a day, and he was getting exhausted. He stomped emphatically, trying to burn out the storm of thoughts flooding his mind. Maka Kura, his weapon, his bonded weapon, had just informed him that he was his father. The prick had lied to him, but deep down, it didn't surprise him as much as it should have. No, he should've known. The way Maka Kura talked to him, yelled at him, told him what to do, like he was some kind of child. *Screw him.* He'd never talk to Maka again, or Samaja, whatever its stupid name was. He shook his head. No, Maka Kura. He absolutely refused to call the weapon Samaja.

"How many more steps until we reach the top?" he whined.

Lillian offered only a half-smile. They walked forever, climbing to agonizing heights. Torches lit the dark stairwell intermittently. His stomach roared from lack of food, but Zanera and Kelindra were captured or taken or lost, and he had no clue where they might be. He would reach the surface as fast as he possibly could. For them. Whatever it took. Nothing else in the world mattered. Not Madislak, not Petrovana. He had to reach them. He managed to keep Kasherri's influence and his own dark aspirations at bay, maintaining complete control, just as Lillian had taught him. Thank the gods he didn't have to worry about angrily attacking his friends again. Hopefully, over time, he would be able to exercise the type of control Lillian or Blank Face seemed to have over it. He growled at the thought of his estranged brother.

He heard Lillian panting behind him, pulling him from his thoughts, and noticed his own ragged breathing as he pushed to reach the top of the seemingly endless stairwell. They reached a small, flat area, like a dais, almost as if it was built specifically for people climbing these stairs to rest.

"Can we rest for a bit?" Lillian batted her eyelashes.

"Are you trying to seduce me again?" Leper cocked his head to the side.

"Is it workin'?" she grinned.

"Hmph. Maybe." He smiled.

Two wooden benches were mounted to the stone walls, and Leper took a seat across from her, letting his arms and everything sink onto the bench in complete relaxation of his weary body. Lillian followed suit, lying completely down on her back.

"You don't think they're hurting them, do you? Whoever has Zanera and Kelindra?" Leper leaned his head against the rough stone wall.

"You can't think like that, Lep. We will get to them before anythin' happens. We'll get to Costin, and either Ghost or Ace with his dragon Peridona will fly us to Kordry." She rested her forearm on her forehead.

He checked his pouch of vials just in case. Still nothing. He let out a sigh and glanced at the piece of paper he got from the rain trials that he kept. The riddle that kept popping up in the back of his mind, he didn't pay it much heed, considering all the chaos they'd been navigating.

"Do you think this line refers to what just happened with the barriers? It says, 'only then the shackle shatters when destiny awakens and darkness scatters?'"

"Beats me. But it does sound kinda accurate. The barriers would be the shackles that shattered. And the darkness would be all those beasts rushing up here, scatterin' across the lands." Her stomach growled.

"I just don't get it. Other than the first two lines, everything could match what we did down there. 'Through shadows deep and dreams that teem.' It's creepy as shit down there, but what the hell does 'veiled beneath the moonlit pledge where whispers bind the gleaming edge' mean? There's no moonlight down there." He folded it back up and put it in his pocket.

"Probably just some dumb paper, Lep. I wouldn't read into it too much. Should rip it in half, and we can each eat a half. I'm starvin'." She gave him a sidelong glance.

"You could." Leper chuckled. "Turn into a chicken and lay us some eggs. Or a pig, and I'll just take a few slices from the back."

Lillian burst out laughing as she sat up. "I don't think it works like that. We could just cut a chunk of yer broad–ass chest and eat that."

Leper flexed his pectorals, staring down at his chest.

"*Gods*, I was jokin'!" She laughed harder. "You're actually considerin' it, aren't you?"

"I'm thinking about a lot of things right now. Eating my own meat might be one of them." He chuckled.

"Bleh." She made a puking sound. "Yer disgustin', thanks." Her eyes wandered up and down the length of him. "I could certainly sink my teeth into you." She flashed her teeth.

Leper chuckled and tried to mock her accent again. "Yer teeth or yer claws?"

"That an offer...or?" Lillian fired back in her lowest possible register, mocking him right back.

Leper couldn't contain himself as a bubble of laughter rolled up his throat, and he let out a genuine burst of laughter. The hallway echoed with the sound of delight and happiness, something he hadn't experienced since the day Nalecht's henchmen showed up in Kordry.

The laughter quickly faded as he recalled that moment and the ensuing misery they'd all been put through. The pain of loss that set him on this course. Nalecht's first attempt to acquire the shard of Theora was when he tried to kidnap Zanera and Kelindra. He killed Leighth's family, her brothers. She wasn't even twenty years old. He briefly touched the shard of Kasherri to make sure it was still there. Their last piece of leverage, if everything Zanera mentioned in the letter was true. If they were okay... His pulse quickened as he continued to consider everything that could be going wrong. His face tightened, and panic flooded his mind.

"We need to go," he said grimly.

Lillian got to her feet quickly. "I know. I feel it too."

"Feel what?" Leper stood beside her.

"The dread." She forced a smile and began walking again.

"You're almost to the surface," Maka said quickly and quietly in his mind.

"Fuck off," Leper shot back.

They climbed for another hour before they came to another doorway, brown and yellow in color, with the crest of Xaneth Harbor on it. A dragon's face. Where in the hell were they?

They opened the door and found a desk with scattered papers on it. A torch mounted to the wall burned lowly. No guard, though it seemed like some kind of office. Leper went to the desk and flipped through the papers. Nothing.

"Where the fuck did we end up?" Lillian breathed, her hot breath landing on his neck, sending chills prickling along his skin.

"I have no idea." Leper sighed. "I just hope Ghost is okay after all that time I was gone."

"I'm sure Delinah and The Former took care of her," she offered.

The bottom three levels had only one or two prison cells each. The rest of the levels had ten to fifteen cells until the surface level. A whole new wave of worry flooded Leper's mind. What if they were in a city? Any city likely wouldn't let him, as a Chernzerk, just waltz out of their dungeons. He couldn't let the guards see him. He'd be thrown right back down here or executed. Maybe Lillian should scout ahead and bring back food until they find an alternate route. He didn't feel like fighting his way out, and he sure as shit wasn't going into a prison cell again.

As if she could read his thoughts, Lillian said, "We'll find a way out. I'm with you."

"How did you know?" Leper locked eyes with her magnificent green gemstones.

"It's all over yer face." She grinned. "Let's go."

Leper nodded, and they ascended to the lowest level of the dungeon. The dragon–face symbol on the walls confirmed they were in Xaneth Harbor. How they got so far from Costin, Leper didn't know, but it didn't matter; he needed to breathe fresh air and see the sun. Lillian led the way, and as they crested the stairs to the bottommost level with its only two cells, Lillian immediately turned around, trying to block his view.

"No! Don't look there!" she pleaded.

It was too late. Leper glanced over her shoulder and saw Harmony. Bruised, battered, and missing an eye, shaking uncontrollably. He almost let out a sigh of relief until he glanced into the other cell. There she was, in a beautiful gown of blue, green, and purple with streamers hanging off the sleeve-length arms. Her bare back showed her soft skin, that delicate softness he missed for weeks on end.

His heart cracked, plummeting to the floor. Rage resurfaced as he watched her mouth locked with his brother's—but not Madislak. No, not the one she was supposed to marry for political power. She kissed him with everything she had and couldn't seem to get enough.

How many times must his heart be stomped on by this man before he realized he was no friend? Blank Face—the traitorous, menacing piece of shit. How many times would he let this world, these people, stomp on him like he didn't matter?

A lancing pain raced across his chest. He couldn't produce words as his mouth fell open, hanging there at their frantic embrace. They survived. Beaten and bruised, ragged and starving. They experienced literal hell to get this shard for the good of their friends and to keep it from Nalecht, and this was the thanks they got.

At that moment, Leper realized that perhaps Nalecht wasn't his only enemy in this, but the ones he considered friends. The one he considered his love, lover. The reason behind the stunning gown didn't even matter; he knew exactly what it was for. It didn't matter anymore. None of it mattered anymore. He was merely a tool to be used by all these backstabbing, ungrateful hypocrites.

"Leper. No!" Maka frantically called in his head.

That only made it worse. Fuck them. Fuck them all and this world. *I will burn it all to the ground.*

As the shard of Kasherri shot a pulse of darkness into his mind, it fused with his own vengeful thoughts. Leper didn't even bother to resist as his consciousness slipped, giving way to the insistent hunger for vengeance. The hatred, anger, and greed. His blood boiled, roaring through his temples. His knuckles turned white as his fingernails dug into his palms.

Chapter Twenty-Seven

L illian stiffened. There was no coming back from this. No return to that place of peace and happiness.

She grabbed onto his arm. "Look at me, Lep!" she pleaded.

His eyes slowly opened and glazed over, a black shimmer flickering across them before fading. Her father had warned her—if she ever saw that look in any Chernzerk's eyes, they were lost for good. There was nothing she could do to stop it. Nothing anyone could do. He lost himself to this anger, this hatred, and he will never come back.

Her heart cracked into a million tiny pieces, not for herself, but for him.

A tear rolled down her cheek, landing soundlessly on the cobblestone floor of the two-cell room. She didn't bother wiping it away. They had sent her a broken, uncontrollable, hurting man, and she had gone through hell and back with him. Her stomach twisted, aching from either wounds or hunger—she wasn't sure which was worse.

"No." She whimpered. "Don't give in now, you've come so far!"

All that work, all that progress—gone.

When she first found him in Costin, he'd been a volatile, impulsive mess. She helped him work through it, helped him find stability until he could grasp onto something real, find that anchor. The others glanced at each other, shocked and uncertain, but for the first time in her twenty-four years, she didn't know what to do.

"Leper!" She hollered right in his face. But he just stared off in the distance, like he couldn't see her, like he wasn't there.

She had no idea how to pull him back from this.

Her father, Oubank, never told her how he kept pulling Samaja back when he lost control. She never thought she'd have to do it for someone as uncontrollable as Samaja.

She shook his shoulder, but his face was so hollow, "Leper, please, don't do this!"

She had helped Leper fight his demons, regain control. As a Chernzerk, that kind of balance took years to master, but he had been doing it—fighting it off in the hallway after they escaped. He had been doing so well.

And now?

Her heart shattered when she saw the look on his broken, furious face. The moment his gaze flicked from Harmony's cell to the one beside it, she knew. Even after all his doubts, after everything he questioned about their relationship, he had held on. Held on long enough for it to be resolved.

None of it mattered.

Even after everything, even after a month of uncertainty, not knowing if they would live or die, he had been laughing again. Joking. Smiling. Actually smiling.

And it took all of five seconds for this bitch—this selfish, fucking tramp—to wash it all away.

If he went to kill her, she wouldn't even stop him at this point. Petrovana deserved whatever venomous insults were about to spew forth from his mouth. If he decided to end her, maybe she deserved that, too.

Leper's frantic breathing and heaving shoulders suddenly slowed to a calm, nerve-racking, calculating pace. A shudder ran down Lillian's spine as Leper leveled Petrovana with a smile that looked like death itself.

"You really are nothing more than a fucking tramp. I should've listened to Lillian this whole time," Leper said, his voice low.

Blank Face came to a sobbing Petrovana's defense. "You don't understand. We thought you were dead."

"Well, it certainly didn't take either of you long to get over my death, then." He gave a sidelong glance at Harmony. "Or has this been going on longer?"

"No. Leper, honey," Petrovana blubbered. "I swear. It just happened. I... I can't explain it."

He tossed Maka Kura at the cage, and it slammed against the bars in front of Petrovana, causing her to jump back. "Enough excuses, you dumb whore." He paced back and forth. "You can't explain it, kind of like you can't explain that third spell you hide from everyone?" Leper growled.

Lillian's head snapped to Petrovana. "What did he just say?" Her mouth hung open.

"It's four now," Petrovana confessed.

Lillian's mouth almost hit the floor as she let the word slip. "Soulreaver."

Petrovana's eyes snapped to Lillian. "What?" She frantically ran to the bars. "What did you call me?"

No, she wasn't about to give this bitch an inch of information, not after what she just did to Leper.

"Nothin'," Lillian snapped. "What I meant to say was dumb wench."

"Lillian, please tell me," Petrovana pleaded from behind the bars, her tears streaking down her face.

"You're a gods-damned freak. That's what she said. An abomination. And you wonder why no one likes you," Leper's voice was so low and steady it gave Lillian goosebumps.

A tiny, beautiful girl with black hair in pigtails, the ends colored red and green, whipped around the corner yelling, "I got the—"

Her announcement got cut short as Leper lunged. She barely had time to react before he was on her, snatching her throat in a vice grip. The keys clattered to the ground. She yelped and slammed her hands down on his arm, trying to break his hold.

"You want to help them?" he snapped. "What a shame."

Blank Face flickered in and out of transparency, trying to blink beyond his confinement—but he couldn't.

"Leper, she's helping us!" He reached through the bars. "She's a friend."

"Oh, Blank Face has feelings now, does he?" Leper's eyes narrowed as the girl squirmed.

"Leper, stop it! You don't know who she is. I know you're mad, but this ain't you, even if they all deserve a beatin'," Lillian said, gripping his arm.

"Oh, we're past a beating. There's only one thing they deserve. And once I kill this little inconvenience so Blank Face can watch her die, like I had to watch Rinawen die, then I'll start with them." His arm tensed, his grip tightening. "After they're dead, I'll destroy this entire city and move on to the next until it's all gone."

The girl choked, coughing against his hold.

"Lep! Stop it! She's innocent!" Lillian yanked on his arm.

"Her name is Intiva," Blank Face said quickly.

"Shut yer fuckin' trap, idiot." She shot him a warning glare.

Leper's grip faltered, and Lillian shoved him back. But he recovered fast, lunging for the keys. If he got them, both Blank Face and Petrovana were dead.

Hell, part of her wanted to let him do it.

But if, somehow, he ever snapped out of this, it'd only bring him more grief. He wasn't a killer. Not really. And even if he hated Petrovana now, he might not always. He could be capable of forgiveness.

Lillian dove for the keys. Leper shoved her aside, but she twisted midair, landing on her feet and spinning to strike. Her fist slammed into his face, and his head rocked back, but he had the keys in his hand.

"Leper, stop this!" she snapped, her patience fraying.

He didn't. His free hand shot out, grabbing her by the throat. He slammed her back into the cell bars. She gasped, struggling for air, and before she could break free, Intiva ripped the keys from his grip and tossed them into the cell so he couldn't reach them. He turned and growled angrily at her.

Lillian's scimitars hissed free as dread coiled in her gut. She didn't want to do this. She didn't want to hurt him. But she would if it meant saving him from himself.

Leper bolted for Intiva. Lillian dashed in front of him and swung low, aiming for his leg. He deflected with Maka Kura, their eyes locking.

"Leper," she rasped. "Please don't make me do this."

His gaze held nothing. No warmth. No trace of the man she had fought to save.

"I don't know why you're sticking up for them." His voice was hollow. "Out of respect—and only respect—I'll start with this shit-hole town. Consider this a once-in-a-lifetime mercy. If I see either of you again," he pointed at Petrovana and Blank Face. "I'll snap her pretty little neck like the twig she is."

Then he was gone. Just like that. He grabbed a handful of Intiva's robes and dragged her up the stairs.

Lillian's legs trembled beneath her.

There was no snapping him out of this. Not now. Maybe not ever.

The realization hit like a punch to the gut, leaving her breathless.

They lost him forever.

Her father's words echoed in her head: *Their minds don't stabilize until they learn to separate the magic in their veins from the darkness that corrupts it.*

Dread crawled up her spine. If Leper was truly gone—if he had hit that breaking point—Madislak wouldn't let him roam free, tearing through cities. No sane ruler would.

Like an incurable pet, he'd have to be put down.

Above, the shrieks of guards shattered the silence, followed by the sickening thuds of bodies hitting the ground.

Leper trudged up the steps, dispatching any guard in his way with swift, lethal efficiency. After the thirtieth guard fell to his blades, the rest began to flee. The air grew fresher as he climbed, carrying the taste of freedom and the humidity of the Bay of Disdain. His tattered clothes clung to his body, but he ignored the discomfort. His mind fixated on destroying anything and everything about this city. Then he would move on to another city and another. This world wanted evil, destructive Chernzerk, and they were about to get it.

Everyone always pushed his buttons, urging him to become this person. Enough fighting it. He would let it consume him and destroy everything in his path—every city, until nothing remained. That would show them.

Hunger pangs faded as he reached the last floor, where a captain clad in plate metal armor awaited him with eight other guards.

"Stand down, or I'll use force," the captain commanded, pointing his sword at Leper.

"Kiss my ass," Leper barked, not breaking stride.

Two guards lunged from the side. Leper parried the first attacker's sword to the ground, sidestepped the second swing, and brought Maka Kura down on both their necks in one clean motion. His anger, amplified by the shard, made him deadlier—more confident.

Intiva trailed behind him like a loyal hound, eyes alight with admiration at every fatal strike. "I've never seen such beautiful power, such conviction. I would follow you anywhere."

He ignored her.

Keeping her alive might've been a mistake. He should've snapped her neck in the dungeons, especially if she was going to be this annoying.

"Get Nylor," the captain barked at one of the guards.

"Yeah," Leper mocked, "get Nylor. He needs to die, too."

No sense leaving any stones unturned while he's down here, better tell them to bring his bitch daughter with him.

"When you get Nylor, tell him to bring his stupid daughter, Cylandra, with him. She needs to die, too." Leper hollered at the guards fleeing to get Nylor.

The guard captain lunged, swinging powerfully over his head. Leper crouched, then swung upward, knocking the blow away. The sword vibrated on impact. The captain raised his shield, deflecting Leper's next attacks, but the wooden shield splintered. Leper kept striking, beating the shield until it cracked apart. As he aimed for the killing blow, a searing pain shot across his back from another guard.

A low growl escaped him. As he turned to deal with the attacker, Intiva jumped on the guard's back, ramming two daggers into his chest and taking him to the floor. She looked up at Leper, smiling like a good dog that had just helped.

He rolled his eyes and turned back to the captain, who had finally shaken the broken shield off his arm. The captain charged, swinging wildly. Leper deflected the sword and rammed his shoulder into the captain's midsection, pushing him off balance before arcing Maka Kura downward. The captain's blood sprayed over Leper, its fresh scent a stark contrast to the decay he had endured for weeks.

Intiva had already dispatched the remaining guards by the time Leper finished with the captain. She motioned towards the men and women she had felled, then knelt as if in offering. "For you, my love."

"You assassin bunch certainly are a different lot, aren't you?" Leper offered her a hand up.

"Forgive my forwardness. I can't control myself around someone who takes what he wants. It's... hot." Her tanned cheeks flushed.

"You do understand the dynamic of this relationship, right? You're my prisoner, and if I see either of those two again, I will kill you," Leper said, thinking she needed a reminder.

"Like I said," she batted her large eyes, "I like a man who takes." She flashed open her cloak, revealing a lot of leg and tight, short shorts. "What he wants."

Leper shook his head. *Lunatic.* It made sense that she and Blank Face were somehow friends. A bunch of insane assassins hanging out would probably drive anyone to the brink of insanity. As long as she followed him like a dog and watched his back, he didn't care. It was more loyalty than most had shown him.

He shoved the doors open to the outside and sucked in a deep breath of fresh air, feeling the sun on his face for the first time in seven long weeks. He held one arm over his eyes as they adjusted to the bright light. Even the heat didn't bother him. The putrid smell of the rain trials made this place smell like a dozen freshly picked roses.

Leper blinked a few times as the blinding sunlight finally dimmed to something bearable. Beside it, the Mortis Nightshade—the moon—cast a brilliant purple glow across the sky. His lips curled upward as the shard on his chest thrummed. With it in his possession, he had unlimited magic for Maka Kura. And with the moon visible, the psyrenth magic within the shard of Kasherri surged, growing stronger, feeding his power, feeding the shard's power.

He sucked in a deep breath. "Where should I start?" He glanced around. "What does Tamara love?"

"Gold, power, control," Intiva answered immediately.

"Leper, focus. You're out of control! You don't want this—focus on getting the shards!" Maka Kura's voice rang in his mind, pleading.

No matter how hard Leper tried, Maka Kura always found a way back into his head.

"You're part of the reason I'm like this," he barked back.

He studied the pristine edge of Maka Kura in his hand, remembering—it could cut through anything. A smirk flickered across his face before he hurled it toward the house in front of him. Maka Kura tried to resist, but with the moon out and the shard around his neck, Leper forced him forward. The blade slammed through the walls, sending Maka Kura crashing through the structure. Wood cracked, glass shattered, and moments later, Maka burst from the other side in a storm of debris.

Leper dispatched the second blade, tearing through the building until nothing but rubble remained. Shrieks and screams echoed around him.

Perfect.

Guards swarmed the city, but with Intiva at his side, he cut them down as they marched toward the shipping docks—Xaneth Harbor's lifeblood. Reaching for the shard of Kasherri, he called for large undead to rise. He hadn't used it much, but all the shards functioned the same way. As long as you understood their limits—and your own—you could shape the magic within them however you wanted.

Five massive cave trolls clawed their way out of the earth, as if they'd been waiting beneath the surface all along. Their hands, the size of boulders, flexed with raw power. Jagged yellow teeth jutted from their snarling mouths, gnarled and stained. Two of them hefted clubs as thick as tree trunks—the perfect tools for destruction.

At least twenty shipping docks lined the beach, wooden platforms jutting into the water. This part of Xaneth Harbor was called Crown's Shipyard. The land curved into the sea in a semi-circular shape, with platforms extending outward to make loading and unloading easier. From above, it looked like a crown—wooden spikes rising from its base.

He grinned, imagining the complete destruction of this beautiful shipping harbor. With any luck, it would shatter Tamara's soul.

Along with the cave trolls, Leper and Intiva set fire to every single ship docked in the harbor—cargo, crew, and unlucky bystanders burned along with them. Then they dismantled the platforms, tearing apart the wooden piers that connected the ships to shore. Leper tapped into the psyrenth magic of the shard. Black tendrils snaked out to crush vessels, then did the same to the docks.

Everything was going as planned—until Nylor showed his big, ugly face.

"Well, look who it is," Leper said, his voice buzzing with excitement. "Where's your bitch daughter, Cylandra?"

Nylor narrowed his eyes. "Sailing out of here. Away from you. Away from this evil."

"Yet you stayed here, like the asshole you are," Leper said with a smirk.

Intiva growled beside him, like some vicious raccoon—cute and deadly.

"Do you remember a little girl? Eleven years old. Name was Lillian." Leper raised Maka Kura, pointing it straight at Nylor. "You nailed someone close to her on a cross because he supposedly had horns like me."

"Yes. And I'd do it again. Your kind is nothing but trouble." Nylor gestured toward the burning docks. "You did that, didn't you? Destruction is all you know."

Leper grinned. "You're absolutely fucking right about that. But you're wrong about one thing." He stepped forward. "You won't be doing it to anyone else—because I'm going to kill you. Right now."

A tug on his arm.

He glanced down. Intiva was pointing toward the arena.

"What?" he backhanded her. She rubbed her cheek briefly, then flicked her eyes from the shipping dock to the coliseum.

"I think Nalecht is here," she mouthed.

His eyes moved toward the coliseum where she was gesturing. Sure enough, a tall, slender silhouette—one that looked an awful lot like Nalecht—paced the dais, screaming at a crowd. White hair whipped in the wind. They were so consumed by whatever was happening that none of them noticed the shipping docks burning.

The sight of him only stoked the fire raging in Leper's head. Images of Rinawen's tree engulfed in flames flashed before him, Zanera and Kelindra watching helplessly. The way Nalecht had desecrated her burial ground in front of her own children—mocking her memory—made Leper's grip on Maka Kura tighten until his knuckles turned white.

He blinked away the trance and let out a low chuckle. "Well, fuck me."

His lips twitched upward. Lillian really had rubbed off on him down there.

A bigger, better target.

His pulse pounded. "On second thought, I'll let the undead handle you. I've got a debt to settle."

He reached for the shard, summoning fleshy, skeletal horrors to join his trolls, unleashing them upon Nylor and the others, tearing through the city. He didn't turn to see if Nylor had been overrun or if he'd scurried off like a coward. He didn't care. The only thing that mattered was destruction—burning everything to the ground. House after house, building after building—obliterated, no matter who was inside. And to make sure nothing remained, either he or Intiva set fire to the ruins with a torch.

Nalecht and Tamara were going to see their end coming. And he was going to make damn sure they both suffered for everything they had done.

After a few moments, Intiva pointed across the dirt path. A large two-story structure.

Tamara's manor. *Even better. Might as well kill the Queen of Xaneth Harbor while I'm at it.*

Leper tossed Maka Kura into the air. The blade arced, cutting down the two guards at the front door before he stormed inside.

Another guard swung at him immediately. Leper deflected, using a maneuver Blank Face had taught him. He caught the guard under the shoulder, kicked the back of his leg, and slammed him to the ground. The guard gasped for air.

"Where's Tamara's room?" Leper demanded.

The guard sputtered, "Top...floor, last door on the right hallway."

"Thanks." Leper pointed at the guard, then looked to Intiva. "Finish him."

She smiled wildly and, in a flash, ran her daggers across his throat.

He reached the double doors to her room and hollered her name, demanding she open the door. A woman's voice behind the door claimed she wasn't there. He didn't buy that lie for a second. Leper backed up to the wall, used it to push off for momentum, and rammed his shoulder straight through the wood. Pieces of wood splintered off the door as it rocked back and slammed into the wall.

A redheaded woman shrieked as the door blew apart.

"You!" Leper pointed at her. "You're the bitch that saved Nalecht at Tudela!"

Her mouth chattered as her eyes darted around the room. "I... I'm Jocelyn, Tamara's sister."

"Where's your dragon?" Leper peered through the windows.

She straightened. "Why?"

"I'm a damned dragon slayer, why do you think?" Leper seethed, aiming a chakram at her.

"Leper, no, you are taking this way too far! You're hurting innocents! Forget the destruction and fire. Get the shards! Find Zanera and Kelindra," Maka pleaded.

His ears heated again as white-hot anger ripped through him at the mere sound of his ghostly voice. Leper pushed Maka Kura's voice out of his head and slammed the door shut on him. He would not listen to anything Maka had to say ever again.

"It's Tamara's dragon. I'm just the rider. He won't speak to her," she said.

"Do I look like I give a shit?" Leper crossed his arms. "Where is he so I can kill the bastard, and where's your stupid sister?" He fired back, losing patience.

"The coliseum. Fingin is there in case Madislak tries to pull anything," she said frantically.

"Perfect. And would you say Tamara values her dragon rider?" Leper asked, arching a brow at her.

Her throat bobbed, and she backed away slowly. "Yes. She'll kill you if anything happens to me."

"That's what I was counting on." He turned Maka Kura over in his hands and held out the pointed end.

"What... What are you going to do?" she shrieked.

Leper approached Jocelyn aggressively. She used her arms to block her neck and face, her body shaking in her ivory nightgown. He jabbed her in the thigh.

"Don't want your sister to underestimate the severity of the situation." Leper sheathed his weapon.

Intiva stood by, her button nose twitching as she grinned excitedly. Leper grabbed a handful of Jocelyn's red curly hair and pushed her forward. Her hair, only reaching her chin, didn't offer much to grab, but he managed. He shoved Jocelyn through the doorway, and she hobbled down the hallway to the stairs.

Intiva walked right by his side, a whimsical glint in her eyes. Simply amazing. In a matter of minutes, he seemed to have gained a loyal companion willing to follow him to her ultimate death. *Best prisoner ever.* The joy dancing across her large hazel eyes was unmistakable as they barged out of the manor and marched straight for the coliseum.

"Let's go destroy the last place she holds so dear and make her watch while her sister dies, shall we?" Leper grinned down at Intiva.

"Whatever you desire," she beamed up at him.

Chapter
Twenty-Eight

L illian took a moment and a deep breath, trying to calm the racing beat of her heart as it slammed against her ribcage. Panic ripped through every thought. Would they ever be able to get him out of this? Or would he be permanently altered? She shook her head and motioned for Blank Face to hand her the keys. Problem for another time. Right now, she needed to figure out what the hell happened in the month they were gone. What manner of bullshit had they managed to stir up, and why was Harmony so impossibly quiet?

"How could you!" She pointed her finger at Petrovana. "You stupid whoring bitch."

"I...I didn't mean to. It just kind of happened. We've been together the past month, and it just..." Petrovana yammered.

Lillian's nails dug into her palms. "You sent him to the rain trials angry and alone! Reeling from Rinawen's death. You sent a broken man to his death. I fixed him. I fuckin' sifted through the anger, all the hatred, all the resentment, and grief." She inhaled sharply as another tear rolled down her cheek. She couldn't hold it in. "I had him fixed! He was fightin' off the uncontrollable rage, he was maintainin' it, and you two just fucked everythin' up in two seconds. It was all for nothin'." Her face felt like it was on fire.

Their silence cut through the tension like a blade as Lillian paced back and forth.

"Do you have any idea what we went through down there? The hell we faced? We almost died of poison, from fightin' with Kasherri herself. We fought off a fuckin' goddess and you three are up here traipsin' around like the world ain't goin' to shit. Did you even try to get Zanera and Kelindra to safety, or like anythin' else he asked, did you just say, 'fuck it, we'll let him figure it out'?" Her neck strained as she spat angrily.

They both looked at the ground, Harmony too.

"Where have you been?" Petrovana asked. "Before the rain trials."

Lillian slowly turned her head towards Petrovana. "That's none of yer business. I would've never left if her jackass husband didn't break my ribs." Only a half-truth.

"We tried, Lillian. You think we're in this dungeon for the fun of it?" Blank Face growled.

"There are two of the greatest minds in the world sittin' in this cell, supposedly," Lillian scoffed. "And the best fighter in the world, and you tried?" She mocked. "Apparently not very hard."

"You have no idea what we went through here. Shit, I don't know who we're more scared of—Nalecht or worrying about how crazy man up there would react to us losing the shard of Theora or not getting to Zanera and Kelindra fast enough! His temper doesn't exactly help us think clearly," Blank Face snarled.

Lillian's toes curled in her boots, and it took every ounce of restraint to not reach through the bars and punch him. "He fuckin' knew already!" she bellowed loudly. "Zanera and Kelindra kept him updated on what was happenin' up here on the surface. He godsdamn knew you morons failed, and he was okay with it. Fer shit's sake, he was determined to get out of there and save yer sorry asses because he thought you were gettin' tortured or worse. Nope, turns out yer too busy fuckin' each other to get anythin' done!" Her neck strained, and it physically hurt from how loud she yelled.

"He..." Petrovana's eyes reflected the regret that crossed her face. "He wasn't mad at us?"

"At first, yes, but I told ya, I helped him. I fixed the parts you completely broke the first time. He fought so damned hard to not lose it when he got the last letter from Zanera and Kelindra, when they got abducted, and he won, Petrovana! He pushed it back and focused on savin' them, you, all of us. So, forgive me for defendin' him when he comes up here and sees you dressed for marriage and with yer tongue down his brother's throat."

Petrovana's shoulders sagged. After Blank Face handed her the keys, Lillian began unlocking Harmony's cell.

Petrovana slumped to her knees. "I'm a terrible person."

"Yes. Yes, you are," Lillian seethed, then looked at Harmony. "And what's yer deal? Reckon you haven't made a peep since we got back."

Harmony's mouth opened. "I... C..." She shook her head.

"She hasn't said anything since," Blank Face motioned to her injuries. "That sort of experience is harrowing."

She unlocked Harmony's cuffs, and Harmony threw her arms around Lillian.

"I..." She turned to Blank Face and made hand signals.

Blank Face spoke up. "She says she's sorry for what happened with Madislak, and she's glad you're here now."

Lillian grasped Harmony's shoulders and looked her in the eye, reading her every reaction. "Should I let them out?"

Harmony slowly nodded yes.

"Look, I'm goin' to unlock you, but no more screw-ups. You listen to me and follow directions. Can you manage that? Reckon we're fightin' something worse than just Nalecht, Tamara, and the talisman." She walked to their cell door.

"Agreed," Blank Face said with a nod.

"Deal," Petrovana added.

The lock to the cell clicked open, and Petrovana put her arms around Lillian. "I'm so sorry. Fer everythin'."

"Get off me." Lillian pushed her aside.

"Listen carefully." Lillian uncuffed Petrovana's wrists so she could heal them, then put them back on, still not trusting her. Petrovana didn't bother to fight it, apparently accepting her fate. "The gates, the barriers, whatever you want to call them, between Kalazaar and Malastion are no longer there. In order to get out of the trials, we either die and leave them locked or get out and break them wide open. There is a force of Kasherri's army headed to the surface as we speak. Imps, kobolds, minotaurs, and centaurs. Thousands of them."

All their eyes popped wide with realization. Fear glazed across Petrovana's face as she recoiled. Blank Face, however, remained composed and stoic as normal. She had to hand it to him; nothing seemed to ever faze him.

"That must've been the boom that shook the world." Petrovana glanced at Harmony, who nodded.

"Reckon it was certainly somethin'. Knocked both of us on our asses," Lillian added.

"What do we do now?" Petrovana asked.

"First, yer goin' to tell me what went wrong and what you know about the shards and the talisman situation. Then we're goin' to find Zanera and Kelindra. They might be our only hope of gettin' Leper back," Lillian said, stroking her jawline with her thumb and pointer finger.

Petrovana and Blank Face poured out all the details of their capture, their attempted rescues, and subsequent failures. They recounted Madislak's changed demeanor upon discovering the truth about Harmony. Lillian was taken aback at that news but moved forward anyway. They explained why Intiva was with them, how she helped, and what they thought Madislak was trying to accomplish. Petrovana showed Lillian her four spells, then healed both Harmony and Lillian. Though Lillian wouldn't tell her what she called her or what it meant, she would have to earn that.

In turn, Lillian told them about the Deathbinders, Kasherri, and the talisman's true purpose. She was shocked when they said Harmony already knew about its ability to kill a god. Lillian also informed them of the terrifying fact that it was Ryollin and Aisha's prison, unsure if unlocking it would release their corrupt souls or grant power to the one who unlocked it. Then she explained that taking the shard of Kasherri out of there also unlocked the boundary that channeled healing magic specifically to the dwarves. By the end, they agreed they'd rather leave the souls of the dead gods in the moon prison than risk the unknown consequences.

"But first, we need to quell the ragin' storm of hatred and anger above us," Lillian concluded.

The cuffs fell off Petrovana's wrists as Lillian unlocked them, and she rubbed her wrists, the red ring marks standing out on her pale skin. She felt the magic return to her and immediately healed Harmony and Lillian's wounds. Guilt rattled her mind—she had broken Leper's trust, with his own brother. *What an idiot.* How indecisive could she be? How stupid?

They started their ascent up the steps, with Lillian leading the way. The scene of utter destruction greeted them—guards wide-eyed, mouths hanging open, all dead. She had caused this, sent him into this uncontrollable frenzy.

They not only battled Kasherri's forces, Nalecht, and the talisman's unleashed power, but also themselves. She had to make it right, to show him how deeply she cared for him and to pull him out of this dangerous state of mind.

There was no telling how far he would go, the consequences of his actions in this state. He would never forgive himself for acting like his father. He'd condemn himself to a life of misery, all because of her. Everything she did seemed to go to ruin. She had destroyed her friendship with Lillian, summoned an unparalleled evil, and been banished from her home. When she found a new place that could have been home, she destroyed that, too. There would be no going back after this, no returning to what might have been. Like everything else in her life, she'd managed to eviscerate her own happiness and everyone else's. She didn't bother to protest when Lillian put the cuffs back on her. She didn't trust herself. Why should anyone else trust her?

"Reckon this is all my fault," Petrovana said with a sniffle. "I'm a worthless abomination. A no-good whore."

"Yes." Lillian nodded, matching Petrovana's intensity. "You are all those things."

"Hey!" Blank Face snapped, shoving Lillian's shoulder. "Where were you when Tamara captured us? Where were you for the weeks leading up to all this? Where were you when we couldn't decide how to handle any of this?"

"Don't touch me again, Blank. I swear to Theora I will rip yer head off," Lillian clenched her teeth. "I was gettin' Ace to join us. I was recruitin' The Former to help. I was out gettin' strong allies fer when things went sideways."

"And where is this help? Where are Ace, the dragons, and The Former?" Blank Face clenched his fists at his sides.

"I don't know. I was too busy fightin' fer my life and tryin' to save the man I love from losin' himself to continue what I started," Lillian seethed.

"Exactly what I thought. You're not mad that he saw what he did. Hell, you're probably happy because now that gives you a free path to him," Blank Face spat.

"Yer right," Lillian sighed. "The entire month we were down there, I tried. But it doesn't change the fact that he kept me at arm's length. After my first couple attempts, he stood up for this dumb bitch. Then I gave him his space, out of respect."

Lillian inhaled sharply. "He could've taken me anytime he wanted down there, but he didn't. Out of respect for her." She pointed at Petrovana. "But if you think fer a second in yer stupid brain that I would prefer to see him lose it like this than be with her, yer wrong. I'd rather suffer through watchin' him with her before I wished this on anyone. The agony and torment he goes through—are you really that selfish? Or are y'all too stupid to realize he's never comin' back?"

Blank Face's shoulders sagged, and he looked at Lillian, then to Petrovana. She immediately noticed the regret that crossed his eyes, the sadness. He turned his focus back to Lillian.

Blank Face rubbed his face. "You're... I'm sorry, but you're right."

"Thank you," Lillian spat.

Blank Face lowered his hood, revealing the shiny black nubs on the back of his head where the cut-off marks of his previous horns had been.

"You know, he bears the weight of all of us on his shoulders. Trying to change the perceptions of Chernzerk, fighting for our peace to walk among everyone." He nodded to Petrovana, and she could see clarity in his deep brown eyes. "Perhaps it's time another one of us helps him. Perhaps it's time I stop hiding

in the shadows and concealing my real identity while he feels
all the pressure. But there's something I have to confess before
we go any further." His nostrils flared. "If Tamara, Nylor, or
Nalecht see me with my horns regrowing, they will do anything
to capture me. That's why I always hide a poison to kill myself
within my cloak."

"Why?" Petrovana said, recalling him biting that poison into
Tamara's arm.

His throat bobbed. "I'm Xartazza. The one they've been hunting for, for five years."

Petrovana's eyes flew wide, and she noticed the same expression on Harmony's face.

Lillian shifted her weight. "Who the hell cares?"

"Tamara would've given up everythin' fer you. Why do they
want you so bad? Was it really fer the rain trials?" Petrovana
shrugged her shoulders.

Blank Face shook his head no. "They hate Chernzerk. They
wish to carry out Pasileveo's deeds. They want us all dead.
Cause we're the only ones that can completely destroy the talisman."

"Yeah, we know. Leper's been fightin' against that since he
showed up." Petrovana huffed.

Blank Face's soft brown eyes met Petrovana's, and she sensed
he was recalling something terrifying within him. In utter
shock, she watched a solitary tear streak down his cheek. "You
don't understand the type of cruelty Tamara is capable of."

Lillian interrupted them. "Look, I know yer thinkin' about
somethin' painful right now, and I know what it's like, but we
need to get goin' before there's nothin' left to get to."

Blank Face knelt down, bracing himself with one hand on the
ground. "When Tamara ran out of ways to provoke a reaction
from me physically, she broke me emotionally. She would send...
girls in, against both our wills. Then, when they were pregnant,
she would make me watch them die when they gave birth. The
ones that weren't born Chernzerk, she just left to die, hearing
the screaming and letting them starve to death in my room."

"I..." He stuttered. "I had to shut it off and let the darkness
take over. I couldn't bear it, and it was exactly what she wanted."

"Four of the Chernzerk babies survived, but I have no idea where they are. I've been searching for them. That's why I worked with Nalecht. I thought he might still have them or know where they are. He remained close to Tamara, and I thought I would catch wind of them, anything."

"They don't want Xartazza for the rain trials. They traded them for something and can't find them."

Another tear rolled down his face.

"I lived with that darkness controlling me for years until I ran into Leighth in Ambrosia, and I finally fought back. So, the next time you want to tell me how fucking selfish and what a piece of shit I am for hiding, remember that."

Petrovana knelt beside him, placing her hand on his back and shoulder, offering what comfort she could. What kind of monster would do something so twisted, so vile? What kind of person would treat him that way at the age of... fifteen? Heat boiled in her stomach, her face flushed with rage. The hair on her neck stood on end, and she vowed to use her new psyrenth magic to inflict an insurmountable amount of agony on Tamara when the chance arose. Surprisingly, Lillian didn't offer a snarky response, which Petrovana had half-expected.

"I know this is hard, but how do you know they got away?" Petrovana asked gently.

"The last I knew, Tamara traded them for something price-less, according to Jenkins." Blank Face spat. "That's why I left Xaneth Harbor. I tried to track them, but couldn't find a shrew with a high enough pinnacle to locate them. Every time I tried, it was like they vanished. Their life force is still there, but their location is missing."

Rubbing his back gently, Petrovana moved up to his head, grazing over the glossy black nubs that were now his horns. "I'm sorry that happened to you. We will find them, Blank... Or should we call you Xartazza?"

Blank Face grabbed her hand and squeezed it, then rose to his feet. "Call me what you want."

Lillian nodded. "I have somethin' to tell you guys too. But let's go make sure there's a world left fer me to tell you."

"Agreed." Petrovana flashed a grin at Lillian. "Let's go stop Leper before he does somethin' he regrets."

"No," Harmony finally spoke, catching them all off guard.

"There she is," Lillian blurted.

Her piercing blue eye narrowed on all of them. "Burn. Place. Down," she said slowly, emphasizing each word.

They all shared concerned glances.

Petrovana broke the silence. "I agree. Let's burn this place to the ground and Tamara with it. Screw Madislak's wedding and alliance. He can join us or leave. We'll get the innocent people out and then just level it with fire and ice."

Blank Face arched a brow. "Let's do it."

Lillian's smile was infectious. "Then let's go make our presence known."

"Wait," Harmony forced out again.

They turned to face her as she furrowed her brow in concentration. "No. Hurt. M... Madislak."

At least she was getting her voice back. Blank Face removed the rest of his cloak to reveal plain leather underneath. Petrovana glanced him up and down. His narrow frame was chiseled and rippled with every movement, his physique nearly flawless. The black leather, lined with red, complemented his blond stubble and cropped hair perfectly. With his sides shaved short and about three to four inches of hair on top, his brown eyes were even more captivating than before. Petrovana had to tear her gaze away, feeling her cheeks flush, as she turned back to Harmony, who sported a mischievous grin.

Lillian led the way up as they prepared to dethrone Tamara and decimate her beloved city—whatever parts Leper left for them, at least.

Chapter Twenty-Nine

M adislak's arm stretched across the table, pinned by the knife driven through his hand. He reached with his free hand, but Nalecht swiftly grabbed it.

"This is how it will go. Touch that knife, and I'll add another to your collection. Lie to me, and you'll find another in your arm," Nalecht's voice was cold and ruthless. He turned to The Latter. "Vickus, fetch Thessek. His skills with the ring will be invaluable."

The Latter floated off, returning with Thessek, whose blue and brown attire and face were splattered with blood, wearing a wicked grin. "Ohhh... More games, I see."

Thessek glanced at the table, his eyes widening. "What have you done to the master! Thessek does not play games with the master."

Nalecht's hand seized Thessek's throat. "Unless Thessek wants to meet his end today, he will play these games."

Thessek recoiled, his eyes bulging. "I... I suppose I can make an exception," he stammered.

"Good. Glad we understand each other," Nalecht grinned, then turned his intense gaze to Madislak. "Who is getting married here today?"

Madislak looked at the brown wooden table, debating whether to lie, but the agony from his wounded arm dissuaded him. He remembered how Harmony had answered Thessek under similar pressure. "I am," he admitted reluctantly.

Thessek's ring glowed yellow.

Nalecht's brows narrowed at Madislak, and he slammed both hands on the table, rattling the glasses and silverware. "To whom?" His voice boomed through the coliseum.

For the first time in his life, Madislak felt genuine fear. He closed his eyes, trying to steady his racing heart. Panic surged through him—this could be the end, right here at this table. Nalecht's face loomed closer, the scent of dried meats on his breath overwhelming. The man was on the edge of losing control. Madislak cautiously opened his eyes to meet Nalecht's unnervingly calm gaze.

"Petrovana," Madislak answered slowly. "Petrovana D'leon."

"Was that so difficult?" Nalecht turned his attention to Tamara. "What poison or venom is he talking about, and where is my grandfather's journal?" His voice steadied as he controlled his temper.

"Viper venom. I attempted to poison him with snake venom," Tamara replied hastily.

Thessek's ring glowed red. Madislak braced himself for the impending punishment, fearing they both might end up with another knife in them. Nalecht snatched a knife from one of his many sheaths, preparing to strike Tamara's arm, but Thessek intercepted, grabbing Nalecht's arm and deflecting the blow.

"Not the master!" Thessek cried out. "Use my arm."

Nalecht growled. "That will be your last mistake."

Nalecht moved in a blur and grabbed Thessek by the neck. Taking out his pristine sword, he slowly shoved it through Thessek's heart as he watched the life drain from the struggling man. Then dropped the lifeless body to the ground. He bent down and took the ring from Thessek's finger. Nalecht held it up in the sunlight, tilting his head and admiring it briefly.

Then he glanced at a nearby guard and pointed at Thessek's body. "Clean that up."

The guard stood his ground briefly, then, with a forced nod, began dragging Thessek's corpse off the dais. If nothing else, for some odd reason, Tamara's crew seemed very loyal to her. All of them except her sister, Jocelyn. He wondered if Fingin would show up to defend Tamara, or whether the shards provided enough power that even a dragon wouldn't challenge him.

The smell of Thessek's freshly drained blood filled Madislak's senses, taking over the dried meat breath smell that lingered. The blood from the knife that stuck through his hand started to dry in the immense, dry heat. It would hurt like crazy to pull it out of there now that it had about thirty minutes to dry and heal. He tilted his hand slowly just to make sure it still worked. Pain ripped through him again as more blood pulsed out around the blade. Yep. Still works.

"Let me ask you again, proxy of Ambrosia. What venom?" Nalecht leaned in close to her face.

"Fine," she sighed. "It's green dragon venom. Ace obtained it for me before he left our service. I tried to induce hallucinations with it."

The ring retained its natural brass color, not glowing any color.

Nalecht sneered. "What kind of useless shit is this? It's not working."

The Latter glanced at Nalecht. "I believe it requires an incantation to activate properly."

"Then go find it!" Nalecht snapped, pointing towards where he retrieved Thessek.

He took a seat in front of them. "Hope you're comfortable, because I'm far from finished. We will resolve this, and I will have my answers."

Madislak closed his eyes briefly in relief. They had bought themselves some time, somehow. Perhaps Petrovana and Blank Face would come to his rescue. Though he wasn't sure why they would. He had treated them horribly since their arrival. If he had only listened to them and seized the opportunity to escape when it presented itself, he wouldn't be here now, desperate for an escape. Foolish. He should have trusted his friends. Maybe Harmony had a valid reason for her actions. Perhaps he was indeed to blame for all of this.

He regretted not sending the note in his pocket to Leper, just to confirm whether he was still alive, instead of squandering it on an alliance built on deceit and lies.

He trusted Tamara of all people for an alliance—Tamara, known as the most ruthless of all the monarchs. Even more brutal than Nalecht, but she commanded a fierce loyalty from her followers. Frustration washed over him as he searched for any leverage to escape this situation, instead of dwelling on regret. Any scrap of information that could be crucial.

He would give anything to see his children now and assure them that everything was under control. The thought of them growing up as orphans, losing Lantess due to his reckless actions, weighed heavily on his mind. If he died here today, what would become of Kalazaar? Nalecht would only need one more shard. If he killed both of them now, he would have Petrovana, Blank Face, and Harmony—all three of the most powerful individuals in the world. He had doomed them all, despite their efforts to rescue him.

Opening his eyes, he met Tamara's glare with contempt. *Bitch*.

He started to speak, but was cut off by Nalecht. "I have to hand it to you, Madislak. I always thought you were the type to slash your way through everything. Marrying Petrovana and attempting to sway the shrews—that's a brilliant strategic move."

"Brilliant enough for you to let me go through with it?" Madislak joked, trying to lighten the tension.

Nalecht chuckled dryly. "No. They've resisted my attempts enough. The last thing I need is the king pushing them further in the wrong direction."

Madislak sighed heavily. "So, you'll kill me now. Finish what you started three months ago in Lantess."

"I need what's in your head first," Nalecht replied, raising his eyebrows.

So that's it, Madislak resolved silently. No matter the pain, he would keep the rest of his knowledge to give the others a chance in this war. A tear traced his cheek. He would never see Rylin or Alissia again. He'd wasted so much time fighting this senseless war, never seeing his children grow. What kind of man would Rylin become? Would he follow his father's path? And Alissia?

Beautiful, like her mother. Would she become a leader, a queen, or a fighter like Lillian?

"Just tell me one thing, Nalecht, before I die." Madislak met Nalecht's intense gaze.

Nalecht raised an eyebrow.

"Why?" Madislak's voice trembled. "Why do all this? Why kill so many innocents? Why Leighth's family? What's the point?"

Nalecht burst into laughter. "Oh, Madislak. You have no idea what that talisman is for, do you?"

Madislak shrugged as pain ripped through his arm again. "No. Other than for you to claim more power, more tyranny."

Nalecht let out a long, exaggerated sigh. "I suppose, since both of you are about to die anyway, I can tell you what my grandfather told me."

He paused as both Tamara and Madislak looked at his pointed nose. "When Theora, Amarook, Hathor, and Obidiah killed Ryollin and Aisha with the talisman, they used it to lock their power, their souls, into the Mortis Nightshade. Whoever unlocks it receives that power and will become immortal, like them."

"But there's two locked in there. You're only one person," Tamara blurted.

"Precisely," he groaned. "I would've offered you Aisha's powers, but you clearly cannot be trusted."

Tamara's tanned face turned multiple shades of red. She sputtered to say something, but her anger made her words stay in her throat. There it was. The hair on the back of his neck stood on end. Nalecht, a god. An all-powerful, immortal deity, and he would be entirely unstoppable then. Kalazaar would truly be heading for oblivion if he accomplished that. Tamara was still rage-stricken, clearly seething at the missed opportunity to be immortal. The sight of her misery brought a small ounce of joy to him in this impossible situation.

Madislak took a breath, mustering his strength. If he was going to die here today, he would not go down without a fight. He clenched his right hand, still missing his pinky and ring fingers, readying to yank that knife out of his hand on the table. He slowly moved his hand up and up, and up, resting it on the table and then inching it ever so slowly closer until the opportunity was right there. Just as he was about to make his move—

"Jocelyn!" Tamara's shriek halted his movements.

Nalecht was immediately on his feet, turning toward the coliseum.

"Holy fuck." Madislak enunciated each word slowly.

Marching through the coliseum's large double doors, dragging Jocelyn by the hair, Intiva grinned, walking happily beside him. His brother, Leper—the one they had thought dead—stomped through the entrance, the shard of Kasherri dangling around his neck. The conqueror of the rain trials.

He headed straight for the dais. But Madislak could sense something was amiss from the scowl on Leper's face and the anger in his eyes. There was a chilling fixation in his gaze as it locked onto Nalecht standing on the dais—a look of death.

Leper's eyes briefly shifted to Madislak, confirming his suspicions that Leper was not in control of himself. Even Leper's glare at Tamara didn't distract him as he advanced toward them. Leper stopped about twenty feet away. He came for this fight, and it sent a shudder down Madislak's spine. Nalecht and Leper, two very unstable people with so many innocent people around, and both looking ready to spill blood, anyone's blood.

"Well, this certainly is a very pleasant, very unexpected turn of events. Looks like I'll have all my shards today after all." Nalecht boasted from the dais.

Madislak yanked the knife out of his hand. "Leper! Run!" he hollered.

Leper clutched a handful of Jocelyn's curly red hair, shoving her forward through the coliseum. Blood streamed down her leg, soaking her ivory nightgown. The city on fire behind him, smoke rolling through the sky. He glanced up at the dais and spotted Nalecht. *Perfect.* Two targets in one place—Tamara and Nalecht. It looked like neither of them bothered to inspect the destruction or even care about the people to stop him; they simply sent Nylor to investigate.

The coliseum had a crowd already gathering in the stands as Leper marched in with the bloodied Jocelyn. They were dressed in fine clothes and ready for a wedding, but they were about to get something entirely different. Leper's lips twisted upwards again.

Madislak screamed for him to run. *Not a chance.* Madislak, dressed in plethocyte, stood ready to marry his girlfriend. No, ex-girlfriend. Leper didn't care about relationships anymore.

The scent of lilies and daisies flooded his senses as his boots thudded past the archway at the center of the coliseum. Ten-foot-high walls separated the viewers from the arena. The dais where Tamara, Nalecht, and Madislak loomed had a set of ascending steps. Flower petals littered the dry dirt and rocky ground.

He stood twenty feet from the dais, his loyal dog Intiva at his side. Unsheathing a chakram, he pointed it at Nalecht, then Tamara, then looked to Intiva. "Those two are mine."

"I got your stupid shard of Kasherri, Nalecht." Leper spat his name. "Where's Zanera and Kelindra? I'd like to make sure they're alive before I burn the rest of this shit-hole down."

Nalecht stepped down from the dais, narrowing his gaze. "They're alive and safe for now. Hand me the shard of Kash-erri," he growled.

Nalecht's beady black eyes, level with Leper's, burned with hatred. Leper matched it.

Leper emphatically raised his middle finger. "Not until I see them alive and well. I don't trust you or anyone else here to keep their word. It's been proven to me that it's nearly impossible for anyone these days." He flicked his eyes to Madislak.

Madislak's eyes narrowed on Leper for a brief moment as he clutched his bleeding hand.

"Excuse me, boy? Who exactly do you think you're talking to? I am your Anyth, and if I tell you to give me that shard, you better hand it over." Nalecht paced towards him.

Leper ignored the condescension. Nalecht held up a necklace with six shards dangling from it, then tucked it under his black leather shirt. *Is he taunting me?*

"Guess I don't need this dumb bitch anymore." Leper jabbed Jocelyn in the stomach with the pointed end of Maka Kura and tossed her to the ground.

"Jocelyn! Nooo!" Tamara bellowed. "You'll pay for that, you freak."

"Leper, what are you doing?!" Madislak hollered, taking a step towards Leper.

"Shut up! You're next after I'm done with this pile of crap." Leper leveled Tamara with a death glare, and she closed her mouth. "And as for you, dear brother, I suggest you stay out of this unless you want to die like these two." He pointed between Nalecht and Tamara.

"You've got five seconds to show me Zanera and Kelindra, or I will take those gods-damned shards right off your neck, and I will bury everything you hold dear." Leper aimed Maka Kura in Nalecht's direction.

Nalecht withdrew his sword and slashed at Leper, but he caught it between the blades of Maka Kura.

"No, you give me my damned shard first." Nalecht bared his teeth.

"You'll have to pry it from my cold, dead body." Leper shoved upwards, and as Nalecht's hands flew above his head, Leper kicked hard, sending Nalecht careening backward.

Leper grinned and turned to Intiva. "Correction. This won't take long. Make sure Tamara doesn't go anywhere."

Dust billowed up where Nalecht landed. He rolled, then got to his feet. "You've got some nerve."

"I kicked your ass before. I'll do it again, this time in front of an audience." Leper gave him a toothy smile.

Nalecht's face smoothed out, masking all emotion. In a blur, he rushed straight for Leper, the red spear of Ryollin, and the blue trident of Hathor glowing simultaneously. But Leper was ready, perfectly parrying each swipe. Remembering his sparring with Blank Face and what Maka Kura taught him, he didn't let Nalecht land a single blow. Nalecht continued his attack, two arcing swipes followed by a center stab. Leper twirled out of the way, noting the lackluster and repetitive moves. In no time, he committed Nalecht's entire move set to memory.

When Nalecht swiped once, then twice, and went for the stab, Leper undercut it and bucked under his armpit with his shoulder, slicing across Nalecht's stomach with Maka Kura as he lost his balance.

The crowd gasped. Nalecht sucked in a breath, and the orange mace of Aisha glowed, releasing a yellow light that flowed into the wound, healing it.

Leper grinned arrogantly. "Is that all you've got?"

Maka interrupted Leper's thoughts. "Quit messing around, Leper! We have so much potential if you just focus on what's important! Get the shards and find the girls! Your friends will help you! LISTEN TO ME!" He yelled, and Leper shook his head to get rid of the vibrations in his mind.

"Get off my back!" Leper slammed one of the chakrams against the ground. "I'll tell you when I'm ready to talk to you."

Nalecht yanked a dagger from one of his many sheaths and leveled it at Leper. "Fuck you. I'm going to enjoy ending you."

The sudden speed of Nalecht's twin weapons caught Leper off guard. He reached for his blade—one that refused to obey him—and barely managed to snatch it off the ground. He parried as fast as he could, but no opening presented itself.

His back screamed in agony, likely reopening a small wound. Nalecht's relentless barrage forced Leper to backpedal quickly. Before he could adjust, Nalecht's boot connected with his face, sending him spinning. Immediately, Nalecht's sword swiped across Leper's back. Now his back stung in two separate areas, but the lacerations weren't deep—nothing fatal. *He's going to take his time killing me...if he can.*

Warm blood flowed, and his temperature soared. He squeezed Maka Kura tightly, his knuckles turning white, and whirled around to face Nalecht just as he brought his sword down. Leper deflected it to the side, then grabbed Nalecht's arm and wrenched it forward, sending him off balance again.

Leper regained his footing, ready for Nalecht's next attack. As anticipated, Nalecht launched forward, whirling both sword and dagger feverishly. Leper swatted the dagger down, shoulder-checked Nalecht, and kneed him in the stomach, sending him skittering backward. Nalecht growled in anger, repositioning himself about ten feet from the coliseum wall.

Leper's lips curled upward. He spread Maka Kura apart and brought both chakrams together. A loud clap echoed, followed by a yellow wave of force, as Nalecht shot backward, slamming into the wall. His dagger and sword thudded into the dirt.

The crowd exploded with cheers, but Leper didn't waste time. He rushed over and aimed a swing at Nalecht's neck, going for the final blow. The shard of Ryollin glowed bright red, and Nalecht's hand shot out, grabbing Leper's forearm with a grip so tight he thought his arm might break. Nalecht shoved him backward, and Leper went flying, losing his grip on Maka Kura and slamming into the ground. He crashed into the archway and rolled.

His back throbbed, his body ached, and now his arm hurt, but the overpowering rage boiled within him. He shoved the pain aside and willed himself to his feet, pushing the wooden pieces of the archway off him as the crowd cheered wildly. He held out his hand, and Maka floated back to his waiting palms. The yellow light circled around Nalecht again, healing him. That was fine. Those shards' power didn't last forever—unless you were a Chernzerk and wielded them. Nalecht's face showed nothing but utter hatred as he glared at Leper from the wall.

Nalecht regained his composure, stepped away from the wall, and aimed his hands at Leper. The green axe of Obidiah glowed a vibrant green.

A brief pang of apprehension floored him as he realized he might actually die. He'd forgotten about the elemental properties of the shard of Obidiah. Lightning burst forth from Nalecht's outstretched palm, and Leper reflexively held out Maka Kura, bracing for the impact.

The lightning crackled and screeched, sizzling around him but never connecting. Flashes of lightning circled around Maka Kura, and a large grin spread across Leper's face. Maka Kura absorbed all of it. He didn't even know it could do that; it must have been another evolutionary feature. Nalecht's mouth fell open as Leper admired the little crackles of white light emitting from the curved blade.

The crowd went absolutely berserk, booming and cheering so loudly Leper couldn't hear anything else. He returned his gaze to Nalecht. With a quick wind-up and flick of the wrist, Leper thrust Maka, hurling the blade straight for Nalecht's chest.

Nalecht held up his sword and deflected the blade, but the pent-up lightning energy within Maka Kura was unleashed.

The massive resounding crack echoed so loudly Leper had to cover his ears. An immense flash of white forced him to close his eyes as the sizzling crack of energy sent Nalecht flying into the stone wall, leaving an indent that began cracking and crumbling on top of him. A black spot marked where the energy had been released, emitting smoke and filling his nose with the smell.

Nalecht scrambled to get up, the orange mace of Aisha alighting once again, but this time, no yellow healing light emerged—the shard's power was depleted.

Leper burst out laughing.

He raced towards Nalecht and was on him in an instant. Sheathing Maka Kura, he pulled Nalecht up from the crumbled stone and pummeled his face—once, twice, three times. Then, he shoved Nalecht's head into the dirt floor of the arena. Nalecht's face was bloodied, his eyes disoriented, as Leper slammed his head onto the ground again. Grabbing all six shards,

Leper felt an immense surge of power rush through his veins. He was unstoppable. He'd take his time, savoring every second of this moment. Maybe he'd change his plans—craft the talisman for himself and unleash whatever lay trapped in that moon. It would make destroying the entire planet that much easier.

He called to Aisha, and the orange mace glowed, releasing yellow light that encircled him. The aches and pains vanished, the bleeding stopped, and even his hunger was gone. But he wasn't done with Nalecht. Not by a long shot.

This man had put him and his friends through hell. He destroyed Lantess, killed Gwen, hired the man who killed Rinawen, and sought to exterminate every one of his race simply because they could destroy his precious talisman. Now, Nalecht would pay. Leper grabbed his long white hair and dragged him across the dirt floor back to the archway. Using the strength of Ryollin, he yanked him up and slammed him down again. Nalecht gasped for air, his eyes nearly popping out of his head.

"Fucking hurts, doesn't it?" Leper taunted.

Nalecht heaved a couple of breaths and turned to face him. "I hate you! I hope you rot in the deepest, darkest pit of Malastion!"

"You first, asshole." Leper knelt down and delivered two more punches, sending Nalecht reeling in pain on the ground. He followed up with a kick to Nalecht's stomach as he lay there, groaning.

Turning his attention to the dais, Leper focused on Tamara, now standing beside Madislak. Intiva held Tamara hostage at knifepoint, his lips curling into a sinister grin, ever the loyal dog. Their mouths hung open in complete shock. Madislak looked as though he might collapse at the sight of what had just transpired. *Or is that fear in his eyes, realizing what I'm capable of? If it isn't, it should be.* Leper shouted for Intiva to bring Tamara over. The cheering crowd fell completely silent.

Once Intiva brought Tamara to the center of the coliseum, Leper unleashed his fury on her, too, allowing Intiva to add a couple of blows for good measure before tossing her down on top of Nalecht. Leaning over the beaten and bloodied mess of both of them, Leper screamed, "Was it worth it, provoking me!?"

But he wasn't finished. He scanned the crowd, now silent. Were they actually concerned for the queen who had brought them nothing but misery? *What a joke.*

He called to the shard of Theora, and two massive hands burst from the ground. Raising his arms, he clenched his fists—earth and stone mimicking his movements—then slammed them down onto a section of the coliseum. The structure collapsed, dragging anyone still breathing into the crumpled mess of stone and wood.

"Stop it!" Tamara screamed. "You're destroying my city!"

Intiva silenced her with a punch to the face, then another to the stomach. He turned the shard of Obidiah toward the ruined stands and unleashed a massive cone of fire. Flames roared as they consumed the arena, shrieks and cries rising from the people in the stands as they were engulfed in flame.

"I will fucking kill you, and I will enjoy every second of it, you horned freak!" Nalecht snarled through clenched teeth.

He had been so caught up in the destruction that he'd nearly forgotten Nalecht was still here—still breathing, still waiting for his end.

Leper smirked. "Well, that would require you to be alive past today. And that sure as hell isn't happening."

Leper heard approaching footsteps but ignored them. Then, he heard two things thump to the ground.

"Leper? Why are you killing everyone?"

Leper froze in his place. He recognized that little voice.

Chapter Thirty

L eper turned around slowly. *No. No, no, no, no. Not them, not here.* He'd completely forgotten about them in his blind rage to kill these people. Larnadix had tossed Zanera and Kelindra to the ground like they were nothing. He must've walked in the entrance gates behind Leper while he was beating the crap out of Nalecht and Tamara. Rage rolled through Leper's system, threatening to burst like a pressurized pipe. His eyes connected with Zanera and Kelindra, and the disappointment and sadness in their eyes immediately lifted the haze from his mind. The simmering anger, greed, and jealousy floated away. He rushed over, helping them up and gazing into Zanera's green eyes, then Kelindra's innocent brown eyes. They were everything to him—his anchors, and they always would be.

His breath hitched, and his chest constricted.

Gods, they must think I'm some kind of monster. I've killed so many people in my rage. I've...

They were his anchors, not Lillian. This whole time, he'd been searching for one—how could he have been so foolish not to realize it was the ones he considered his little sisters? That was why Rinawen had appeared in the rain trials—she had been the clue, the sign pointing him toward the truth.

He let out a sigh of self-disgust.

He turned his attention to Larnadix.

"Why would you bring them here? Do you have no human-ity left?" Leper snapped, breathing in more power from the shards.

"You and I both know I'm not their father. Let's quit with the pleasantries," Larnadix snarled. "Give us the shards, or you all die."

Before Leper could respond, Larnadix began to change.

The short, chubby figure Leper had known melted away as his body stretched and transformed. He shot upward, now standing nearly as tall as Nalecht. His hair grew long, falling in silver waves streaked with earthy brown, and his elven ears elongated to a sharp point. Dark tattoos writhed across his skin; one was a distinct mark—two crossed axes, Axeladdle's old insignia before it got destroyed.

Leper's heart slammed against his ribcage repeatedly as recognition struck.

"Pasileveo." He gritted his teeth. He recognized him merely from his resemblance to Nalecht; they looked identical.

Pasileveo—*Larnadix*—grinned wickedly. "*Gods*, it feels good to shed that fat, useless skin. It's a blessing that his stupid bitch wife died when she did. All that whining and demanding— 'Do this! Do that!' I was about to put a knife through her myself. And the smell of her... ugh." He gagged for effect, his twisted glee making Leper's blood boil.

Not only had they burned her tree and disrespected her home, but now he mocked her. Leper gripped Maka Kura and swung violently at Pasileveo—only to feel the cold sting of steel pierced his abdomen. He glanced down to see Tamara's shimmering falchion protruding from his body before it vanished as she yanked it free. He gasped.

"That's for what you did to my sister!" Tamara gritted through clenched teeth.

Leper glanced toward where he had left Jocelyn. Madislak was helping her up the dais steps, disappearing from view.

Rough hands yanked his head back by the horns. Nalecht's bloody, bruised face came into view as he seized the shards and tore them from Leper's neck. The force sent Leper stumbling backward.

Then—suddenly—his mind cleared. The dark whispers of the shard of Kasherri fell silent. No more commands to submit. No more corrupting pull. Even in the midst of chaos, pain, and the certainty of death, it felt... freeing.

"These belong to me." He held the shards in Leper's face, his breathing ragged.

Leper placed his hand over the hole in his stomach, trying to stop the bleeding, but was unable to see the wound in his back. Warm, oozing liquid flowed through his fingers, carrying the sharp, metallic scent of iron and something darker, like charred wood and burnt cinnamon. He wobbled over to Zanera and Kelindra, pushing away the agony that hounded him. Nalecht, Tamara, and Pasileveo circled them, and Leper prepared to defend them with anything he had left.

Tamara lunged at him, and he brought his arm up to block, but Intiva intercepted, slashing Tamara in both legs and then across the abdomen. Nalecht grabbed her, lifting her the same way Leper had. With a flick of his arm, he hurled her across the arena. She hit the ground hard, tumbling into a motionless heap.

She was either dead or unconscious.

Another blade connected as Leper was distracted by the flying Intiva, and another fresh wave of agony roared through his gut. He winced as Pasileveo yanked his blade out from Leper's back after running him through. Leper turned to face him, calling Maka Kura to his side, but he was too weak to catch the blade, and it fumbled through his fingers onto the ground.

"Stop it!" Kelindra shouted. "You're killing him."

Another lancing pain ripped through him as Nalecht quickly ran his short sword through Leper and wrenched it back out.

"No!" Zanera yelled, trying to shove Nalecht away. Leper fell to his knees, reaching for her to tell her to run. Nalecht stood over Leper, an evil grin spreading across his face, enjoying every second of this, just as he had said he would. Leper clutched his stomach with one arm and used the other to keep himself upright as he retched up blood.

He couldn't even protect Zanera and Kelindra anymore; he brought them here. They were his anchor and his weakness. He'd failed them, failed Rinawen, failed every single one of his friends. He promised Rin he would look after them. How could he do that if he were dead?

"Somebody help us!" Kelindra screamed.

Pasileveo backhanded her, and she fell to the ground. Rage engulfed Leper's every thought. He shoved aside the pain from his wounds, pushing himself up and calling Maka Kura to fly at Pasileveo. One blade sailed over, deflected by Pasileveo, but the other struck him across the back of both knees, sending him to the ground. Leper's head erupted in a blinding pain, and he fell to one knee, clutching his head. His vision blurred momentarily, and when it cleared, Nalecht was leaning over him. Without the shards, Leper had no magic left in him.

Pasileveo limped over and put his hand on Nalecht's shoulder. "Take those shards, forge the talisman. Hurry before the other binder shows up and takes them."

"I plan on seeing his death with my own eyes, my king," Nalecht argued.

"NOW!" Pasileveo yelled. "His friends are here somewhere, and at the rate you screw shit up... Well, I'm not taking any chances. I'll make sure he dies, slowly."

"Yes, my king." Nalecht took one last glance at Leper and ran.

"Nalecht," Pasileveo called, and Nalecht turned around. "Once you're out, summon the undead. We've no need of this place anymore."

Leper blinked, his vision blurring again. Kelindra was in a panicked sob, holding on to him for dear life. Zanera helped him lie down on his back.

"Run," Leper squeaked out. "They are pure evil."

"Shhh," Zanera said, pressing on his stomach with her narrow hands.

"Find Lillian. Red hair. She's a badass like both of you. She can protect you better than I ever could," Leper grunted through the pain. "Or Petrovana. Purple eyes."

His stomach burned in agony, and he let out several pained groans as Pasileveo stood over him, grinning sadistically. The backs of his legs seemed to have healed.

"Or King Mad..." Leper was able to push out.

"You... You're not going to die!" Zanera cried.

"Where are your vials, Leper?" Kelindra asked urgently.

Leper grunted, then said, "All gone, destroyed."

Panic flushed Zanera's face, draining it of color. "No..."

Leper put his hands on their faces, turning them to him. "I love you both, and I'm so proud of you. I'm so, so sorry I got you involved in all this. Please. I'm going to die. I'm begging you, please go. Find Lillian."

"I will..." Zanera fought back the lump in her throat. "I will not leave you here. You're the only family we have left."

Leper's heart swelled with pride. He had never been so loved, so blindly accepted by anyone as completely as these two girls. He truly wished he had taken the time to listen more to his friends and be a better person to all of them. Perhaps he wouldn't be in this situation if he had. Dizziness engulfed him as his body felt cold, and darkness took over.

Zanera Xentoth knelt over Leper's body as his eyes slipped shut and he lost consciousness. She had just witnessed the most traumatizing experience of her young life. All three of them had run him through with their weapons. Her pulse pounded in her temples, and her breathing became erratic, her chest heaving at an alarming rate. Kelindra sobbed and patted Leper's face, trying frantically to wake him up. They couldn't lose him. He was all they had left, the only one she trusted as much as she had trusted her mother when she was alive. Now he lay on the ground in this miserably hot, dry, dusty coliseum.

Pasileveo stood over him, watching him die with a sick, twisted smile on his face. This disgusting man had deceived them for years. He wasn't their father, not even close. He was someone else. Something she had discovered, which caused him to become more aggressive and lock them away in a dungeon to use as leverage for this exact moment. Exploiting their closeness—if she hadn't been so careless, so reckless—she wouldn't have cost Leper his life today. *No... I will not let him die today.*

She ripped the bottom half of her yellow shirt and the sleeves that went down to her elbows off.

"Kelindra, help me pack the wounds," she cried. They started pushing the cloth into his stab wounds.

Kelindra tried to rip off the sleeves of her blue shirt as well. Zanera helped her, and they continued to bandage him as best they could.

Pasileveo chuckled and paced around them, with a wicked grin. He raised his sword and started to swing downward.

Zanera snapped her head to him. "I won't let him die! Not because of you!"

"Go away, ugly man!" Kelindra shouted.

He took two long strides and arced his sword down at them, and she scrambled to grab one of Leper's chakrams—but it wouldn't budge. Either they were far too heavy, or they simply wouldn't work unless he was the one wielding them.

She snatched Kelindra and dove out of the way just in time, his weapon whooshing by them.

Zanera whipped her head around, searching desperately for anyone to call for help, but the crowd had scattered in the chaos. Tamara hobbled back toward the dais, and King Madislak had vanished. The little assassin girl was still unconscious. There was no one.

Tears welled in her eyes, but she blinked them away.

Her gaze landed on a dagger, abandoned on the ground. She snatched it up and hurled it with all her strength at Pasileveo. The blade sank into his neck. He wailed, stumbling backward.

Leper had said Lillian, Petrovana, or Madislak. But where were they? She didn't want to run. Not when it meant leaving him here, defenseless against this... thing.

"His back," Kelindra said, pulling Zanera from her search.

"We need to roll him over." Zanera braced her hands under his shoulder. She would do her best to keep him alive and hope someone came to help them.

She heaved up, her muscles and veins bulging as she pushed, but couldn't get him rolled over.

"How much do you weigh, you moose?" she mouthed.

Then she tried again, her knees sliding out from under her as she pushed with everything she had. Kelindra hopped over and put her small hands on his hips, and they pushed again.

"Come on," she gritted as her tears hit the ground. "Please."

"He's going to die, Zee," Kelindra said, bawling.

"One more, Kelindra. We can do it." Zanera nodded to her when they got ready, and they heaved.

Zanera's heart thundered in her chest as she pushed and pushed. Her knees slid into the same spot as before, the ground beginning to tear through her black pants and scrape her skin, but she didn't care. They got him halfway there, just a little more, and he would fall to the other side. Kelindra slipped too, and his body started to fall back down.

"No!" Zanera chirped, putting everything she had into it, throwing her shoulder into his for more support, but she didn't possess enough muscle to stop his body from falling back flat. Just then, a white hand reached under his back, catching him and pushing him the rest of the way over.

"Momma!" Kelindra screamed excitedly.

Zanera looked up and saw her mother's beautiful green eyes and long blond hair, just like hers, smiling at her bravery. *Gods*, she missed her mother. Tears started flowing for a whole different reason, rolling down her cheeks and dripping onto the dirt floor.

She nodded and smiled at them.

Pasileveo roared as he tossed the dagger back at them. Rinawen batted it away with a burst of blue force, and Zanera glanced over to see that he was no longer in human form. He was eight feet tall with dark black skin and solid red, menacing eyes. Three large talons protruded from his hands, sharp as blades. Black, rough horns curled straight back on his head, and a tail that looked like a whip hung from his backside, swinging back and forth like a cat's. He swung his massive taloned hand at them, and Rinawen held up her arm. A blue light pulsed, halting his attempted strike, and with the flick of her arm, he was sent careening backward.

Her visage flickered, and she disappeared as quickly as she came.

"Mom, don't go," Zanera pleaded. "I'm so scared he's going to die and we won't have anyone. Nalecht's going to remake the talisman!"

Zanera watched her mother disappear into nothing again and immediately started wrapping Leper's back with his own shirt. Glad to see her mother again, no matter how briefly, it put a flicker of hope in her chest. She wouldn't have stopped him for nothing, right? There must be a reason she saved them, and him. Her pulse thumped harder and harder as her hands trembled while she tried to stop the bleeding.

"I told you to stop that! He's going to die today!" Pasileveo sneered and raised his large three-taloned hand to strike again.

"I won't let you kill him!" Zanera shot back.

"I don't care. We have nothing left to lose, Kelindra." Zanera locked eyes with her sister.

Kelindra slowly nodded to Zanera, seemingly understanding her determination to stay, even if it meant risking their lives too.

"You have your whole life ahead of you. Don't throw it away for some Cherno," Pasileveo hissed.

Zanera held out her hand, and Kelindra grabbed it as they both shed a few more tears, then covered Leper's back with their bodies. Zanera closed her eyes, her heart racing so fast it might explode, squeezing Kelindra's hand once more, bracing for the final strike.

But the blow never came. A loud clang of steel followed by a whoosh erupted behind them, and a deep voice boomed. "You will not touch them."

Zanera blinked away tears and whipped her head around. It was King Madislak, thumping Skyrunner against his shield, his face honed and focused on Pasileveo.

Pasileveo picked himself off the ground and snaked his tail behind Madislak, unnoticed, until it whipped straight for Madislak's back.

Another figure appeared, tall and slender, with small nubs on the back of his head, short blond hair, and stubble on his face. The man's hands moved impossibly quick. He sliced off the end of the tail headed for Madislak's back, and it recoiled quickly. With deadly grace, he positioned himself beside Madislak and pointed his dagger at the demon.

"To get to them, you go through me," he snarled.

"Blank Face." Pasileveo's voice dripped with disgust.

Immediately after, a large black shade panther roared through the gates, pouncing on the demon. It sank its teeth into Pasileveo's shoulder, ripping him backward onto the ground. The panther let out a loud, reverberating roar that echoed through the entire city, sending a prickle down Zanera's spine.

Then, with a shift, the panther transformed into a redheaded woman twirling two scimitars. That had to be Lillian.

"Fuck you, fuck yer evil goddess, and fuck Anyth Nalecht," she gritted.

Madislak and Blank Face stared wide-eyed in utter shock, and Zanera's mouth fell open. Leper never mentioned she was a shapeshifter or that she was a Chernzerk like he was. Her glistening white horns sparkled in the sunlight, starting at her temples and wrapping around her head.

"Kelindra!" Zanera shot up. "Come on. They'll take care of that thing! We need to find a healer."

Zanera grabbed her sister's hand, and they sprinted toward the exit—until a fleshy, bony hand clamped around her ankle. She yelped, stumbling, and shrieked, "Ew! Ew! Ew!"

Then, all around them, fleshy skeletal beings began clawing their way out of the ground. The undead army from the shard of Kasherri. Within moments, they were surrounded by the disgusting smell of decay and rickety flesh beings. Zanera glanced back at Leper, still motionless on the ground. For a moment, she thought they'd saved him, but as hundreds and hundreds of these creatures emerged, she knew. And that small flicker of hope that ignited when her mother arrived suddenly went out.

Zanera looked around at the red, hungry-eyed skeleton-flesh creatures crawling out of the ground, leering at them. She pulled Kelindra close. Madislak and Lillian were in a heated battle with the big black demon, too focused to notice her. Blank Face was locked in combat with a strange mohawk man she didn't recognize. They'd have to fight their way out.

Backing away with Kelindra, Zanera moved towards Leper's body. Suddenly, she felt a hand on her arm and yelped. She turned to see the assassin girl with the multicolored hair, holding out a dagger.

"Do you know how to use this?" the girl asked, flicking her eyes between them.

"No," Zanera shook her head. "Why are you helping us?"

The girl pointed at Blank Face. "I'm Intiva. I owe that man my life, and he owes me a lot of gold." She grinned and pointed to Leper. "And I'm pretty sure I'm in love with him."

Zanera moved Kelindra behind her. "Just stay behind me, Kelindra. I'll fight them off."

"Go for the heads," Intiva said, whirling into motion.

They would have to carve a path out of this arena to get out of here alive.

Intiva moved like Blank Face but a little slower, ripping through a wave of five skeletons in no time as heads rolled to the ground. Zanera hollered and charged, dismembering the first creature in her path. Something brushed her arm, and she shrieked.

"Ew." The squishy flesh pressed against her, and she instinctively swung high, severing its neck with ease.

"That's it, keep going," Intiva encouraged.

Intiva continued her flurry of attacks, and Zanera slowly took down one skeleton after another, finding a rhythm and gaining confidence. But the overwhelming numbers pushed them closer and closer to Leper's body until they were nearly standing on him.

Panic surged through Zanera's veins, her heart hammering against her ribcage. Blood splattered her face and matted the ends of her long blond hair as she swung and swung. Her narrow arms grew tired, and she cursed herself for not spending more time training with weapons instead of being a damned princess. She took a brief moment to catch her breath when one of the skeletons latched onto Kelindra's leg, eliciting a blood-curdling scream.

Intiva, already in motion, whirled to Kelindra's defense. In her focused frenzy, she miscalculated, and a skeleton bit her in the side. Intiva winced and recoiled, pulling Kelindra back with her.

"We need to carve out a path. We can't kill them all. I'm sorry, but he is...lost." She blew a kiss from her hand to Leper.

An eagle's cry from above caught their attention.

"Ghost!" Zanera cheered.

Ghost flew at breakneck speed, slamming into two rows of skeletons and scooping about a dozen of them up in her taloned lioness paws. She shot upwards, soaring to about a hundred feet, and dropped them. Banking in a circle, she landed gracefully over Leper's body and let out a deafening screech. The sound was so loud and piercing that Zanera, Kelindra, and Intiva covered their ears. The skeletons shuddered and shook, and even Pasileveo, in Deathbinder form, recoiled in agony at the pitch and severity of the cry.

Ghost spread her wings, shivering her entire body, her feathers standing on edge down to the tips of her wings and neck. With a quick thrust, the feathers flew off like thousands of little arrows, incapacitating a wide area of skeletons. The feathers returned, and Ghost shuddered again, bringing them back into place.

Zanera looked into Ghost's beautiful golden eyes, speckled with silver. They looked sad yet hopeful. Ghost's rainbow-colored feathers sparkled in the sunlight, making her look magnificent. She angled her head toward Zanera, then dipped her front shoulder. Taking the cue, Zanera quickly ushered Kelindra onto Ghost's back and got on in front of her, tying the large saddle straps around Kelindra's legs and body, then anchoring them down on the buttons, but the straps were large, and the restraints were still loose around her legs.

"Get yourselves out of here. I don't even know where to tell you to go, or your name," Intiva muttered.

"It's okay, Intiva. I'm Zanera, and this is my little sister, Kelindra Xentoth. Should I become queen one day, you will always be welcome in Kordry," Zanera replied. "I think Ghost has a plan, and I'll just follow her lead."

"Thank you. If you save him, if he lives, tell him I'll never forget him," Intiva said.

"He's never mentioned you before," Zanera tilted her head to the side. "But if you go back, tell the others Nalecht has all the shards, he's going to reforge the talisman; they need to stop him."

Intiva nodded. "Now go, before it's too late!" She hustled off toward Blank Face.

Ghost gripped Leper in her paws, crouched, and then took flight.

"The dwarves in Costin can heal. Should we go there?" Zanera leaned down toward Ghost's head.

Ghost squawked and climbed into the air, almost halfway out of the coliseum. Freedom was finally in sight. Hopefully, Ghost knew where to go, and they could heal Leper.

Zanera saw Pasileveo's tail flying toward Ghost as they ascended.

"Look out!" she yelled.

But it was too late. The demon's tail whipped up, wrapping around one of Ghost's legs. Ghost let out a cry of agony, clawing for purchase on Leper's body with her other three paws. She became unstable, swaying back and forth in the air, her wings whipping frantically in an attempt to break free. Zanera felt Kelindra's arms tighten around her waist.

"Hold on, Kelindra!" Zanera yelled, tightening her thighs around Ghost.

Ghost tried to whirl around but lost control, flying straight for the coliseum stands and threatening to barrel right through them. Zanera averted her gaze from the quickly approaching stone steps, only to see Leper falling from the sky, plummeting toward the ground.

Chapter Thirty-One

T he army of the dead rose around them. Lillian spared a quick glance at Zanera and Kelindra as she batted several undead back down. Intiva, luckily, was helping. Refocusing on the large black demon in front of her, she watched as it spewed fire from its mouth at Madislak. He deflected the blow masterfully with his gold and red rune-covered shield. They'd been in a deadlock with this beast for far too long, making zero progress, even with Blank Face's assistance. Blank Face was now engaged in a fierce duel with The Latter.

Lillian batted away the demon's arcing tail and dashed in, slicing the back of its knees. The wounds healed instantly. No matter how many times she cut through its skin, it regenerated, seemingly unfazed. Only when the demon focused on her long enough did Madislak get a chance to strike it with Skyrunner. If only she could transform into a dragon and devour it, but that shift was beyond her current capabilities. Smaller creatures were possible, but a griffin was the largest she could manage, with larger forms requiring more practice and focus.

Pasileveo swung his three-clawed hand at Madislak, who rolled out of the way. The demon then turned his attention to Lillian, standing directly below him. He kicked at her, but she expertly rolled aside as his tail whipped around and his talons slashed down. Lillian crossed her scimitars above her head in an X, accepting the blow from the tail as it sliced across her stomach. The initial sting felt like a whip, but then came the burn, as if the tail carried fire. She shoved upwards with her scimitars and launched into a frenzy.

Slicing across his abdomen, Lillian spun away from the next swipe of his talons and cut into his arms. She looked upwards and swung at his neck with her left hand as he crouched over. Another connection, but also another immediate healing, even at his neck.

Anger rolled through her. Her face heated, and her blood boiled. She launched into a rage-driven series of attacks, piercing his skin another eight times while guarding against his strikes. Nothing. Her chest heaved, and her arms tingled. She was exhausted and tired of fighting. It had been non-stop since the rain trials—fighting, running, fighting, running.

He sucked in a large breath, ready to unleash a stream of fire, until a loud shriek from... Ghost! The demon recoiled, shuddering and stumbling against the ten-foot stone wall.

Madislak scrambled over to Lillian. "Whatever we're doing, it's not working. We've been at this constantly; neither of us can keep this up," he panted. "Not to mention someone needs to chase down Nalecht; he's getting away with the shards."

Lillian glared at him. "I noticed. I cut into him a hundred times, and it doesn't even faze him. You need to hit him with that sword. I don't have Idelthian steel." Her chest heaved. "Let's not waste this opportunity that Ghost gave us. Let's kill this thing, then we'll figure out Nalecht."

Madislak nodded. As they went to finish off Pasileveo, The Latter slammed into them, with Blank Face close behind. They all got knocked to the ground, but the two assassins were so focused on their duel that they got back up impossibly quick and continued the fight. Blank Face swung, but his blow missed The Latter's neck by inches.

The Latter retaliated with a brutal headbutt, and blood immediately streamed from Blank Face's nose. Snarling, Blank Face drove his fist into The Latter's gut as their brawl raged on, crashing through the waves of skeletons surrounding them.

"He won't let me. Every time I try, he focuses on me and ignores you. We could use Blank's help, too. Should we help him finish off The Latter?" Madislak spat as he picked himself off the ground. "Where the hell are our shrews?"

"One of them is still cuffed, and I have the keys. Petrovana ain't who we thought she was." Lillian rolled her shoulders. Pasileveo was now back on his feet, their brief opportunity gone thanks to these dumbass assassins. Ghost's distraction had only bought them a few precious seconds.

"No, we can't help him. Those stupid assassins are fightin' fer superiority like a bunch of dumbasses would. If we interfere, they'll likely cry about it, and I don't have time for whinin'."

"He's coming to," Madislak said, motioning toward Pasileveo. "I don't know if we should flee or keep trying to kill it."

Lillian stepped toward Larnadix. "Reckon we have to keep tryin'. Zanera and Kelindra never gave up on Lep, and I won't give up on them."

Madislak nodded.

Lillian charged headlong at Pasileveo as he shook his head and regained his footing. Madislak followed closely. Pasileveo swiped down at her with his back hand, but she vaulted over it and rammed her scimitar into his left eye. To her surprise, as she yanked it out, he reared back in pain, swaying and flailing wildly. He crushed skeletons in his path and put a hole in the wall he had just been using for support—a hole that led out of the arena into the crowd stands.

Then he turned, and his eye was back. *Son of a bitch.* His tail whipped skyward, and she followed it to Ghost, who was trying to fly Leper's limp body, with Zanera and Kelindra on her back, out of the arena. The half-eagle, half-lion squealed in pain and lost control of its flight. A crash at that velocity, and none of them would survive.

"Madislak, stab him! He's going to kill those poor girls!" Lillian yelled, more fear in her voice than she anticipated.

Madislak landed an impressive blow on Larnadix's abdomen, and he recoiled again, but this time the strike didn't heal like normal. Lillian pressed her attack, desperately trying to keep Pasileveo distracted so Madislak could continue cutting him apart piece by piece.

Pasileveo inhaled sharply, a deep breath, and instead of a stream of fire, he launched a ball of flame. It connected with the ground in front of them and exploded. Lillian went flying backward, flames licking her body and clothes. Sweat poured out of every pore as she smelled herself burning alive. She hollered in agony, rolling across the dirt to extinguish the flames. A cooling sensation touched her skin, smelling like... ice?

She skidded to a stop just in time to see Blank Face drive both daggers into The Latter's neck before tossing him to the ground. He'd won—finally. Now they could move past this arrogant struggle for superiority and focus on what really mattered.

Harmony stepped forth from the hole in the wall, her ice tattoo drained. Pasileveo roared, yanking his tail—still connected to Ghost—back towards himself. Ghost lost all control, careening wildly towards the stands, and Leper plummeted in free fall from fifty feet in the air.

Lillian glanced at Madislak, then turned to Larnadix.

Madislak, with steam rising off him as well, pointed towards the air. "Go!" he commanded, like the king he was.

Lillian got to her feet, transformed into a griffin, ran a few steps, and launched herself skyward.

Madislak easily swatted the skeletons around him down. Relief flooded him as Harmony arrived, helping with the fire. *Thank the gods.* Petrovana was still cuffed with no magic, tucked into the hole in the wall Pasileveo had created while thrashing about. Harmony only had forty seconds for her spell to recharge. Hopefully, when it did, she could help with this annoying Deathbinder.

He had never fought anything like it. Pasileveo wouldn't let him land a blow unless he managed to catch him off guard. Good luck with that. The rampant smell of decay filled his nostrils, and he could taste his own salty sweat leaking profusely down his face and into his mouth. But he resolved to let no one get hurt by Pasileveo anymore, who was now solely focused on Harmony, his proxy, his queen—if she'd still have him.

Madislak sprinted, making up ground as Pasileveo stalked towards the hole. Shoving skeletons aside, he plowed through them with sheer strength and force, rambling his way towards Harmony. He wouldn't get there in time. Pasileveo was nearly upon his shaking queen; he needed to be faster, cover more ground quicker. *No.* He narrowed his gaze on Pasileveo. *Not today, asshole.* He sucked in breath through his nose and channeled his inner strength, from the warrior he'd always been and always would be.

Blank Face appeared in front of Harmony and Petrovana, ushering them away as Pasileveo slammed his hands down where they had been standing and missed. The Deathbinder latched onto the wall and started pulling, threatening to bring another massive chunk of wall down in the process.

Madislak continued sprinting past the ache in his legs and burns on his arms, his mind formulating a plan, crazy as it seemed. He broke through the last line of skeletons about thirty feet from Pasileveo and pushed his legs to the max, covering the next ten feet quickly and tucking Skyrunner across his back. Madislak sprang into a somersault, angling his shield to face the ground. He pushed off with all his might, and a yellow force wave erupted from the shield, vaulting him through the air. He went higher and higher... *oh shit, too high, TOO HIGH.*

He was about fifteen feet in the air now, wobbling like a circus performer on a tightrope. Taking one more glance at Harmony, he straightened himself and leveled a gaze of utter focus on Pasileveo. On his descent, he masterfully withdrew Skyrunner and slammed it right through Pasileveo's arm, severing his hand. Madislak landed on both feet, dropping to a knee to absorb the impact as Skyrunner crashed into the ground with a resounding thud.

The ground shook and vibrated. Dust fell from the seats and the canopy above as it seemed the whole world trembled at the impact. Cracks spread from under his feet, reaching twenty feet towards the center of the arena.

A few seconds later, the ground erupted in a white wave of light, blasting the demon and slamming him into the wall at the other end of the coliseum. *What the hell was that? Did that kill him?* The wave took all the skeletons with it, definitely killing them as bones scattered and flew everywhere.

Ghost crashed into the stands.

Madislak's gaze snapped to Pasileveo, whose black skin simmered as he struggled back to his feet, unsteady. Skyrunner had flung him fifty feet, and in an instant, the skeletons swarmed him again.

Madislak glanced towards the stands, ensuring the girls were safe, then hurried around the broken wall. Blank Face, Harmony, and Petrovana were all okay.

He'd make sure they stayed that way, then refocus on the demon. But they needed someone to locate Nalecht and the shards. If Nalecht had already escaped and summoned this army, they had to stop him from reforging the talisman.

First, though, they had to survive this. With Leper unconscious and enemies closing in from every side, getting out of this predicament was easier said than done.

"Blank, Zanera, and Kelindra just crashed with Ghost above us. Can you check on them?" he ordered.

"Yes." Blank Face disappeared.

"Are you both okay? I'm so sorry. I'm such an—" Madislak got cut off.

"It's okay. Reckon we all have a lot to regret right now," Petrovana interrupted.

He turned to Harmony, a tear escaping his eye. "Please forgive me. I don't know what I was thinking."

"Is. Thing. Dead?" Harmony responded.

Madislak arched a brow.

"Is the Deathbinder dead?" Petrovana explained.

"No, Skyrunner did something I didn't know it could do, but he was getting up slowly. The skeletons formed around him like they were protecting him, though," Madislak said, pointing towards the other end of the coliseum.

His head pounded in response. He likely wouldn't be able to pull off another move like that anytime soon.

"Why are you still cuffed?" He motioned towards Petrovana's wrists.

"That's a long story, one that can wait until we're out of this predicament. I'm assumin' Nalecht has all the shards? Considerin' this army of the dead ain't fightin' for us?" She rubbed her temples.

Madislak nodded. "Yes... They... ran Leper through several times. Zanera and Kelindra tried to save him. I don't know if he's still alive, but something tells me he's somehow holding on. Nalecht took the shards and ran off to make the talisman. We have to get out of here and try to stop him."

He looked over his shoulder for Lillian but saw only skeletons flying at the hands of a shaded panther. A loud roar emanated from the end of the coliseum, and Madislak's shoulders drooped.

"Guess that means he's ready to fight some more. What do we have to do to kill this damn thing?" Madislak threw his arms up in defeat.

Harmony ran a finger across her neck, then pointed at herself, then at Madislak, and finally out the hole. "Fight."

"I won't risk losing you," he argued.

She walked up to him, narrowing her gaze, her piercing blue eye leaving no room for argument. "Fight," she said again.

Madislak let out a defeated sigh. "Ignoring your advice was the worst thing I've done in my life. I'll not make that same mistake twice."

Her lips quirked up in a half grin, and he led her out of the hole.

Setting Leper down, she glanced around at the skeletons that circled them. There were too many of them for her to contend with right now. She needed to clear them away so she could get him to safety.

Shifting into a shade panther, Lillian ripped, clawed, and used her mace tail to blast through them, bludgeoning most as bones and flesh flew wildly around her. She marveled at the transformation; these creatures were built for utter destruction and terror. Her senses sharpened. The overwhelming stench of rotting flesh burned her nose, nearly unbearable. Every detail stood out in stark clarity: specks of dust floating in the air, glistening droplets of sweat and blood. Even their footsteps, fifteen feet away, echoed loud and distinct in her ears. An ultimate weapon of chaos, and she planned to utilize every sense that came with it.

Dispatching a pack of skeletons in seconds, she spared a glance across the coliseum where Madislak had somehow subdued Pasileveo temporarily. Then her attention turned to Leper, still unconscious on the ground. Sniffing him, she found he was still warm but with a weak pulse that might be failing. He had been unconscious too long. They needed a healer urgently, or he would surely die. With Ghost crashing into the stands, Lillian desperately hoped Zanera and Kelindra were safe.

This is shit. It's all going to shit fast. Only a miracle can save us. The undead army had overwhelming numbers, a Deathbinder they couldn't kill. Zanera and Kelindra couldn't reach safety, and they were lugging around this limp body. Meanwhile, Nalecht was reforging the talisman, and Kasherri's unleashed army was heading to the surface. *We're fucked.*

She transformed back into a griffin and carried Leper over to where Petrovana still stood. Arcing high enough to glimpse both Blank Face and Intiva helping Zanera and Kelindra onto Ghost's back, she noted that Ghost seemed disoriented but not too badly hurt. Unfortunately, she would have to rely on her old best friend—the source of much of their internal misery—to heal him. She hated the idea of uncuffing Petrovana. She'd almost rather fly to Costin and risk it, but time was scarce, and they needed her now. Spotting Leper's chakrams on the ground, she saw them slowly eroding into dust and fluttering away. *Shit, shit, shit. He's dying.*

Madislak and Harmony were pressing the big black demon, and Harmony's ice magic proved to be a game-changer, forcing him to retreat or face certain death. Now they only had the skeleton army to deal with, which should be manageable with their combined skills. The civilians who didn't know how to fight or lacked weapons were the only ones truly at risk. She swooped down and laid Leper's body in front of Petrovana, then returned to her regular form.

Petrovana's eyes widened in shock as she stared at Lillian's horns, but they didn't have time to debate it as Madislak and Harmony rounded the corner.

"I'm gonna unlock you. Heal him," Lillian said as she pointed at Leper.

Petrovana nodded. Lillian pulled out the key and unlocked her magical cuffs. Petrovana leaned down and placed her forearm on Leper's stomach, where the wounds were.

There was a commotion in the stands, and Ghost soared over them, followed by a loud, disturbing roar from behind the dais.

"Fer fucks sake, now what?" Lillian barked.

Blue shimmering scales carrying a red head, and Tamara flew over the coliseum, snapping at Ghost. The girls screamed, and Ghost beat her wings faster, taking off like an arrow. The dragon's golden eyes, outlined in red, landed on them as it emitted a low growl.

"After them!" Tamara bellowed. "He tried to take my sister from me; let's take them from him!"

Evil bitch.

Fingin's clustered horns curved around the top of his head, then twisted and entangled like a crown as he lurched and pounced skyward, Zanera and Kelindra screaming the entire ascent.

"Fuckin' heal him now! We need our gods-damned dragon slayer!" Lillian erupted, panic thick in her voice.

Petrovana closed her eyes and poured more magic into the wounds; a yellow healing wave flowed around him. Her face paled, nose bleeding immediately, followed by her eyes.

She looked up wearily, eyes laced with sadness. "I... the wounds are too old and too severe... I can't."

"I don't give a shit! Do it again!" Lillian seethed.

"We'll both die," Petrovana pleaded. She rubbed the back of her head briefly, and her eyes lit up with recognition. "The power, from Kasherri, the river in my mind... I—"

"What are you babblin' about?" Lillian screamed. "We don't have time fer yer fuckin' useless thoughts right now."

"I don't know if it'll work; I don't know if I have enough magic left in me now," she muttered.

Lillian put her hands on her hips. "We don't have another fuckin' option right now, do we!?"

Harmony tilted Skyrunner up as Madislak held it and sliced her palm. "Channel." She held out her hand.

Petrovana's eyes widened. "You know the risks. It could claim both our lives—I've seen it with my own eyes. It's not worth it. It's too unstable, Harmony. Overdraw, underdraw, oversaturation, undersaturation—it's all life-threatenin'. Then we're all dead, and fer what?"

Harmony said through clenched teeth, "Channel."

Petrovana winced, then held out her hand to Lillian, who gladly sliced her palm with her scimitar.

Petrovana inhaled sharply and grabbed Harmony's hand. The surge of their combined magic made their skin shimmer as she pressed her palms to Leper's wounds once more, her tattoo fading with the effort. This time, the yellow light was blinding, and as the magic flowed, a faint aroma of fresh rain and wildflowers filled the air.

Acknowledgements

First and foremost, I want to thank my family. To my loving wife, thank you for your endless support and patience throughout this journey. To my kids, Haley, Peyton, and Addyson, you've brought so much enthusiasm and joy to this process. You've encouraged me in ways you may not even realize, and I am so grateful.

To my brother, Daniel, who has been by my side through every part of this process, reading, theorizing, helping with marketing, giveaways, and distribution ideas, you've been there every step of the way. To my sister-in-law, Miranda, thank you for your creativity and support, for pushing me to think differently about marketing and distribution. To my sister, Faith, I owe you for your sharp eye on detail and for catching the little things I missed in those final passes. To my sisters, Margaret and Jenny, thank you for your support and encouragement, and to my parents, thank you for believing in me and standing behind this dream.

To my friends Andrew and Tim, thank you for pushing me to keep going, to be better, and to never give up on this passion. To Jonathan, thank you for helping me brainstorm ideas, from giveaways to booth setups, and for always challenging me to think outside the box.

To Miblart—thank you for bringing this world to life with your incredible maps and covers across these books.

To the readers, you are the lifeblood of this story. Every page you read, every message you send, every time you tell a friend about this series, you keep Kalazaar alive. Your passion, your theories, your excitement when new chapters arrive, all of it fuels me to keep going. This is your journey as much as it is mine, and I am forever grateful for your support.

And finally, to my two AMAZING editors. Ali Bumbarger, I can't thank you enough for your incredible work. You've carried so much of this story on your shoulders with your developmental edits, your sharp eye for character flaws, and your deep knowledge of this world. You know almost as much about Kalazaar as I do, and your contributions are beyond words.

And to Pam Hines—thank you for your copyedits that go far beyond grammar and punctuation. You've helped me refine line flow, offered resources and programs to sharpen my craft, and guided me toward growth at every step. You always go above and beyond, and I am endlessly grateful for everything. This book would not exist without you two!

Thank you all for walking this road with me and for helping me bring these stories to life.

Enjoying the Journey?

If you enjoyed this book, would you take a moment to leave a review? Your words help other readers discover the Shattered Divinity Universe, and they mean the world to me as an author. Reviews don't have to be long, even a sentence or two makes a huge difference.

Thank you for standing with me on this journey. Every review, every recommendation, every word of support helps keep this world alive and growing.

How to Connect
With Me

Thank you for picking up this book and stepping once more into the Shattered Divinity Universe. You are part of a growing band of warriors and legends, and your support means the world to me. I promise to keep building this world bigger and brighter, with stories that will pull you in, challenge you, and give you a place to belong.

If you would like to connect with me, the best place to start is my website at aarondyoder.com. There you can find all my social links for Facebook, Instagram, and TikTok, and you can also sign up for my newsletter.

When you join, you will receive Leper's origin story (as soon as it's finished), a tale that holds more than it first appears. Hidden within it are hints that might just point toward the saga still to come, though I will leave it to the sharpest among you to notice.

This is only the beginning. Through my site and my newsletter I will keep you updated on contests, giveaways, meet and greets, book signings, readings, and future travels to different cities where I hope to meet you in person at comic cons, renaissance faires, and beyond.

Thank you for reading, thank you for believing, and welcome deeper into the Shattered Divinity Universe. The adventure continues, and I am honored to have you with me on the journey.

About the author

Aaron D. Yoder is the author of the Shattered Divinity trilogy, an epic fantasy saga of betrayal, sacrifice, and redemption set in the world of Kalazaar. His storytelling blends fast-paced battles with deep emotional arcs, exploring themes of forgiveness, resilience, and the strength it takes to rise after loss.

Aaron's journey as a writer is fueled by a lifelong love of fantasy worlds and the belief that stories have the power to carry people through their darkest seasons. Drawing inspiration from mythology, raw human emotion, and his own perseverance, he crafts tales where flawed heroes fight impossible odds, and still find hope.

When he's not writing, Aaron is a devoted father, a full-time worker with a physical job, and an advocate for indie authors and bookstores! He is passionate about helping new voices find their place in the publishing world, whether through collaboration, giveaways, or building community.

Aaron lives in Pennsylvania, where he continues to expand Kalazaar's lore and build the foundation for his next saga. His debut novel has already captured readers with its rich worldbuilding and unforgettable characters, and this is only the beginning of his journey.

"Stories remind us that even the most broken can rise again. That's why I write."

Coming in 2026

F rom *Shattered Legacies*
The final book of the Shattered Divinity Series

The journey that began with betrayal and sacrifice races toward its last reckoning. Bonds of blood and spirit will be tested in fire, and the fate of Kalazaar will be decided in a clash of gods and mortals.

This is the heart-pounding, emotional conclusion you won't want to miss.

Everything was dark, his eyes didn't open but Leper knew exactly where he was. He lay on the ground, bleeding out because of his own stupidity. He could feel Maka Kura's presence, that hum but he couldn't see or hear anything. An emptiness swallowed Leper whole... Nothing took shape in the pitch blackness, his body like a sack of stones, heavy, immobile, useless. Then, something shifted. His weightless body floating through the endless expanse of... nothing.

A hard thud slammed him back into that crushing, stone-like weight. How had it come to this? A few images flashed in his mind, Lillian setting him in front of Petrovana and then shifting back into her Chernzerk form. His anger, his arrogance, it had gotten him killed. He tried to feel his abdomen, where the three swords had pierced through him, but his arms and hands wouldn't move. "Fight!" Maka Kura's voice echoed through the swirling pit of grief consuming his mind. He'd been reckless, furious enough to believe he could take on Nalecht, Tamara, and cut down anyone in his way. The darkness in his mind, twisted further by the shard of Kasherri, had consumed him. It wasn't until Zanera and Kelindra dragged him out of that spiral that the madness loosened its grip. To them, he must've looked like a monster. That was when they ran him through, stabbed him right through the stomach, three times.

He couldn't manage a curse, couldn't even growl in defiance. This was the ultimate failure of his life. He couldn't save Rinawen, and nowhe'd failed to protect Zanera and Kelindra. He'd sealed their fates, along withthe rest of his friends. He had brought the last remaining shard Nalecht neededstraight to him, practically handed it over.

A monstrous wave of regret washed through him, so powerful it caused physical agony in his chest. Lillian had warned him, warned him what it would feel like to be the reason his friends died. She'd seen it coming, and still, he hadn't listened. He hadn't listened to the one person he could trust with not only his life but Zanera and Kelindra's. Even Maka had warned him.

His face couldn't produce tears. If it could... he would have shuddered, but he was trapped in this motionless shell.

He tried to move his body but couldn't. The clinking of chains told him exactly what he needed to know. He knew why he couldn't move, he was shackled to a wall, metal chains wrapped tightly around his wrists, chest, abdomen, and legs. Thick, unforgiving links dug into his skin, binding him in place, rendering him motionless. Not that it mattered. The overwhelming regret and grief kept him still, paralyzed.

"Leper... fight!" Maka Kura's voice echoed again in his head.

Leper shut his eyes. "Why do you care? You abandoned me and Blank Face. If you hadn't been such a worthless father, maybe I would've turned out better. "

His head throbbed as Maka Kura's voice hammered back, full of intensity. "This isn't about you or me! This is about Zanera, Kelindra, Lillian, Madislak, Harmony, Petrovana, Blank

Face, Ace, Leighth! Don't you see? What started with you and
Rinawen has grown into something bigger. They need you to
fight!"

Images flooded Leper's mind. He saw his own broken body,
lying there. Zanera and Kelindra flinging themselves over him,
desperately trying to save him in the face of a Deathbinder.
Pride surged through him. They were scared, but they loved
him. Loved him for *who* he was, not *what* he was. Warmth
coursed through his veins, roaring to life, and he wiggled his
fingers.

"FIGHT!"

Leper yanked against the chains, the sharp metal sinking
deeper into his skin. But he was too weak, too drained. His
mind spun, locking up his limbs. He'd slaughtered thousands of
innocents. Threatened Madislak, again. Turned on his friends.
Sworn to kill anyone who got in his way. He was no better than
his lunatic father.

Leper rested his head against the cold wall behind him and
pulled again. The chains didn't budge. He stared into the black
abyss, no sensetrying to break free, he deserved this, whatever
it was.

"These are metal bands. I can't break through them," he
muttered with a sigh.

A booming cackle echoed from the darkness, one all too familiar. The same laugh that resonated in the rain trials each
time they thought they defeated Kasherri. Which could only
mean she was here, somewhere. *No.* He wouldn't get to be with
Rinawen, he wouldn't get to see her shining face. His mind
whirled faster. He would be stuck in this endless torment and
never ever see Rinawen again.

"Try. Harder. "Maka Kura enunciated each word with fierce
precision.

Another wave of images surged through his mind. Madislak,
fighting the Deathbinder with raw fury. Blank Face, removing
his hood and robe, joining the battle. Lillian, revealing her true
form and embracing the beast within. Then came the array of
the undead, crawling from the ground, Intiva, Ghost, everyone
fighting together, protecting him.

A flicker of hope, quickly followed by rage, ignited in his chest. He pushed again, straining with all his might. His chest heaved up and down against the pressure, but still, the chains held fast.

"Imagine my delighted surprise to find you on my doorstep," came a sultry, sweet voice. Kasherri's entire form apparated in front of him. Her taloned feet clicking against the stone as she paced, her nasty three-eyed face twisted in an ugly grin.

Panic washed over him. After his victory over her in the Rain Trials, an eternity in her clutches promised to be anything but pleasant.

"I told you, you can't kill a god, Leper," she spat his name like a curse. "But now, you will be mine forever. "Another cackle erupted from her toothy maw.

Leper couldn't muster words, so he spat in the goddess's face. There was no point in being rational, not when there was no escaping this. His fate was sealed the moment she appeared. This was a one-way ticket, and he'd be on the losing end for a long time to come.

Her wicked smile vanished as her long, taloned fingers wiped the saliva from her face.

It was replaced with a different, more calculating grin. "Oh, you will pay for that. "

Why isn't she retaliating? Maybe his fate wasn't sealed yet. Leper strained against the chains, every muscle in his body burning with effort. Sweat poured down his face, his arms slick with moisture. He pushed until his breath gave out, slumping back against the wall, the chains the only thing keeping him upright.

"Come on, Leper. Don't give up now," Maka urged, his voice softer this time, less commanding.

More images followed. Ghost with Zanera and Kelindra, all fighting valiantly to save him. Then, the massive blue face of the dragon, Fingin, soaring after Ghost. Zanera and Kelindra screamed in pure terror.

Tamara's voice cut through the chaos as she pointed at the fleeing griffin. "Kill them! He tried to take my sister from me, let's take them from him!"

Leper sucked in a deep breath through his nose and braced himself against the wall.

Rage boiled through him like a furnace struck by a powerful bellow, igniting a fire deep in his core. His face flushed with heat, his ears tingled as disgust simmered beneath his skin.

He gathered every ounce of strength he had left, summoning it from the deepest, darkest corners of his being.

"Not. Fucking. Today." He growled.

With everything he had, Leper lunged from the wall at the wicked goddess.

www.ingramcontent.com/pod-product-compliance
Lightning Source LLC
Chambersburg PA
CBHW030222120726
47903CB00005B/1324